The Bloodstained Key

The Heart Stones, Volume 1

Charity Rau

Published by Charity Rau, 2023.

THE BLOODSTAINED KEY

First edition. November 28, 2023.

Written by Charity Rau.

To all the girls for whom my stories scared them into calling their parents before the sleepover was over - Hope this one thrills you even more!

Chapter 1

Marianna stood at the top of the elegantly curved staircase. The crowded ballroom below was a gaping mouth of gossipy busybodies ready to swallow her whole. She didn't think she could do this. Two years. It had been two whole years since she'd learned the ship Will had been on disappeared. Time was such a funny thing. It felt so much shorter and so much longer than two years.

She clutched the gold painted railing, the ridges and planes of the expertly carved wood underneath soothing her and forced herself not to look over at the corner of the ballroom where she'd first realized she loved Will. Why did tonight's ball have to be at Lord Rotari's manor, on the anniversary of Will's disappearance?

The announcer called her name, and in a haze, she lifted her heavy muslin skirts and mechanically started down the stairs. Hundreds of eyes turned to face her. She sucked in a breath, focusing on the scents of the food, trying to identify each dish's ingredients. Spiced chicken, garlic and basil, and fire-roasted potatoes smothered in the cook's secret sweet sauce.

She reached the end of the stairs and panic flooded through her as so many pairs of eyes met her own. Susan darted forward and grabbed her arm pulling her effortlessly through the people into a quiet corner.

"Mari, are you okay?" her friend squeezed her arm.

"Yes, just.." Marianna blew out a breath.

"They're like vultures, right? But you are going to dance tonight, right? Accepting a dance with somebody, doesn't mean you're being unfaithful to Will."

"No." Marianna sighed. "Until he comes back, I can't enjoy things like dancing." She pushed her palms against the wall as if bracing herself to face another night of stares and whispers. She was an oddity in Anderian society, pining over a sailor who had been missing for so long.

Dancers swirled past them, a rustle of colorful skirts and swinging coattails. The orchestra played louder, building to a crescendo. Susan started to speak, but Marianna shook her head. It was impossible to hear anything over the music.

Susan pulled Marianna away from the crowd and into an isolated alcove. Her voice was gentle as she whispered, "Don't you think it's about time you start to consider that Will might not be coming back?"

Marianna stared at the tiled floor as she twisted the wooden ring on her finger. She didn't answer.

"It's been two years. Do you know what people are saying? That you're crazy. Soon no one will consider marrying you." Susan sank down onto the plush rose-colored cushioned bench, tugging Marianna to sit down next to her.

Susan meant well. She knew as well as anyone how cruel high society could be, and status could only protect one for so long, before they'd be on the receiving end of said cruelty. Marianna had to be pretty close to the end of that mercy, but that didn't matter. She wouldn't give up on Will.

"I don't care what they say. I must believe Will is alive. If I don't keep believing my heart will break." A sob broke loose, and tears streamed down her face.

Susan pulled her into a hug. "Shh, don't cry. I won't talk about Will anymore."

Marianna sucked in a deep breath and let it out. Susan handed her a handkerchief, and she dried her face.

"I am crazy. Look at me. I'm a mess. Why do you stick around?"

"Because you're my best friend. Besides, I like being the friend of the crazy girl."

Marianna laughed. "You're a good friend."

Susan snorted and waved her hand dismissively.

"Seriously, I don't know how I would have made it this far without you." Marianna smoothed out the handkerchief.

Susan reached over and squeezed her hand. "You ready to go back?"

"I guess I have to." Marianna smiled weakly as they rose. She clutched the cameo that hung around her neck, wishing for her mother, before they headed back into the ballroom.

Marianna's sister, Annette, swirled around the room in the arms of a handsome soldier. His blue uniform was freshly pressed, the gold epaulettes and buttons glistening in the soft candelabra light of the ballroom. Anderian dress uniforms were so elaborate, people from other countries often mistook high-ranking soldiers for royalty.

"I am happy for Annette." Marianna watched her sister dancing with her suitor. "She loves Matthew. I hope this disturbance everyone keeps talking about doesn't escalate into a war. It would be horrible if he had to go to war."

Susan's husband, Daniel, walked over to them. "Good evening, Marianna." He took her hand and bowed.

"I don't mean to be rude, but I overheard your concerns. I don't think you need to worry. The king's soldiers have everything under control."

He released Marianna's hand and tilted his head toward the strangest looking man in attendance, his bright blue hair and beard making him hard to miss. "Lord Bludington has a definite interest in you, Marianna. He's wealthy too."

Susan nudged her husband and shook her head.

Marianna rolled her eyes. "Well, I'm not interested in him, and money would be the last reason in the world I would marry." She turned and strode away, but not fast enough to miss Daniel and Susan's next words.

"She's still pining for your brother?" Daniel asked. "Is she ever going to get over him?"

"She loved him deeply, and you're not helping things by suggesting the oddest man in the county as a suitor for her," Susan hissed.

Marianna walked faster. Did everyone have to keep talking about how tragic she was? She knew she was pathetic, pining over a boy who was probably dead, but she didn't need everyone constantly reminding her of that fact. Her thoughts were interrupted as she plowed into something solid.

"Watch out there. Are you okay?" The low, gravelly voice was accompanied by a strong hand grabbing her arm and steadying her.

She sucked in a breath as an icy shiver raced down her spine. "Uh, yes. I'm fine." Marianna extracted her arm from Lord Bludington's grasp and took a step back. He had never approached her before, and up close, the shocking blue of his hair and beard made her eyes sting.

"I was coming to see you, but you beat me to it. May I please have this dance, Lady Marianna?"

Goosebumps raised the tiny hairs of her arms, and she resisted the urge to rub them. Why was she so scared? The man was strange, but it wasn't like he could hurt her here in a ballroom full of people.

"Milady?"

Still perturbed by the comments Daniel made and the odd reaction this man had caused her, she snapped out her answer. "No, I don't think so. Now, if you'll excuse me." She pushed past Lord Bludington, walked through the ballroom door, down the hallway, and into the ladies' lounge.

Mrs. Garbedeau, a tiny gray-haired woman who also always wore some shade of gray, stood in the center of the room. Today she wore a gown of silvery satin so pale it nearly looked white. A dark gray shawl knitted from fine silk thread draped over her shoulders. Dozens of women of various ages were huddled around her.

Marianna hovered near the wall, walking as quickly as her voluptuous skirts would let her, praying the old woman wouldn't see her. The last time she'd gotten stopped, the old woman had held hostage for three hours telling wild tales. Mrs. Garbedeau was the biggest gossip in town and never missed an opportunity to let everyone in on what she knew.

"I hear he's in the market for a wife again."

A chorus of twitters came from the group as Mrs. Garbedeau continued. "And he's the richest man on this side of the Obsidian River."

A woman at the fringe of the crowd broke in, "But isn't it strange that something tragic has befallen every one of his previous wives, though."

Mrs. Garbedeau leaned into the group and lowered her voice. "That hardly matters when he's nearly as rich as the king."

This brought an audible gasp from several of the women.

Marianna reached the other side of the room and was ready to push through the door into the inner chamber when the old lady's next words stopped her.

"I hear he's quite interested in the Locklear girls. Especially the older one."

"What? The merchant's daughters?" Tarlie scoffed, tossing her mane of perfect golden curls, and crossing her arms. "But they're not truly nobility, not by blood. Their father just managed to do well selling his wares."

Of course she would be the first one to protest. Her father was one of the highest-ranking nobles in their town.

Tarlie's mother laid a hand on her daughter's shoulder, the gigantic rings she wore on every finger shimmering as the light hit them. "Don't worry, sweetcakes," she crooned. "He won't be able to ignore your beauty. You have as much of a chance as any other girl, if not more."

Marianna didn't wait to hear anything else. She pushed through the door into the luxurious inner room. White circular chairs formed of intricate iron twists filled the room. Plush red cushions lined their seats. The soft scent of roses filled the room. Strings of rose petals crisscrossed the ceiling around three large chandeliers. Teardrop crystals hung from the golden chandeliers casting a soft golden glow around the room.

Marianna dropped into the nearest chair with a sigh. She was seriously getting tired of all these parties. She should be grateful, because whether she liked it or not, Tarlie was right. Her family wasn't noble by birth. Father had made such a fortune that the upper class had welcomed him with open arms, especially after he'd purchased a manor worthy of nobility. Money could buy a lot, but it was never the important things like happiness or true friendship.

As Marianna leaned back in her seat, another woman spoke from behind the wall.

"He's so strange. And his hair! I know of no one else who's ever had blue hair; it doesn't seem natural."

Marianna didn't recognize the voice, but she agreed with this woman.

"Oh nonsense!" Mrs. Garbedeau exclaimed. "Some people look for gossip and slander where there is none. I don't care if he is a little bit strange. With his fortune he can be as strange as he wants to."

Tarlie laughed boisterously. She was welcome to him. Unfortunately, it didn't seem that Lord Bludington was interested in her. Marianna hadn't seen him go near her once all night. And that was saying something considering how desperate Tarlie was for his attention.

"Where did he come from? How did he obtain such a vast fortune?" the same cautious woman from before asked.

"Well, that's easy enough to answer." Mrs. Garbedeau's voice grew quieter, and Marianna found herself leaning closer to the wall, straining to hear her next words.

"It's his mother's fortune. She died many years ago. I don't remember when. He had a sister too, but she died not long after their mother. Fragile women in their family. I don't know anything about his father. By the time they moved here, he'd been out of the picture for years. It could have been one of those situations where he worked for the king, if you know what I mean."

Marianna could imagine Mrs. Garbedeau wiggling her eyebrows as she said it, like it was a secret. But everyone knew the king occasionally employed men, assassins essentially, to protect the kingdom from those deemed threats. When they didn't return home from an assignment, the king would provide a bounty for the families including a manor and a higher title.

It made sense. Bludington's family showed up with no father in the picture to claim the biggest manor around, armed with an unseemly amount of wealth. If that was the case, Bludington had certainly had his fair share of hardships. Guilt pricked at her. She had been judging Bludington so harshly. But still, guilt and pity couldn't erase the sense of unease she felt whenever she was around the man.

She sighed and rose. She'd heard enough. It was time to go home. Slipping out the back door and down the servant's hallway, Marianna avoided the room where all the women were still gathered around Mrs. Garbedeau. Because she'd played here as a child, she knew all the best ways to sneak out.

The sweet scent of roses greeted her as she stepped into the gardens, releasing some of the tension from her neck. The stables stood outside the garden, and she picked up her pace as the evening chill sent shivers down her spine. Out of sight of all the nosy women, she gave in to the urge to rub her arms.

Lord Bludington... ugh. It wasn't just the blue color of his hair and beard. He'd had at least three wives already. Their deaths were shrouded in mystery. No one knew what had happened to any of them, and the stories only grew stranger and stranger with the passing of time.

And he lived in that gothic castle up on Friar's Hill, miles away from anyone. So dark and melancholy. Marianna wrapped her arms tighter around herself as she entered the stable and found her family's groom.

She was ready to go home. Her brothers, James and Henry, wouldn't care, but Annette wouldn't be pleased, which is why she hadn't told her. Annette didn't understand how difficult these things were for Marianna. Annette was the life of the party, easily making friends wherever she went. Everybody loved her, and she still had her love to dance with.

"Brent, I'm very tired, but I'm sure my brothers and sister will be here all night. I'd like to go home. You can bring the carriage back to get them."

Brent gave a little nod. "Yes, ma'am. The carriage will be ready shortly if you want to wait outside."

Marianna nodded and stepped back out into the cool night air. Within minutes, the carriage appeared. Brent offered his arm, helping her into the carriage before climbing to the top and signaling the horses forward.

When Marianna got home, she went to the parlor to say goodnight to her father. As she entered, he was overtaken by a fit of coughing. Worry flooded inside of her, and she clutched her heavy ballgown skirt, lifting it as she hurried over to him. He was getting worse with each passing day. She should have stayed home with him, but Annette had thrown a fit when she suggested it.

"Father, are you okay?"

He motioned to the little table sitting next to his chair where a pitcher of water sat. Marianna quickly poured a glass for him.

"We should call a doctor. You've had that cold a long time."

He shook his head. "I'm fine, dear. It comes with old age, I'm sure."

"You're not old."

"I'm getting there. Did you have fun tonight? Dance with any handsome men?"

Marianna turned away. "All balls are fun."

Her father took her arm and pulled her back toward him. "I'm so sorry about Will, my dear. If I could do it over, I would never have sent him away.

Will you please forgive me?" He stood up and gathered Marianna into his arms.

She rested her head against his shoulder, and her voice came out muffled. "It's okay, Father. I still believe Will is coming back. He promised me he would, and I have to hold on to that."

Her father sighed, pressing a kiss to her forehead. "Good night, my dear. I love you very much."

Marianna turned and went to her bedroom. Despite all her insistence Will was coming back, she was losing hope. He might really be dead, and that thought was shredding her heart to pieces.

Marianna's eyes flew open. Her room was dark. What time was it? She sighed, punched up her pillow, and rolled onto her side. She stared into the dark and tried to fall back asleep, but she no longer felt tired.

After several more minutes, she heaved herself up. She barely held back a yelp as her feet struck the cold floor. She rummaged around in her nightstand drawer until she found a match. After lighting her bedside candle, she headed for the stairs.

The library was the one place she could count on being lit. Because her father often suffered from insomnia, the servants kept the fire and lanterns going all night. Marianna reached the ground floor and inched along the hallway that led to her favorite room in their house.

Something thumped against the wall out of the view of her candlelight. She held her breath and stopped. Who was creeping about at this hour? She inhaled deeply. Probably the servant who kept the fire lit.

"Wilson?" Marianna called out in a shaky voice. There was no answer, just another thump as a long shape rolled toward her, stopping right before it knocked into her. The shape unrolled itself into a boy.

"Thomas? Whatever are you doing up this time of night?" She had a pretty good idea why Thomas was up. His father was a notorious drunk, and likely Thomas had made himself scarce to avoid a beating.

Thomas's father worked for the next-door neighbors, and one day Marianna had discovered Thomas huddled behind a bush in their garden, crying and trying to hide a black eye. Marianna finally managed to get Thomas to tell her what happened, and she had been furious, going to her father and insisting that they must do something to help.

But her father had said it was out of their hands. Their neighbors knew what kind of man Thomas's father was but refused to press charges against him. The best they could do was offer Thomas a place to escape from his father when he went into one of his drunken rages. Marianna had a special key made for Thomas. She'd threaded it through some yarn, making a necklace the boy could wear under his shirt.

Thomas had only taken them up on the offer of escape a few times, and Marianna hadn't seen him in weeks.

"Aww, I needed to get away for awhile, Miss Marianna." Thomas ducked his head, but not before Marianna saw the glisten in his eyes.

"And I know the perfect place to escape." Marianna held out her hand to Thomas. "Come with me?"

Thomas lifted his head, and a grin covered his face. "The library? There're still more stories we haven't read, right?"

Marianna nodded, and Thomas grabbed her hand. She squeezed it and led him to the library. At the door, Thomas dropped her hand and raced inside to find the book. It was a book of fairytales from Marianna's mother. Her mother had been a huge supporter of the arts, making sure the girls were well-read and knew about all the famous painters and musicians. Out of all of them, though, Marianna knew her mother's favorite artist had been Stincosa, the writer of the fairytales.

Marianna used to keep the book in her room, but once she had started reading the stories to Thomas, she put it in the hidden shelf in the library. Thomas loved retrieving it from there, and it was as safe as it had been in her room.

Thomas handed the book to Marianna and plopped onto the fluffy pillow by the crackling fire. Wood smoke mingled with the scent of old books as Marianna took her seat in the velvet armchair.

She ran her hands lovingly across the cover of the fairytale book. Made of fine mahogany leather with golden lettering, it evoked a thousand memories of her mother. Marianna could have easily lost herself in them, but the eager-eyed boy wasn't so patient.

"Find the one about the donkey and the pig!"

"Okay," Marianna laughed. She had read that fairytale to Thomas at least half a dozen times, but it was his favorite, so she found it and began reading. Soon Thomas was asleep, and Marianna's eyes were starting to feel heavy as well. She closed the book and pulled the knitted blanket from the back of her chair to cover Thomas.

"Good night, sweet boy," she whispered as she covered him. She found Wilson in the kitchen and let him know about the guest they had in the library before returning to bed.

Chapter 2

"Is Marianna still asleep?" James asked. He stood at the bottom of the stairs with Annette and Henry. Marianna paused on the staircase to listen.

"Last I checked she was," Annette said. "Father said she was upset last night, and I wanted her to get as much sleep as she needed."

"Will she ever get over Will? It's been two years, but you'd think it'd happened last month." Henry shook his head.

Marianna covered her mouth to keep herself from protesting aloud. Even her family thought she was pathetic.

"She loved Will. Things like that can't be healed like a physical injury. It takes much more time. We need to be there for her," Annette reprimanded.

Everyone was quiet after that, so Marianna slipped up the stairs. At the top, she coughed loudly and stomped down. Her siblings stepped out of the parlor and met her at the bottom of the stairs.

"Hello, sleepyhead." James said. He'd always held a special place in her heart, even more so after Will's disappearance. He was always making her smile. He and Henry may have been twins, but they were as different as night and day.

"I guess I was more tired than I thought." Marianna offered a weak smile.

Her smile disappeared when she noticed the army bag strung over James' shoulder. Henry held a similar bag. A knot formed in her stomach. Ever since they had turned sixteen, she'd known this was a possibility. That they could get called to the army.

She swallowed hard, pushing the words out past the lump lodged in her throat. "What's this? Are you going somewhere?"

"Sorry, Sis. We've been called to the border," James said.

"Where is the fighting taking place?" Marianna bit the inside of her cheek. She couldn't bear to think about them leaving. Especially when there was a chance they wouldn't come back.

"There shouldn't be much trouble, but the king decided he wants as many reinforcements as possible to let the rebels know we mean business. We were waiting for you to wake up, but we've got to leave. Couldn't go without saying goodbye to our favorite big sister." James pulled Marianna into a bear hug. He was trying to hide it for her sake, but he was clearly thrilled about this new adventure.

"I love you," he whispered.

"I love you, too." Marianna choked on the last word. She pulled away from James and turned to Henry.

He squeezed her shoulder and said, "I love you too, you know."

She threw her arms around him, hugging him tightly. "I know you do. Be careful, you hear me? And take care of one another." She cleared her throat trying to get rid of the frog that had claimed residence there.

"We will, don't worry. I promise to keep an eye on James. I won't let him do anything stupid," Henry said, shooting a glance at his brother.

James shook his head, not taking the bait. "We'll be back soon," he called over his shoulder before they walked out the door.

But there was no guarantee they would be back. Experience had taught her that much. Tears pooled in her eyes, and she blinked rapidly, trying to hide them from Annette.

She needed to think happy thoughts. They would be back, and it would all be fine. A seed of doubt lingered in the back of her mind, but she ignored it. Taking a deep breath, she put her arm around Annette's shoulder as they followed their brothers outside. The boys hopped into the carriage, waving as it rolled down the street and out of sight.

As they turned to go in, Marianna asked, "Where's Father?"

"He wasn't feeling well this morning. After he said goodbye to the boys, he went back to bed. I'm worried about him. He's had this cold for a while now. He should see a doctor, but you know how he is about that." Annette wrapped her arms around herself, a distressed look on her face.

"He was coughing last night, but he insisted he was okay. If he doesn't get better soon, I'll call the doctor," Marianna reassured her sister.

Later that night, Annette helped Marianna pin up her long, dark hair. They were preparing for another party.

"I don't know how we can keep having parties every night when war is looming over us." Marianna sighed.

"I think people need it to take their minds off of all the bad in the world," Annette replied.

Marianna's mind swirled. Her sister could be so naïve sometimes. Avoiding the problems in Anderi would probably guarantee war would come. Not that Marianna could deal with thinking about it tonight. Not when her brothers had been sent to the front lines.

"Do you think Matthew will get sent to the border?" she blurted out. Anything to keep her from thinking about Henry and James on the war front.

Annette paused, looking at Marianna's reflection.

"I don't know. If he does go, I hope he asks me to marry him first. If something happens, and he hasn't asked me..." Annette's voice trembled as she continued. "Well, there would always be a piece of me wondering if he wanted to marry me."

Marianna gasped. "Annette, how can you say that? He will ask you. If you could see the way he looks at you, you wouldn't have any doubts." She reached back and squeezed Annette's hand.

"Thanks, Mari. It means a lot to hear you say that." Annette went back to her sister's hair.

It didn't take her long to finish, then Kendra came in to help them get into their dresses. Marianna's dress was a royal blue silk, with cream lacings on the bodice. Ivory lace trimmed the quarter length bell sleeves. It was a bit old-fashioned, but it had been her mother's dress, and she loved wearing it.

"Thank you, Kendra." She pulled up her heavy skirt and headed for the door. "Ready, Annette?"

Annette's dress was a vivid pink, with the more modern puffy cap sleeves and a high waistline. She pulled on long white silk gloves before picking up her skirt and joining Marianna at the door.

"Yes, of course." She smiled at Kendra, and soon they were in the carriage headed to the party.

Within minutes, the carriage pulled to a stop in front of a grand mansion. Matthew opened their door. He helped Marianna out first, before taking Annette's hand.

"You look beautiful, Annette," he whispered, a little smile on his face as he helped her out. He weaved her arm through his and escorted her into the house.

Marianna took her time climbing the steps, giving them their space. It sometimes seemed awkward when it was the three of them, but Matthew was a sweet young man, his calm sensibility a perfect match for Annette's flighty impulsiveness, and he was always willing to include her in their activities.

How different things would have been if Will had been here. Tears formed behind her eyes, a lump growing in her throat. She swallowed hard and forced the tears back before finding her way to the ballroom. She hadn't enjoyed balls and parties since Will had disappeared, but according to proper society she was required to attend them.

Before she had even reached the threshold of the ballroom, a hand stopped her.

"May I please have this dance? I promise I don't bite, and you wouldn't refuse a man twice." Lord Bludington's garish blue hair and beard assaulted her eyes. His eyes matched his hair perfectly. Though there was a smile on his face, his eyes bored into hers. Like he was staring straight into her soul. Cold chills scampered down her back, and a jolt of fear surged through her.

She was reacting foolishly. He was an ordinary man. Sure, his reputation with his wives was a bit murky, but not enough to warrant an official investigation. And people respected him, always trying to get his attention, get an invite to his strange manor. So there was nothing to worry about, right?

She gulped in air, then let it out. She needed to dance with him, to prove to herself she was behaving foolishly. Before she could clear away the thoughts, she heard herself say, "Yes." Lord Bludington smiled at her answer and led her onto the dance floor.

The murmurs increased as they entered the ballroom. Everyone was talking about her. The sight of her on the dance floor again after being absent from it for two years was sure to fodder gossip for days, maybe even weeks, but she could hardly think about that. Her heart pounded so hard she was sure it would race right out of her chest. She breathed deeply.

Lord Bludington chattered away about the war and the weather and other inane things. Things went flying by with dizzying speed, but at least she hadn't forgotten the steps. Her palms were clammy with sweat, and she hoped Lord Bludington hadn't noticed.

She wished to be in the lounge room with all the women who considered themselves too old to dance. Every house had one filled with books and games. Typically, she would be deep into a book by now, but not today.

Today had to be the day she gave in and danced with someone. She thought she'd feel more guilty, like she was betraying Will. But it was hard to feel guilty when her heart was pounding like a racehorse. She had to concentrate to keep breathing normally.

When the music finally ended, Marianna pulled away from Lord Bludington and muttered, "Thank you. Please excuse me."

She hurried away so fast that she didn't realize she had walked straight into a web of nosy old ladies.

"Do you fancy him?" Lady Portense grabbed her arm.

"Tired of sitting on the sidelines, eh? About time you got back out there." A lady she didn't recognize patted her on the shoulder as if she'd fought a giant and come back victorious.

"He is quite a catch!" Mrs. Garbedeau snickered as she scooted closer, her shoulder bumping into Marianna's.

"But no one knows what happened to all those girls he married. I wouldn't go anywhere with him, not even for a million cullers." Lady Harrington crossed her arms while pushing in closer.

Marianna waded through, pulling away from the grasping hands, until she was out of the ballroom. She hurried down the brightly lit hallway to the powder room. With a quick glance around to ensure no one was there, she headed for a private corner and sank down onto a padded red velvet bench.

The Harringtons had one of the nicest manors, and their powder room was far bigger than anyone else's. Gilded mirrors of various sizes and shapes hung on all four walls, making it seem even larger than it was. Plush grape carpet covered the floors, so soft that Marianna immediately removed her shoes and let her feet sink into it. She leaned back against the cushiony chair, resting her head, closing her eyes against the multiple reflections staring at her.

Her heart beat erratically, and her mind was muddled. Emotions swirled through her like a tornado. This was ridiculous. Why was she so frightened? It was one dance, but it was her first time back on the dance floor in so long. And it hadn't been with Will. Her heart clenched, and her hands shook.

The door opened, and Susan's head appeared around the corner. "Are you okay? Why did you hurry away like that? Did Lord Bludington say something to you?"

Marianna shook her head and shoved her hands under her skirt. She stared down at the blue velvet of her dress and took a deep breath. "I don't know. He didn't say anything to me, but whenever I see him, I feel scared, and I get chills. There's something very strange about him, besides his blue hair. I mean, why is his hair even blue?" She lifted her head and stared at her friend.

"You're being silly. He's an ordinary man who happens to have a strange hair color. Maybe he dyes it that color, who knows?" Susan sat down and put an arm around Marianna's shoulder.

"I know it sounds silly. It is silly, but he really scares me."

"It's going to be okay. You danced with him once. You don't ever have to dance with him again. Come on, let's go back to the party."

Susan pulled Marianna to her feet and led her back out to the ballroom and watched her like a hawk, never giving her a chance to escape to the lounge. Although Susan tried all night to get Marianna to dance with many different gentlemen, Marianna managed to find excuses to be alone. After the turbulent emotions one dance had given her, she couldn't imagine trying another.

After putting up with the party for a few hours, Marianna found her sister and pulled her aside. Her head was pounding from the stress of the night, and the ballroom atmosphere was only making it worse.

"What's the matter?" Annette asked.

"I have a headache. I'm going to leave, and I'll send the carriage back for you."

"Are you sure you're okay? You did the same thing last night and the night before. You should try to enjoy these parties. I'm really worried about you."

"I'm fine. I have a headache, and I'm leaving now," Marianna snapped. "All these people care about is their stupid parties. They don't care about the war looming. They don't care about the soldiers' lives at stake. They don't care about the poor people barely getting by, which is the whole reason people want to fight." Marianna hadn't meant to get so angry or loud.

A couple of nearby people stared as Annette grabbed her arm and ushered her outside. "Calm down. I was just expressing my concern." She squeezed Marianna's hand.

A flash of guilt shot through Marianna for taking her issues out on her sister and causing a scene.

"I'm sorry I snapped at you. But I'm okay. I just need to go home and rest." She squeezed back five times, the special signal she had made up after their mother had died and Annette was inconsolable. It meant 'I'm always here for you.'

Annette stared at her for a moment before squeezing the code back and then nodded. "Okay, but you don't have to worry about sending the carriage back. Matthew will take me home."

Annette pulled Marianna into a quick hug before walking away. Marianna watched her go, then turned to the cloak closet to retrieve her wrap.

Once inside the carriage, she leaned her head back and closed her eyes. Maybe she'd wake up to find this was all a horrible dream. Will wasn't missing, and she didn't even know who Lord Bludington was. If only…

Chapter 3

The next few weeks were not easy for Marianna. They heard nothing from her brothers, and the rumors circulating the ballrooms claimed the rebellion on the border was becoming worse each day.

Marianna worked hard to avoid Lord Bludington. He sought her out at every ball even though she'd made it clear she was not interested in him. How could he still be interested in her? If she were any colder to him, she'd be downright mean.

She was sure Lord Bludington viewed his chasing after her as a game, one many young men of Anderi indulged in, though he was old to be partaking in such nonsense, as he was at least nine or ten years older than Marianna. If she continued to ignore him, he would get tired and move on to someone who would be easier to catch.

Marianna's father was getting weaker, although he insisted he was fine. He was coughing more, horrible deep-throated coughs. He spent most of his time wrapped in a blanket, sitting in the chair next to the fire in his office.

One morning, Marianna came downstairs and found her father this way. He held a letter, a tear rolling down his cheek.

She rushed to his side. "Father, what is it? Are Henry and James okay?"

Her father looked up, swiped at his eyes, and hurriedly folded up the letter. He tried to straighten up but started coughing.

"Here, drink some water." Marianna reached for the glass on the side table and handed it to her father. He took it and swallowed a few sips. Finally, his coughing subsided.

"The boys are fine as far as I know, Marianna. I'm getting melancholy in my old age. I'd better get busy with my work."

He set the glass down and stood up, but coughing racked his body and he nearly fell over. Marianna stepped forward and grabbed his arm, trying to support him. Her father clutched his chest and fell against Marianna. She staggered under the weight.

"Wilson, Wilson, come quick!" Marianna called for the butler who had worked for her family for as long as she could remember. The tall, sturdy man rushed into the room. He grasped her father by both shoulders and eased him back into the chair.

"Give him some water," Wilson said.

Marianna picked up the glass and held it to her father's lips. He took a few sips and nodded.

"Wilson, can you take him upstairs? I'll send for the doctor."

Her father started to shake his head and opened his mouth to speak.

"I don't want to hear your excuses, Father. This has gone on long enough. You are quite sick. Your face is flushed, and you can't even speak without being overtaken by a coughing spell. Wilson, help him upstairs."

Her father didn't protest this time, showing how sick he really was. It scared Marianna to see him so weak. Her father, who had always seemed strong enough to do anything, now becoming feeble.

Marianna sent Brent for the doctor, then turned back to the study to see what she could do to help her father with his business. He had taught her how to keep track of the accounts and manage stock, but it had been a while since she had helped him, and she wasn't sure where to begin. Once again she wished she'd had the opportunity to go to a higher learning institute, but such a dream cost an exorbitant amount.

She sighed as she walked farther into the room. The letter her father had been reading caught her eye. It was lying on the floor. She picked it up and read it.

Merchant's Bank

352 Elm Lane

Dear Sir Henry Locklear,

According to our records, we still have not received your payment for the loan against your manor. You have until the 3rd May to repay this loan, or we will be forced to foreclose on the property. As this payment is already late, there will be a penalty fee of three hundred cullers added to the total payment you owe Merchant's Bank.

Total payment – 35,000 cullers

Sincerely,

Charles Dudley

President

Marianna gasped. "Thirty-five thousand cullers? That's more than Father makes in a year. How could it be this bad?"

She ran over to where her father kept the account books, pulling out the last one and flipping it open. Her eyes ran over the pages. The bank was correct. Father was terribly behind on the bills.

As she continued to flip through the pages, she saw her father had lost two other merchant ships besides the one Will had been on. And half of the merchandise on the last incoming ship had been damaged by a storm. The ship had also been severely impaired by the storm. No longer sea-worthy, it was waiting in port to be repaired.

There was no money for the bills or the repairs. The bank wouldn't lend them anymore money, and there was only one ship left to bring in merchandise.

Marianna looked to see when it had last left port. March 3rd, less than a month ago. There was no way it would be back with the goods to pay the bank bill before the bank would foreclose.

Marianna slammed the book shut and sank down into the chair behind the desk, putting her head in her hands. No wonder Father was sick.

This was why he'd refused a doctor. They couldn't pay for a visit, but he needed to see one or he was going to die. She sighed heavily. There must be something she could do.

The door opened, interrupting her thoughts. Annette stepped into the room, stopping inside the doorway. "Are you okay? The doctor is here. He'll help Father, and he'll get better."

"Come in and close the door."

Annette came in and sat down in the chair across from the desk.

Marianna cleared her throat, struggling to come up with a way to break the news of their encroaching poverty to her sister gently. Nothing came to mind, so she blurted it out.

"There's no money. None, and in a little over a month, the bank will take our house. I don't know what we're going to do."

"What do you mean, no money?" Annette's eyes went round in disbelief.

"Just what I said, Annette. I don't know how we were unaware of it, but it's the truth." Marianna shoved the account book and letter at her sister. "Look for yourself."

Annette took her time reading the letter and looking through the account book. "What are we going to do? What about the doctor?" Panic filled Annette's eyes and her breath hitched as she spoke.

Marianna laid a hand on her sister's shoulder. "I don't know, but we'll think of something," she assured her sister even as her own mind filled with doubt.

Taking a deep breath, she tried to calm herself. "For now, go find out what the diagnosis is and how much the visit will be. Come back and tell me."

Annette slipped out of the room and returned several minutes later.

"The doctor says he's not sure what's wrong with Father, but he has some medicine for the cough. He'll be back next week to check on him again. It's going to cost us fifty cullers. Where are we going to get it from?" Annette barely managed to get the words out as her eyes filled with tears.

"Come with me." Marianna led her sister upstairs and into her room. She reached in her top dresser drawer and dug around until she found a little golden key. Walking over to the ornately carved chest that sat in the corner, she fit the key in the lock. Coins jingled inside of the sapphire blue silken bag she pulled from the trunk.

"That's your dowry. You can't use that." Annette laid her hand on Marianna's arm as if to stop her.

"Well, it's not like I'm going to need it anytime soon, and where else are we going to get the money?"

"But your dowry? Marianna, are you sure?"

"At least it's not yours," Marianna said as she counted out the appropriate amount of money. She handed it to Annette. "Go give it to the doctor and tell him we'll see him next week."

When Annette hesitated, Marianna pushed her toward the door. "Just do it."

"Okay," Annette whispered before leaving the room.

Marianna put the rest of her money away, then rested her head against the box. She didn't know what to do. If only her beloved fairytales were true, then she would have a fairy godmother to help her out of this mess.

Chapter 4

The next two days, Marianna's father stayed in bed. By the third day he insisted he was well enough to move down to the parlor to sit. Marianna busied herself washing and putting away the linens. They went through so many of them.

Ellen and Kendra insisted it was no problem for them to do the linens, but Ellen already did so much work, and washing linens wasn't really in Kendra's job description. No other lady's maid position would require the maid to wash the linens. And besides, she liked doing the washing. It gave her some alone time, time to get lost in her thoughts and not have to worry about anyone else.

She'd just shut the closet door when an unfamiliar voice greeted her father in the parlor. Hadn't he been alone in there when she'd brought him breakfast? She took a step closer to the parlor door.

Goosebumps scattered across her skin. What was Lord Bludington doing at their house?

"It has been a pleasure talking with you, sir. I do hope we can reach an agreement soon, for your sake as well as mine." Bludington's voice echoed down the hallway.

In another minute, he'd be in the hallway. Marianna rushed the other way, desperate to get away before the man came out into the hall, but she was too late. The door opened and Lord Bludington stepped out.

"Ah, Miss Marianna," he called after her. "How are you this fine day? I nearly missed you. I'm so glad I didn't."

With dread, Marianna slowed and turned around. She forced a tight smile onto her face. "Fine, thank you. If you'll excuse me, I have things to attend to."

She whirled around, but before she could take a step, he reached out and grasped her arm.

"If I didn't know any better, Miss Marianna, I would say you're scared of me." Despite the teasing lilt of his voice, the smile on his face was cold, and his eyes were steely. Marianna lifted her chin.

"What utter nonsense. I do, however, have things that need my attention. I don't have time for silly games." She jerked her arm from his grip and stepped away from him.

"Well, I wouldn't want to keep you from your tasks, but I hope you speak the truth about not being afraid of me, as I anticipate that we will see much of each other in the near future."

Before Marianna could semblance a reply, Lord Bludington turned and walked out the front door. Marianna shivered. What could he mean? She'd managed to avoid him so far. Rubbing her arms, she shivered again.

"What did he want?" Annette asked as she came down the stairs.

"I'm not sure. He was talking to Father."

"Girls," their father called to them. They entered the parlor and found him sitting in his favorite spot in front of the fire, wrapped in a thick wool blanket. He coughed as he shifted into a more comfortable position.

"Since you were out in the hallway, I assume you heard Lord Bludington leave?"

"Yes. What did he want?" Marianna asked.

"Girls, sit down. I'm afraid I have some bad news." He motioned to the plush, royal blue love seat that sat across from his chair.

Marianna sank into it, the fuzzy velvet caressing her palms as she braced herself for more bad news. Her eyes glazed over as she stared past her father at the curtains that matched the love seat perfectly. They framed the window, pulled back with ties. Sunshine shimmered through the glass, belying the thick tension filling the room. How much more bad news could she take?

Their father explained about the misfortune that had struck his ships and how they now had no money. Annette started to interrupt him, to tell him that they already knew all this, which pulled Marianna from her stupor. She stopped her sister with a swift kick to her shins. Annette glared at Marianna, but let their father go on.

"...and this is what it comes down to, girls. I never wanted things to end this way, and I'm not going to force either of you to agree, but if one of you don't accept this offer, we will lose our house, our ships, everything."

Apprehension swirled through Marianna's stomach. Before her father even voiced the offer, she knew what it was. She closed her eyes and swallowed hard. There must be another way. It couldn't come down to this.

Annette's voice sounded far away as she asked, "What offer, Father?"

"Lord Bludington has asked for one of you girls to accept his marriage proposal. He is interested in Marianna, but if she won't accept, he is willing for you, Annette, to take her place. He says he's tired of being alone in his big house and longs for companionship. I didn't even know you girls were that well acquainted with him, but he seems to think very highly of you both."

Their father's speech ended when he fell into a coughing fit. He reached inside his blanket, pulled out a handkerchief, and wiped his mouth with it.

"Shh, Father. Rest a moment. Don't upset yourself over this. We'll be okay," Marianna said as she handed her father a glass of water. A sad smile spread across his face as he took a drink.

"You girls are so good to me, so like your mother." He handed the glass back to Marianna, reaching for her other hand as he did so. He pressed a kiss to it, then clasped her small hand in both of his large work-worn ones.

"I didn't want things to work out this way, but our situation is dire. Bludington agreed to pay all our debts in addition to giving a generous annual allowance to our house. I'll not decide who is to marry him. And if neither of you agree to do so, we will do our best to stick things out together in the poorhouse. I need to give him an answer before the bank forecloses on the house. Once the two of you have decided what you are going to do, I'll let him know."

Father's eyes closed wearily, and he rested his head against the chair. The recent events were taking a toll on his already fragile health.

"Let's talk upstairs," Annette whispered and turned to leave.

Marianna started to extract her hand from her father's, but his hand tightened around hers.

"Marianna, I am truly sorry about Will. If I could go back and do it over again I would. He was a decent young man, and he would've made you a good husband." His eyes glistened with tears as he spoke.

Marianna tried to pull away, afraid of the overwhelming emotions threatening to overtake her, but her father held tight. "It's okay, Father. You don't have to keep apologizing. It's not your fault the ship sank." The words were a whisper, her voice wobbly.

"No, Marianna, it isn't okay, and you need to hear what I have to say. It was partly because of my selfishness I sent him away like that. It was one of the most foolish decisions I have ever made. I wanted to keep you with me a little longer."

Another coughing fit overtook her father, and his shoulders shuddered with the force of it.

"It's okay. Don't talk anymore. Just rest."

He shook his head, pushing away the glass of water she offered him, before continuing. "If I hadn't sent him away, none of this would've happened. I rarely tell you girls how much you mean to me. I love you both, dearly, and I know because of my foolish choices, you are both suffering. I'm so very sorry."

Her father had sent Will out on the ship because he wanted her at home with him longer? She'd thought her father believed Will was not good enough for her, that his pride in their wealthy family name was why he always got so upset about Will.

Her heart swelled with emotion, and tears fell down her face. She leaned forward and kissed her father's forehead.

"It's okay, Father. I've already forgiven you. Annette and I both love you so much. Rest now. Everything will be okay, I promise. You've always taken care of us, now let me take care of you."

Her father nodded, seeming satisfied that he had said all he wanted to. He leaned back against his chair and closed his eyes. Within minutes, he was asleep.

"Sleep well, Father," Marianna whispered before trudging up the stairs.

She cracked open her bedroom door, bracing herself for a discussion with her sister. Annette was always full of opinions and ideas, but not always well thought out ones. Her sister was already asleep, sprawled across Marianna's bed fully dressed.

The recent events were taking their toll on her normally vibrant sister. Marianna pulled the folded blanket from the end of the bed and spread it over Annette. She softly kissed her forehead and went to Annette's room to sleep for the night.

Marianna was in a dark tunnel. She couldn't see anything, but the cold, stone walls pressed in on her. She wanted to scream, but her throat refused to function. A blue light came towards her. No, wait, it wasn't a light. It was hair, a beard. The face that belonged to the beard came into focus. Lord Bludington spoke.

"There's nothing to be afraid of, Marianna. Are you afraid of me? There's nothing to be afraid of, Marianna." He repeated that line, louder and louder, breaking into uproarious laughter. As quickly as it had started, the laughter stopped.

He spoke again, his fiery blue eyes piercing her with their brightness. "I ALWAYS get what I want, Marianna."

His mouth formed a large, evil smile, and his shiny white teeth glistened against his hideous beard.

Marianna gasped awake. Kendra stood over her, holding a wet cloth against her forehead. Marianna grabbed the cloth away as she sat up trying to understand what had just happened.

"Are you okay, Miss Marianna? You were thrashing about so, I thought you might be sick. You are very hot to the touch."

"I'm fine, Kendra. Thank-you. I'm not sick, you can go back to sleep."

"As you wish, ma'am." Kendra gave a little curtsey and left the room.

She knew now more than ever that she would do whatever it took to keep herself or her sister from marrying Lord Bludington. There had to be another way to get her family out of debt. There were things that could be sold, maybe she could get a job... Ideas whirled around in her head, and she got up, pulling out paper to form a plan.

Chapter 5

Sunlight was streaming through the bedroom window when Marianna was finally satisfied with the plan she had laid out. She climbed off the bed with papers in hand and walked to her room to see if Annette was awake. She opened the door to see her sister standing before the mirror smoothing out the wrinkles in her dress.

"Sorry for stealing your bed last night. I was more tired than I realized. Sorry we didn't get to talk either." Annette dropped her hands and stepped toward her sister. She motioned to the papers Marianna gripped. "What's all that?"

"My plan. So that neither of us must marry that awful Bludington."

"You always go on about him, but really, what's so bad about him? I mean besides being a little older and having blue hair, both things which he cannot help. Give the poor man a chance. He hasn't done anything to you, and it was generous of him to offer to help us."

Marianna wasn't sure how to put her feelings about the man into words. "He has an aura of evil or something. Every time I'm around him I get a feeling."

Annette laughed. "That's ridiculous. You can't say someone is evil because you have a feeling about him. Are you sure this isn't about Will?"

"Do you want to marry Bludington?"

"Of course not! Matthew may propose to me any day now, so why would I consider Bludington?"

"Oh, so since I'm the oldest, I'm expected to marry him then?" Marianna crossed her arms over her chest. Annette could be so spoiled and selfish sometimes.

Annette's eyes went wide with innocence as she stared at Marianna. "I didn't say that." She shrugged one shoulder, her voice quiet.

"Well, then what did you mean? If you're not going to marry him, and I'm not going to marry him, how do you propose we pay our bills?"

Annette shook her head. "I don't know. I haven't thought that far."

Marianna didn't say anything. She stared at her sister and sighed. Annette wasn't always ready to listen to Marianna's plans even though Annette never had any kind of plan in place herself.

Annette sighed. "I'm sorry, I didn't mean to be so thoughtless. Let's see what your plan is."

They poured over Marianna's outline together, with Marianna doing some explaining when necessary.

"I don't know. It might work, but talking to the banker... They don't let women walk in to talk to bankers."

"I'll take Wilson with me. I've already explained everything to him last night, and he's willing to help with it all. We got into the war office."

"Yeah, but the banker's office is in the back, and you'll have to get pass other people."

Her sister had a good point. All the Anderian banks were the same. Lots of mid-level people in the main part of the bank to go through before getting to the banker. The banker was the only one who could grant loans or extend payment times. It was hard enough for an average man to get in to see the banker, but it was unheard of for a woman to see him. Still, she was determined to try.

"It has to work," Marianna said stubbornly. "We need to get started now."

She sent Annette to gather the servants and composed herself to speak with them. She did not want to let them all go, but there was no help for it. Her father wouldn't like it, so she would tell him about it later, but they had no money to pay servants.

She was releasing everyone except Wilson, knowing they would need his help with their father. Everyone would get an exemplary letter of recommendation, and she was sure it wouldn't be long before they would all find another position.

Marianna took a deep breath and went downstairs to where the servants were gathered in the parlor. "I'm so sorry to tell you, but with the misfortunes our business has suffered, we are going to have to let you all go. We no longer have the funds to pay you."

A few of the younger servants gasped, but most of them were calm. They knew this was coming. She gave them the last of their wages—taken from her dowry—and said some tearful goodbyes, especially to Cook and Ellen.

"I'm sorry about your bad luck, Miss Marianna, but this is our home too, and we couldn't possibly leave. Don't worry about paying us. We're family," Cook said.

"That's right. Your mother would be ashamed of us if she knew we left you in your time of need." Ellen had been housekeeper since before Marianna was born. "We'll be right here with you, helping you get through it."

"There might not ever be money again. We might not ever be able to pay you," Marianna stammered, tears filling her eyes.

"It doesn't matter. It's settled, we're staying!" Cook nodded emphatically.

"Yes, absolutely!" Ellen added.

Tears streamed down Marianna's face as she hugged them.

"You both have always been so good to Annette and me. Thank you. From the bottom of my heart, thank you."

"There, there now. Dry your tears and go see to the rest of your business now. Ellen will take care of the auditor when he gets here." Cook wiped Marianna's tears away with the tip of her apron.

Seeing the surprised look on the girl's face, Cook said. "Wilson already explained your plan to us, and he won't be taking any payment either until everything is back to normal."

"But it might not ever be back to normal," Marianna protested.

"Don't you worry, dear. We have faith in you. You have your mother's grit and courage, and you'll be ready to face whatever comes up against you." Ellen smiled as she pushed her toward the door. "Go on, that banker is waiting on you."

Marianna nodded and went out to the front steps. The loyal servants' words had boosted her spirits. The carriage was already waiting for her, Wilson standing patiently at the open door.

She smiled and squeezed his hand. "Thank you so much. I'll do my best to get everything back to normal." She stepped up into the carriage.

"I know you will." Wilson winked and closed the door.

Once they reached the bank, Wilson helped Marianna alight from the carriage. "Would you like me to walk in with you, Miss Marianna?"

"No, thank you, Wilson. If I need you, I'll send someone out." She shook her head as she stared up at the towering brick structure. If she needed to sneak around the bank to get to the banker, she didn't want to have to drag Wilson into it.

She sighed. This was it. What happened in this building would determine her future. It didn't seem fair for a future to be decided in a cold, lifeless place such as this.

Inside, the building was pristine. It gleamed with cleanliness, the walls a stark, smooth white. Everyone was all business, and no one smiled.

The tellers were all busy, but one man stood by himself near the door. He had a little carnation pinned to his lapel, so Marianna knew he worked at the bank. He was doing nothing, so she walked up to him.

"Excuse me, sir. Could you show me to Mr. Dudley, please? I have some business I need to conduct with him."

He raised an eyebrow. "You? You're just a girl. What business could Mr. Dudley have with you?"

"It's about my father's loan and the mortgage on our house."

"And why isn't your father here, miss?"

"He's very ill and couldn't come out." It wasn't exactly a lie, as her father was ill. He just didn't know she was here.

"I'm sorry, but banking business is not done with women, and certainly not girls. Excuse me," the man said as a gentleman came toward him.

He stepped away from the door to greet him. Mr. Dudley must be behind that door. The men were deep in conversation, taking no notice of her.

She reached out and twisted the knob. It was unlocked. She breathed a sigh of relief, glanced back at the men, then slipped through the doorway, closing the door behind her.

A long, deserted hallway, as pristine as the lobby of the bank, stretched before her. At the end was a door with a plaque on the front that read, *Charles Dudley, President.*

Taking a deep breath, Marianna lifted a fist and knocked tentatively. She waited a moment. Maybe he wasn't there. What would she do then? She didn't know if she could get past the guard a second time.

A gruff voice shouted through the door. "Was that a knock? If you're going to knock, do it right."

Marianna waited a few seconds more, and after hearing nothing, knocked again, louder.

"Come in," the same gruff voice called to her. She hesitated a split second before pulling open the door. A man bent over the desk, peering at some account books. Without looking up, he said, "Well, what do you want? I haven't got all day. Let me hear it."

Marianna swallowed hard. He wasn't even looking at her. She needed to stay calm. She could do this.

Marianna cleared her throat and began speaking. "Um, sir, I'm here about the Cloverfield mortgage."

At the sound of her voice, the man's head shot up. He jumped out of his seat and came toward Marianna. The rest of her words lodged in her throat as she took a step back.

"What is the meaning of this? How did you get back here?"

"I, uh, walked back here."

"Are you being impertinent, young lady?" The man's eyes were bulging and the veins in his neck looked like they might pop out of his papery skin.

Marianna's heart raced. If she couldn't get him to calm down, she would be thrown out of here before she even had a chance to talk to him. She took a step forward.

"Women don't belong in banks doing a man's business," he yelled.

Marianna took another step forward and laid a hand on the man's arm. "Please, sir, I'm very sorry to trouble you, but my father was too ill to come. Why don't you sit down, and maybe I can get you some tea?"

At her words, Mr. Dudley calmed some. He slapped her hand away, but he sat down.

"No, no, I don't need any tea. State your business." Mr. Dudley's voice was curt, and his eyes were skeptical. "What's so urgent that a father would send his daughter to take care of business?"

Marianna skirted the question and launched right into the speech she had mentally prepared. "Sir, I'm here about the mortgage on Henry Locklear's, home, Cloverfield. He's my father, and it's been our home for many years. If you can give us some more time, we can pay you back. There is a merchant ship with loads of goods headed back this way, but it won't arrive until the beginning of June at the earliest. There is enough merchandise on it to pay you back, if you can give us until then. Please, sir."

Marianna hoped this was true. She had no idea how much merchandise was on the ship, but if she could have some more time, she was sure she could come up with the money.

"Please, if you could give us a little more time." She sounded like she was begging, but she was desperate. She hated the tears that pricked her eyes. She hoped Mr. Dudley couldn't see them.

Mr. Dudley rose from his chair, and a myriad of emotions Marianna could not read flashed across his face. He placed his hands down on the desk hard. Marianna flinched and closed her eyes to ward off more tears.

"Do you have any idea what it's like managing funds with the war going on? I haven't got any spare money lying around anywhere. In fact, I haven't even got all the money I'm supposed to have because the king believes he can just commandeer it for the war." Spittle flew from his mouth, barely missing Marianna as it arched past her.

"No, of course not! You should be at home knitting things for the soldiers, not here at my bank, trying to conduct business like a man." Mr. Dudley didn't even pause for a breath as he continued bellowing. "So, this is Locklear's game then, is it? Time! He's always asking for time. He's lost so many merchant ships that were coming to pay me, I can't even count them all. And now he sends me his weeping daughter to try to soften me with womanly wiles. OUT, woman! This is low, even for Locklear." Mr. Dudley pointed to the door.

Marianna couldn't move for a moment. She was so angry at the insults this banker so freely gave her hard-working father. Mr. Dudley came around and grasped her arm, shoving her toward the door.

Marianna yanked her arm away. "My father works hard I'll have you know. He is ill now, and it has put him behind, but he doesn't know I'm here.

I had thought to save him some grief, but I can see you have no heart, so that won't be happening. I can see my own self out, thank you."

Marianna stomped out of the room, down the hall, through the door, and across the lobby until she reached the front steps.

Wilson was waiting there with the carriage. "So, it didn't go well, Miss Marianna? Don't worry, we'll think of something."

She shook her head, unable to say anything around the knot in her throat. He helped her into the carriage and shut the door quietly behind her.

The tears she'd been trying to hold back escaped. She leaned her head back against the carriage and closed her eyes against them.

The only thing left was the money from the sale of the household items to the auditor. If Annette didn't get enough money from that, their options would be the poorhouse or Bludington.

Chapter 6

Annette was waiting at the door when Marianna and Wilson pulled up in front of Cloverfield. She ran down the steps to meet Marianna, slowing when she saw her sister's face. "He didn't give you the time, did he?"

"No. How much did we get from the auditor?"

"Not enough to pay the bank. There's barely enough to pay for necessities for six months. And this came with the post today." Annette handed Marianna an envelope made of fine linen paper. The return address listed Lord Bludington as the sender. Marianna ripped it open and pulled out an invitation.

"A five-day party? Is he crazy? How can he think we have time for such frivolity when we're on the verge of losing everything?" Marianna threw it down onto the table.

"He's assuming one of us is going to accept, and we no longer have any worries. Or this is his way of convincing one of us to. Either way, we'll have to go. It's already been printed in the papers along with the guest list. If word gets out we refused, people will start talking." Annette's eyes were big with worry.

"Who cares about the stupid gossip anymore?"

"We will if our other creditors find out our true financial state. Then they'll be down our necks for money too."

Despite not wanting to believe it, Marianna knew there was truth behind Annette's words. They would have to go.

"He's trapped us into this." Marianna sighed and rubbed her forehead. "What else was in the mail? Anything from the boys?"

Annette shook her head.

"That's too bad," Marianna said. "They might be able to send some money. We still have a little time. Maybe we will hear from them soon. Just because we go, doesn't mean we have to enjoy the party. When did the invite say it begins?" Marianna had been so angry, she'd hadn't paid attention to the dates.

"In two days. Lots of our friends will be there too. It'll be fun. Try to avoid Bludington as much as possible. Come on, we must start packing." Annette grabbed Marianna's arm and pulled her toward the stairs.

Annette was fifteen. Of course she would love a party like this. It wasn't fair that Annette had to deal with all this when she should be enjoying parties and balls. This was good for her, and Marianna couldn't ruin it by spreading her despair over things. She forced a smile, then followed her eager sister up the stairs to help her pack.

Chapter 7

Two days later, Marianna and Annette headed for Thunderwell, Lord Bludington's estate. After a tiring day's drive, their carriage halted in front of the monstrous building.

It was made of gray stone and stood four stories tall. A single tower rose from the back of the house, giving the manor a castle-like appearance. Dark clouds lingered above the tower setting a pall of gloom over the mansion.

She'd known it was big, but this was gigantic. It looked like the places described in Annette's mystery novels, the ones where the heroine didn't make it out alive. Goosebumps prickled her skin, and Marianna rubbed her arms as she stepped out of the carriage and walked toward the house.

She glanced back to see Annette close behind, staring up at the hall, a look of awe on her face. Marianna and Annette had grown up in luxury, but their manor was nothing compared to this. There had to be at least twenty bedrooms.

When Annette noticed Marianna's eyes on her, she quickened her pace and grabbed ahold of Marianna's arm. "Well, if you do marry him, this would all be yours. No wonder he's so willing to marry without a dowry."

"I'm not going to marry him, and besides, this place is terribly gloomy looking." Marianna rang the doorbell. A moment later, a tall grim-faced woman opened the door.

"May I help you?" the woman asked in a monotone voice, her face expressionless.

"Um, yes. We're here for the party. Marianna and Annette Locklear." Nerves formed a tight ball in Marianna's stomach. The house seemed an unlikely place for a party, and the housekeeper an even more unlikely hostess. Marianna almost expected to be turned away.

"Oh yes, come in." She opened the door wide and spun around. "Follow me, please. I shall send some men to fetch your bags," the housekeeper uttered in the same tone.

She led them into a dark entryway and down a long hallway. Laughter chased by quiet murmurs echoed down to them, and light crept out under the double doors that stood at the end of the hall. At least the people who were already here seemed to be having a good time.

The housekeeper pushed open both doors and motioned for the girls to go in. Marianna barely managed to hold back a gasp. It was magnificent!

Three massive chandeliers hung from the ceiling, filling the room with light. The marble floor gleamed in a swirling pattern of pink and white. It grabbed the light from above and reflected it around the room.

The walls were a mint green. People filled the ballroom, laughing, talking, dancing. A long table filled with food and drink stood against the far wall.

She never would have expected this. Maybe she was imagining the gloom before. Marianna glanced at Annette. Delight covered her face as she moved to the center of the room, spinning as she went, taking everything in.

Matthew met Annette in the middle of the room. She grasped his hands, and he twirled her into the crowd of dancers. Marianna turned away, hoping to find Susan. Instead, she nearly slammed into Lord Bludington. She bit back a gasp, trying to school her features so he wouldn't know he'd surprised her.

"Welcome, Miss Marianna. I'm so glad you and your sister could make it. Come, greet your friends." In the cheerfully bright room, Bludington's beard and hair no longer seemed so garish.

"Thank you for inviting us. This looks like it will be a wonderful party," she said sincerely.

Bludington took her arm and led her to a small group where many of her friends were clustered. Susan latched onto Marianna. After making small talk for several minutes, she pulled Marianna away from the rest of the group and dragged her over to a deserted corner.

"Marianna, you'll never guess what I found out today. Bludington has had this ballroom closed for several years, ever since his previous wife died. He opened it up just for you, and when he found out you like books, he also opened the library, which had been locked up even longer, ever since his first wife died. She loved the library. Marianna, he's doing all this for you!"

Susan was glowing with the information she had gleaned, but Marianna still couldn't bring herself to like Bludington.

"Don't get so happy. I don't think I can marry him."

"Is this still about Will?" Susan's voice grew soft. "I'm sorry, Mari, I'm not trying to be mean, but you've got to let him go. He'd want you to be able to move on and find some happiness in life, not mourn him forever."

Marianna was silent for a few minutes. If only Susan knew. It was so much more than Will. In fact, the events of the last several days had kept her so busy she hadn't even thought about Will. A cringe of guilt flashed through her for so completely forgetting about him.

"I'm sorry. I know it hurts, but it's the truth. You have to move on."

"It's not just that, Sue. There's so much I want to tell you. Is there somewhere we can sit and talk privately?"

"I think so." Susan led Marianna through some open double glass doors. Several iron benches lined the edge of a brick terrace. It was well lit by lanterns that formed a half circle around the terrace. A little farther down, a well-cared for garden grew, and a bright floral scent hung in the air.

The girls claimed one of the iron benches, and Marianna told Susan all the things that had happened in the last few days, leaving out only a few details.

"You mean if you married Bludington, he would pay off your father's debt and give him more money to live on? Marianna, why ever would you consider trying to get out of such a thing? He must care a lot about you if he will go to all that expense to get you."

"You don't understand. There is something very strange about him. He gives me the creeps."

"That is the most ridiculous thing I have ever heard." Susan stood up then, her voice getting louder, as she paced across the terrace. "Blue hair doesn't mean there's something wrong with him. He was born with it. I've never known you to be like this, to hold something that one can't help against him." She stopped pacing and stared at Marianna.

"You need to snap out of it. You can help your family here. It's not as if you'd be marrying the devil, and there'd be some benefits. I mean, the man is rich as Midas, and think about the parties you could host in that magnificent ballroom." Susan walked over to Marianna and took her hands. Her voice softened.

"Think about your family. They need you right now. They are here, now, living and breathing. Will is not."

Susan's words stung, but there was some truth to them. Marianna did pride herself on not holding things one couldn't control against a person. But still, she got such a bad feeling whenever she was around Bludington. And all his other wives had died. Would she die soon if she married him?

Susan pulled her into a hug. "I promise I won't say any more about this, if you promise me, you'll think about what I said." Marianna nodded, unable to speak, fearful that she might cry.

"Come on, let's go back to the party. We might be missing a lot of fun." Susan pulled Marianna off the bench, and they went into the ballroom.

As they entered, Bludington walked over to them. Marianna glanced at Susan who smiled, squeezed her hand, and walked away. Bludington gave a little bow.

"May I have this dance with the prettiest lady here?"

Marianna knew she couldn't be rude, and as she had no real reason for disliking the man, she gave a little curtsey and accepted.

She spent the rest of the evening in Lord Bludington's company. He was courteous and thoughtful, and his eyes no longer seemed piercing, but Marianna still couldn't get rid of her unease. She breathed a sigh of relief when Bludington announced it was time to turn in.

He rang for the servants, and they came to the ballroom doors and waited for their instructions. He called a maid over to where he and Marianna were standing.

"This is Betsy. She'll be your lady's maid while you're here and will show you to your room. Good night and sleep well." Bludington bowed and kissed her hand, turning to give orders to the rest of the servants.

"This way, ma'am," Betsy said and walked out of the ballroom. Marianna held back, glancing over the people still waiting for room assignments. Her sister occupied in conversation with Matthew, and Susan gave her a little wink and a smile.

Marianna sighed and rushed out of the room to see Betsy disappearing down the hall. She ran to catch up with the girl, but Betsy didn't even seem to notice her charge had not been with her the whole time.

After a few more turns, and a climb up some stairs, Betsy stopped in front of some double doors. She pushed them opened and stepped aside, waiting for Marianna to enter.

In the center of the large room stood a queen-sized bed covered with a downy comforter, white with little blue flowers. Blue and white pillows filled the head of the bed, and matching curtains adorned the windows. One window had a cushy window seat. Another was actually a glass door that opened out onto a balcony that overlooked the gardens.

On one of side of the room, a bright blue chair sat in front of the fireplace. A bookcase sat to the side of it. On the other side of the room, near the window seat, was a washstand and mirror. And above, lighting up the beautiful room, was another chandelier, not as big as the ones in the ballroom, but still impressive.

"When you're ready for the lantern light, miss, pull the bell, and Marcus will come and put the chandelier out." Betsy pointed to a bell rope.

"I'm ready now. After he does that, you can help me ready for bed. I'm very tired."

Betsy nodded and pulled the rope before leaning against the wall to wait. Marianna went over and sank down into the blue chair. It was so comfortable, she could've fallen asleep right there. Bludington must really be trying to impress her. She had never seen such luxury before. A chandelier in a bedroom. It was madness.

A knock at the door interrupted Marianna's thoughts. She nodded at Betsy to let the man in. Marianna turned to see how Marcus would put the chandelier out. He came in with a long pole. On the end were four snuffs, in a row. Marcus made quick work of snuffing out each candle on the chandelier, while Betsy lit a lantern. He bowed to Marianna and left the room, then Betsy helped Marianna into her night clothes.

"I'll be back in the morning, ma'am. Have a good night's rest." With a little bob, Betsy exited the room. Marianna climbed into bed. As she fell against the soft mattress, she let out a sigh.

She was glad Betsy had said she'd be back because Marianna would never be able to find the dining room on her own. This place was massive, but so beautiful, she could only wonder what else Bludington had planned to try and impress her.

Chapter 8

Marianna awoke to a knock on the door. What time was it? Her eyes flew open as she tried to pull herself from the dregs of sleep. Where was she?

Sunlight glistened off the crystals hanging from the chandelier above her, filling the room with rainbows. The events from last night came rushing back to her.

"We're not at home anymore." Marianna groaned, rubbed the sleep from her eyes, and sat up. "Come in."

Betsy ducked in through the door and bobbed down in a deep curtsey. She avoided looking directly at Marianna.

"I'm so sorry, miss. Everyone else is up and about, and your sister insisted I wake you. She said you would not want to miss any of the party events."

Marianna's heart softened. She knew how persuasive and insistent Annette could be. This poor girl was probably afraid she would lose her job here.

"It's fine, Betsy. I'm glad you woke me. I shouldn't like to be the only one still in bed. Come, help me get ready for the day."

Betsy looked up and smiled. "Yes, miss," she replied as she rushed to get Marianna's dress out. The blue and yellow cotton day dress didn't require as much help as a ballgown would have, but Betsy still arranged it perfectly for Marianna to step into before buttoning up the back and tying up the bodice laces.

She escorted Marianna to the dressing table chair and started on her hair. "Don't worry, miss. I know how to do all the current styles." Marianna smiled into the mirror, her eyes catching Betsy's. "Something simple is fine. I don't go through this much trouble at home."

Betsy seemed desperate to please her, and Marianna hoped her smile was reassuring. Was she afraid of losing her job? Surely Bludington hadn't threatened something like that, had he? Although many members of high society would fire servants for far less than messing up a hairstyle. She'd heard of people firing servants for something as simple as spilling a drink.

After Marianna had dressed and Betsy had put up her hair, another knock came at the door.

"Go ahead and get it Betsy," Marianna said, expecting to see her sister or Susan. The door opened, and she turned to look. She barely kept from gasping. Lord Bludington stood at her door.

"Good morning, or I should say, afternoon. I hope you slept well."

"Yes, very well, thank you."

Did everyone know she was the last one up? She averted her eyes and smoothed out imaginary wrinkles in her dress.

"Might I escort you down for the light lunch being served in the dining room? I'm sure you're quite hungry."

Not knowing what else to say, and not having any clue where the dining room was located, Marianna agreed. Bludington took her arm. They went through a myriad of hallways and down some stairs until they stood before yet another set of gilded edge double doors. Did every room in this place have double doors?

Inside there was a long dining room table that stretched across most of the room. The guests were already seated. Marianna flushed as Lord Bludington led her past everyone down to the end. Susan watched her with a little smirk on her face. Annette was also grinning widely.

Bludington was attentive during the meal, checking to see that Marianna had everything she needed. As the meal ended, he leaned close to Marianna and whispered in her ear. "After lunch, I have something I would like to show you, if that's satisfactory to you?"

The food in her stomach curdled, making her nauseous. Marianna pulled back, unnerved by Bludington's closeness. Having no reason to object, she nodded her agreement. Why would he want someone who was not interested in him? She wasn't exactly a stunning beauty.

Soon people began scooting their chairs back, going off to whatever entertainment they had planned for the afternoon. Bludington pushed his chair out and stood. He held out his hand to Marianna. With a little sigh, she took it.

He tucked her arm under his and led her down yet another hallway. When they reached a set of intricately carved wooden double doors, he pulled Marianna to a stop. Carved fairies and mermaids frolicked up and down the edges of the wood. Marianna reached out and traced the outline of a fairy.

"This is exquisite. Who did these carvings?" They looked like La Guardia's work.

Bludington smiled and shrugged. "I had this room prepared for you. I understand you love books, so take any you want from this room. You can come here anytime you want to read or look through them. Make yourself at home." He pushed open the doors.

Ceiling to floor bookshelves lined the entire perimeter of the room, except for a small portion of the far wall that housed the fireplace. On each wall was a sliding ladder, granting easy access to even the highest shelf.

In front of the fireplace, sat two love seats and a sofa. In the middle of the room was a desk and a table, giving plenty of room for one to do research. All the furniture was made from a deep mahogany wood with blue velvet seat cushions. The sapphire blue carpet was plush, and Marianna's boots sank into it. From the ceiling hung another golden chandelier. Even though she didn't trust this man, she was amazed by this generous gift.

"It's beautiful," she breathed. "Thank you." She grasped his hand.

"I'm happy to see that I have finally done something to please you. I will leave you now to the books. Enjoy." With a little bow, Bludington backed out of the room and closed the doors behind him.

Marianna spent all afternoon in the library poring over the books. Every book she had ever heard of and wanted to read was there. All her favorite books—the ones she loved to read repeatedly—were there, and the couches were comfortable enough to sleep on. It was one of the most peaceful afternoons Marianna had had in a very long time. Much too soon, Bludington returned.

"Are you ready for dinner? I see you've taken my advice and enjoyed yourself." He motioned to the numerous books spread out on the desk, table, and sofa. Marianna felt slightly embarrassed at the mess she had made.

"Yes, sorry. I didn't realize it was so late. I'll get all this." Marianna bent down, scooping books up into her arms. Bludington pulled the books away from her and set them back down.

"No, no, don't worry. This is why there are servants. There is a man in charge of seeing to the order of this room. He'll have everything back in place before you can be back in here again." Bludington offered her his arm. She accepted it, and he escorted her back to the dining room.

This time Marianna tried to pay special attention, so she could find her way back to the library. When they reached the dining room, Marianna was confident she knew the route.

During dinner, Bludington was again attentive to all of Marianna's needs. She began to feel smothered, afraid that she would have to spend another evening dancing with the man. Although his hair and eyes seemed less harsh than they had at first, she still wasn't comfortable around him.

As everyone left the dinner table, Marianna managed to slip away from Bludington and join Susan in the ballroom. Susan saw her coming and grabbed her arm, pulling her away from the crowd.

"Oh, Marianna, he's absolutely taken with you. I heard he showed you the library and it was so wonderful that you spent all afternoon there. Was he with you?" Susan's eyes glittered with excitement, and her hand clung tightly to Marianna's arm.

What was this? Why was everyone trying to set her up with this man? Why couldn't everyone leave her alone? She didn't get in their business. Marianna pulled her arm out of Susan's grasp.

"No, he wasn't with me. The library was nice enough, but you don't marry someone for their library. I have to talk to Annette." Marianna whirled away from Susan and wandered through the crowd of people, searching for her sister.

Several people tried to stop her, to offer congratulations, but she barely acknowledged them as she pressed on through the crowd. She moved faster, desperate to get away from all the questions and silly remarks.

The colors of the girls' dresses swirled before her eyes. The heat from all the bodies in the room was overtaking her, and she stumbled. A firm hand caught her before she fell to the floor.

Marianna looked up into the concerned eyes of Matthew. Annette reached out and squeezed Marianna's other hand.

"Mari, are you okay? You look a little flushed."

"I'm just hot. I think I need some fresh air."

Annette and Matthew led her out to the terrace and made her sit on one of the ironwork benches. Annette sat down beside her and put an arm around Marianna's shoulder. Matthew stood at Annette's side.

"Are you okay? Do you need anything?"

Annette ignored Matthew's questions and began talking. "It's all the excitement, Mari. Bludington sure has gone to a lot of trouble to convince you to marry him. He seems quite sweet. I think you two would make a nice couple."

Marianna never said she would marry him. In fact, she made it obvious she intended not to. She would've shared her thoughts with her sister, if she hadn't been ready to pass out. Instead, she ignored her sister's comments, closed her eyes, and leaned her head against the back of the bench.

She'd wanted to talk to Annette about how distressed Bludington had been making her, but it was clear she was just as enamored with him as everyone else seemed to be. She didn't want to have that conversation in front of Matthew anyway. He was sweet, but she wasn't sure he didn't have loose lips, and the last thing she needed was someone spreading the news that she wasn't interested in Bludington.

"You both go back to the party. I'm fine, just a little tired. The fresh air is helping." Marianna opened her eyes and looked at her sister's doubtful expression. Marianna reached out and squeezed Annette's hand. "Seriously, I'll be okay. Go. Have fun dancing with Matthew." Marianna pushed Annette forward and smiled at Matthew.

"You're sure you don't need anything? A glass of water, maybe?" Matthew offered.

"I'm fine, but thank you. Go do what you should be doing—enjoying the party."

With one last look, Annette and Matthew left Marianna and joined the rest of the merrymakers in the ballroom. Marianna closed her eyes once again. She took several deep breaths, and the beginning of an idea came to her.

She jumped up and walked to the edge of the terrace into the grass that lined the side and around the manor until she reached the back door. She climbed the steps and tried the doorknob.

It opened, and she peered around inside. No one in sight. Perfect. She slipped in and closed the door behind her.

Marianna was pretty sure the dining room was down the hall to the left. So that meant the library would be that way too. She turned but was soon lost in the maze of hallways.

She tried to turn around and go back the way she came, but that only made her more confused. She stopped to think. Lighted candles were mounted in even intervals, casting eerie shadows on the walls. They leapt large before dancing back smaller, repeating the cycle over again and again. All the hallways looked the same—dark and gloomy. How did anyone ever find their way around this place?

Around the next corner, Marianna saw a hallway she didn't think she had been down before. It was darker than any of the others. She walked over to the closest candle and pulled it from its holder before starting down the unlit hallway.

It was colder and longer than any of the others had been. She couldn't see the end. She wrapped her arms around herself and considered turning back, but she'd come this far, so she might as well find out what was down here.

She walked for several minutes before the hallway ended against a wall. A painting hung in the center of the wall, and to the right of it was a door.

What kind of room was this, and why was it all by itself? Marianna stopped at the door and tried to open it. It was locked. She bent down closer to the doorknob, noticing a tiny keyhole underneath it.

She examined the painting, her eyes widening at the gruesome scene. A dwarf, with hair the same color as Bludington's, clutched a kneeling blonde girl, her back against his chest. He held a dagger to her throat. The girl's eyes were full of terror as she stared across the fire. On the other side of the fire, a hag in tattered gray robes held her hands out in supplication, as if pleading with the dwarf to let the girl go.

Why would one have such a gruesome painting? She wanted to turn away, but she couldn't help but peer closer.

The hilt of the dwarf's knife glistened in the flickering candlelight. A wolf's face encrusted with red jewels for eyes glared out at Marianna. She swallowed hard and took a step back. The eyes followed her movement.

Were the eyes watching her? Marianna let out a choked laugh. She was being silly. It was a painting.

They eyes got brighter. She took several steps to the side. The eyes followed her movement.

They were definitely watching her. Marianna whirled around and came face to face with a tall, skinny man.

His face was pale and gaunt. His eyes were a gray so light they looked almost colorless. The light from his candle reflected off his skin and eyes, making him look like a ghost. Marianna choked back a scream.

Chapter 9

"Who are you?" Marianna whispered.

The man said nothing. He stared at her for a long moment, his face glowing eerily in the candlelight. Was he a ghost? Was that why she hadn't heard him coming? Was this place haunted? But a ghost couldn't hold a candle, right? Marianna's thoughts raced as she tried to determine what was real and what wasn't.

The man spoke, halting her spiraling thoughts. "I'm Dunsten, the butler. I think a better question is, who are you, and what are you doing in this part of the house? No guests are allowed back here." His voice was quiet but steely, and his pale eyes bored holes into Marianna as he waited for an answer.

Marianna cleared her throat and tried to make her voice strong. Her words still came out hoarse. "I'm Marianna Locklear, part of the party group. I was looking for the library, but I'm afraid I got turned around. If you could show me back to the ballroom, I would be most grateful."

Dunsten stared at her, and Marianna thought he was going to deny her request, but then he gave a little bow and wordlessly started back down the hallway. Marianna shivered and ran her hands up and down her arms. She ran to catch up with Dunsten, who was walking very fast.

After a dozen turns through the maze of hallways, Marianna finally saw the double doors that led to the ballroom. Dunsten stopped a few feet in front of them and turned to Marianna. "Here you are, miss. I suggest you do no more touring of the house on your own." The words were unoffensive, but his tone made them sound like a threat.

Marianna nodded and rushed into the ballroom.

It looked as she had left it. Dancers whirled around the floors. People gathered in groups talking, and still others were gorging themselves at the food-laden table. The normalcy slowed her racing heart. Maybe she had been overreacting. She wiped her hands down her dress and sucked in a breath.

She found Susan and hurried over to her. Her friend looked distressed and started talking before Marianna even had a chance to say anything. "Where have you been? I couldn't find you. Are you okay?"

"I have to talk to you, in private." She grabbed her friend's arm and started dragging her toward the terrace.

"Mari, what's the matter? You look terrified, like you've seen a ghost or something."

"I thought I did," Marianna muttered.

"What did you say?"

"Nothing." They reached the terrace, and Marianna glanced around. Once she was confident they were alone, she pulled Susan to a bench and told her about the spooky hallway with the weird painting.

"I'm really scared. I knew there was something creepy about Bludington."

"What? I don't understand. I mean, I agree the painting is a little weird, and the butler might look strange, but you still can't call a person evil because of that." She reached over and squeezed Marianna's hand reassuringly. "I'm sure it was scary. You got lost in a strange place. Don't let your imagination go wild. I think you're stressed."

"Why won't anyone believe me? It's not my imagination. Something is weird about this place." Marianna pulled away and stood up. She paced back and forth across the terrace, trying to come up with a way to explain what she was feeling.

At that moment, Bludington stepped out onto the terrace. Marianna halted and looked over at Susan in panic. "Did he hear me?" she whispered. Susan shook her head helplessly.

"There you are. I wondered where you'd gone off to," Bludington said as he reached the girls.

Marianna swallowed the nervous lump in her throat and managed a strained smile. Her knees nearly buckled, and Bludington reached out to support her.

"Are you all right, Miss Marianna? You look a little pale."

"Oh, I'm fine. A little tired, I suppose." Marianna gave a nervous little laugh.

"Yes, she'll be fine. She tends to get overexcited at parties." Susan pulled Marianna into a hug and whispered in her ear, "Forget all that nonsense you've dreamed up in your head, and you will be fine." Smiling at Marianna, Susan walked away.

Marianna stared after her, wishing her friend understood how much Bludington frightened her. She turned back to him, a smile pasted on her face.

"If you don't mind, I think I'll turn in now. As I said before, I'm quite tired."

"Of course. I'll call for Betsy."

In a minute Betsy was there, leading Marianna up to her room and helping her ready for bed. The chandelier had not been lit, so Marianna didn't have to call for Marcus. She was thankful because she was ready to sleep. Sleep gave her freedom from the worries that were facing her now, and the bed here was amazing. She fell back against the downy pillow and was fast asleep in minutes.

Betsy came to wake Marianna the next morning. "Miss Marianna, Lord Bludington has big plans for today." She pulled open Marianna's wardrobe and selected a pale yellow dress with mint green lacing and trim. Where had that dress come from?

"This will be perfect." Betsy held up the dress and swayed.

"Plans, what kind of plans?" This didn't sound good. And now Betsy had been instructed to pick out her clothing, from a stash Bludington had? Had the dress belonged to one of his dead wives? Marianna stared at the dress uneasily.

"Oh, don't worry, these are good plans," Betsy assured her. "He invited all your friends and your sister to come along."

"Along on what?"

Betsy motioned to Marianna to change out of her nightdress. Marianna rolled her eyes but did as Betsy asked. Betsy laced Marianna up into the yellow dress before answering.

"Just as I thought. Perfect!" Betsy exclaimed.

"Where did this dress come from?" Marianna asked as she stood in front of the mirror.

Betsy was right. The dress was flattering on her. Her dark curls made the yellow color pop and the dress fit like it had been made for her. She fingered the tiny mint-colored bows that lined the neckline.

"Oh, Bludington had a wardrobe prepared for the party. Dresses of all shapes and sizes, for any of the ladies to choose from, but I think some were made with you in mind."

That practice wasn't unheard of in Anderi, but only the wealthiest of wealthiest ever did so. She'd had no idea that Bludington thought about anyone else, and a sliver of guilt shot through her.

Before she could say anything else, Betsy pushed her into the dressing table chair and began arranging her hair.

"Lord Bludington is taking you all out. First, a carriage ride to the lake, and then a picnic. And if you're lucky, you'll get to go out on the boat."

"A lake? I haven't seen a lake around here."

"That's because it's the opposite way of town. It's past the village where I'm from. And it's beautiful. The water is so clear it sparkles in the sun. And there are all these weeping willow trees." She sighed. "I would love to take a boat ride out on it, but I've never had the chance."

"Well, perhaps you could come with us," Marianna said.

Betsy's eyes grew wide. "Oh no, miss. I didn't mean that. I wasn't fishing for an invitation."

"You didn't. I asked. Do you want to come with us?"

Betsy hesitated a split second, desire flashing through her eyes. "Oh, no ma'am! I couldn't do that. It wouldn't be proper. If I showed up to go on a trip with the lords and ladies, I'd surely be dismissed. And I can't lose this job, Miss Marianna. I just can't."

"I insist you come, as my lady's maid. I might need assistance out there so far from the manor. You can't be let go for following a guest's directions."

Betsy's eyes sparkled as she bobbed into a curtsey. "No, I certainly can't. If you insist, I suppose I'll have to come."

Moments later, they were climbing down the manor stairs. In the drive, stood a white and golden carriage hitched to four beautiful black horses with flowing manes and tails. It was open-air with three red velvet bench seats. Bludington stood next to it along with Annette, Matthew, Susan, and Daniel.

"Isn't it beautiful?" Annette rushed over to her sister and grabbed her arm.

"Yes, it's lovely." Marianna turned to Lord Bludington. "I'll require my lady's maid on this outing." She motioned to Betsy, who still stood on the manor steps.

"Of course, whatever you need. There's plenty of room on the driver's bench for another person," Lord Bludington said waving up at the carriage.

Marianna took a step back. The creepy, ghostly man from the previous night sat in the driver's seat.

She swallowed hard and schooled her features. Of course she would see him again. He was the butler.

"Thank you." She forced the words out, before shooting a glance at Betsy.

Betsy smiled and waved, nearly bouncing up and down with excitement. Lord Bludington helped Marianna onto the first bench seat and the others climbed in behind them.

The horses galloped forward at a breakneck speed. Marianna's heart lurched and she grabbed the side of the carriage in a death grip. She relaxed a little as the horses hit their stride and the carriage settled into the rhythm. Clearly Bludington wanted to show off.

As the carriage rattled down the road, wind blew into Marianna's ears making it impossible for her to hear her friends behind her. She sighed and turned to Lord Bludington.

"I didn't know you had a lake on your property," she yelled over the wind.

"It's out on the edge, past the manor village."

Marianna nodded. She said nothing as she enjoyed the passing scenery. Vibrant green fields dotted with black horses, golden fields of wheat that shimmered in the wind, and cornfields full of emerald stalks with waving heads of yellow fur.

She had expected to go through the village, but the carriage skirted it, and all she could see was the fountain where the townspeople would gather to get water. Hardly anyone was at the fountain as they bounced past it. That was odd. It seemed like everyone would be there at this time, trying to stock up on the water they'd need for the day.

"I thought we might have to go through the manor village," Marianna yelled.

Lord Bludington shook his head. "There's not much to the village, I'm afraid. Hardly anyone even lives there anymore."

"Oh." Marianna nodded. That was even stranger. How could he have such a fine place, but no people living in the village to help him maintain it?

Before she could think on that anymore, the carriage rounded a bend and the air turned cooler. A large body of water appeared like a sparkling diamond in the distance. Fresh, crisp air filled her nostrils, and she breathed in deep as the carriage slowed.

Within minutes it pulled to a stop in front of the lake. Sunlight danced across the water. A wooden dock stretched halfway to the middle, and several colorful rowboats bounced next to it. Large weeping willows lined one end of the lake. Their branches swept back and forth so gently they could put someone to sleep if one watched them long enough.

"It's so pretty," Susan said as Daniel helped her down from the carriage. She looked over at Marianna with a knowing grin. "This is a perfect day for a picnic too!"

"Yes, and rowboats!" Annette turned to Lord Bludington. "Please say we're going to take the rowboats out."

"Of course, whatever you want. There's plenty to do here at Thunderwell. I want you to have a chance to enjoy it all." Bludington turned to offer his arm to Marianna. "But first, let's eat."

Dunsten jumped from the driver's bench and helped Betsy down. She slipped behind Marianna and followed at a discreet distance. Dunsten grabbed a huge picnic basket from the back of the carriage and hauled it over to the shade of a weeping willow tree. He spread out a blanket and opened the basket. There was roast chicken, cheese, sourdough rolls, grapes, strawberries, and even some chocolate squares.

Everyone sat down and dug in. "So, Annette, what do you think of my Friesians?" Lord Bludington motioned to the black horses that were now milling about grazing on the bright green grass.

"They're beautiful," she breathed. "I love Friesians."

"Me too," Bludington agreed. "I have a new filly. My grooms don't have time to train her properly, so I was thinking you'd like to have her."

Marianna jerked her head up and stared over at Annette. Excitement covered her face.

"Really, you're going to give her to me?" she asked.

"If you want her, she's yours."

"Oh, wow. Thank you! That's so generous. I've always wanted a horse of my own. Thank you so much!" Annette jumped up and ran over to give Bludington a little hug. She raced back over to Matthew and chattered away about all she could do with her new horse.

Bludington looked over at Marianna, a wry smile on his face. "It doesn't take much to make her happy, huh?"

Marianna nodded silently. What was his game here? How could he want to marry her so badly? She shoveled food in her mouth so she wouldn't have to say anything.

Soon the lunch was finished, and Annette decided it was time to take out the rowboats.

"We've got the yellow one," she called as she raced toward it. Matthew followed at a more sedate pace.

"I'm glad your sister's having such a good time. What about you?" Bludington asked as he led Marianna toward the rowboats.

"Oh, fine. It is a beautiful day." Marianna looked around for Betsy. When she spotted her, she motioned her over. "I'll need Betsy to ride with us in case I get seasick. She has my smelling salts and other medications."

Marianna had never been seasick in her life. She'd grown up wandering about her father's ships, often climbing up on the masts all the way to the crow's nest, but it was the only excuse she could think of. Betsy beamed as she squeezed in next to Marianna.

"Don't worry, milord. I won't make a sound." Betsy made a zipping motion across her lips.

Lord Bludington laughed. "Why, Betsy, you can talk if you want. We don't mind." Confusion spread across Betsy's face, and she looked at Marianna. Marianna shrugged her shoulders.

"All the same, I'll stay quiet. I'm only here for my miss." She nodded and closed her eyes as if that would help her keep quiet.

"So, what book do you like best in the library?" Bludington asked Marianna.

"Hmm," Marianna paused. "That's a hard question. How could I choose one book? I suppose if I had to, it might be *The Big Book of Fairytales*. There are so many different stories, it would almost be like having more than one book. And fairytales are my favorite kind of story."

"Why is that?" Bludington asked.

Marianna thought a moment before answering. "I suppose because life is rarely a fairytale, but it's kind of nice to imagine that somewhere, maybe in some other world, someone is living a fairytale life."

"Interesting," Bludington murmured, his eyes pensive.

What was he thinking? Maybe she shouldn't have told him that.

"You're a bit of a scholar, aren't you?" Bludington asked.

"I suppose, though I never had any formal training above the schoolroom."

"Would you like to?" Bludington leaned forward.

"What do you mean?"

"Well, the Strausburg Institute is not far from here. You could attend some classes there."

"Do they accept female students?" Marianna asked with a snarky laugh. He was crazy. The only place she could go was Tarn's Institute for Women. She'd have to go overseas, and he'd never let her leave the country if they were married.

"I could persuade them to let you attend."

"Seriously?"

"Most definitely." Bludington eyes were earnest. Of course, this was probably dependent upon her marrying him.

"Hmm, it certainly is something to think about," Marianna answered.

The sky darkened as clouds rolled in.

"Row in, a storm is coming," Matthew yelled as he rowed his and Annette's boat toward shore.

They made it back to the dock, but light rain fell as they rushed for the carriage. Dunsten clucked the horses into action, and they sped back to the manor. They arrived just in time, as the massive dark clouds that hung low over the manor poured rain upon them.

Marianna dashed into the house behind the others, managing not to get too wet. A shiver ran down her spine as she looked out at the storm. Why did darkness always hang over the manor?

Chapter 10

After the picnic, Marianna went to the library to read. All the books from the day before had been returned to their proper spaces. She sighed. She would have to hunt them all down again, but she did remember where most of them had come from.

As she walked toward her favorite shelf, something caught her eye. On the side table sat a pamphlet that hadn't been there the day before. Marianna picked it up.

The Strausburg Institute - the finest higher learning establishment in Anderi. Over 100 courses of learning to help you cultivate the life you want to have.

Marianna flipped it open and read through the courses. This was amazing. Could Bludington really get her a spot? Her finger traced over the course that read *Novelist – Read and study the greatest works of our time and learn how to write your own outstanding work.* It went on to list all the novelists who had attended Strausburg.

Why was she even thinking about this? It was highly unlikely that even Bludington could get her a spot. Besides, would it really be worth it to marry him for this? Marianna snorted and hid the pamphlet under some books.

She went over to one of the shelves and located the book she hadn't had time to finish yesterday, pulling it out. She struggled to concentrate as her mind kept wandering back to the pamphlet and the possibilities it represented.

Would it really be so bad to marry him for the chance to attend her dream school? It would be the opportunity of a lifetime. Marianna shook her head. She couldn't think like that. She slammed the book shut and stuffed it back onto the shelf as the library doors squeaked open.

Lord Bludington had returned. He escorted her to dinner and was so attentive, passing her the sauce for the chicken, and refilling her wine glass. She had everything she needed before she realized she needed it.

After dinner, everyone moved to the ballroom, and Bludington engaged her in the first dance. As the music started up, Bludington swung Marianna close to him.

She gasped. Bludington had never pulled her so close before. A wild gleam shone in his icy blue eyes. Her heart raced and for one wild moment, Marianna thought he knew about the wandering she had done the previous night.

He spun her out in a twirl, and as she turned to meet him, the gleam was gone. She must have imagined it. She was being crazy, thinking he was out to get her.

As her sister and Susan had pointed out, he had been nothing but gracious, going out of his way to see all of Marianna's needs were taken care of.

"So, Miss Marianna, have you enjoyed your time here?" His voice was kind and friendly.

"Yes. Thank you for your hospitality."

"I'm pleased you have enjoyed it. Come, I have someone I want you to meet." Bludington led her off the dance floor and over to a thin, reedy man with salt and pepper hair. A single spectacle hung from a chain on his coat's breast pocket, and he held a polished black cane.

"Professor Drakir," Bludington said. The man turned, a questioning look in his eye. "This is the exceptional young lady I was telling you about. She's a perfect candidate for your first female student."

A broad smile covered the professor's face as he reached out to accept Marianna's extended hand. "A pleasure to meet you, Miss Marianna."

"The pleasure is all mine. I've heard so many good things about Strausburg and would love to attend classes there." Marianna couldn't hold back her smile, her heart filling with joy. Maybe this was possible. Maybe she could go to Strausburg.

"I would love to have you. Once I've convinced my fellow board members it's time to have a female student, I shall let you know, and you will have the first spot." Professor Drakir's eyes gleamed with joy, but Marianna struggled to keep the smile on her face.

He was the only one who'd agreed to this? There were ten board members! She knew this had been too good to be true. It could be years before the other nine members agreed. She should have known better than to get her hopes up.

Marianna barely managed to maintain conversation with the professor. Though it couldn't have been more than five minutes, it felt like hours. Finally, Bludington whisked her away, back onto the dance floor, oblivious to her distress at the news.

"I don't suppose you've made your decision yet?"

His question interrupted Marianna's thoughts. Wait, what? Was he going to make her decide early? Her pulse quickened and her palms grew slick.

He spoke again. "As I can see you have not, I'll retract that question. There's still time, and I won't ask you again until the time is up. Let's not talk of it since it makes you uneasy." Bludington smiled, rambling about inconsequential things.

Marianna wasn't listening. Her mind was on the proposal she had to give an answer to. Maybe she could do it. He didn't seem as bad as she first thought. And the time she would have in that library. Maybe she could get into Strausburg within a few years. She wouldn't even see him that much since this manor was so large. There was still time for her to decide.

For some reason Marianna couldn't identify, she felt the need to hold back. She didn't fear Lord Bludington anymore. The feelings of unease were mostly gone, but something about giving in to Bludington's proposal didn't seem right.

Before she knew it, the night was over, and Betsy appeared at Marianna's side to take her to her room. Marianna readied for bed quickly, but sleep eluded her, her mind dwelling on the looming proposal. She tossed and turned trying to put it out of her mind. Finally, in the early hours of the morning, she drifted off into a restless sleep.

A long hallway emerged before Marianna. The blue haired dwarf from the painting stood at the end of it. He raised his wolf-headed knife high above his head, and ran toward her, the ruby eyes pinning her to the spot.

He was coming to kill her! Marianna wanted to run, but her legs were like ice, frozen to the ground. She tried inching her feet forward, but they refused to move.

She needed to get out of here! With a yell, she lunged forward, her legs finally cooperating.

She ran through the unfamiliar maze of Bludington's hallways, going deeper and deeper into the maze with no idea of how to get out. The dwarf came closer. He could nearly reach out and touch her.

She tried to run faster, but a hand grabbed her hair and tugged her backwards. She whipped around trying to break free, only to find that dwarf was no longer a dwarf, but Lord Bludington. He gave her one of his creepy smiles and raised the knife above her throat. Marianna screamed.

Chapter 11

"Miss, are you all right?" Betsy hovered over Marianna, concern etched across her features.

Marianna couldn't answer, her lips frozen with fear. She shook her head, her mind spinning as she tried to discern reality from her nightmare.

"Miss Marianna, you had a nightmare. It must have been awful to make you scream so." Betsy took Marianna's hands in her own, rubbing them, trying to bring warmth back to them. "You're okay now. Nothing will hurt you here. Take some nice, deep breaths."

Marianna drew in a shuddering breath.

"That's it, miss. In and out, in and out." Betsy breathed deeply with Marianna and soon Marianna had calmed.

She let out a final deep breath before asking, "How did you know what to do?"

"I have five younger brothers and sisters. I had to learn quick how to calm distressed people." Betsy grinned as Marianna chuckled.

"Thanks." Marianna smiled.

Betsy jumped up from the bed and pulled out a beautiful blue day dress. She helped Marianna ready for the day, and Marianna went down to breakfast.

Several people were already there, but Bludington was not among them. Marianna breathed a sigh of relief. She couldn't bear to face him after that horrible nightmare.

She found her sister and pulled her aside. "I had one of those dreams again, only this one was worse. He was trying to kill me."

"You really need to get a hold of that wild imagination or soon you'll be having dreams about me killing you." Annette laughed.

Marianna stared at Annette. It was easy for her to laugh it off since she didn't have to worry about marrying him. Marianna couldn't believe her sister was still acting as if this was nothing. She should at least feel bad Marianna was having such horrible nightmares.

Regret flashed in Annette's eyes. "I'm sorry, Mari. I shouldn't make light of it, but it was a dream. Sometimes I dream wild things like that. It's scary, but you must put it out of your mind knowing that it's not real. Come, Lord Bludington is here. We need to sit down." She pulled Marianna back toward the table.

Marianna froze. Bludington held out her chair, smiling. The smile was a creepy one, like when she'd first met him, like the one from her dream.

It was just a dream. She couldn't make a scene. Dozens of eyes followed Marianna as she walked on leaden feet to the chair. She sat down, shivering when Bluebeard's fingers grazed her shoulders as he pushed her chair close to the table.

Marianna chanced a look up, afraid he would comment, but he didn't seem to notice. He smiled and leaned down close to her.

"I heard you had a nightmare. I'm very sorry. I hope that won't scare you away." He laughed like he'd told a great joke, then sat down in his own seat. He said nothing more to her, other than to see she had what she needed, the creepy smile pasted on his face the entire time. Nausea roiled up in her stomach.

He was a creep. She hadn't imagined it.

Marianna finished the meal in silence, wishing the time would go faster. Finally, it was over, and she jumped up. "Lord Bludington, thank you again for your hospitality, but my sister and I must go now. I need to see to my father. He has been ill as you know."

"Oh, of course. I understand your concern." With a look of surprise, Bludington hurried to his feet. He motioned to a manservant, whispered in his ear, and sent him off to do the task assigned to him.

"Henry is seeing to your baggage and carriage. They should both be ready in minutes. Allow me to escort you to the door."

A confused Annette rose to her feet. She looked down at Matthew in dismay. This had not been the plan—to rush out immediately after breakfast. Marianna had told her last night they would be staying until after lunch.

Before she could protest, Marianna had her by the arm, dragging her along toward the door. Matthew jumped up and followed.

The carriage was waiting at the door. Bludington took Marianna's hand and helped her in, then bowed, pressing a kiss to her hand.

"May your journey be safe and quick." He returned to the house to see to the rest of his guests. Annette and Matthew were hugging and saying a tearful goodbye.

"Oh, come on, Annette. You'll see him tomorrow. I can't wait to be gone from this place."

Annette glared at her sister. With a final farewell, Matthew helped her into the carriage, and they were off.

"Just to let you know, Miss Rush-away-fast-as-you-can, I will not see him for some time. He's going to the border." She turned her tear-filled eyes away from Marianna to look out the window.

Marianna swallowed hard, letting out a whoosh of breath. "I'm sorry. I didn't know."

"I don't get why you're so angry, Marianna. Bludington is practically offering you the world, and you're scared off by some stupid nightmare? He would even pay for you to go the Strausburg Institute. That's all you've ever wanted, and you would make history. You'd be the first woman to ever go there." Annette shook her head.

"It doesn't make sense. I think, even if you won't admit it to yourself, that this is about Will. It's highly unlikely he's coming back, and our family's survival is on the line. Just because you'd rather go to the poorhouse than marry Bludington and live in his mansion, doesn't mean father and I would like to join you there." Annette's eyes flashed with anger.

"I haven't decided for sure, yet. There's still time." Her reply was weak even to herself.

"Time for what? We've expended ourselves already and there is nothing left. Except for a decision to be made." Annette rolled her eyes and turned away.

The rest of the ride she refused to speak to Marianna. Marianna knew she deserved it, because even though she said she hadn't made a decision, she knew she had.

Chapter 12

The carriage shuddered to a stop in front of Cloverfield. Wilson opened the door and helped Marianna and Annette out. He whispered something to the driver before turning back to the girls.

"I'm afraid I have a little bad news."

"What? Is it Father? Our brothers?" Annette's voice was hoarse. She grabbed Marianna's arm, her earlier anger forgotten.

"Why didn't you send for us? I knew we never should have gone to this party," Marianna said.

"Calm down, and I'll tell you." Wilson laid a reassuring hand on each of the girls' shoulders. "We still haven't heard anything from your brothers. It's your father, but he's okay. He got worse last week, and the doctor has sentenced him to bedrest for the next couple of weeks. But he's already feeling better than he was, trying to get up and see to things around the house. I wanted to tell you before you we went in though, because we need everyone helping to keep him in bed. The doctor said if he doesn't stay in bed until the cough is gone, it will get worse, and eventually it will kill him."

"Just because he stays in bed doesn't mean the cough will never come back. And if he does stay in bed and it comes back, what then?" Marianna asked. Annette didn't say anything, her eyes were fixed on Wilson.

"I understand your worry, but for now, let's deal with the most imminent crisis—keeping your father in bed. Let's not borrow trouble. If we face that problem, then we'll deal with it. Come, your father's waiting to see you."

Marianna and Annette followed Wilson upstairs to their father's room. He sat against some pillows. When he saw them, his eyes lit up. He motioned them forward and took their hands in his own.

"Ah, my two princesses. How was the party? Did Bludington bestow you with all the gifts you deserve, trying to convince you to marry him?"

"Father!" Marianna couldn't believe he was making a joke about this.

"He did for Marianna. He gave her a library full of books and the most beautiful guest room. He said he could secure a place for her at Strausburg Institute and even introduced her to the dean. He opened and cleaned rooms that hadn't been used in ages..." Annette rambled on about the party.

Marianna was ready to protest, until she saw how much her father was enjoying the conversation. He'd been so sick and so worried about everything. She might as well let him imagine with Annette until she was ready to break the news that she wasn't going to marry Bludington. What could a few days of imagination hurt anyway?

Marianna left the room, tired of hearing Bludington's praises sang. After she'd left, Annette must have told her father something about Marianna's hesitation to say yes, because for the next several days, no one made any mention of the proposal. Although Marianna was sure it had to be weighing on the back of Annette and their father's minds like it was hers.

Every day Marianna ran to check the mail as it was delivered, hoping for news from her brothers. None came, and their financial situation was getting worse. All of Marianna's dowry money was gone, and only a little money remained from the items they had already sold. Not much remained, but Marianna had one more thing she could try to sell.

She opened her bottom dresser drawer and pulled away the garments to reveal the wooden box her mother had left her. Horses danced across the cherry-colored wood. She traced the carving, remembering when her mother had given it to her.

She'd only been ten years old, but she'd known her mother was dying.

"This is my most precious treasure," her mother had told her. "My father got it on one of his many adventures. The box is made from the finest wood in all the lands. It comes from Cherry Forest, and this box was hand carved by the famous carver La Guardia."

Her mother sighed, then continued, "I've always wanted to go to Pangolie, but it appears I'll never make it there. Someday you can go for me."

And at the time it had not been such an outlandish idea. Up until her mother had gotten sick, Marianna's father had regularly taken them to exciting new places on his ships. But then her mother fell ill after catching an unknown illness on one of those trips. That had been the end of it. Her father had refused to take them anywhere else despite their desperate pleading.

Marianna gently opened the box remembering more of her mother's words.

"Go on, dear. Open it. See what's inside."

Inside lay a beautiful cameo. A woman's head and torso were carved out of the stark white shell that was set into a baby blue one. Even at that young age, Marianna knew the blue shell was the rarest kind. They came from only one place. The shores of Carid, a southernmost island. It was a place few people dared to go because few ever returned home.

In recent days, it had become even more infamous, and many people even refused to buy goods from there, claiming it was the Devil's Island. But it was so rare, surely she would be able to sell it somewhere.

She pulled it from its bed of red velvet and wrapped it in her silk handkerchief. The handkerchief was one of the few things she had kept when selling off all their goods. Because it'd been her mother's, she hadn't been able to part with it. She didn't really want to part with the cameo either, but it was the last valuable thing she had left.

This had to work. She hurried downstairs and out to the waiting carriage.

By mid-afternoon, Marianna was feeling discouraged. She hadn't found a single person interested in buying the cameo. She'd had varying responses, from those who kicked her out of their stores at the sight of a product from Carid, to those who commented on the beauty of the necklace but then apologized as they explained they didn't buy products from there.

She now sat in front of the last shop in town where the crotchety old owner might be willing to buy such a product. Mr. Maxon had numerous odd things in his shop. If he could make money from something, he didn't really care where it came from. Marianna climbed from the carriage and pushed the shop door open. A bell jingled, announcing her entrance.

Damp, murky air greeted her, and the musty smell of unused things filled her nostrils. It took her eyes a minute to adjust to the dark interior. The shop was cluttered and dusty. Old lamps and furniture filled one side, while the other side was lined with shelves of trinkets.

There were intricately blown glass dishes, little figurines of horses and bears and such, and fine silverware. The next shelf held books, and if she hadn't been here for such an important reason, she would have browsed through them.

Another shelf held elaborately welded daggers and knives and a couple of full-sized swords. Her brothers would love this place. Sadness swelled up inside her at the thought her brothers. Were they okay? Were they staying warm and getting enough to eat? She hoped so.

A long counter filled the middle of the room. Mr. Maxon stood behind it, looking up from the old clock he was examining. His round wire spectacles slipped down his nose. "What do you want?" he growled. His white hair stuck up in tufts are all around his head.

"I'm sorry to interrupt you, Mr. Maxon, but I have something I think you might want."

He waved her over dismissively. "Well? What is it? I haven't got all day."

Marianna rushed forward, pulling the silk-clad cameo from her pocket. She gently unwrapped it and laid it on the counter for Mr. Maxon's inspection. He murmured as he picked it up.

"I haven't seen one of these in years." He pushed his spectacles up and held the cameo closer. "It's definitely real. Amazing." He set it back down.

"But there's a reason I haven't seen one of these in ages. They don't sell anymore. Sorry, girl, but I don't want it." He pushed it back toward Marianna.

Desperation threaded through her. He had to buy it! This was the last place. Marianna pushed it back toward Mr. Maxon.

"But it's extremely valuable. I even have a cherry wood box carved by La Guardia that I'll throw in with it." Marianna hadn't wanted to sell the box too, but she no longer had any other option.

"Not that valuable anymore, girl. Haven't you heard? Carid is a Devil's Island. No one will talk about the place, much less buy goods from there." He walked down to the other end of the counter.

Marianna picked up the cameo and followed him. "Please, sir. In another year, all that Devil's Island foolishness could be over, and this'll be one of the most prized possessions to own." She thrust the cameo at him. "Look at it. How smooth and fine the carving is. And it's set on the brightest blue shell available."

"This hasn't been a most prized possession in years. And it is unlikely to become one again anytime soon." He gently pushed the cameo back toward Marianna. "I'm sorry, girl. I've heard about your troubles, and I understand why you want to sell this so. But even if I wanted to, I couldn't get any money for it, much less the small fortune you will need to pay off all your debts."

He sighed and continued, "Your mother was a kind and generous woman. She didn't deserve the early death she got. You're better off keeping this along with her memories and finding another way to pay off your debts. Marriage to a stranger isn't always as horrible as it sounds. I know some people who made quite a life from it."

Tears pooled in Marianna's eyes. She blinked rapidly as she clutched the cameo to her heart. She stepped back. Did everyone in this infernal town know about Bludington's offer? She wanted to be angry, and yet she couldn't be.

She never seen such a kind look in Mr. Maxson's eyes before, and she remembered how her mother had always been nice to him. As a child, she hadn't understood her mother's kindness.

"Life isn't always kind to people, and sometimes that makes it hard for them to be kind to others. We must be kind to these people, because they need it the most," her mother had told her when she'd asked why she was nice to mean old Mr. Maxon. It had meant something to him. Not enough to buy the cameo from her, but still it was something.

"Well, thanks anyway, Mr. Maxon."

He nodded and she hurried out to her carriage. Wilson helped her into it.

"No luck?" he asked.

Marianna shook her head, unable to speak for fear the tears would fall.

"It'll be all right," he assured her. "Something will work out. It always does." He gave her a small smile as he climbed onto the driver's seat. He clicked the horse into action. Despite his reassurance, Marianna had a sinking feeling. It seemed the only way out of the poorhouse would be to marry Bludington.

Chapter 13

Someone pounded on the door. Who could it be at this hour? Marianna put down her book and darted downstairs. Wilson was pulling the door open as Marianna reached the landing.

"Hello, I'm Dr. Forester. Lord Bludington sent me over to look at Mr. Locklear. I understand his condition has worsened."

"Uh..." Wilson looked back at Marianna, a questioning look on his face.

Marianna hurried to the door. Seriously, Dr. Forester? There was no way they could afford him. He was known throughout the land as one of the experts in treating coughing conditions like her father's. His price reflected his expertise.

"Hi, Dr. Forester. It was so kind of you to come, but I'm afraid we can't afford your services. Our family physician has been keeping an eye on my father." Marianna started to turn away.

"Oh, no. You misunderstand. Lord Bludington is paying all my fees as well as the price of any treatment deemed necessary." Dr. Forester took a step forward as he rushed to explain.

Annette walked into the hall, just in time to hear the doctor's last words. Her face brightened as she hurried over to the door and clutched Marianna's arm. "That's wonderful," she squealed.

Marianna was tempted to slam the door shut in the doctor's face. Bludington had to have his hand in everything. If it hadn't been for the horrible shape her father was in, Marianna wouldn't have hesitated, but this could mean life or death for her father, so despite her misgivings, she opened the door and welcomed the doctor in.

His exam didn't take long, and his news was positive. "This is a very treatable condition. He simply needs to take this medicine until the cough is gone. I happen to have a bottle with me here. I will leave it for you. When you run out, you can get more from Tay Thomas's Apothecary in town. Here's a prescription for it."

He handed Marianna a half sheet of paper with the long and unpronounceable name of the medicine written on it. "Be sure you get another refill once this bottle has run out. It won't be enough to fully treat your father."

Marianna gratefully took the little brown bottle and nodded, but inwardly she cringed. How much would the refill be? She was sure it would be more than they could afford.

That thought never occurred to Annette as she joyfully took the bottle from Marianna and mock kissed it. "Oh, you life-saving beauty you. Our father will be well in no time."

"Mari, Mari." Annette came charging into the room. Marianna jumped up from her desk and met Annette at the door.

"What is it? Is it Father? Is he okay?" Marianna couldn't believe her father could be having trouble. For the past four days he'd been taking the medicine from Dr. Forester, and he'd been doing wonderfully.

Annette pushed the brown medicine bottle into Marianna's hand. "Well, for now, but there's only two doses left."

Marianna shook the nearly empty bottle as if that could somehow magically make more medicine appear inside. "I'll go down to the apothecary first thing in the morning."

"But how are we going to pay for it?" Annette's eyes were wide and fearful.

Marianna had no idea but tried to sound confident. "I'm sure I still have a bit held back in my dowry. I can use that."

Annette shook her head. "There's no way there's anything left from that. I've seen all the things you've been using it for."

Annette was right. There wasn't a cent left in Marianna's dowry, but she ignored her sister as she walked to her desk and sat.

"I'm tired. And I've got to get these inventories down before bed. Don't worry. It'll be fine. I'll take care of it in the morning."

Annette looked at Marianna dubiously, but she nodded. "Okay, well, good night, then."

"Good night."

Marianna waited until the entire household was asleep before beginning her search. She knew there were still some undiscovered hiding places her mother and father had put spare bits of change, and she was going to find all of them. It had to be enough for the medicine. It had to.

By the time the sun peeked over the horizon, Marianna was satisfied she had located every hiding spot, but her bounty was much less than she'd hoped. Maybe it would be enough? But that was a big maybe.

She skipped breakfast and didn't bother waking her father or Annette as she grabbed her shawl from the hook by the door and walked out into the cool morning air. Wilson had already hitched the horse to the carriage and was waiting for her. She climbed in, and they were off.

Within minutes they had reached their destination. "Would you like me to go in with you, Miss Marianna?"

"No thank you, Wilson. I'll be fine." She managed a small smile before clambering down from the carriage. It wasn't a large building, but it was bright and clean with a giant window that allowed sun to light up the entire place. Marianna took a deep breath. She looked down into her silk bag that held the few coins she had found. With another sigh, she pulled the drawstring tight and hurried into the apothecary.

As she pushed the door open, a bell tingled and the overlapping scents of various oils greeted her. Bright sunlight reflected over hundreds of jars that lined the shelves, casting a rainbow of color across the floor.

It was warm inside, and a surge of hope flashed through her. Maybe Mr. Thomas would be kind and generous. She made her way to the counter and tapped the little bell that rested on top.

After a second, a stocky man pushed past the red velvet curtains hanging in the back. He wore no jacket, only shirtsleeves, khaki-colored pants, and the blue and white striped apron that marked him as the druggist. He came to where Marianna stood waiting.

"Good morning, miss. How can I help you?" His gray eyes were warm, and his tone was friendly.

Marianna pulled the prescription paper from her bag and handed it to the man. "How much to fill this, sir?"

The man whistled. "Ooh, the fancy stuff. Don't see many orders for this around here. But I do have some in stock. Do you have the original bottle, or would you like to purchase one?"

Marianna nodded and dug through her little bag. "Yes, somewhere in here." She pulled it out and set it on the counter.

Mr. Thomas' eyes narrowed. "Oh, one of Dr. Forester's patients, eh? No wonder you got the fancy stuff."

Marianna shook her head. "No sir, not regularly. My father's been so ill lately, and a family friend paid for his services." She hated to label Bludington a family friend, but her main priority was getting the medicine her father needed.

"Well, to get a refill of this is quite expensive. It'll be 150 cullers."

Marianna barely held back a gasp. 150 cullers? How could one bottle of medicine be so expensive? She had only managed to scrounge together 60 cullers. She sighed, pulled the money out, and plopped it onto the counter. "How much can I get for this?"

The shopkeeper shook his head. "I'm sorry, miss, but we only sell it by the bottleful. It's much too expensive to be trying to separate down into smaller amounts."

"Please, sir, my father's very ill, and this is all I have. If we don't get more medicine, he could die." Marianna fought to keep the desperation out of her voice.

"I understand, but I can't help you. Ask your rich friend to help you out," the man said firmly. "I'm sure he would want to see your father regain his full health if he paid for Dr. Forester to come see him."

Marianna hesitated a second, wanting to plead with the man some more, but she could tell he wasn't going to be swayed by anything. To ask Bludington for more help, though? It was bad enough that they'd had to accept his help in the first place.

You could always just marry him, a traitorous voice whispered in her head. Marianna shook her head, forcing the thought away. She hastily gathered up her coins from the counter and headed for the door without a word.

Chapter 14

The day before Bludington was to arrive for the answer to his proposal, Annette came to Marianna's room and shut the door behind her. "I gave the last bit of medicine to Father. It's gone." She sat on the bed facing Marianna, who was writing in her journal.

Annette leaned forward and tapped her sister on the arm. "So, do you have your answer ready? He's coming tomorrow, you know."

Marianna averted her eyes, staring aimlessly out the window. She knew he was coming tomorrow. Knew they were out of options and time, she just didn't want to admit it.

"Well then, I guess your answer hasn't changed, so I'll marry Bludington," Annette announced.

Marianna jerked her head up. "Are you crazy?"

Annette crossed her arms, her gaze steely.

Marianna dropped her pen and lunged forward, grabbing Annette's arm. "You can't be serious. What about Matthew?"

"He's going to war, and he might not come back. Besides, he's never actually asked me to marry him. I'd rather not waste my time dreaming about an impossible dream while my family suffers, especially when I can do something about it."

The words stung, but thoughts were crowding into Marianna's mind so fast, she could hardly think.

"You're not really going to do this, are you? You love Matthew, and I know he cares about you. What will he say when you tell him? You don't know that anything is going to happen to him."

"You'd rather I refuse Bludington, send us to the poorhouse, and our father to his grave? You do realize that if we go to the poorhouse, he'll die. There'll be no medicines and no doctors there. I've made my decision, and

I'll not listen to you try to talk me out of it." Annette rose and stomped out of the room, slamming the door behind her.

Marianna sat in silence for several minutes, unable to think. She had never thought her exuberant, younger sister would dream of accepting Bludington's proposal, but Annette had carefully thought through the consequences of what would happen if they refused Bludington—something Marianna had not done.

Emotions swirled through her. When had living life become so hard? Could nothing be easy? Her throat tightened and she felt the urge to run and never stop as tears pressed against the back of her eyes.

She rose from her bed and grabbed her cloak from the closet. She pulled it on and went out behind the house where there were several acres of open land. It was too stony to farm, and the grass was patchy, making it unsuitable for raising animals. It was worthless land, but Marianna loved it.

It had been a long time since Marianna had walked across it. It had been something she'd done with Will. She reached the low stone wall where Will had told her he was leaving, climbed onto it, and sat down. This was where he had given her the little wooden ring she always wore. She looked down at the ring, twisting it.

She remembered the day Will had given her the ring as clear as if it were yesterday...

Will held Marianna's hand as they strolled across the field. Bits of grass and a few dandelions had managed to poke up among the rocky terrain. When they reached the crumbling wall, they stopped.

Will released Marianna's hand and shrugged out of his jacket. With a sweeping bow, he flung it over the wall.

"Your throne, my lady." He took her hand, helping her climb up to sit.

"I can't believe you have to leave tomorrow. My father is crazy. I've begged him not to send you on the ship, but he won't listen to me."

Her father had insisted Will go on this trip. It was one of the longest and most dangerous of her father's trading routes, but it was also the most profitable. Her father assured her that after this trip Will would have earned the necessary funds for them to live their life together in the manner Marianna was used to. She'd told her father she didn't care about that, but he wouldn't be swayed.

She took a deep breath, trying to hold back the tears that threatened to let loose in a deluge. She had promised herself she wasn't going to do this—cry when they said their goodbyes—but she was beginning to think she wouldn't be able to keep that promise.

Will squeezed her hand. "Hey now, it's not all that bad. I'll be back before you know it, and I'll bring you back the most marvelous things."

Marianna chuckled. "I know you will, but all I want is to be with you."

Will stepped closer to her, putting his hands on either side of Marianna, and leaning in until their foreheads touched. His eyes sparkled like the sea on the sunniest day. Marianna's heart raced as a thrill rushed through her. It was a thrill she had only ever felt with Will, and she'd had her fair share of suitors.

Every boy in town wanted to become part of the richest merchant family. But for Marianna, it had only ever been Will. The old society ladies scorned her, telling her she was foolish for giving up her choice of the most eligible bachelors for a sailor's son.

"Our power lies in choosing the man most accomplished in growing our wealth, not choosing one who doesn't have a clue what to do with even a hundred cullers." Mrs. Garbedeau had repeatedly tried to discourage Marianna from seeing Will, but Marianna hadn't listened. She knew what her heart wanted, and it wanted Will.

"I tried to convince my father to let us all go on this trip, but he wouldn't hear of it. Ever since Mother..." She didn't have to finish. Will already knew.

"Someday we'll go anywhere you want," he said. "The beaches of Carid, the ancient ruins of Darne, the Cherry Forest of Pangolie, to see the city lights of Elonai. Or to Cargives, so you can go to Tarn Institute."

That was why she loved him. He understood her in a way no other boy ever had, and he supported her dreams. Sometimes she thought he understood her even better than Annette did.

Will leaned forward and pressed a gentle kiss to her lips before pulling back. Marianna leaned forward, eager for more, but she stopped when the jacket tugged underneath her. She braced herself and started to say something, but Will spoke first.

"Sorry!" He lifted one hand to steady her, while the other dug in his jacket pocket, trying to extract something from it. "Not exactly how I imagined that going," he muttered.

"Imagine what going?"

He didn't answer but dropped to one knee and held out the object he had removed from his pocket. It was a wooden ring, and carved inside was the inscription: *All my love, always, Will.*

"Marianna Locklear, will you marry me?"

Marianna leapt from the wall, bent down, and threw her arms around his neck.

"Yes, a thousand times yes!"

Will managed to stand up, pulling Marianna with him. She offered him her hand. He slipped wooden ring onto her finger, then lifted her hand and kissed it. "I'm sorry it's not a diamond, but when I get back, I'll get you the best ring money can buy. I'll let you pick it out if you want."

"This one is beautiful. Even more so because you made it." Marianna lifted her hand and admired the ring. "It's all I need."

Will pulled her close, wrapping his arms around her waist. She bounced up on her toes, clasping her hands behind his neck, her fingers brushing the edges of his golden curls.

"You deserve more though. That's one reason I'm glad I'm going on this trip. If we come back with all we think we will, your father said he make me a partner in his business." He smiled down at her.

"It won't be dangerous though, will it? Marianna asked.

"Not any more dangerous than any other trip."

"But the things they're saying about the Isle of Carid? What if they are true?"

"You know the gossips in this town. They can make up a horrendous story about their own children and spread it around faster than spreading butter on bread, and some of them have."

Marianna laughed. That was certainly true, but she still felt a niggling doubt. It disappeared when Will leaned forward and kissed her.

Marianna sighed. Maybe Will was part of her reluctance to say yes to Bludington. She'd been so selfish. All she'd thought about was how this wouldn't work for her. She hadn't even thought about what would happen to Father if they had to go to the poorhouse.

She didn't love Bludington. He scared her, and there was something creepy about his manor, but she couldn't let her sister go there. Tears pricked at her eyes as she took in a deep lungful of air.

If Will had never left, they wouldn't be in this mess. She choked back a sob as tears streamed down her face. She cried for her lost love. She cried for her father and sister. She cried for her brothers who could be in harm's way. She cried because she knew what she had to do.

"Will, I don't know if you can hear me. I don't know if you are dead or alive, but I want you to know I'll always love you. I have to marry this man, Bludington. I don't want to. The only man I'll ever want to marry is you, but I have to. I can't let Annette do it, not when Matthew's waiting for the war's end to marry her. Our father will die, and we'll both be in the poorhouse if I don't. But I'll love you forever, Will."

The tears flowed faster now, and Marianna could hardly see, but she lifted her hand to her lips and tenderly kissed the ring. She gave up holding back the sobs and let all her grief and uncertainty pour out.

By the time she had calmed herself, the sky was already getting dark. She slipped off the wall and started toward the house. It was quiet when she got there, and most of the lights had been extinguished. She tiptoed to Annette's room and cracked the door. She peered in and saw her sister in bed asleep.

She'd wanted to tell her that she'd decided to accept Bludington's offer. She would have to be the first awake. Bludington was sure to be here early.

Chapter 15

The next morning, a carriage rattled up the drive. Marianna ran to the window. She pulled back the curtain and peeked out. Bludington stepped down, looked up, and raised his hand in greeting.

Marianna stepped back, her heart racing. How had he known she was up here? It was impossible for him to know which room was hers. She swallowed hard, taking deep breaths. She had to go downstairs before Annette got there and accepted Bludington's offer. She could do this.

She pushed away from the window and hurried downstairs, making it into the parlor as Wilson led Bludington inside. When he saw Marianna was already there, he lifted his brow in surprise.

Wilson reached out and squeezed her hand. "I'm always here for you, Miss Marianna. If you need anything, just send me a message." His voice was low, his gaze serious. Clearly he had concerns about Bludington as well.

Marianna bit her lip and nodded, fighting the apprehension threatening to drown her. Wilson gave little bow and left the room.

"Ah, Miss Marianna. You are here, I suppose, with your answer." Bludington took her hand and kissed it.

"Yes, Lord Bludington. My answer is yes," Marianna blurted out before she could lose her nerve.

"I'm pleased to hear that, though I fear you're not happy to give me that answer. I have something which might make you feel better about it."

Heat flooded her cheeks as she watched Bludington pull something little out of his pocket. She'd hoped her reluctance wouldn't be so obvious.

All thoughts fled once Bludington opened the box in his hand. It contained a ring with the biggest diamond Marianna had ever seen. Slightly smaller amethysts lay on either side of it. Bludington removed the ring from the box and held out his other hand for Marianna's.

Wordlessly, she gave it to him. He saw the wooden ring that already nestled her ring finger, and a flash of something crossed his face, too quick for Marianna to even tell what it was. He slid his ring down to rest on top of the little wooden one without saying a word. Next to Will's ring, Bludington's ring seemed garish. Marianna took a deep breath, willing herself not to cry.

"It's beautiful, thank you," Marianna heard herself say, not sure where she'd found the courage to speak.

"Your father told me your birthstone was amethyst. I'm glad because they always look so nice next to diamonds. I can assure you no one else in the city has a ring this fine or of this design. It's an original." Bludington apparently thought her emotion was due to the giant ring he was giving her.

Annette walked in. Marianna heard her but was still staring at the massive ring. It didn't matter, since Bludington began talking as soon as he saw her sister.

"Hello, Miss Annette, do come in. Good news, your sister has agreed to marry me."

Shock covered Annette's face. The sisters stared at one another only a moment before Annette rushed forward and grabbed Marianna in a hug.

"Congratulations," she said loudly, then pulled Marianna into the hallway and whispered, "Are you sure?"

Marianna nodded. "I want you to have your chance to be happy. I already had mine, even if it was cut short."

"Thank you. Remember I'm here whenever you need, and I'll always love you no matter what."

"I know. I love you, too."

The girls stepped back into the parlor and Marianna turned to face Bludington.

Bludington pulled a scroll from his coat. He walked over to the table and unrolled it. "I've already drawn up the betrothal agreement. You need to sign here." He motioned to the line at the bottom, then handed the document to Marianna.

19 May

An agreement of betrothal is formed between Lord Grason Bludington of Thunderwell Manor and Lady Marianna Locklear of Cloverfield House. A yearly sum of 5,000 cullers will be at the Lady's disposal as well as a weekly allowance of 200 cullers for her family. Upon the unexpected demise of the Lord, the Lady will receive all his worldly possessions and wealth. Upon the unexpected demise of the Lady, the Lord will no longer provide an allowance to the Lady's family. Upon the signature of both parties, this will become a legally binding contract.

Marianna bit back a gasp when she read the yearly sum Bludington was making available to her. But if something happened to her, the financial provision for her family would cease. Not that she would have expected anything else from Bludington.

Most spouses didn't even offer a pension to the family. Well, she would have to be very careful at that creepy manor of his. She grabbed the pen and scrawled her name at the bottom with a wince.

Bludington took back the document, rolled it back up and stuffed it inside his jacket. "Your father and I already agreed that you should transition to Thunderwell Manor. You'll want to get familiar with your new home. Besides I'll also have to be going away for a bit before the wedding, so you'll have the place to yourself."

Apprehension crept through her. Alone, in his creepy manor with his strange servants? But what could she say? She'd already signed her life away to him.

"But all the little details as to where we have the wedding and who is invited, I leave in your capable hands, Miss Marianna. I have business to see to at the bank." Bludington bowed and left the room.

Marianna sighed and collapsed into the closest chair, slid down, and leaned her head against the chair back. "At least he's keeping his word and paying the overdue bills and the mortgage. You'd better keep an eye on Father to see he spends the allowance wisely. I don't know how often I'll be able to send extra money."

"You'll be okay, Marianna, won't you? I wasn't trying to force you to make this decision when I said I'd marry him."

Marianna sat up and leaned forward. "I know, Annette, and yes, I'll be okay. You said before the man is rich as Midas. I'll have the wonderful library and a beautiful bedroom, a chance to go to Strausburg Institute. Bludington's not so bad, once you get past the blue hair. And I'll love exploring all the hallways in his house."

Marianna forced a smile as a shiver passed through her. She hadn't been able to stop thinking about the hallway with the strange painting. And what was in that locked room?

Chapter 16

All too soon, Lord Bludington returned to take Marianna to Thunderwell. Wilson carried out all her luggage, and Bludington directed where to put it in the carriage. Marianna paced the front hall as Annette watched her.

"Mari, are you sure your all right? You look a little pale."

"I'll be fine." Marianna gave Annette a weak smile.

Their father came into the room. He reached out to Marianna, and she ran to hug him.

"My dear darling daughter. I love you so." He sighed. "Are you sure this is something you want to do?"

Marianna nodded against his shoulder, and he sighed heavily.

"If only I had made different choices." His voice cracked, and Marianna pulled back.

"No, Father. This isn't your fault. I'm old enough and smart enough to make my own decisions now."

A single tear trickled down his cheek. "If you need me to come, write to me."

Already the fresh bottle of medicine Bludington had brought with him that morning was working. Her father's face was flush with healthy color, and he hadn't coughed once while talking to her.

"Don't worry about me. Concentrate on getting well."

He gave her a small smile and squeezed her hand.

Bludington charged through the door. "Ready, my lady? Your carriage awaits." He swept out his hand and bowed deeply.

Annette laughed, her eyes darting over to her sister.

Marianna smiled. "It's fine," she mouthed then turned to Bludington. "I'll say goodbye to my family, and I'll be ready."

He nodded, for once seeming to pick up on her cues, and stepped outside to wait for her.

Marianna's father gathered her in one final hug. "Remember, if you need me, I'll come," he whispered.

Annette squeezed Marianna so hard she could barely breathe. "You're positive you're going to be okay? You should've asked if I could have come with you."

"It's a bit early to be asking favors, especially since he's already been so generous. But once I'm able to, I'll have you come visit."

Annette nodded. "You're really okay?" She pulled back and stared into Marianna's eyes as if she could tell by looking how Marianna was truly feeling.

Marianna nodded and laughed. "Of course. I have a gigantic mansion with a glorious library to attend to. What more could I want?"

Marianna pushed away from her sister, hoping Annette couldn't hear the crack in her voice, or see the fear in her eyes. She stepped outside. Bludington handed her up into the carriage, climbed in, and sat opposite her.

Annette ran out, peering into the carriage before the door was shut. "I love you, Mari. If you need me, I'll come."

Before Marianna could respond, the carriage door slammed shut as if issuing the edict for the rest of her life—imprisonment with a man whom she did not love and who scared her witless.

Chapter 17

Bludington didn't talk much during the ride to his manor, and eventually Marianna fell into a light sleep. When the carriage rattled to a stop, she woke to find they were pulling up to Thunderwell.

"Welcome home, my lady." Bludington hopped out, reaching to assist Marianna.

Once she was on the ground, he took her arm and led her up the stairs. They were met at the door by the scary man Marianna had encountered in the mysterious hallway.

"Lady Marianna, this is the butler, Dunsten." Bludington motioned toward the thin man. "Are the servants gathered?"

"Yes, my lord," Dunsten replied with a little bow. He stepped back to allow Bludington and Marianna to enter.

Bludington led Marianna inside and down several identical-looking hallways, before stopping at a door Marianna had not seen before.

"This is the small dining room, where we will eat when we have no other guests. Right now, the servants have been gathered here for introductions. Some of the groundskeepers and stable hand aren't here now, but you'll meet all the household staff." Bludington pushed the door open, and Marianna followed him into the room.

He'd called it small, but it was far bigger than the dining room at the Locklear estate. On the far wall, about thirty servants stood in a line.

"I would like everyone to meet your new mistress, Lady Marianna. Each one of you will introduce yourself and state your job, starting here." Bludington motioned to a woman Marianna recognized from her previous visit.

"I am Mrs. Strunk, the housekeeper." Mrs. Strunk bowed, and the next person spoke.

Marianna looked down the long line of servants to see everyone from the housemaids to the stable hands were there. She only recognized Betsy, the lady's maid who had assisted her when she'd stayed here before. After Betsy introduced herself, Bludington leaned down and whispered into Marianna's ear.

"I take it she was satisfactory. Would you like to keep her as your lady's maid?"

Marianna nodded and smiled at Betsy. Betsy smiled back, lowered her eyes, and bobbed into a curtsey. Marianna knew she would never be able to remember all the servants' names, but she tried to take note of the household servants.

After everyone finished their introductions, Bludington dismissed them all but the housekeeper, the butler, and Betsy.

Betsy came forward and curtsied again. "I can show you to your room now, if you're ready, my lady."

Marianna glanced at Bludington, who was talking to Dunsten and Mrs. Strunk, then nodded.

Bludington paused his conversation with the other servants, turning to Marianna. "Betsy will find you when it's time for dinner. You're free to do whatever you like until then."

Marianna nodded, then followed Betsy to her room. Free to do whatever she'd like? What did that mean? She'd only be allowed some time to do as she'd like? What would she be required do with her other time?

Marianna rubbed her forehead and closed her eyes for a split second. She opened them to see a worried look on Betsy's face.

The maid touched her arm. "Are you all right, ma'am?"

"I'm tired. It's been a long day. I think I'll lie down for a short nap before dinner."

"All right, ma'am. And here we are. It's a good thing too. You look worn out. You'll feel better with a good rest."

Betsy opened the door. It was the same room Marianna had stayed in during her previous visit. Marianna was surprised but said nothing. She'd enjoyed this room and was glad she'd get to keep it.

Betsy pulled back the covers. "You climb in and sleep, ma'am. Is there anything else I can help you with?"

Marianna sighed and leaned against the soft pillow, closing her eyes. "No, thank you." She yawned and was soon fast asleep.

Chapter 18

Something cold and wet pressed against Marianna's skin. It tugged at her, beckoning her from sleep. She tried to ignore it, but there was a voice too, an insistent one. Marianna forced her eyes open.

Betsy stood over her, holding a wet cloth to Marianna's forehead, her face full of concern. "My lady, are you all right? It took me such a long time to wake you, I was worried you were sick."

Marianna blinked several times. Where was she? What day was it?

The answers assaulted her mind. Bludington's house. She was to be married. To Bludington!

She sat up abruptly, knocking the cloth from her head.

Betsy stepped back. "What is it, my lady?"

What time was it? It was dark out. Had she missed dinner? Where was Bludington?

Marianna took a deep breath. Her thoughts slowed as she began to think more clearly. Betsy hovered nearby, gripping the wet cloth so tightly water dripped onto the floor.

"I'm so sorry, Betsy. I was sleeping so deeply, I forgot where I was. I sleep like that whenever I get really tired. Did I miss dinner?"

Betsy's shoulders relaxed and her grip loosened. "No ma'am. It's time for dinner now, but we could take a few minutes for you to freshen up."

Marianna climbed out of bed, taking the cloth from Betsy. She caught sight of her reflection in the mirror above the wash basin and grimaced. Her eyes had dark bags under them, and her hair was sticking out all over the place. "Oh, I look horrible!"

She grabbed her comb and pulled it through the tangles until they were gone. She dipped the rag in the cool water and washed her face, holding it against the bags under her eyes for a few seconds. It helped clear the last of the fogginess from her brain.

"Okay, I'm ready. I hope they haven't had to hold dinner for me."

Betsy led Marianna to the small dining room. Marianna tried to take note of the corridors so she could begin to find her own way through the house, but they were going so fast, it was hard to keep track.

Betsy stopped abruptly, and Marianna almost tumbled into her. "Here we are, miss."

Out of breath, Marianna smoothed her skirts and breathed deeply. She pushed open the door, steeling herself for what she feared might be an unpleasant scene.

There was only one place setting and more than enough food for two people spread out on the table. Dunsten stood to the side along with two maids. When he saw Marianna enter, he stepped up to the chair behind the place setting and pulled it out.

Was Bludington not coming to dinner? Marianna took a few hesitant steps forward and sat down. Dunsten pushed the chair in and stepped back. Shivers darted down Marianna's back as she eyed the butler. He said nothing and didn't look at her. The candlelight glistened off his pasty white skin, and his gray eyes glowed.

The maids began heaping food onto Marianna's plate. If she didn't stop them, they'd fill her plate until there was no room left on it.

"Thank you, that's enough."

The maids stepped back without comment. Marianna scooped up a bite of toasted apples, their sweet cinnamon fragrance made her stomach growl. She glanced around the room embarrassed, but the servants stood still, saying nothing.

Where was Bludington? Was he so mad she'd held up dinner that he wouldn't eat with her? Or had she taken so long he was already finished? But what did it really matter? The less she saw of him, the happier she'd be.

She took a deep breath. The smell of exotic spices and freshly baked bread made her mouth water. A dish of fresh greens topped with little tomatoes sat in front of her. It was slightly sweet and perfectly complemented the bite of fish next to it. She set aside a bowl of fresh berries topped with a sprinkling of sugar and cream to eat last.

The main course was tender beef brisket on top of a bed of twisted Pangolie noodles. She'd only had the dish once before, and it was as good as she'd remembered it. The noodles were only made in countries to the far north which made the dish hard to come by. More proof of Bludington's vast wealth that he'd been able to ship the noodles here.

Although she was glad Bludington was not there, her curiosity finally got the better of her. She took a deep breath, turning toward the butler. "Dunsten, where is Lord Bludington?"

"He had things to attend to, ma'am, and took his meal in his study. He does that quite often," he replied without making eye contact.

Marianna crossed her arms, rubbing them as if she could rub away the fear the butler sparked inside of her. What was his problem with her? Was he still angry he caught her nosing around that one time?

Dunsten bowed before returning to his statue-like pose next to the wall. Both Dunsten and the two maids maintained their motionless stance the entire time Marianna was eating. They only broke from position when she needed more to eat or drink. It was unnerving. At home, their meals had always been casual events, with Wilson, Cook, and Ellen often joining them at the table.

Was this how the meals always were, or were they keeping an eye on her? Marianna rushed through her meal so she could get away from the prying eyes of the servants. When she finished eating, she saw Betsy had slipped through the dining room door and was standing inside of it, waiting for her.

"Would you like to go back to your room, or maybe to the library, my lady?"

"Oh, yes, let's go to the library."

Marianna wanted to be able to find the library on her own, so she paid careful attention as Betsy led the way. The candelabra Betsy carried cast eerie shadows on the wall. It had to be objects in the hallway making the shadows. Maybe mirrors or portraits, or a vase or two atop some little tables, but it was too dark, and they were moving too fast for Marianna to tell.

It reminded her of the night she'd found the hallway with the strange dwarf painting. She shivered and scanned the hallway looking for that dark corridor.

One more turn and they were at the library.

"Are you okay, my lady? Do you need a blanket to ward off the chills?" Betsy asked.

"Oh, I'm fine. Just a passing shiver. I'll be reading here for a few hours if you could come back later? I'm not sure of the way to my room."

"Of course, my lady."

Marianna spent the next several hours reading in the library. She was so absorbed in her book that the strange new world she now lived in faded into the background.

The library door groaned as someone pushed inside. A crash sounded as the figure stumbled into the closest shelf, sending books tumbling to the floor.

Marianna jumped up, dropping her book, and grabbing the lantern from the side table. "Who's there?"

The lantern light fell across the shelves of books, reflecting off the golden trim and casting a shine on the smooth wood floor before reaching the doorway.

Betsy knelt in the shadows scrambling to gather up the fallen books. "Oh, it's me, Miss Marianna. I'm so sorry I startled you. I guess I should have knocked first."

"Betsy." Marianna sighed in relief before continuing. "It's fine. I'm jumpy tonight. Let me help you." She rushed over, setting her lantern on the table before bending down and picking up a couple of books.

"You needn't help me, my lady. It's not your job." Betsy protested.

Marianna ignored her and continued putting books away. "I totally lost track of time. I was so absorbed in my book."

Betsy stuffed the last of the books into the shelves. "Were you ready to go back to your room?"

"Yes, it's getting late, and I should be readying for bed." Marianna followed Betsy back to her room.

Chapter 19

Marianna awoke to light streaming through the windows. She sat up and stretched. After a minute, she heard a faint knock at the door.

"Come in."

Betsy peeked around the door before pushing through it with a tray of food.

"Oh, how nice. Breakfast in bed." Marianna smiled.

"Yes, Ma'am. I thought you might enjoy something special after I gave you such a fright last night." Betsy bobbed a curtsey and brought the tray to Marianna.

"Oh, I had forgotten about that. You mustn't let that worry you anymore. I'm not going to fire you, although it was nice of you to bring me breakfast in bed. After I'm finished, I'd like to go to the library, but maybe this time I can lead and see if I know the way."

Marianna found she did know the way to the library from her bedroom. Betsy only had to correct her once. At the library, Marianna pulled her journal from her pocket and started drawing out the floor plan of Thunderwell. It would take her some time, but she was determined to learn how to get around the massive place without getting lost.

A strange, scuffling noise came from the hall. Was someone out there? She tiptoed to the library door and peeked out. No one was in the hallway, but one of the doors at the far end of the hall was cracked open with light leaking through.

A tittering laugh echoed from that room. Marianna stepped out and crept toward the sound. She peered through the crack. Two maids huddled together, waving dusters over a dresser in a pretense of working, though it seemed all they were really doing was gossiping.

"You know his first wife Miss Lillianna cried all the time. She feared Lord Bludington. She would have these horrible night terrors. She wrote to her father constantly begging him to come get her," a tall, thin maid whispered. Her dark curls peeked out from the fluffy white cap all the maids wore. Marianna recognized her from the staff introductions and was pretty sure her name was Carrie.

The other maid's eyes looked like two large buttons as she said, "Really?" Short and plump with a bright orange braid that stretched down her back, Marianna had no trouble remembering her name was Leah.

"Her father refused to come for her, and she fell ill." Carrie hesitated before adding in a stage whisper, "And in less than a week she died!"

"Seriously? Of what?"

"That's the thing. The doctor couldn't find anything wrong with her. Not physically, anyway. Everyone said she died of fright, and that horrible unending fear is what killed her."

The maids moved farther away, pushed open a door that led to another room, and stepped inside. The voices faded to a hum, and Marianna could no longer make out what they were saying. She eased the door open enough to squeeze through, so she could follow the maids.

She crept into the room and came face to face with a black bear standing up on his back legs, his mouth frozen in a roar. Marianna bit back a scream as she stumbled back.

Light from the fireplace reflected off the glassy eyes and her heart raced in time to the words she kept thinking over and over to calm herself. It was just stuffed. It was just stuffed.

She took several deep breaths as she took in the rest of the room in the dim light. A red fox was mid-leap atop a large wooden desk. Under the fox, was a hare. Above the fireplace mantle, three deer heads with large racks stared at her. In the opposite corner, a lion stood proudly, and in front of him, a rhino was frozen in mid-run.

What was this place? No one was inside, though the fire was lit. Maybe it was for the maids? The room was so large, it had to be above the ballroom. Marianna didn't know anything about Bludington being a hunter, but then again, this practice of taking your kills and displaying them like trophies was frowned upon now, so maybe he didn't want people to know.

A laugh came from the next room, and Marianna remembered why she was there. She crept as close as she dared to the door the maids stood behind, pressing herself against a wardrobe in the one corner where there were no animals. Hopefully it would be enough for the maids not to notice her if they suddenly came back into the room.

"Of course, I wasn't here then, but I've heard the stories. They say her screams woke the whole house. Everyone would have felt sorry for her if they could have gotten any sleep. Cook said everyone wandered around here like zombies until the—"

"Is it true that fear can really kill person?" Leah asked.

"I don't know, like I said I wasn't here during that time, but that's what everyone who worked here then says." Carrie said. "It's really a shame. That man has had more than his fair share of tragedy. You know all his previous wives died tragically."

"That sounds like bad luck for this new girl," Leah replied.

Marianna sighed and rested her head against the wardrobe.

"How did the others die?"

Carrie answered in a whisper. Marianna pressed closer to the wardrobe and strained to hear. How had Bludington's other wives died?

Somewhere down the hallway a door slammed.

"That'll be Dunsten. Come on, now. We have to get back to work." Carrie's comment was followed by the clatter of buckets. "If he catches us piddling around in here, we'll be in trouble."

The maids swept back through the doorway into the room where Marianna hid. She slid down farther behind the dresser and held her breath. Neither one of them even paused as they left the room. The door shut behind them with an ominous thud.

Was Dunsten out there? All Marianna needed was for him to find her sneaking about again. She took a deep breath and waited.

The hallway stayed quiet, but Marianna kept waiting. She didn't want to take a chance she might run into Dunsten. Her knees ached from crouching so long. It had to be safe to go out into the hallway now.

She got up and stretched. Her muscles protested, and she nearly fell over. She regained her balance, and carefully opened the door. Dunsten stood there, his piercing gray eyes staring at her with a disapproving glare.

Chapter 20

"Miss Marianna, what are you doing in this part of the house? Have you lost your way?" Dunsten asked.

Marianna took a deep breath. She refused to be bullied by this creepy man. "Not at all. As lady of the manor, it is my job to know my way around, is it not?"

Without waiting for him to respond she brushed past him and strolled down the hallway. Her heart pounded like a racehorse. She squelched the desire to look back and see if Dunsten was following her, and she barely managed to keep from running all the way back to her room.

As soon as she turned the corner, she opened the first door she saw and rushed into a sitting room, pulling the door shut behind her. Plopping onto the nearest loveseat, she struggled to calm herself. Her hand gripped the curved arm of the chair, and the satin fabric clung to her sweaty palms.

Where had she found the courage to say that to Dunsten? And what was she thinking? She did not want to make an enemy of him. He seemed to be second-in-command of this place, and he already disliked her.

The room was dark, the curtains pulled tight across the windows, adding to her unease. She couldn't even tell what the color scheme of the room was, just that it was all dark colors. Why was it so dark?

She shifted in her seat and listened for footsteps. What if Dunsten had followed her around the corner? She had been so worked up, she hadn't paid attention. She sucked in another breath and tried to focus on her breathing.

She couldn't stop thinking about the story that maid told about Bludington and his first wife. What'd happened to the other two wives? How in the world had no one cared to tell her about this? Her chest tightened. Her throat squeezed in on itself, and she gasped for breath. She had to calm down.

This was getting her nowhere, and all she needed was to pass out in a fearful panic attack and become fodder for the servants to gossip about. She reached up and clutched her mother's cameo that hung around her neck. Her thumb rubbed the raised shape of the lady's head.

"In... out. In... out," she chanted to herself. Her heart rate slowed and finally she could breathe normally again.

She didn't know how long she had sat there, but it was long enough for Dunsten to have come and gone. Now she had to find her way back to her room and Betsy. She was dying to question Betsy about Bludington and his previous wives. She knew the girl hadn't been here long, but as wild as the gossip was among the servants, it would be impossible for her not to know something.

She rose from the couch and cracked the door open. No one was around. She took a deep breath and stepped into the hallway. Not knowing where she was, she turned back the way she'd come hoping it would lead her back into a more familiar part of the manor. After wandering down several more hallways, she turned the corner and nearly ran into Betsy.

"Oh, Miss Marianna there you are. I'm so sorry I nearly ran into you." She grasped Marianna's arm to keep from knocking into her.

"I've been looking for you. I was afraid you were lost." She glanced around furtively, then lowered her voice. "Especially when I heard Mr. Dunsten griping to Mrs. Strunk about how the new wife-to-be was getting an attitude with the servants, and deciding she was queen here."

Marianna gasped. "He said that?"

Betsy nodded, a smirk covering her face. "I knew you had to be wandering around, and Mr. Dunsten must have found you. Whatever did you say to him?" Betsy's smirk turned into a full-size grin that covered her face.

"I simply told him that as lady of the house it was my duty to know where everything was. And then I left him in the dust." Marianna still couldn't believe she'd said that to him. She sobered as she remembered her words could have negative effects. "You don't think he's going to get meaner now, do you?" she asked Betsy.

"Who knows?" Betsy shrugged. "I'm still enjoying the moment, and you should too. I don't think Mr. Dunsten has ever had anyone stand up to him. Maybe it'll make him nicer."

Marianna raised her eyebrows.

Betsy shook her head. "Yeah, you're right. I don't think anything could do that."

"How do we get back to my room, anyway?" Marianna asked. "I need to talk to you, but I don't want to do it now." She glanced around. No one was in sight, at least that she could see, but she knew better than to assume anything around here. She had learned that the hard way.

Chapter 21

Once in Marianna's room, Betsy poured her a cup of orange and spice tea. She knew it was Marianna's favorite and one of the few things that could help her relax.

"Here, miss. Have a sip."

Marianna clutched the cup with both hands as she brought it to her face and breathed in its spicy sweet scent. The smell alone made the tension in her muscles ease. She took several sips before talking. "I heard something today. Those two maids, Carrie and Leah, were gossiping about one of Bludington's previous wives."

She told Betsy all she'd heard then asked, "What do you know about any of his other wives?"

Betsy stared at her for a minute. "I don't know about any of that. You know that's gossip. None of those maids were even here then. About the only ones who would really know anything are Mr. Dunsten and Mrs. Strunk."

Marianna gave Betsy a look. Those were the last two people she would ever ask about anything, and Betsy knew it.

Betsy shook her head. "I know," she said. "I know you would rather die than ask either one of them anything." Her eyes widened, and she gasped. "Oh, I didn't mean that literally. Bad choice of words. I'm sorry, Miss Marianna."

"Don't worry about that, Betsy. I didn't even notice your choice of words." Marianna shook her head, her mind swirling. It was so strange. Who ever heard of someone having so many spouses die on them?

"The only thing I do know about," Betsy said, "is that there were three wives before you. Three silver cups in the kitchen with their names inscribed on them: Lillianna, Carianna, and Elianna. I remember because it is weird how they all have names that end in 'anna.' Come to think of it your name ends in 'anna' too." Betsy paused for a moment. A look of uncertainty covered her face.

Her name followed the same pattern as Bludington's three dead wives. A shiver darted down Marianna's spine, and she clutched her teacup so hard her knuckles whitened.

Betsy rushed to assure her. "I mean, I'm sure it's a coincidence. It doesn't mean anything."

She fell silent then, busying herself with cleaning up the tea tray. She poured the last of the hot water from the pot into Marianna's cup, gathered up the untouched cookies, and was ready to carry it all back down to the kitchen when Marianna broke the silence.

"Silver cups, huh? What's the deal with that? I don't think I have one."

Betsy shrugged. "I think it is still being made."

"What?" Marianna asked. "How do you know that?"

Betsy cleared her throat nervously. "Well, I did overhear Mrs. Strunk talking to the silversmith in town the other day. She was spelling out your name, and she yelled at the man, telling him to make sure he got it right this time. You would have already had a silver cup if he had spelled your name right the first time.

"What are these cups even for?" Marianna asked.

Betsy shook her head. "I'm not sure. The old ones sit up on the highest shelf in the kitchen. No one is allowed to touch them, not even to clean them. Mrs. Strunk cleans them herself. It is amazing because that's about all the actual work she does. Most of the time she's busy bossing everybody else around."

"Did the other wives drink out of these cups?" Marianna asked.

Betsy shrugged her shoulders helplessly. "I don't know."

"I think it's time you told me everything you know about this, Betsy." Marianna could see she was about to protest. "I mean it. Even if you think it is just rumors. How else am I going to deal with this?"

"Okay." Betsy sighed then sat the tea tray down and collapsed onto the chair in the corner. "Now look, I haven't heard much, and I do think it's all rumors, but apparently, all three of the wives met some kind of tragic death. I don't know any specifics, but everyone claims Bludington was the reason they died. Some say he was a beater, but that seems unlikely. Don't you think? I mean he never even comes to see you so..."

"I agree, but I do feel scared of him sometimes. I don't really know him, and he's never actually done anything to me. It's a feeling I get." Marianna sat down and leaned forward. She rested her head on her hands and sighed. "What else?"

"Huh?" Betsy acted like she hadn't heard what Marianna said.

"Don't play dumb with me, Betsy. What else do people say about him?"

Betsy swallowed hard and cleared her throat. "Well, this one is silly. I mean, it's obviously a rumor." She laughed weakly.

"Betsy, tell me!"

"Okay." Betsy sighed. "They say..." She shifted nervously on the loveseat, her eyes darting about the room.

"Well?" Marianna asked. "Out with it. What do they say?"

"They say he is directly responsible for the deaths. Like he killed them or something." It all came out in a rush.

This was so unexpected that Marianna couldn't think of anything to say. She stared at Betsy.

Betsy started laughing uproariously. "Oh, but it's such ridiculous a rumor. These people will think of anything to entertain themselves."

Marianna still stared at her. It did sound ridiculous. How could he have even gotten away with such a thing?

Betsy grabbed her arm, and all her laughter vanished. "Marianna, are you okay? I'm serious. It's a silly rumor. You know that, right?"

"Of course," Marianna said. "It's so obviously outlandish, I couldn't think of anything to say." She forced a smile and squeezed Betsy's arm. "Thanks for telling me. I don't want to be the only one who doesn't know what the rumors are."

Betsy nodded, but still stared at Marianna, her brow furrowed.

Marianna pulled Betsy to the door. "Let's go for a walk in the gardens. I need some fresh air." She couldn't bear to spend anymore time thinking about this.

Betsy's face relaxed. "Okay, yes, let's." She followed Marianna out to the gardens.

Marianna sighed lightly thankful Betsy had told her about the rumors. She hated being in the dark, and at least now she knew some of the rumors were too outrageous to be true.

But a tiny part of Marianna couldn't forget that some of Bludington's servants believed he'd killed his wives. Something had to make them think that. Marianna just wasn't sure what that was.

Chapter 22

Later that night, Betsy turned down the covers and dimmed the light once Marianna had climbed into the bed.

"My lady, I'll be in the next room, if you need me. Are you sure you're all right?"

"Yes, Betsy. I'm worrying about silly things. I'll be fine though." Betsy nodded and left the room.

Marianna tossed and turned before falling into a dream-filled sleep. She was in the hallway with the dwarf painting. This time instead of seeing Bludington, she saw Dunsten, his pale skin glowing.

He seemed to be floating down the hallway, coming toward her like a ghost. He lifted one arm without saying a word and pointed at her. He was coming closer and closer. Instead of eyes, he had dark hollow circles.

Dunsten lifted both arms and reached for her throat. Marianna screamed. Her eyes flew open. Cold sweat made her nightgown cling to her skin. Her breaths were ragged as she tried to orient herself.

Betsy stood over her, a light held high in her hand. "You're okay, my lady. It was just a nightmare."

"Did I scream out loud?"

"Yes, my lady. I don't think anyone else heard you though. This place is so big, and no one else has a room in this wing of the estate."

"That's good. I'm sorry I woke you, Betsy. Could I have some water? My throat is sore." Marianna hoped no one had heard her scream. If Carrie or Leah heard it, she would be the talk of the manor all the next day.

"Of, course, Lady Marianna." Betsy went over to a little table that held a pitcher of water and an empty glass. She poured some water and carried it over to Marianna.

"Call me Marianna. My lady is so formal, and I'm not really nobility." Marianna drained the glass and handed it back to Betsy. The maid set it down before pulling a chair close to the bed. She bent down, picked up a bag, and pulled out the knitting needles with half a blue and green scarf hanging from it.

"I'll stay here with you until you fall asleep, and I'll be near in case you have another nightmare."

Betsy sat and began knitting. Marianna laid back and turned away from the light. She felt rather childish for having a maid sit with her, but at the same time she felt strangely comforted by Betsy's presence. Soon she fell into restful and dreamless sleep.

The next morning, Marianna awoke early. Betsy had fallen asleep in the chair next to the bed. Hopefully she didn't have a crick in her neck. At least Marianna had one ally in this strange place. She slipped out of bed and crept over to the washstand where she washed her face and hands in the tepid water before heading to the dining room.

Marianna stood by the table in the dining room surprised she'd found it empty. Was she up too early for the servants? Maybe she could find something to eat on her own. She walked over to the door the servers with the food always came through.

The door swung open at her touch. She stepped into an unlit hallway. Light crept out from under another doorway at the end, so she ran her hand along the wall as she walked toward it. She felt for the doorknob, and the door swung open.

Heat spread over Marianna's body, and a dozen delicious scents taunted her nose. Freshly baked bread, sizzling bacon, fresh oranges, and dark roasted coffee beans. Her stomach growled as she gaped at the sight before her.

Maids bustled around a large table. Leah was filling a tray, and Carrie was pouring drinks into cups. Another maid kneaded dough, and another was cutting up vegetables. The cook was bent over the oven pulling something from it. Conversation flowed as fast as the people were working.

Everyone was crammed together around the oven and the table that took up most of the floor space in the kitchen. There was no room for Marianna to go any farther, so she started to turn around when a maid looked up and saw her.

"Oh, milady, do you need something? You really shouldn't be in the kitchen. It's only for the servants."

The cook's head snapped up, and she took a step toward Marianna. Conversation ceased, and everyone turned to stare. The cook's gaze bored into her. Wasn't anyone around here friendly?

Marianna cleared her throat. "Um, I was looking for some breakfast. I wasn't sure if everyone was up yet, so I thought I could get some myself..."

Incredulous looks covered the servants' faces. The cook was the first to speak.

"Dear me, my lady. You never need to be getting breakfast on your own. That could very well cost any of us our jobs. Didn't you see the bell rope in the dining room? You are to pull it if you need anything. Go sit down in the dining room, and I'll have something out to you in an instant."

A bell pull? How had she not seen that? It wasn't as if anyone had taken any time to explain to her how things worked around here, so how was she supposed to know?

She sucked in a breath, and her eyes darted about. The silver cups Betsy had told her about were still at the forefront of her mind, but where could they even be stored in such a crowded place?

"Come now, my lady." The cook moved forward and began pushing her out the door.

Marianna thought she wasn't going to find them before the cook herded her from the kitchen, but then she spotted the floor to ceiling shelves that filled a little alcove in the back. And on the topmost shelf was a glint of silver. That had to be them.

Marianna desperately wanted to get a closer look, but it was clear that wouldn't happen in the middle of the day. The cook made a shooing motion as she pushed the swinging door open. "I promise I'll have the food out to you in less than five minutes."

Marianna took a tiny step forward as she scanned the room once more. There had to be a ladder or something to reach those tops shelves. Even the stately Mrs. Strunk wouldn't be able to clean them without assistance.

"Come now, girl. Whatever are you waiting for?" Cook put her hands on her hips and glared at Marianna. Afraid of being caught looking at the silver cups, Marianna gave the cook a weak smile and turned to the door. And then she saw it. A foldable wooden stepladder tucked into the opposite corner of the shelves.

Satisfied that was all she needed to get a closer look at the cups, she started to push through the door. She would have to find a time when the kitchen was empty to come back and take a closer look at them.

When the cook saw that the hall was unlit, she grabbed Marianna's arm and stopped her. "How did you get here with no light? Leah, go get Peter. Tell him the hall needs to be lit, now!"

"Yes, ma'am." Leah gave a little bob and scurried out of the kitchen through a small door on the opposite end which Marianna had not noticed before.

The cook was still holding Marianna's arm. Suddenly she dropped it as if realizing what she had done.

"Oh, I'm so sorry, my lady. Here, let Carrie get you a chair, and you can sit until the hall is lit." Already Carrie was moving toward Marianna with a chair pulled out from under the table.

Marianna sat for a few minutes while the servants readied everything. As soon as Peter arrived to light the hall, she was rushed out to sit at the dining room table. In less than five minutes, a plate full of delicious smelling food was in front of her. There were two giant berry filled hotcakes, a pile of scrambled eggs, and three slices of thick cut bacon. Marianna eagerly dug in.

After eating alone for several minutes, the door opened, and Marianna looked up to see Lord Bludington enter. He looked shocked to see her there, but quickly replaced that look with a smile.

"Miss Marianna, I see you've risen early today." He took a seat opposite of Marianna, pulling the notorious bell pull Marianna had neglected to notice, and Cook came in with a plate of food for him. He took little bites, swallowing quickly before speaking again.

"I'm sorry I have not been around lately. It's the busy season for me. The only meal I take in here is breakfast, and it's usually so early you are still asleep. I hope all is according to your comfort."

Marianna nodded, still too surprised to speak. She began shoveling food into her mouth, hoping Bludington wouldn't notice she was desperate to escape his presence. He spoke again as if they were having a leisurely conversation.

"You might want to take a stroll through the gardens if you haven't had a chance to do so yet. Everything is blooming, and it is quite lovely. Don't be afraid to wander the house either. This is your home now." He took another few bites of food.

It was nice to know she could wander wherever she wanted. The way Dunsten was always lurking about hadn't made it feel that way.

"I'm sure you're looking for ways to occupy your time. If you would like to have guests, feel free to do so. Let Mrs. Strunk know so she can arrange accommodations for them." With a little smile, Bludington wiped his mouth, stood up, gave a bow, and left the room.

Marianna paused mid-swallow, surprised he was already done eating when she had been the one pouring food down her throat. She remembered to swallow, but the food caught, and she began to choke and cough. She grabbed her glass and gulped some water. After a minute, she was able to breathe again.

It almost seemed like he had done that on purpose – made her nervous, then got up and left like he had the upper hand. Maybe he even meant to make her choke. Maybe he was trying to kill her.

But that was ridiculous. What possible motive would he have for killing her? He could be having fun at her expense, but that wasn't the same as a murder attempt. She needed to find some more things to occupy her time before she went crazy.

Chapter 23

Betsy was wringing her hands when Marianna entered the room. When she saw Marianna, she ran over to her and bobbed down in a curtsey, keeping her eyes down while she spoke. "Oh, my lady, there you are. I didn't know what had happened to you, and after last night I was afraid something horrible might befall you. I'm so sorry I wasn't awake before you. That's inexcusable and if you want to dock my pay, I understand. But please, please don't fire me."

Marianna reached out and took Betsy's arm, pulling her upright. "Look at me, Betsy."

It took a minute, but Betsy finally raised her eyes to Marianna's.

"I've already told you I don't want to fire you, and I've told you to call me Marianna. You're the only friend I have here. I'm not going to get rid of you. I need you to help me keep my sanity."

Betsy gave Marianna a small smile, so she continued. "Now, I want to go exploring, but I can't ever find my way around this monstrous place, so will you come with me?"

"My lady..."

"Marianna, remember?"

"Miss Marianna, I can't be friends with a lady. It isn't done."

"Why ever not? What if I command you to be my friend?"

Betsy rubbed her hands down her apron and cleared her throat. "Well, I suppose I would have to then, but what will everyone say? They'd say I was putting on airs."

"I don't care what they say, and who is here besides more servants and Lord Bludington? He won't even know since he's never around. What do you say? Will you be my friend?"

Betsy gave Marianna a little smile and nodded.

"All right, come on, then. Let's go exploring." Marianna grabbed Betsy's arm and pulled her out the door and down the hall.

Betsy showed Marianna the entire east wing of the house. It was filled with more bedrooms. Some were suites, with a sitting room in the middle and a bedroom on either side.

"This east wing gets used the most for parties and things. Back here is the servants' quarters, but you probably don't want to go through here."

"Yes, I do. I want to see your room."

"It's much different than yours. You should stay in the elegant part of the house."

"Betsy, you said you were my friend, and I want to see your room. I don't care if it's not elegant. That doesn't matter to me."

Marianna stepped up to the door that was almost hidden by an alcove. She opened it, and immediately saw the difference between this part and the finer part of the estate. The hall was narrow, and no candle holders hung on the dingy gray walls.

Betsy bent down, picked up a lantern from the floor, and lit it. The light did little to brighten the hall. Betsy started walking and pointing out the doors to different servants' rooms. Near the end of the hall, she stopped and pushed open a door.

"This is my room." She stepped back to allow Marianna to look inside.

A single bed was pushed against the far wall. A table with a lone candle sat next to the bed. The candle was burnt down to a couple of inches. Two dresses, just like the one Betsy was wearing, hung on pegs on the wall adjacent to the bed. That was all the room contained. Marianna took in the room and then turned to Betsy.

"This is all you have? What about a water pitcher? Surely, Bludington wouldn't deny you that."

"It's in the common room. We all share one."

"All the servants share the same one?"

"It really isn't so bad. It's all we know. We've all grown up sharing everything. Please don't go to Lord Bludington about this, it will only make him mad, and possibly make things worse for you."

Marianna wondered how Betsy knew what she was thinking. Wait, make things worse for her. What did that mean?

Betsy must have seen what Marianna was thinking since she rushed to say, "I don't know what I meant by that. I'm sure it wouldn't change the way Bludington treats you. I only meant it would be worse for us. Please, don't go to him."

Marianna wanted to question Betsy further. She didn't believe Betsy's excuses about the Bludington comment, but the fear in Betsy's eyes stopped her. She was really terrified of losing her job, even though Marianna had assured her that wouldn't happen.

But maybe she didn't have that power. At home the servants had always been treated like part of the family, but she knew that wasn't the case in some places. Was Lord Bludington an unfair and unkind employer?

"Don't worry, Betsy. I won't talk to Bludington about it. Now, show me where this common room is, and no reasons why I shouldn't see it. I'm lady of the house, right?"

Betsy swallowed hard, gave a tiny nod, and left her room. Marianna followed her down the hallway to the door at the end. Betsy opened it up and motioned her inside.

There were a few couches and chairs, all muted browns and grays, and rather worn. Two tables, one on each side of the room, held water pitchers. The walls were the same dismal gray as the hall. There were no wall hangings or any décor of any kind. The wood floor was scuffed and scratched and only added to the gloominess of the room.

"This is it. Through that other door is another servants' hallway, where all the stable hands and gardeners stay. I'm not allowed to go back there. None of us girls are. Those men talk bad and have horrible manners, at least that's what Mrs. Strunk says." Betsy pointed over to the end of the hallway. "The door at the end of that hallway leads outside."

Marianna opened her mouth to comment on the depressing atmosphere of the room, but before she had a chance to say anything, Betsy grabbed her arm and began pulling her back down the hallway towards the main part of the house. They were moving so fast, that Marianna nearly lost her train of thought.

Once they reached the main hallway, Betsy dropped Marianna's arm and started to speak, but Marianna wasn't paying attention. A figure hovered in the corner. She caught a glimpse of his face. It was Dunsten. He moved back in the shadows, staring at her with his ghostly-looking eyes, his face expressionless. A shiver darted down her spine as she forced herself to turn away and pretend she hadn't seen him.

"... and I don't think you have really seen all the main house yet. There're two different sitting rooms, a parlor, and a sunroom. Of course, you've already seen the dining rooms, the library and the ballroom." Betsy was rattling on, unaware of the way Dunsten had been watching them.

She took Marianna to each of the rooms she mentioned, chattering cheerfully as if she could wipe away the grim picture of the servants' quarters from Marianna's mind.

Marianna was able to see how all the hallways of the estate connected to each of the main rooms. The two sitting rooms were in the same hall as the dining rooms. The parlor and sunroom were down the same hallway as the library.

The sitting rooms and the parlor were ornately decorated and gave off a pretentious and stiff atmosphere. Straight hardback chairs that looked like they could have been thrones, pristine rugs with complex designs woven through them, all deep colors like gold, maroon, green, and cream. Marianna wouldn't dare take any food or even a drink into them.

The sunroom, however, was beautiful. Sitting in a corner of the manor, two of its walls were all glass. Two comfy-looking couches sat facing each of the glass walls. The view was of the garden. A stone path led through brightly colored flowers of pink, yellow, purple, and white, until it ended at a rose trimmed gazebo.

Off to one side, was a koi pond. Sunlight glistened off golden and white fish as they darted about a statue of a woman in a long, flowing gown. She had a wreath of flowers on her head and a pitcher in her hand. Water poured from the pitcher into a bowl that sat on a little pedestal, and once it was filled, the water streamed over the side and down into the pond.

"This is amazing," breathed Marianna. "I can't believe I didn't find this room before. It's right down the hall from the library. Is my bedroom right above this room? The view of the gardens seems to be the same."

"Yes. This room is especially beautiful when you come here in the morning. Since it faces the east, the sunlight comes pouring through, lighting the room up brighter than any chandelier could."

Marianna let out a little giggle and fell back against one of the couches. She sank into its softness, pulled a pillow from behind her, and held it tight against her chest. "Maybe I really can be happy here. Come on, Betsy sit down, and don't give me any excuses. I command you to do it if that makes you feel better."

Marianna grabbed Betsy's arm and pulled her down onto the couch. At first, Betsy sat straight up, stiff as cardboard, but after several minutes she relaxed against the back of the sofa. "It's not that I don't want your friendship, it's just... I really can't lose this job. My mother is ill, too ill to work. And my Da, well he got injured in a mining accident and didn't make it through the night."

"Oh, I'm so sorry." Marianna turned to face Betsy.

"It's okay, it was a long time ago, but Mother started going downhill after that. She gets sicker every year." Tears glistened in Betsy's eyes. She scooped up the end of her apron and swiped at them.

Marianna reached out and squeezed Betsy's hand. "That's hard. My father's been ill for a year now too."

Betsy smiled through the tears. "Yeah." She lifted the edge of her apron. A green stalk was stitched up into yellow petals that surrounded a circle of black.

"My mother made this especially for this job. I told her not to worry about it, but she insisted. She was so proud that I had my first real job working in a manor and everything. She's always called me her sunflower. Says I brought sunlight and joy into her life from the moment I was born and every day since."

Betsy's voice tightened, and she took a shuddering breath. "I'm the oldest of eight. Sasha's next and she's only twelve, so she can't even get a proper job. She helps old Mrs. Denny with the Sanderson children." Betsy barely took a breath before exclaiming, "Oh, they're so bad!"

The expression of horror that covered Betsy's face while talking about the children made Marianna laugh.

"No, they really are that bad," Betsy insisted. "I had to watch them for awhile before I got this job, and they run around like little hooligans, and wouldn't listen to a word I said. Mrs. Denny can't even keep up with them anymore. But it's not a real job and only pays a couple cullers. Still, it's better than nothing." Betsy sighed.

"What about your other brothers and sisters?" Marianna asked. "How old are they?"

Betsy's face brightened, and it was obvious she loved her siblings. "After Sasha, there's the twins, Donald and Ronald. They're ten. Then there's Ava Marie, who's eight, Conner who's seven, Porter who's five, and Daisy who's four."

"Wow, so little! I remember when Annette was that little. I bet the little ones are fun."

Betsy nodded. "Yes, I love them to pieces. I used to watch them a lot, before I moved here. Now it's Sasha's turn whenever she's home." Betsy's voice was wistful.

"You must miss them. I know I miss mine. Especially with the boys being off who knows where with the rebellion. Speaking of which, have you heard any news about that or seen a paper anywhere?"

Betsy shook her head. "We don't get the paper all the way out here, but my mom always gets them. Next time I stop home, I'll bring you the latest ones."

"Would you? That would be wonderful!" Marianna sighed and leaned back against the sofa. "It's so strange here. There are wonderful things, strange things, and some downright creepy things. But I'm very glad I have you, Betsy."

"I'm glad I'm here too, miss."

They were both quiet then, watching the setting sun cast a rosy, orange glow over the garden. After a long while, Betsy hopped up, a look of distress on her face.

"Oh, Miss Marianna, I'm sorry. I forgot myself. It's already past dinnertime. Look, it's starting to get dark."

"It's okay, Betsy. I can still get some food. Come on, we'll go get something from Cook."

Marianna led the way to the dining room, and this time she pulled the bell pull to order some food. The cook grumbled something about Marianna's missing dinner but brought her some food anyway. Betsy had disappeared through the kitchen door, and after several minutes reappeared.

"Betsy, I'm going to take this plate upstairs. Go get your food and bring it too."

There was a strange look on Betsy's face, but she said, "I'm ready now, Miss Marianna."

"What about your food? Surely you didn't eat it all already?"

"No, when we miss dinnertime, we don't get anything to eat." Betsy's voice was low, and her eyes were down.

Marianna looked around the dining room, and then grabbed Betsy's arm and pulled Betsy up to her room. When they were inside with the door shut, Marianna handed her plate to Betsy.

"Here, eat some of mine. I can't finish it all anyway. And it's my fault you missed dinner." Betsy looked ready to refuse and started to hand the plate back to Marianna.

"I command you to eat some!" Marianna said in a voice gilded with laughter. Betsy gave a little laugh and began to eat. Soon they had the food polished off, and Betsy was helping Marianna get ready for bed.

"I had fun today, Betsy. I'm glad you're my friend." Marianna threw her arms around Betsy. She pulled back and said, "We'll go exploring again tomorrow. I can hardly wait."

Marianna plopped down onto her bed, falling back against her pillows and closing her eyes as she pulled her covers up. She opened them enough to see Betsy blow out the light and tiptoe to the door. Her eyelids slid shut, and she nestled deeper into her covers.

Betsy must have thought she was asleep, or she couldn't hear her as she whispered, "Goodnight, Miss Marianna. I'm glad we're friends too. I only pray that you will be safe here."

Marianna's eyes flew open, but all she saw was Betsy's back as she crept out the door.

Chapter 24

The next morning, Marianna jumped out of bed, the despairing thoughts from last night forgotten after a good night's rest. She had made a friend in this depressing place, and today they were going to finish exploring the manor, but first she needed to write to her family again.

Marianna opened her journal and noted the date. She'd been here at Bludington's manor for five days. Only five days? It had certainly seemed longer. She was surprised she hadn't heard back from anyone yet.

She had written to her father, Annette, Susan, and her brothers as soon as she had arrived at Thunderwell. She hadn't expected a reply from her brothers, of course. Mail to and from the army was never on time and sometimes lost altogether. She would've expected to hear back from Susan and her sister though. Her sister especially, since she'd promised to write every day.

Maybe this time she'd get a reply. She drafted letters to everyone on her list again, telling them about her days at Bludington's manor. She left out the scarier bits, like the way Dunsten seemed to be always following her around, and the horrible story she'd heard about Bludington's first wife. She was tempted to tell Annette but was afraid her sister would tell their father who would worry for her and take a turn for the worst.

She begged for information about the war and her brothers. She couldn't believe how isolated from everything she was out here. As wealthy as Bludington was, it seemed like he could find a way to keep in better contact with the rest of the world.

She finished the final letter, folded it, and slipped it into the last envelope she had. She would have to find out how she could obtain some more stationary. She dipped her stamper into the hot blue wax and pressed the shape of a butterfly onto the envelope, sealing it closed.

Unbidden, tears filled her eyes as she recalled the day her father had taken her to the stationarier's to pick out her own stationary. It hadn't been long after her mother had passed. She'd taken over her mother's duties as the primary letter writer, and her father had noticed.

"Such a fine letter writer deserves her own personal stationery set," he told her, pride in his voice as he patted her shoulder.

Marianna had never been to the stationarier before, so just going there was exciting. The sharp scent of ink mingled with the fresh smell of new paper. Hundreds of kinds of paper lined the walls in display cases.

On one, shelves held dozens of different kinds of seal stamps, and right under them sat a rack that held the wax melting cups. In the center of the store, were tables filled with boxes of different kinds of envelopes, ink pots, various colors of feathered pens, and baskets filled with little stars of sealing wax in every color of the rainbow.

Marianna's father walked over to the counter at the far wall and told the shriveled old man huddled over the counter, "We need everything - letter paper, envelopes, wax, and a seal stamp. Even a pen and ink pot."

The old man's eyes lit up with greed, and he scurried out from behind the counter. "Right this way, sir! I only carry the best products," he said in a gravelly voice. He led them over to the seal stamps, the most expensive of the products Marianna's father had listed.

"I have seal stamps in iron, for those who prefer a sturdier model." He lifted the wooden handle of a display piece to show the solid rounded iron end. "And we can have whatever shape you would like engraved on the end." He set the iron piece down and picked up the next one.

"And we have them in silver for those who prefer a finer model." He paused, setting the silver seal stamp down after showing the shiny silver end. He picked up the next one. "Or in gold, for those who prefer a kingly seal stamp." He gave Marianna a wink. Clearly the gold model was the most expensive one, and he thought he could sway her to buy it.

"I'll take a silver one," Marianna blurted out. A hint of a scowl crossed the man's face, and Marianna knew her instincts had been right. The man was quick to rebound, pulling out a book and flipping through its pages, pausing to point out various designs that could be engraved on the bottom of the seal stamp.

"And what would you like engraved on your seal stamp, miss? We have unicorns,"—he flipped forward a few more pages— "or a tiger or lion, if you prefer something more fierce." He waved his hand over a page filled with wild animals, before flipping some more. "Or perhaps you'd prefer a flower of some kind?" He pointed out several elaborate flower designs.

Marianna shook her head. She already knew what she wanted. "A butterfly, please, sir."

This time the old man couldn't hide his scowl as well, and Marianna's father caught a glimpse of it.

"Whatever the lady wants is what we are going to get." He smiled down at her, giving her shoulder a squeeze.

The old man muttered something unintelligible then flipped to a page full of butterfly designs. "Which one would you like, miss?" he asked in an exasperated tone.

It only took Marianna a moment to find the one she wanted. A simple outline of a butterfly. "And blue wax, please." A blue butterfly. Her mother would have loved it, and that's exactly why she chose it.

She'd found some stationary lined with hand-painted blue butterflies, a more expensive choice that made the old man smile with glee. She also chose some blank cream-colored envelopes the same color as the letter paper, a royal blue feathered pen, and a pot of blue ink.

She carried all her loot—except for the seal stamp which would be delivered after the butterfly had been engraved on it—home and proudly showed her brothers and sister. They had all been duly impressed.

Marianna sighed, pushing away the memory and the stray tear that had somehow escaped. She hadn't expected such a wave of homesickness to flood her over a simple memory from long ago, and there were other things to be done today. She couldn't sit around and mope. Plus, she still had some exploring to do with Betsy.

Cheered by that thought, she jumped from her chair and headed to the front parlor where she left the letters in a silver tray for outgoing mail.

Chapter 25

She found Betsy waiting outside the dining room door.

"All right, what part of the castle have I not seen? I haven't seen the part with the tower. Where is that?"

"That's in the south corner, Miss Marianna. I don't know if you want to go there. It's dark and dingy."

"I want to see the whole house, Betsy. No matter what state it is in, so lead the way."

Betsy led her down to the south corner and into a dark hallway. At first, Marianna thought it was the hallway with the dwarf painting, but then she saw that doors lined either side. There had only been one door in that creepy hallway.

"All of these bedrooms look the same. Furniture covered with sheets, dust everywhere, quite messy. They haven't been used in a long time." Betsy opened a few doors for Marianna, and Marianna saw that what Betsy said was true. The rooms were in a deplorable state.

"Why haven't they been used in so long?"

"I guess because there's never been enough people here to fill them up."

"No one ever cleans them?"

"If they are not going to be used, Mrs. Strunk says it's a waste of time to clean them."

Marianna raised her eyebrows. It was a shame there were so many unused rooms.

Betsy closed the door, then led the way to the end of the hall where a wooden door stood. She pulled a key from her apron pocket and unlocked it.

"This is the door to the tower. I figured you would want to see it, so I got the key from Mrs. Strunk. She wasn't too happy about it, but since you're the mistress there's not much she can do." The door popped open on squeaky hinges. It shuddered a few times, then stood still.

Marianna heard a faint noise. She grabbed Betsy's arm. "Shh, listen." They listened for several seconds, and the noise came again. "Did you hear it? I can't tell what it is, but I think it's coming from below us."

A flicker of fear passed through Betsy's eyes. It was gone so quickly that Marianna wondered if she'd imagined it.

"It was the wind. It couldn't have come from below us. We're on the ground level, unless it was dirt shifting."

Betsy walked through the door, and began climbing the narrow, wooden steps. They creaked with their weight. Maybe it hadn't been such a good idea to insist on seeing the tower. Marianna held tightly to the spindly, iron handrail as they ascended.

"Has anyone been up to the tower lately?"

"Oh, Lord Bludington comes up here quite frequently. I'm not sure what he does up here. There are rumors... Well, they're just rumors." Betsy picked up her pace.

"About what?" Marianna hurried after her.

"I really shouldn't tell you. It would be like speaking bad about the master of the estate."

"Well, as mistress, don't I deserve to know what people are saying?"

"I suppose so." Betsy hesitated before adding, "Some people say he has a magic cauldron up here that he mixes things in."

"What, like a witch's pot?" Marianna let out an unbelieving laugh.

"I told you it was a rumor."

Bludington did scare her sometimes, but a wizard over his pot stirring up spells? That was ridiculous. Marianna laughed again as she imagined Bludington hunched over a black pot, stirring and stirring.

"Miss Marianna, what is it? Are you okay?"

By this time, Marianna was laughing so hard that she had to stop climbing. She gripped the rail, trying to control her laughter, but the harder she tried to stop the worse it got. Finally, she was able to breathe out between laughs.

"It's just... Bludington over a pot... it would be a hilarious... sight."

Betsy laughed nervously. "That would be a funny sight."

Betsy still seemed scared, so Marianna did her best to calm herself as they continued climbing.

They reached a door like the one at the bottom of the staircase. Betsy unlocked it and pushed it open. The circular room had one large window opposite the door that let in plenty of light.

In the center of the room stood a table with numerous glass tubes filled with liquids of a variety of colors. An apparatus of twisting wires and tubes that Marianna knew alchemists used also sat on the table.

"Lord Bludington is an alchemist? That's why people said he stirred up spells in his pot." Marianna stepped close to the table to examine the liquids.

Four tubes in the back caught her eye. They were filled with a substance that looked an awful lot like blood. Why would Bludington have blood in tubes?

Even as she thought this, Marianna reached out to take hold of one of the red-filled tubes. Betsy grabbed her hand and pulled her back.

"Don't touch. Some of this stuff could be poisonous. Didn't you want to see the view from the window?"

Betsy pulled Marianna away from the table, but Marianna kept her eyes on the strange tubes. She stared at them until a cool breeze distracted her. Turning, she looked out over the land below, surprised at how high the tower was. "No wonder it took us so long to climb those stairs. We are really high up."

"Yes, and we'd better start back downstairs, or we'll be late for lunch."

Marianna allowed Betsy to pull her toward the door, but she couldn't help looking back for another glance at the tubes. She suddenly shivered, frightened by some unknown reason, and turned toward the stairs. She hurried down them, passing Betsy in her rush.

"Miss Marianna, what is it? Don't run, you might fall."

Betsy's voice brought Marianna back to her senses and she slowed down. She looked back at Betsy's worried expression.

"Sorry, I got a little chill. I'm fine now, though."

When she reached the bottom of the stairs, Marianna pushed opened the door and stepped into the hallway. As she did so, she saw the departing back of a person. She was sure it was Dunsten.

Why was he always around? He scared her, with his ghostly looks and unrelenting stare. Marianna shivered again and wrapped her arms around herself.

Marianna smiled at Betsy, trying to hide her fear as they went to the dining room for lunch. They made it just as the servers were setting the table. Betsy started for the kitchen, telling Marianna she would return once she had finished eating.

After lunch, Betsy took Marianna through the rest of the house, leaving out Bludington's quarters. Marianna didn't want to risk the chance of running into Bludington unexpectedly. It took them a few hours, and Marianna still hadn't seen the hallway with the painting of the dwarf.

"Betsy, when I was visiting here, I found a hallway with no doors except for one at the end. It had a painting of a dwarf hanging on the wall at the end of the hallway. Is that hallway a part of Bludington's quarters?"

Betsy looked surprised. A flicker of something passed through her eyes. Marianna couldn't quite tell what it was. "I don't know of any hallway like that, Miss Marianna. Are sure you didn't see it in one of your nightmares?"

Marianna stared at Betsy for a long time. She was sure Betsy was lying to her about knowing where the hallway was, but the flinty look on Betsy's face said she was not going to budge from her story. Finally, Marianna let out a sigh.

"I know it was real, perhaps you don't know where it is located." Marianna turned and went into the library. "I'll be reading for the rest of the afternoon, Betsy. Come get me for dinner."

Marianna closed the door on Betsy's departing back and took a seat on the sofa. She didn't get a book but stared into space thinking. Something weird was going on here, and it had something to do with that hallway. Marianna was sure of it. If Betsy didn't want to help her, she'd have to find it on her own.

Chapter 26

After dinner, Marianna headed for the kitchen. She peeked through the door. Leah stood at the table chopping vegetables. Several other maids whose names Marianna couldn't remember attended to other tasks. There was no sign of the cook.

Perfect. The cook probably wouldn't have let the maids talk to her. Marianna slipped inside. "Leah, could I speak with you for a moment, please?"

All the maids looked up, shock on their faces. Apparently, they were not used to being spoken to by the mistress of the house. One stepped back, and two others whispered to one another, looking ready to dart out of the room.

"Y-yes, milady?" Leah stuttered, vigorously rubbing her hands on her apron.

Leah was afraid of her? Seriously? Leah was at least three inches taller than Marianna, and Marianna clearly didn't have much authority here.

"You're not in trouble. I just want to speak with you." Marianna motioned for Leah to come into the dining room.

Leah looked apprehensively at the others. Two maids shrugged their shoulders, and another nodded her head, so Leah followed Marianna.

"How long have you worked here, Leah?" Marianna tried to make her voice friendly, but it was clear Leah was still afraid.

"Um, three years, my lady."

"Oh, good. Maybe you can help me with something. I am still familiarizing myself with the house, and I was wondering if you knew where the hallway was with the dwarf painting. It's a dwarf with a blue beard, and he has a knife in his hand."

Leah's eyes widened, and she answered before Marianna even had a chance to finish explaining. "I don't know of any such place, my lady. I only work the kitchen and the bedrooms. I've never seen such a place." She was obviously lying, but her eyes were wide with fear.

"Are you sure you haven't passed it when you were doing your duties? There is only one door in this hallway and the painting hangs at the end of it."

"I know nothing, milady. Nothing at all." Tears puddled in Leah's eyes, then trickled down her face.

Great. Now she was making servants cry.

"It's okay if you don't know anything about it. You're not in trouble. But tell me, who, besides Cook, has been here the longest of the maids?"

Leah looked relieved not to have to answer any more questions and replied quickly. "That would be Carrie, my lady. She has been here five years."

"Okay, thank you. Go tell Carrie to come here."

Leah bobbed a curtsey and rushed out of the room. Marianna rolled her eyes and let out a sigh. How could they fear her? Dunsten had made it clear who was in charge here when Bludington was not around.

At home, where she did have power over whether a maid stayed employed, no one had been scared of her.

Carrie stepped into the dining room. Up close, she looked to be in her mid-thirties, and she didn't look as scared as Leah had, much to Marianna's relief.

Carrie's gaze was firm but respectful as she met Marianna's eyes, and Marianna was beginning to think she might not get any information from her. She explained about the hallway once more. Carrie waited patiently until she had finished, then spoke quietly.

"I know of no such place, my lady, and I have been here five years. Perhaps it was another estate where you saw this hallway?" Carrie's tone was polite and sounded sincere, but a flicker in Carrie's eyes made Marianna believe she was lying.

Cook burst into the room, interrupting their conversation. Her eyes flashed with anger.

"What is this? You're disturbing the help and bringing them to tears. I can't get the proper standard of work out of them if you insist on scaring them." One hand flew to her hip, and the other waved a spatula around in the air. "What is it you're so determined to know, anyway? If anyone can answer your questions, I can. I've been here over ten years."

Marianna once again explained about the hallway.

Cook's eyes widened, then become veiled. "Sometimes it's better to leave things alone, rather than go digging up old things that don't matter anymore. All you'll find is trouble. Anyway, I know nothing of such a place here, and I have been everywhere in the estate at one time or another," Cook huffed.

She turned to Carrie. "Back to the kitchen. What are you standing around for when there's work to be done?" Cook swatted at Carrie with the spatula, and Carrie rushed away. Without another word, Cook followed Carrie into the kitchen.

Marianna sighed, disappointed, but not surprised that she hadn't learned anything new. She left the dining room and went to the library, looking for a book to take her mind off the hallway everyone insisted did not exist. She found a book of gothic tales and soon became absorbed in it, losing track of time. It grew dark outside, but Marianna only noticed enough to light a candle.

A door slammed, and Marianna's light went out. She screamed, jumping out of her chair.

A single candle made shadows dance across the wall as a figure came toward her. The sparse light flickered across a ghostly face before the light vanished.

Footsteps shuffled closer. Marianna's throat tightened as a wave of fear washed over her. Unable to think, she only knew she had to get out. She ran to the window and fumbled with the latch.

A cold hand grabbed her shoulder. She screamed as the hand tightened and roughly pulled her back.

Chapter 27

Knocked off balance, Marianna stumbled and would have fallen if not for the tight grip on her arm. She tried to pull away, barely squashing the scream that rose in her throat, but the grip didn't loosen. Until it suddenly pushed her backward. Her arms pinwheeled as she struggled to find something, anything to help her regain her balance in the darkness.

She collided with something both soft and hard. A chair, one of those fancy velvet ones with the wooden arms and legs. She gripped the arm of the chair, the grain of the wood pressing patterns on her palm. A match scratched across something. A hint of smoke teased her nose, and a little flame appeared in the darkness.

A tall, hooded figure stood in front of her, the face veiled so she couldn't recognize it. His long dark cloak was wrapped around him so that it was all she could see. It touched the floor, covering his shoes. Next to him a candle sat on a little round table, the light glinting off the silver object he was hurriedly burying beneath his cloak.

Was that one of the silver cups? Why wasn't it on the shelf with the others? The figure stepped closer, looming over her as he spoke. "What are you doing in the library at this time of night?" Dunsten growled.

Of course it was Dunsten. Marianna's racing heart slowed a little. With Dunsten, she knew what she was dealing with. At least, she hoped so.

"I, uh, I thought Lord Bludington said this room was for me." Marianna gulped in air. Her voice grew stronger as she added, "I didn't know there was a curfew on it." Her grip on the chair relaxed.

"It's dangerous for a young girl like you to be wandering around the castle at night. I'll escort you back to your bedchamber." Dunsten pulled her from the chair, his grip tight and painful, and Marianna winced.

He loosened his hold before yanking her toward the door.

"Could you slow down, please? You're practically dragging me. I'm not going to run away."

Dunsten merely grunted as he moved so fast that the flash of shadows on the walls made Marianna dizzy as they twisted and turned through the maze of hallways that led back to her bedroom. When she saw the old-fashioned suit of armor standing like a sentry at the end of one hallway, she sighed with relief. The next hallway was her own.

At the door to Marianna's room, Dunsten gave a stiff bow. His cloak fell open enough for Marianna to catch a glance underneath. The silver cup sparkled in the candlelight, and she was sure she could see an M, an A, and an N.

Was it her cup? And if so, why did he have it? Questions swirled in her mind like a hurricane. She could hardly think straight.

"I would stay in my room at night, if I were you, Miss Marianna. There are things going on here that you cannot understand." Dunsten's hollow eyes bored into hers, as if he could tell by looking at her that she would try this again.

"What things?" What exactly is going on here?" Marianna demanded.

Dunsten made no response. He stared at her expressionless, his hood still flopped over his head making him look like a villain from a fairytale. Marianna stared at him, but he remained speechless and motionless.

Finally, she shoved open her door, marched inside, and slammed it behind her, not bothering to say anything else to Dunsten. She was tired of being bossed about by him.

Hadn't she been given permission to wander where she wanted? Bludington hadn't given her any parameters on where she could go and when. And she was to be the mistress of the place. What was Dunsten's problem?

Betsy met Marianna inside the doorway. "Are you okay, Miss Marianna? I didn't know where you had gone, and Dunsten came and questioned me. He scares me."

"He scares me too. He came into the library like a ghost. I had just finished reading *Lady Eltringham*, and my light went out when he threw open the door."

"Oh, that's the one where the manor is haunted by that ghost, and Lady Eltringham has to figure out why, right?" Betsy's face lit up.

"Yes, you've read it?" Marianna paused, surprised Betsy knew the story.

Betsy nodded her head. "My mom taught us all to read, and when I got here, Cook would bring us girls books from the library each week. She claims reading keeps us sharp, and when we're sharp, we get more work done." She smiled. "Truthfully, I think she has a soft spot and doesn't want anyone to know it."

Marianna nodded, but her mind was still on Dunsten and his strange behavior. "You know it then. Part of the problem was that my mind was still in the story, but for a minute, I was sure he was a ghost. He always hovers around like one. I can't help but wonder if he's following me or something."

Marianna didn't wait for Betsy's help as she reached behind herself, grasping at the ties on her dress. "Why would he do that, though? Is he spying on me for Bludington?"

She ripped her ties loose and shrugged out of her dress, tossing it to the ground. She pulled off her petticoat and camisole and threw them down as well. Betsy scrambled to pick them all up as Marianna pulled on her nightgown and continued talking.

"Bludington hasn't told me anything I couldn't do, so why would he have someone spy on me? In fact, Bludington told me the other day that I could go anywhere I wanted in the manor. But I can't help the feeling that there is somewhere people don't want me to go. And Dunsten said some strange things to me about not wandering around the house at night but wouldn't tell me why. Is there something I should be afraid of?"

Marianna whirled to face Betsy who stood still, her arms full of Marianna's clothes. "Oh my, Betsy. I didn't mean for you to have to pick everything off the floor like that."

She pulled things from Betsy's arms, folding them up and putting them away. "I just got so angry."

Betsy tried to take the clothes back, but it was useless. "Really, it's okay, Miss Marianna. It's my job."

Marianna ignored her, putting away each piece of clothing. "Do you know anything, Betsy?"

"I don't really know, Miss Marianna. I think it's unlikely that there's anything for you to be afraid of here. Dunsten likes to lord his position over others by scaring them, telling them... weird things."

"What kind of weird things?"

Betsy shrugged. "I don't know. Things like certain hallways being haunted and such. I think he told one girl she'd be sorry if she went into Bludington's wing of the house. Things like that. It's just made-up stuff."

"I don't know. I've had this feeling—even before I moved here—that something was not right about Bludington. But my friends and my sister managed to convince me otherwise. Bludington enforced their convictions in his goodness. He gave me this room, the library, and threw that large party just for me, when he hadn't given a party in years. And now that feeling..." Marianna sighed before continuing. "With everything that's happened lately, it's gotten stronger."

Marianna climbed onto her bed and slipped her legs under the covers. She leaned back against the headboard and closed her eyes, trying to calm the swirling emotions. She opened them at the sound of Betsy's voice.

"Miss Marianna, you're overwrought at what happened with Dunsten. I assure you, you are safe here. I will do everything within my ability to see that it remains that way. Now, you need to go to sleep. You'll feel better in the morning. I'll stay here in the chair until you fall asleep." Betsy pulled up the covers and patted Marianna's shoulder.

Marianna smiled weakly. "I suppose you're right," she said as she slid down against the soft mattress. "You don't have to stay here, Betsy. I'll be fine."

"I have knitting to catch up on, and I can just as easily do it here as in my room. Besides, we're friends, remember, and that means we watch out for one another."

Pleased Betsy made a reference to their friendship, Marianna fell asleep with a big smile on her face.

Will came toward Marianna, but something was strange about him. He seemed to be floating instead of walking. He was calling out to her, but she couldn't hear what he was saying. He got closer and his form changed. He became Dunsten and he was screaming at her.

"Why did you do it? Why did you agree to marry Bludington? I thought you loved me!" Dunsten's pale face leered closer to her, and Marianna screamed. He grabbed her and shook her. Her eyes flew open. Sweat dotted her forehead and trickled down her back. Her breaths came in heaving gasps.

Betsy's worried face peered over her. "Miss Marianna, are you okay? It was another nightmare."

Marianna grasped for the wooden ring still on her finger and twirled it around. It had just been a nightmare. That was all.

Betsy dabbed her face with a wet cloth, and she took in a few more shuddering breaths before she was able to start breathing normally again.

"It was a nightmare, Miss Marianna. You're safe," Betsy assured her.

Marianna rubbed her eyes and sat up. "This one was worse than any of the others. Will was there for a minute, and then he turned into Dunsten." Marianna grimaced.

"Will? Who is he?"

"Will is..." Marianna paused and swallowed hard, "was, my first true love. I don't think I'll ever love anyone else like I loved him. Do you think Will would understand why I married Bludington?"

"If he truly loved you, then he would most certainly understand," Betsy assured her.

"I wanted to believe... I mean I did believe that he was still coming back, for so long," Marianna's voice wobbled. She blinked rapidly, trying to erase the tears that had flooded her eyes.

"What happened to him?" Besty asked in a whisper.

"He was lost at sea. They were on their way to the Isle of Carid..."

Betsy gasped and covered her mouth with her hand. "Oh, I'm sorry, Miss, but it's just, they call that place the Devil's Island. Why were they going there?"

"Well, they left for there before that name became popular. They are so many rich goods there. Jewelry, rugs, exquisite pottery. It's one of my father's favorite places to buy goods."

Marianna settled back against her pillows. It was clear she wasn't going to go back to sleep easily. "I went there once when I was just a little girl."

Betsy's eyes widened in shock. "Really? What was it like?"

"It was beautiful. The beaches were covered with sparkling white sand, and the water was so blue and clear, you could see all the bright, colorful fish that swam beneath. And the shells, well," Marianna reached under the neckline of her nightgown and pulled out the cameo she had been unable to sell. After that incident, she had taken to wearing it all the time, grateful to still have a piece of her mother that hadn't been pawned off to no avail.

She held it up to the candlelight for Betsy to examine. "This is made of the blue shell that washes up on the beaches. They say Carid is the only place you can find it."

She smiled remembering the day her father had given her mother the necklace. "We gathered a bucket of shells on the beach in the morning and then later that day, my dad took my mother to a jeweler where he had this made especially for her."

"It's beautiful," Betsy breathed. She reached out a hand to touch it, but then drew back.

"It's fine. Here you can hold it." Marianna reached behind her neck and unclasped the necklace, placing it in Betsy's hand.

Betsy held it up examining it in the light, before handing it back to Marianna. "It's very nice. You're lucky to have something like that to remember your mother by."

Marianna nodded. Tears again assaulted her eyes, and she turned away from Betsy and took a deep breath.

"Anyway, Will never came back. I feel so bad. I haven't thought about him in a long while. I've been so occupied with exploring and adapting to this strange, new place." Her throat tightened and a tear escaped, trickling down her cheek. She drew in a shuddering breath and turned back to Betsy.

"What if he is still alive? Now I won't be able to marry him. Maybe I've made the worst mistake of my life." She could no longer hold back the tears, and they streamed down both cheeks.

Betsy pulled her close, wrapping her in a comforting hug. "There, there, Miss Marianna. It isn't all as bad as that. The way I see it, Will truly loved you, and he would understand the need for you to protect your family." Betsy patted her back and continued.

"Anyway, in your dream it was really Dunsten. It's probably another way he's haunting you. He's a strange, frightening man. It's not surprising you have bad dreams about him, especially when you think he might be following you around."

Marianna's tears turned to sobs, and Betsy rocked her back and forth. "Let it all out. It's okay to cry. Sometimes it's the only way to ease the pain."

Once Marianna had calmed enough to speak, she pulled away. "You're such a good friend, Betsy. I don't know how I would survive this place without you."

Betsy smiled. "You're a good friend too. I've never had a friend like you before."

Marianna reached over and squeezed Betsy's hand. "Thank-you. I'm all right now, as long as I can sleep without nightmares. You should try to get some sleep too."

Betsy nodded, sat back down in her chair, and picked up her knitting. "I will, don't worry about me. I'll be here until you fall asleep."

Marianna soon drifted off, and she slept through the rest of the night without any more dreams.

Chapter 28

After dinner the next day, Marianna sent Betsy to her room to pack, insisting she take a few days to see her family. Betsy hadn't gotten any time off in the several months she'd been working for Bludington.

Betsy was ecstatic, but also hesitant. "I'd love to go see my family, but only if you'll be all right."

"Yes, I'll be fine! It's only for two days."

Betsy paused one final time in the doorway, a smile on her face. It didn't hide the worry in her eyes, though. "You're sure, Miss Marianna?"

"Yes!" Marianna laughed. "I'll spend my time in the library, reading."

Betsy sighed. "All right."

"Tell your family I said hello, and someday I'd love to meet them."

Betsy's face brightened. "Oh, they'd love that. I'll be sure to tell them."

She darted out of the room, and Marianna went and sat on her bed to wait. She tried to read, but it was hard to concentrate when all she could think about was her impending plan.

She got up, walking onto her balcony, drinking in the warm evening air. Jasmine mingled with the scent of roses and peonies. Orange, pink, and purple streaked across the sky, the soft light creating a glow over the garden below.

Marianna leaned forward, resting her arms atop the balcony's stone rail. The rocky surface scratched her skin, but she didn't mind. It was like she had stepped into a scene from a fairytale, and she wanted to stay in this moment a little longer, to forget her worries and soak in the magic of twilight.

Marianna waited until all the light had left the sky and she could no longer hear the din of the servants tending to the gardens below before going into her room.

She cracked her bedroom door open, listening. All quiet. Closing the door, she walked over to her bed and pulled her journal from under the pillow. There were so many twists and turns to get lost in, but Marianna was confident she could find her way to the kitchen.

Flipping to the page where she'd been drawing out a floor plan of the manor, she traced the path to the kitchen reassuring herself it was embedded within her brain. Marianna desperately wished to add a path to the hallway with the dwarf painting, but one thing at a time. She needed to concentrate on tonight's task—getting a look at those cups.

She put the journal away and picked up the lantern on her bedside table then opened her door slowly, listening. Nothing. She crept down the hallway to the stairs, scurried down them and through the dining room, rushing straight to the kitchen.

Marianna stopped abruptly, gasping. Carrie, Leah, and another maid stood over the sink. Leah was pouring steaming water into it, while Carrie scrubbed and rinsed a dish before handing it to the third maid to dry.

At Marianna's gasp, all three turned to face her. Carrie dropped the dish she held back into the dishwater, grabbing the towel from the third maid and wiped her hands dry. She tossed it back to the girl and hurried over to Marianna.

"What is it, miss? Are you okay? Your face is so pale." She pulled a chair out from the table, gesturing for Marianna to sit.

Nodding, Marianna sat, speechless. She knew the servants were worked hard, but they had to go to bed at some point, right?

Carrie gave Leah and the other girl a glare and waved her hand toward the door. The other girl scurried out, but Leah hesitated. Carrie huffed as she cocked a hand on her hip, shaking her head vigorously. Clearly, she was a protege of Cook. Marianna barely held back a giggle at that thought. Leah sighed and trudged out of the kitchen.

Carrie turned back to Marianna. "Would you like something to drink?" she asked with a smile.

Marianna nodded too stunned by Carrie's hospitable behavior to say anything. The last time they had spoken, Marianna had gotten the distinct feeling that Carrie didn't like her. Maybe it had been her imagination. Maybe this was all her imagination. What secrets could some silver cups hold anyway?

Unable to help herself, Marianna stared over at the shelf that held the silver cups. The back of her neck tingled, and she was sure Carrie's sharp eyes were on her.

"Oh, someone told you about those, huh?" Carrie asked.

Marianna glanced over at Carrie, afraid she would become tight-lipped again, but Carrie's face was still relaxed as a wistful look crept into her eyes.

"I would love to see them, but they aren't letting anyone look at them. It's like Mrs. Strunk has spy eyes on them or something." Carrie met Marianna's gaze, a knowing look in her eyes. "If you think you're going to get the chance, you'd better abandon that idea now. I've tried on three separate occasions to climb up there, and every time someone mysteriously shows up to thwart my attempt."

Her voice grew solemn, and she narrowed her eyes. "And I was one of the lucky ones. Alanna got caught. She was up on a ladder, her hands a fraction away from touching one of the cups when Dunsten found her."

Carrie paused long enough to gasp in a fresh breath of air. Her eyes sparkled with excitement, and any doubts Marianna had about her being the primary source of gossip at Thunderwell were erased. "He fired her on the spot and forbade her to ever have contact with anyone here again. No one has seen or heard from her since."

Marianna sucked in a breath, ready to speak before she lost the courage to ask the questions swirling through her head. "Why won't they let anyone look at them? Are they valuable?"

Carrie shook her head. "I don't know. Nobody does, except Mrs. Strunk or Dunsten. They're the only ones who've been around long enough to have known all Lord Bludington's wives." Carrie rolled her eyes. "And they aren't talking about anything."

"I guess they are pretty valuable," Carrie said as she plopped a cup of tea onto the table in front of Marianna. "They're made of silver. And you know there's only one place left to mine that, and not many people are willing to go there."

"The Isle of Carid," Marianna whispered.

Carrie nodded, her eyes wide as if she was surprised Marianna had said the name out loud.

Cook hustled into the kitchen. "Milady, whatever are you doing in here again? I told you no matter the time of day or night all you need to do is ring the bell pull, and we'll bring you whatever you need."

"Oh, she came in from the gardens, ma'am." Carrie threw Marianna a wink as she continued. "She was about to pass out, she was spending so much time in the sun today. I rushed her right in here to a chair and fixed her a nice cup of tea." Carrie lifted the teacup she had set in front of Marianna proudly.

The cook's gaze darted about the room as if she didn't believe a word Carrie had said. But seeing nothing suspicious, she huffed. "Well then, girl, make sure everything is cleaned up before you turn in for the night. I don't want to come into a messy kitchen in the morning."

She turned to Marianna. "And where is your lady's maid anyway?" She shook her head and didn't wait for an answer as she hustled back out the door muttering. "Make 'em ladies' maids, he says. That's what happens when you try to turn scullery maids into ladies' maids. They don't know their place." The kitchen door swung shut muffling the rest of the cook's words.

Marianna glanced over at Carrie. A smile covered her face as she let out a little laugh. Marianna couldn't help but laugh also.

"Don't pay any mind to her. She's more bark than bite." Carrie leaned close and whispered conspiratorially, "She always feeds the scraps to the stray barn cats."

Marianna smiled at that. She had already begun to understand that Cook was a softie under all her bluster.

"But anyway," Carrie said, "you're getting one of your own."

Marianna's first thought was that she meant a cat, but then Carrie nodded up at the shelf that held the cups.

Oh, right. That's what Betsy had told her too.

Goosebumps prickled her skin, and a knot of unease settled in the pit of her stomach. She wrapped her arms around herself, rubbing her arms vigorously, wishing she could rid herself of fear in her belly as easily as she could the goosebumps.

"Cold, miss?" Carrie asked. She walked over and retrieved a shawl from one of the hooks on the wall, throwing it around Marianna's shoulders. "It's mine, and it's clean. I laundered it yesterday. Keep it as long as you need."

Marianna smiled at her gratefully and pulled the shawl tighter around her. She watched Carrie bustle around the kitchen, cleaning up the last few dishes.

There was a specific plan for these cups, but one that only Bludington, probably Dunsten, and maybe Mrs. Strunk knew about. But what kind of plan for some cups had to be so secret?

Marianna thought about the lab room she had seen up in the tower. All those tubes and wires. And those four little vials all by themselves in a corner that looked like they were full of blood. Why were there four of them?

Marianna tried to stop her racing thoughts. She hoped her imagination was running away from her, but the knot in the pit of her stomach told her otherwise.

Chapter 29

Marianna awoke with a start. Rain pattered against the roof in a steady beat, and for a minute, she couldn't remember where she was. The smell of dying embers reminded her. She was in Bludington's manor.

What had woken her up? Was it that dream? It hadn't exactly been a nightmare, but it wasn't pleasant either. She had been dreaming of Will. It was a strange dream where he was the captain of his own ship, but a deranged boy kept chasing after him.

Maybe it had been the rain. Marianna sighed. She was not getting back to sleep now, so she threw off her covers, stepped into her slippers, and pulled on her robe. She would go to the library and read. She picked up the book she had finished before falling asleep, then grabbed the bedside candle and lit it.

The candlelight flickered with each step she took down the long hallway.

She paused when she heard voices. They were coming from a cracked doorway inches away from her. Who else was up and about at this time of night? Wasn't that a spare bedroom? There weren't any visitors here. She hadn't seen anyone in the house besides the staff since she first came to live here two weeks ago.

She crept closer and peered into the room. Carrie and Leah. Of course. Apparently, they'd made this their sitting room. Two of the blue velvet plush chairs were huddled around the lit fireplace. The women sat in them, knitting as if they belonged in this room.

Not that Marianna could blame them. She'd seen the servants' quarters. Mrs. Strunk must not know about this, as Marianna was sure the stern woman would never allow the servants to use the main manor rooms, even though over half of them sat empty and were rarely ever used.

Marianna leaned in closer to the door, straining to hear their conversation. Their needles clacked together in between their hushed words making an odd symphony.

"He does seem to bring about bad luck for women. It's already touched the new mistress," Carrie whispered.

"Oh, really? Why do you say that?" Leah asked, scooting closer.

"Just some things I've heard. Dunsten said she won't sleep without Betsy in the room to keep watch over her."

What? That wasn't true. As if Dunsten was a reliable source.

"Whatever happened to his second wife?" asked Leah. "You never did finish telling me."

Even from the crack in the doorway, Marianna could tell Carrie was excited to share the gossip. She sat up a little straighter and cleared her throat. "Oh yes, she had the night terrors too. Maybe that's why this new lady has a maid stay with her at night. She could already be having the night terrors."

Leah nodded. "It wouldn't surprise me. She seems a bit jumpy."

Jumpy? Leah was the one who had acted like a frantic little mouse when Marianna had questioned her. Marianna shifted her candle to her other hand so she could move closer to the door.

Anyway," Carrie continued, "the second wife, Carianna, had increasingly worse night terrors. They say it got so bad she would wander the halls like a zombie. Finally, one day after a particularly bad night she packed her bags and ran away. She didn't even try to lie about it. She trotted out the front door with all her things and commanded some grooms to hitch up her carriage for her. When the groom brought the carriage around, she insisted she didn't need any help from them. She took the reins from the boy, climbed in, and started the horses off at a gallop. Ten days later, over in Hydesville, the sheriff found her carriage turned over.

"All her clothes were still there, but she was missing. The horses pulling the carriage had turned up back at the stables, and no one knew what had happened to her. She just disappeared."

"How can anyone manage that?"

"Well, the sheriff didn't think she'd disappeared. He thought she had fallen down the bluff. The carriage had turned over right at its edge. He figured she'd had an accident."

"They searched for her body, right?" Leah asked.

Carrie snorted. "Of course. They searched for days. Bludington demanded answers. I imagine he was feeling quite traumatized after all that had happened with his first wife, but nothing was ever found."

A chill skittered down Marianna's spine. Somewhere down the hall, a door slammed. Marianna's candle went out. Lightning flashed through the room. Thunder cracked, sounding like a giant whip terrorizing the sky. Marianna stumbled in the darkness, knocking against the wall.

Leah dropped her knitting needles and squealed. "It's Carianna's ghost. She's come to haunt us all."

"Hush, foolish girl," Carrie hissed. "It's a flesh and blood person, and they're spying on us." She jumped up and headed for the door.

Marianna righted herself and turned back toward her room. Without a candle she couldn't see anything but if she stayed here, she'd be caught. She found the wall, and using it as a guide, she crept away from the doorway.

When Carrie pushed the door open, Marianna pressed herself against the wall hoping Carrie couldn't see her. After several moments, Carrie stepped back into the room.

"Whoever it was, they're gone now." Carrie's voice grew fainter and fainter as she stepped farther into the room.

Marianna let out a breath and keeping her hand on the wall, hurried back to her room.

Chapter 30

The next night, Marianna made another plan. She knew now more than ever she had to look at those cups. She would see they were ordinary cups, and she could rid herself of the terrifying thoughts that continued to plague her. She would have to sneak down to the kitchen in the dead of night. Betsy would be back tomorrow, so she had to do it tonight.

She had taken several books from the library, but it was as if fate was against her. She wanted to stay awake but couldn't. Her body refused to cooperate, her eyes drooping despite her best efforts to keep them fully open. She caught herself falling asleep twice before the thud of her book hitting the floor woke her for a third time.

She stood and stretched before pacing around her room. Had it been long enough for all the servants to have gone to bed? She couldn't tell. She knew some of them stayed up into the wee hours. But they had to sleep sometime.

The hall clock chimed. Three o'clock. Surely everyone was in bed by now. She sucked in a deep breath, steeling herself for the task ahead. She picked up her candle, cracked her door, and peered out.

Everything was silent and dark. She slipped into the hallway, pausing at the top of the stairs. Hearing nothing, she tiptoed downstairs and through the maze of hallways.

Inside the dining room, she slowed her pace, stopping before the swinging doors to the kitchen. She stood as close as she could to them without knocking them open, and made herself count to one hundred, while listening to see if anyone was on the other side. Still nothing but silence.

She pushed through and took in the room, ready to explain she was looking for a glass of water, but the kitchen was empty and clean. Nothing remained but the scent of freshly baked bread mingling with the smell of the roasted spiced vegetables which had been served at dinner.

She'd never seen the kitchen empty and had begun to believe it never would be. Silence and darkness made it eerie. The flickering flame of her candle cast a small circle of light that barely lit up a few feet in front of her. The rest of the kitchen was nothing but shadows. A huge, hulking one lurked in the corner.

Was that a man? Maybe she wasn't alone after all. But it didn't move. She took a hesitant step forward and nearly laughed at herself when she realized the shadow was merely the pantry cupboard.

She was being silly, and she had something to do. If she wasted time worrying about every harmless shadow, she'd get caught. The story Carrie had told her about the maid who'd been fired came back to her now. Dunsten couldn't fire her, so what would he do to her if he caught her nosing around in here?

She shook those thoughts away and hurried to the corner where she'd seen the stepladder. Setting her candle onto the table, she grabbed hold of it and tugged. It wouldn't move. She tried again, pulling harder. It still wouldn't budge. It had to be stuck on something.

She picked up the candle and shone its light all up and down the stepladder. There on the floor she saw it. A doorstop had been pushed up against the ladder, holding it in place.

Bigger than most doorstops, this one was the size of a small dog. It was made of stone, rough and gray. At first, Marianna was afraid she wasn't going to be able to move it on her own. But finally it gave way, sliding across the floor with a screech.

Marianna paused, hoping no one had heard it, hoping it seemed louder than it was. All was still quiet, so Marianna pulled the stepladder out of the corner and dragged it over to the shelf. Every bump and bounce sounded ear-splittingly loud, like the cymbals in an orchestra. But no one stormed the kitchen, so Marianna kept moving.

Once at the shelf, she noticed a lantern sitting on the third shelf up. That would be much better than the single flame from her candle. She carefully leaned the ladder against the shelf, plucked her candle from the table and used it to light the lantern. She twisted the little knob to turn the lantern light up. Perfect.

She turned back to the stepladder. In her struggle to unfold it, it crashed to the floor—a noise much louder than any of the others she'd made. Sure the whole house would charge into the kitchen to see what was making the racket, Marianna stood frozen in place, staring at the fallen stepladder, holding her breath.

When no one appeared, she scrambled to pick up the ladder and unfold it. It was a bit taller than she had first thought, with four rungs about a foot apart. She scooted it up as close to the shelf as she could get it. Her heart pounded and her hands were clammy. Her throat was so dry it hurt to swallow, and she was beginning to think she had developed a fever from all the stress of the night. She swiped a palm across her forehead, and then wiped both palms off on her nightgown before grabbing hold of the ladder and ascending.

She stopped at the second to last rung, reaching up toward the cups. Her fingers were still inches away. She'd have to climb to the top of the ladder. She glanced toward the floor nervously. It was so far away already, and the top would easily add another foot to that distance.

But she was determined to get a look at the cups. She took a deep breath and braced herself against the shelf as she stepped onto the top of the ladder. It wiggled back and forth for a precarious second before going still. Marianna perched there and let out the breath she'd been holding.

Eye level with the top shelf, she saw there were now four cups. She hadn't noticed this from the floor because one of the cups had been tucked back behind the others. Her cup must be here now. Had Dunsten been bringing it here the other night when he had scared her so badly? No one had said anything about it to her.

She reached forward and pulled the first cup toward her, leaving fingerprints everywhere she touched. She should have thought of that. Now she was going to have to climb down, get a rag, and climb back up to wipe away the evidence of her snooping.

She took the first cup down and tilted it into the lantern light. It glistened, its surface so shiny she could see her reflection in it even in the dim lantern light. The orb of the cup distorted her face making it look longer and skinnier than it was.

Marianna turned the cup over. Large, elegant script covered the other side. *Lillianna*. Bludington's first wife. It was true. Each wife had a cup. One of the cups must be hers.

She started to put the cup back onto the shelf, but something reddish shimmered inside. She turned the cup sideways, so the light would shine inside it. Streaks of the reddish color lined the inside of the cup, horizontal rings that twisted all the way around it.

Was that... blood? Marianna hated that her mind immediately jumped there, but the streaks had the unmistakable reddish-brown color of dried blood. What else was even that color? Maybe some herbs or something? Marianna couldn't imagine how they could create streaks that would stay like that in a cup. Did all the cups have this reddish stuff in them?

She shoved the cup back onto the shelf and pulled down the next one. It looked the same as the first one, except instead of Lillianna, *Carianna* was engraved on it. She tilted it to look inside it.

The same reddish-brown stains lined the inside of this cup. She pushed it back onto the shelf desperate to see the third one. She pulled it down. *Elianna*. And the same stains inside. She set it back up onto the shelf slowly, eyeing the final cup.

Her cup, she assumed. She wanted to look at it, but she didn't. What would it mean if the stains were inside her cup as well? What would it mean if they weren't?

She reached out hesitantly, pausing before pulling the final cup toward her. Taking it down, she examined the outside. In the same script as the others, her name was emblazoned on the front. She took a deep breath and tilted it toward the light. She squeezed her eyes shut, then forced them open. Stark, clean silver shined back at her.

Goosebumps tickled her arms, and a shiver scampered down her spine. Her breath hitched. Her palms grew damp with sweat, and the cup slipped from her grasp. It fell in slow motion until it clattered against the stone floor.

Why did Bludington have cups for all his wives? And why did all the dead ones have blood in theirs? She could think of a thousand horrible reasons and not a single good one. Her vision blurred and her head spun. She needed to get off this ladder. She needed to sit down.

Somewhere in the distance a door slammed, bringing her to her senses. She couldn't get caught looking at these cups. What if that maid that had looked at them hadn't gotten fired? What if she'd been killed?

On shaky legs she climbed down the ladder, grabbed the fallen cup, climbed back up and using her skirt, furiously wiped her fingerprints from the cups. It took longer than she expected to get the cups clean, and by the time she climbed down, the rooster in the chicken pen right outside the kitchen door was crowing.

The servants would be up and about any moment now. Hurriedly, she folded the ladder back up and shoved it into the corner before turning out the lantern. Then she grabbed her candle from the table and hurried back toward her room.

Flickering light shone out from under doorways. A dim lull of faraway voices chattering, and hurrying footsteps let her know that the manor was waking up. Dizziness threatened to overtake her. She broke into a run, praying she wouldn't run into anyone before she reached her room.

She twisted and turned through the maze of hallways, and finally reached the stairs. The noises seemed louder. Was someone behind her?

She didn't even pause before darting up. Her candle flame flickered out, but even that didn't cause her to slow. She ran down the hallway to her room, and barely managed to keep from slamming her door as she burst inside.

She dropped her candle, leaned against her door, and slid down to sit on the floor. She never should have sent Betsy away. Now more than ever, she needed her. She wasn't safe here, and Betsy was the only one she could trust.

Chapter 31

The next morning, Marianna took a book to the gardens to wait for Betsy's return. The events from the previous night unnerved her, and she was glad Betsy was coming back today. She had only been in the gardens for half an hour when she heard the rattle of the old horse cart Betsy had borrowed to get home.

Marianna darted down the garden's stone walkway, through the gate, and up the little dirt path that led to the front of the manor. Betsy waved as she pulled the pony to a stop. She hopped out of the cart and ran to greet Marianna, stopping short of hugging her.

Marianna grabbed her and pulled her into a hug. "You can hug me. I've missed you. All kinds of crazy things have happened here while you've been gone!"

Betsy's eyes widened. "Really, like what? Everything's okay, though, right?"

Marianna nodded. "Of course, you know how my imagination is. It likes to run away with me. But I have a lot to tell you. Not now, though." Marianna glanced at the groom waiting to take the pony and cart back to the stables, and Betsy nodded. Who knew what ears could be listening and reporting back to Dunsten?

Marianna took Betsy's arm and started pulling her to the house. "Anyway, tell me. How was your family?"

"Oh, wonderful!" Betsy stopped walking, reached into her bag, and pulled out a silky white handkerchief with some blue hydrangeas embroidered on the corner. She handed it to Marianna. "My mother made this for you."

Marianna glanced at Betsy. "Betsy, this is amazing! How did your mother get her hands on a silk handkerchief?"

Silk was a highly prized commodity, and Marianna knew how hard it was to get some. Even as a merchant, her father struggled to obtain enough to bring back and sell to buyers.

Betsy shrugged. "My mother has her ways."

"It's so beautiful! And how did she know I loved hydrangeas?"

Betsy giggled. "I told her."

Marianna nodded. "She's doing better, then? Your mom?"

"Yes, so much! I'm glad you told me to go. I feel better leaving my family to come and work here now that I know how well she is doing."

"And your siblings? How are they?"

"Doing well. Crazy and wild as always."

Marianna and Betsy talked all the way to the house. Once inside Marianna's room, Marianna told Betsy all about the cups and the information she had gleaned from Carrie and Leah about Bludington's second wife. Betsy's eyes widened, and she covered her mouth as a tiny gasp escaped.

They talked for so long, Marianna was startled to hear the hall clock chime six—time for dinner.

Marianna and Betsy walked down together, parting ways at the dining room door. Marianna sighed, resigned to eating alone again, but when she pushed open the door, she saw Bludington sitting in his place at the head of the table.

When Marianna entered, Bludington jumped up and hurried over to pull out her chair. "Miss Marianna, welcome. Have a seat."

Unsure of what Bludington was suddenly doing at dinner, Marianna hesitantly took her seat. She glanced at the servants who stood by the wall waiting to start serving. None of them moved and no one made eye contact, so she had no idea what they were thinking. She glanced at Bludington. He smiled before hurrying back to his seat.

"Isn't it lovely to be able to have dinner together for once? I'm afraid my business rarely allows me time to have a leisurely dinner, otherwise, I would join you every night."

Two maids entered with steaming trays. They handed them off to the servants by the wall before dashing back into the kitchen. Ginger, soy, and some other spice Marianna couldn't quite place greeted her nose, and her stomach rumbled. The servants set the dishes onto the table and began to heap food onto Marianna's and Bludington's plates.

Bludington looked at Marianna, awaiting an answer.

Oh, right. He had asked her if it was lovely to have dinner together. Not really. Marianna forced a smile onto her face and nodded her head. Spiced chicken and noodles filled her plate along with a side of roasted broccoli and pineapple.

She loved spiced chicken, and pineapple had been a rare treat since it had to be shipped in from the south fast enough to not spoil. Despite this, Bludington always seemed to have a plentiful supply of it. She dug into the food with relish.

"How have you been occupying your time? Enjoying the library?"

Marianna struggled to swallow the piece of chicken she'd just stuck in her mouth. "Um, yes, the library is wonderful. Thank you."

"And what else have you enjoyed? Have you been to the stables yet?" Bludington delicately cut a piece of chicken in half before taking a bite.

"No." Marianna shook her head, surprised she and Betsy hadn't made it that far in their tour of the place. They had been sidetracked by other things. She glanced up at Bludington.

She had a sneaky suspicion he already knew how she'd occupied her time. How could he not? She was now almost certain that Dunsten followed her around everywhere. Why else would he do that but to report to Bludington?

However, Bludington didn't seem to notice the glance or have any inkling about what she was thinking.

"I've really enjoyed the gardens."

Bludington nodded. "Oh yes, the gardens are magnificent, aren't they? Though, it's not as if I can take any credit for them. My landscapers handle all that." He chuckled. "What else? Surely you've had time to explore." He looked at her questioningly, innocently. Before he raised his glass to take a sip, the edges of a smirk formed at the corners of his mouth.

Was he taunting her? Did he already know where she had been? Sneaking a look at the cups, creeping into random rooms at night, hunting for that mysterious hallway. But he'd told her she could go anywhere she liked, that this was her home now too. So why did she feel like this was a test or a game he was playing with her?

She swallowed hard. "I've explored the house some."

Did her voice sound as raspy to him as it did to her? She cleared her throat and tried again. "I love seeing how the rooms are all decorated differently, but there are so many not being used. It seems a shame."

This time Marianna knew she saw a smirk. He wasn't even trying to hide it.

"And what would you suggest we do to solve that problem?"

"Hmm, I guess I haven't really thought about it. I don't suppose there is much we could do with them right now."

"Hmm," Bludington answered.

What did that mean? At least the smirk was gone. Maybe she should come right out and ask him about the hallway.

Her heart raced and her throat tightened. She reached for her water glass, but her hands were so clammy it slipped from her grasp and crashed into the table spraying everyone in the vicinity before crumbling into shards.

Pain shot through her palm, and she gasped. A line of blood appeared, oozing across her hand. Marianna squeezed her hand shut and closed her eyes, willing the moment of dizziness to pass. What was wrong with her? She didn't normally get queasy at the sight of blood, and she didn't normally drop dishes at dinnertime.

"Are you hurt?" Bludington jumped up from his seat and rushed over to her. He reached for her palm, but instinctively she pulled back. A look of surprise covered Bludington's face.

"It's okay," he said softly. "I want to see how bad it is. I can help you." He held out his hand, reaching for hers.

She hesitated for a second, then relented and gave him her hand. It was bleeding badly enough it needed to be treated. And what was he really going to do to her here in front of all his servants?

He gently took her hand and looked at it. "*Tsk*, this is deep. You must have squeezed the glass as it broke." He glanced up at her questioningly.

"Um, I guess I did." Marianna shrugged her shoulders. She hoped he couldn't read her thoughts on her face.

He picked up one of the fancy linen napkins and pressed it to her hand.

"Mrs. Strunk probably won't be too happy you did that," Marianna said.

Bludington smiled. "Well, Mrs. Strunk isn't the lord of the manor, is she?"

"I guess not, but it's probably ruined now." Marianna nodded to the blue floral napkin with the white background.

"It's fine," Bludington assured her. "We have dozens of those exact napkins and like the excessive bedrooms, they rarely get used." Bludington's eyes twinkled as he smiled down at her.

Was he… teasing her? She hadn't known he had had a jovial bone in his body. His smile broke into a laugh, and she couldn't help but laugh a little too.

"Dorian," Bludington motioned the servant over, "go retrieve the medicinal kit."

Dorian nodded and took off wordlessly. Within a minute he was back carrying a square brown case. He lifted it onto the table and popped it open. The inside was divided into rows, the top of which had several glass bottles of varying sizes. Some held little white pills and others held murky liquids. The next row contained some metal tools like little scissors and pliers, all held in place by small leather straps. On the bottom row were several neat rolls of gauze and bandage wrappings.

"Wow, you're really prepared for medical emergencies," Marianna said. At home, they only had a little box filled with some bandages and gauze and one bottle of pain-relieving pills. Medical supplies were expensive, and she had never seen such a vast array of supplies in a person's private home.

"When you have this large of a place to manage and so many staff doing some dangerous things at times, you have to be prepared," Bludington replied.

Dangerous things? How many dangerous things were his employees doing? Marianna tried to keep her thoughts from showing on her face.

After another minute, he lifted the napkin and peered at Marianna's cut. "Excellent, the bleeding has mostly stopped." He pulled out some salve and gauze, then treated and bandaged her cut with little effort.

Marianna felt no pain and marveled that this strange man could have such a soft, gentle side. Maybe there was more to him than met the eye. Maybe she had been wrong in all her assumptions about him.

Chapter 32

After dinner, Marianna went back to her room and paced restlessly. She couldn't shake the uneasy feelings. Was her first instinct about Bludington so off? He had been so kind just now, treating her injury and checking to see that she was doing well here. Still, something seemed off.

Betsy sat in a chair knitting more of her scarf, watching Marianna pace. "Miss Marianna, are you sure I can't get anything or do anything for you?"

"No. Let's go to the library."

"The library? Now?" Betsy stared, looking as if she thought Marianna had gone mad.

"Yes, now." Marianna headed for the door, and Betsy slowly followed. Marianna sped down the hallway, pausing when she saw Leah slip around the corner on Carrie's heels. She grabbed Betsy's arm and pulled her against the wall. Betsy gasped.

"Miss Marianna..."

"Shh," Marianna hissed, a finger pressed against her mouth.

Betsy's eyes widened. "What?" she mouthed.

Marianna pointed down the next hallway. Both girls watched as the maids ducked into an unused room.

"What are they doing?" Betsy whispered. "That's not a room being used right now, and no one has been assigned to clean it."

Marianna started down the hall motioning for Betsy to follow.

"Are you sure that's such a good idea?" Betsy stood pressed against the wall.

"Yes, why wouldn't it be? Come on, we'll miss what they're saying." Marianna headed back down the hallway without waiting to see if Betsy had followed.

She reached the room and cautiously cracked the door. She pressed her eye against the opening. Carrie and Leah were huddled in the corner by the dresser looking at something.

"This is the only thing left of her," Carrie was saying.

"What exactly happened to her?" Leah asked.

"One day she got up early, before even Cook was up, and slipped out without anyone seeing her. She took her horse from the stables and rode out to the cliffs that overlook the sea. And then..." Carrie paused, shaking her head. "Such a shame really. I ought not talk about it."

"What are they saying?" Betsy pushed in next to Marianna, trying to get a peek into the room. Marianna glared at her and made a shushing motion.

"Sorry," Betsy mouthed.

"Well, I suppose I can tell you. If you promise not to be going around spreading the tale," Carrie said.

Leah nodded her head. "Of course not. I try not to ever gossip about the lord and lady of the house."

"Well, okay then," Carrie said. "So, she got to the cliffs. No one was there, but everyone knew she had been in a state for the last several weeks, so there was really no doubt in anyone's mind about what happened."

"What?" Leah asked.

"Well, she jumped of course."

"She jumped off the cliffs?"

Carrie nodded solemnly. "It was a horrible time around here for a while. Not that I was here then, but I did hear all about it since I was hired not two weeks after it happened."

"She died? Did they find her... I mean," Leah hesitated then whispered, "her body?"

Carrie shook her head. "They were still searching when I came on. All they found was this, and of course her horse was still there, waiting for a mistress who would never return."

"Then how do they know for sure she died?" Leah asked. "Maybe she ran away too."

"Look at this. Right here. What do you see?"

Leah peered closely at the object Carrie held between them. "Oh." She looked up, eyes wide. "Is that blood?" she asked in a horrified whisper.

"Yes."

"But that still doesn't prove she died for sure. Maybe she got hurt before running away."

Carrie huffed and yanked the cloth away from Leah. She stuffed it into the open drawer, then slammed the drawer shut.

"Would a live person haunt those cliffs?" Carrie crossed her arms.

"Haunt? You mean like a ghost?"

"I don't know anything else that haunts, do you?"

Leah shook her head. "No. So that's why no one will take the cliff path into town. And that's why Caden and Jay always take the horses to graze in the eastern field instead of the western one."

Carrie nodded her head. "It's about time you caught on to the stuff going on around here."

"So how exactly does her ghost haunt the cliffs?"

"How do you think? She cries and screams and calls out Bludington's name. And not in a loving way, mind you. She says it like a curse. One time she even appeared as an apparition to Dunsten. At least that's what the grooms claim. They say he came back from the cliff path, face even whiter than normal, yelling for Elianna to stay away from here. Bludington ran out and shushed him up, but by then it was too late. Everyone who was here had heard."

Leah's eyes were like saucers. Marianna didn't think it was physically possible for her to open them up any wider.

"And Dunsten isn't easily rattled," Leah said in awe.

Carrie snorted. "Easily rattled? Have you ever even seen Dunsten disturbed by something?"

Leah shook her head.

"That's right, Dunsten does not get disturbed by things. The fact that he came back in stone cold fear is proof that those cliffs are haunted." Carrie brushed past Leah and picked up her cleaning bucket.

"It's time to get back to work. We've wasted enough time already. Get your stuff and come on." She gestured to the other cleaning bucket on the floor and then headed for the door.

Marianna barely had enough time to grab Betsy and pull her into the next room before Carrie strode out and down the hall with Leah right behind her.

"Is that for real?" Betsy squeaked. "Are the cliffs really haunted?"

Marianna shrugged her shoulders. "I'm not sure I believe in all that haunting stuff. But…" she trailed off thinking. "There's only one way to find out."

"No, Miss Marianna, please. Can't we leave this one alone?" Betsy placed her hand on Marianna's arm.

"You're not afraid of a little old ghost, are you Betsy? Come on, we have about an hour of daylight left. Plenty of time to ride to the cliffs and back." Marianna bounced out of the room and headed straight for her bedchamber.

"Who said it was a little ghost? It sounded to me like she's an angry, vengeful ghost. Particularly toward people from Bludington's manor." Betsy gasped. "And you're going to be his new wife. She'll be even more angry at you." She trailed after Marianna, still trying to convince her that this was foolishness.

When she reached her bedchamber, Marianna went straight to her wardrobe and pulled out a royal blue riding skirt. "This is perfect! And here's one for you too," she said as she pulled out an identical skirt in green."

"Miss Marianna, I couldn't wear any of your clothes!"

"Why not? We're friends, aren't we?"

Betsy gave a hesitant nod, her eyes wide, like a wild animal's caught in the hunter's sight.

"Well, that's what friends do. Share clothes." Marianna thrust the green skirt at Betsy. "Come on, try it on!" Betsy's still frightened gaze darted about the room before she timidly took the skirt and tried it on.

"It fits perfectly. I knew it would," Marianna exclaimed. She quickly changed into her riding clothes, and they headed to the stables.

Chapter 33

Outside the barn, half a dozen silky black horses milled about in the lush grass field, enjoying the feast. In the opposite field, two young stallions chased each other, their feathered manes and tails waving behind them. They created a picture fine enough to be a painting.

Marianna still couldn't believe Bludington had given one of these horses to her sister. They were some of the finest horses available. One alone was worth a small fortune. Marianna sighed as she followed Betsy into the barn.

Inside the barn, dozens of grooms darted about, mucking out stalls, filling troughs with hay and corn feed, and hauling in water buckets. The earthy scent of horses mingled with the sweet, grassy smell of hay that didn't quite hide the scent of horse dung.

High vaulted ceilings with skylights made it as bright inside as it was outside. Gold filigree Friesians trotted across the strip of wood that joined the triangle roof to the base of the barn.

Betsy stopped one of the grooms. "Jay, we need a couple of gentle horses to ride."

The young man set down the bucket he was carrying. A riot of dark curls fell over his forehead, and he shook his head, tossing them back.

"Gentle horses? Are you joking? These horses aren't old nags." Jay snorted.

He wore a cream-colored work shirt with the sleeves rolled up to his elbows, heavy dark brown pants, and tall rubber boots. He flashed Marianna a flirty smile before looking back at Betsy.

Betsy put her hands on her hips. "You know what I mean. Just rideable horses—ones that won't try to throw us the first chance they get."

Jay chuckled. "I suppose I could do that for you and your friend." He glanced over at Marianna and winked.

Betsy slapped his arm. "Jay, this isn't any friend," she hissed glancing back at Marianna. "This is the mistress of the house."

Jay's eyes widened. He instantly became serious. "My lady." He gave a bow. "I'm so sorry. I had no idea. If I had known, I would have never been so presumptuous. I assumed Betsy would not have brought you out here without any warning." He glared at Betsy. "Please forgive me. I really would never assume to be so bold."

It seemed like Marianna garnered that response everywhere she went. He probably thought she was going to fire him, but she highly doubted she had the power to do that.

"It's fine," she said. "I'm glad Betsy has good friends here." She smiled reassuringly at the groom.

"I think I know the perfect horses for you ladies. Caden," he called. "Go get Saturn and Jupiter."

A slim boy of about twelve nodded at Jay and then ran from the barn. Several moments later he returned with two mares. One was silvery-white, and the other was the same silky black as the rest of the horses. Jay stepped forward and took the lead of the silvery horse.

"This is Jupiter," he said. "This fine mare is for the lady of the house. Lord Bludington purchased her specially for you, my lady."

"Oh." Marianna hadn't known Bludington had gotten a horse for her. "Why didn't he give me one of the ones he already had?"

"He wanted something special for you. He sent Toma, the head groom, out to purchase her for you. Lord Bludington had a long list of requirements and only trusted the best of horsemen to go and find one for you."

Jay had an annoyed look on his face as he motioned for Caden to do something. Caden jumped forward and cupped his hands forming a stirrup.

"Here, miss," he said. "Go ahead and step up. I'm real strong. I promise I won't drop ya."

Marianna chuckled. "I'm sure you won't, Caden. And thank you for being such a gentleman." Caden blushed bright red, but true to his word he didn't drop her. Jay helped Betsy onto her horse, and then the two were off to the cliffs.

The closer they got, the more the horses started dancing, pulling against the reins and snorting, reluctant to keep going. Before they even got to the edge, Marianna could hear the surf pounding against the rocks below. The sky darkened and the wind picked up, whistling across the path.

"I don't think we should go any farther. We can see the cliff from here." Betsy's voice cracked. She pulled her shawl tighter around her shoulders with one hand. Her other hand gripped the reins so tightly her knuckles were white.

"Why don't you stay here with the horses?" Marianna climbed off Jupiter and thrust her reins at Betsy. Betsy stared at them.

"Where are you going?" Betsy yelled over the wind.

"I want to get a good look at the cliff's edge."

Betsy's eyes widened, and she shook her head. "What if you fall?"

Marianna rolled her eyes. "I'll be careful. I certainly don't want to fall." She pushed Jupiter's reins into Betsy's clenched hand and patted the jittery horse's neck. "Easy girl," she soothed. "Everything is all right. People have made too much of a silly little cliff."

As she stepped away from Betsy and the horses, a wail pierced the air.

"What was that?" Betsy asked. "It's her. She's warning us to stay away." Her breaths came out in short gasps. "Or she's coming to get us. Maybe she doesn't like it that you're the lady of Bludington's manor now."

Another wail sounded. Jupiter reared up, yanking her reins out of Betsy's hand. Betsy shrieked and clung to Saturn's mane. "That's her. We need to go home."

Marianna jumped forward and grabbed Jupiter's reins before she could go anywhere.

Betsy barely managed to stay in her saddle as Saturn shied away from Jupiter. "Even the horses know this is a bad idea."

"Let's go back to that shade tree we passed a few minutes ago and settle the horses."

"Why don't we just go home?" Betsy pleaded.

Marianna ignored her as she led Jupiter to the shade tree. She stroked her nose and whispered in her ear to calm her, then turned to Betsy. "You wait here with the horses, and I'll be right back."

"You're going back? What if something happens to you? What do I do? If Elianna's ghost gets you, she'll be after me next. This is one of the worst ideas you've ever had."

"It'll be fine. I'll only be gone a few minutes. I want to get a look over the cliff." Marianna had already started walking toward it, calling the last few words over her shoulder. She didn't want to give Betsy a chance to try and change her mind.

She glanced back in the direction of where she had left Betsy and the horses. Hopefully, they would be okay.

A huge cloud covered the last of the sunlight, making it difficult to see much more than the stark, rocky outline of the cliff. Rain sprinkled down, dampening her shawl. Maybe this wasn't such a good idea, but at least it wasn't pouring down rain.

As if the sky could hear her thoughts, it let down a sudden downpour. It took less than a minute for Marianna to get soaked through. She scrambled over the rocks on her hands and knees, desperate to get a look over the edge.

Lightning flashed across the sky, startling her. Her knees fell out from under her, and her stomach crashed onto the rocky surface. Marianna struggled to breathe. Rain sloshed down her face, blurring her vision.

Images of people discovering her body here, at the same place Bludington's third wife had died, flashed through her mind. She couldn't die here too.

She managed to pull a breath in and let it out. In... out. In... out. She would be okay.

She pushed herself back up onto her knees. Though common sense told her to head back to Betsy and the horses, she kept onward. She hadn't come this far for nothing.

Finally reaching the edge of the cliff, she slashed a hand across her eyes, and peered over. Angry waves assaulted the rocks below. Beyond them, seafoam swirled forming a whirlpool of blue and white.

Her head spun and her breath quickened. Heights didn't usually bother her, but this was much higher than it had appeared from the trail. No one could have survived such a fall, and no wonder the poor woman's body had never been found. The sea had probably carried it off to another continent.

She scooted back from the edge and rested for a moment. Rain pelted her unforgivingly. Betsy would be so mad and very worried. Marianna wasn't sure how much time had passed, but she knew it had been more than several minutes.

She sighed and pushed herself up. She needed to get back. Hopefully, the horses hadn't given Betsy too much trouble. She slogged through muddy puddles as quickly as her drenched skirts would allow her.

She had never been so thankful to hear Betsy squeal. "Thank God you're alive!"

Betsy ran toward her dragging the annoyed, soaked horses behind her. They snorted and pawed the ground. "I was sure you were dead. I just knew Elianna's ghost was coming after me next. And if she didn't get me, Bludington sure would. I'd never be able to work in another house in Anderi as long as he was around." She grabbed Marianna into a hug. "Did you see her? Elianna?" Betsy pulled back her eyes wide.

Marianna shook her head. "No, but it's no wonder they didn't find her body. It's rocky, and it's a huge drop. The waves are massive and angry. She would have been carried away as soon as she hit the water." Marianna's hands began to tremble, and her breath quickened.

"Are you okay?" Betsy asked.

"Yes, I think I'm just now realizing how dangerous it was to go up there." Marianna sank down into a nearby rock. "Give me a minute. I'll be okay." She closed her eyes and tilted her head to the sky, letting the torrent cool her face.

"You want to stay here in the rain?" Betsy asked incredulously.

Marianna took a few calming breaths. "No, I'm ready now." She stood and took her horse's reins.

"I'm surprised they haven't sent a search party after us," Betsy said. "With this storm, and the fact that we've been gone for hours."

A chill scampered down Marianna's back. She didn't think anyone back at the manor would care how long she was gone. Or whether she made it back. And she wouldn't have been surprised if they were hoping or even expecting something bad to happen to her on this outing. She knew she couldn't trust anyone except Betsy.

Chapter 34

Jay came running out of the stables as Marianna and Betsy rode up. Caden followed close behind him and helped Betsy down.

"Are you all right?" Jay grabbed Jupiter's reins and helped Marianna off the horse's back. Rain soaked him in minutes. "I didn't know what to do when you were gone for so long, especially with the storm." He swiped back the hair that clung to his forehead.

He wrinkled his brow, and something Marianna couldn't define shone in his eyes. Was it fear? What was he afraid of?

"Yeah, who knows how Lord Bludington would react if we'd told him you were missing. We might have all lost our jo—" Jay's elbow to Caden's stomach ended that thought, as Jay glared at him.

"Well, uh, I mean, probably not. I'm overreacting because we didn't know where you were."

"Just shut up," Jay hissed as he thrust Jupiter's reins into Caden's hands, giving him a sizzling glare. "Take the horses into the stables and see they're properly cared for."

Betsy waved at Jay as he followed Caden into the barn before giving Marianna a weak smile and grabbing her arm. "Come on, we need to get inside, dry off, and have some tea. Don't worry about the boys. They say crazy things sometimes." She laughed nervously, pulling Marianna toward the house.

Marianna glanced back at Jay. He smiled and waved. She waved back, not sure what to think. She hadn't missed the annoyed glare Betsy had shot him before heading to the house. Even the stable hands knew things about this place that she didn't.

Back at the house, Betsy helped Marianna get out of her wet clothes and had tea brought to her room. She whirled around the room like a funnel cloud, picking up a stray piece of clothing here, dusting off the table in the corner, and setting out the tea service.

"Betsy, calm down. Everything is all right. We made it back in one piece." Marianna walked over to where Betsy stood over the teapot and rested a hand on her shoulder.

"Of course, Miss Marianna. I don't know what I'm so worked up for." Tears glistened in her eyes. She rubbed them and cleared her throat. "I'm emotional today, I guess."

"You need to go get out of your wet clothes too." Marianna gently took the teapot from Betsy, ignoring her protests.

"I can certainly pour my own tea. You'll catch a cold if you stay in those clothes any longer. I insist you go change. Then come back here, and we can have tea together, okay?"

"Okay." Betsy gave a weak smile before heading to her own room to change.

Betsy took so long to return, that Marianna decided to go find her. She left her room, heading for the servants' quarters and paused in the hall when she heard voices.

"... that hallway with the painting..."

"... better be careful..."

Were they talking about that hallway everyone insisted didn't exist? Who needed to be careful? Marianna slipped closer to the voices coming through a partially opened sitting room door. She peered in to see Leah and Carrie cleaning the room.

"I can't believe she was asking about it," Leah said. "Something like that is clearly not something to play around with. I only saw the painting once, and I still have nightmares about it. I never want to see it again."

"And well you shouldn't. Just because you're a servant doesn't mean you're safe from the danger. You might not get killed, but the punishment for getting caught there is not much better than death. Maybe even worse." Carrie's tone was sharp. "You'd better stay away from all that, and don't say a word about it to Lady Marianna. Is that understood?"

"Oh, yes ma'am. I would never say anything about it to her."

"No more talk about it." Carrie gathered her cleaning supplies and motioned for Leah to do the same. They headed straight for the door.

Marianna gasped and backed away, rushing into the alcove behind her. She pushed her back against the wall, holding her breath. The two maids walked past, chatting about the dinner menu. When they had gone, Marianna let out her breath in a whoosh.

Something was going on here, and Marianna was determined to find that hall. It was the key to everything. She stepped back into the hallway and hurried for the stairs to the servants' quarters.

She was even more eager to find Betsy now. Betsy had to tell her everything she knew about Bludington, about why everyone was so jumpy around here, and about that hallway.

She was going so fast, she nearly ran into Betsy.

"Oh, Miss Marianna. What are you doing here? This hallway only leads to the servants' quarters."

"I know. I was looking for you. You took so long I was starting to worry."

Betsy laughed. "Oh, I'm fine. Mrs. Strunk had a job she needed me to do that she insisted could not wait. I'm sorry I worried you."

Betsy seemed strangely calm considering how upset she had been when she'd left Marianna's room. And Mrs. Strunk had a job for her? One that couldn't wait? Since when did Mrs. Strunk even assign tasks to the ladies' maid? And what kind of task couldn't wait?

An ominous feeling crept through Marianna, growing with each question that crossed her mind. She couldn't take much more of all this creepy mysteriousness. It was time, once and for all, to find that room and to figure out what secrets it held. She was going to find that room again. Tonight.

Marianna spent the rest of the day in nervous anticipation of what she'd planned for that night. A tiny sliver of doubt crept into her mind as she remembered the maids' words, but she pushed them aside. This was too big for her to ignore. And as her father had always said, she had enough curiosity to kill a cat.

She wandered the gardens and pretended to read in the library, never able to sit still for very long. She ran her hand along one of the bookshelves, pulling out one book, then put it back and pulled out another.

"Those nightmares must still be bothering you. Why are you so nervous?" Betsy asked. "Those dreams didn't come back, did they?"

"Oh, no. I'm fine. I don't know why I'm so restless. It must be a subconscious memory of the nightmares."

"Or maybe because we went to those cliffs. Did you hear her? Elianna's ghost?"

Marianna shook her head. "No, of course not. I'm not sure there is a ghost. Sure, it was sad, but I didn't hear anything except the roar of the surf and thunderclaps."

Betsy stared at Marianna for a long moment but didn't say anything, though it was clear that she didn't believe that explanation.

Night came, and Marianna readied for bed quickly, then dismissed Betsy. Betsy looked uncertainly at Marianna for a few seconds, then finally spoke. "Are you sure you don't want me to stay here, Miss Marianna? What if the nightmares come back?"

"Don't worry, Betsy. I'll be fine. I'm very tired, and I'm sure I'll sleep through the night. Besides, I know you're terribly tired as well. Sleeping on my chair cannot be comfortable."

Betsy stared at her for another second. Marianna faked a yawn and slipped down against the soft mattress, pulling the covers up to her chin. "I promise I'll be fine. Could you get the light on your way out, please?" She gave another yawn and closed her eyes.

Anticipation buzzed through her as she held her breath, waiting for Betsy to leave. Finally, a soft whoosh was followed by the shuffle of feet as Betsy blew out the lantern and left the room. Marianna threw back her covers and relit her lantern. She dressed quickly and slid on a pair of soft slippers.

Reaching into her drawer, Marianna pulled out the candle she had hidden earlier in the day. Afraid the light of the lantern would be too bright and give her away, she lit the candle. She put her journal and a pencil into her pocket, hoping to map out some of Bludington's wing. Then she stuffed some pillows under her blankets in case Betsy should decide to come check on her.

Marianna opened her door and slithered down the hall, heading toward the part of the estate that she had labeled Bludington's wing. It had to be in this part of the house because she'd been everywhere else, even the servants' quarters.

Down the hallway that led into Bludington's quarters, two old-fashioned suits of armor stood on either side of the hallway like sentries.

She stepped closer to the one on the right. Tentatively, she lifted her hand and tapped on the iron chest. A metallic echo filled the hall, and she stumbled back. She hadn't expected it to sound so loud. There was certainly no one in there.

She glanced over at the second suit. It hadn't moved, so she was sure no one could have been in that one either. Still, it was a little creepy.

Setting her candle on the little ledge that jutted out from the wall, she pulled out her journal. She mapped out the hallway before stuffing it back down into her pocket.

She picked up her candle and continued, turning and twisting through the maze of hallways that all looked the same. Golden sconces tilted out from the walls, each one holding an unused candle. Were these candles ever lit? The last time she had been wandering about back here it had been dark too.

Her candle flame didn't cast a very wide circle of light, so it was hard to see much, but she could tell that all the hallways had the same dark gray walls and not much else besides the sconces. She stopped and turned in a full circle, looking for something, anything to help distinguish this hall from the rest.

A scream echoed through the night. Marianna startled, nearly dropping her candle. Where had that come from? She hadn't believed the ghost stories the servants were so fond of telling, but that had been a scream. Who even came back here besides Dunsten and Bludington?

She took a cautious step forward, then another and another. When everything stayed silent, she released her breath and picked up her pace. A sense of unease filled her, but she wasn't quite ready to give up. One more hallway and then she'd return to her room.

Marianna turned the corner and gasped. This was it. She crept to the end and lifted the candle high to get a good look at the painting. Goosebumps scattered up her arms. The flickering flame sent shadows dancing across the picture.

It was so eerie. Was he looking at her? She turned her head to the right and the dwarf's eyes followed. She turned her head left and his eyes followed again. He clutched his captive even tighter, and Marianna was sure the girl's eyes widened.

Marianna blinked. It had to be the poor lighting. Paintings couldn't move.

The dwarf's eyes glowed. The red stones in the knife glittered. The knife blade scraped against the girl's skin. A tiny dot of blood appeared on the girl's neck. Marianna jumped back, her hand covering her mouth, her eyes still glued to the picture.

"Beware of the blue-haired man, or he will be the cause of your death." The dwarf's eyes shined, staring at Marianna as if mocking her, though his mouth didn't move.

She choked back a scream and whirled around. "W-w-who's..." Marianna gulped. "Who's there? Who said that?"

There was no reply except for the slight breeze that nearly extinguished the flame of her candle. Marianna lifted her hand to shield the flame and struggled to breathe.

What had caused that breeze? Was there a door to outside nearby?

It had to be Dunsten. He had done nothing but frighten and intimidate her since she had arrived. Maybe he wanted her gone. Maybe he would hurt her. Marianna's thoughts thundered through her head almost as fast as her heart pounded. Her erratic breathing echoed in her ears.

"Dunsten? Dunsten, if you're here, answer me."

There was no reply.

It had to all be in her head. Was she going crazy? This had been a dumb, dangerous idea. She needed to get back to her room. But how was she going to do that when she didn't even know where she was?

She had to get a grip on her emotions. Marianna sucked in air, finally managing to steady her breathing. She could do this.

She took another deep breath and started back up the hallway. She froze when a faint scream drifted down the hall. More wailing and moaning sounded from below her.

Unable to contain herself any longer, Marianna darted forward taking the first turn she came to. She continued running until she slammed into a person. Hands grabbed her arms. Her candle tilted forward. Something wet and hot stung her hand.

Marianna screamed and yanked away. She pushed her candle firmly back into its holder and held up her hurt hand. The drop of wax had already hardened.

"Miss Marianna, what is the problem?" Dunsten's grim face shone in the lantern light.

Marianna clenched her hand into a fist. She desperately wanted to wipe away the wax, but she didn't want to give Dunsten the satisfaction of knowing he scared her so badly she'd poured candle wax onto herself.

"What are you doing up in the middle of the night? I distinctly remember warning you before that the manor could be dangerous at night. Perhaps one of those dangers is what frightened you so just now. I'll escort you to your room."

His voice became steely as he continued. "But I cannot protect you if you insist on wandering the castle at night. Anything that happens then will be your own fault."

Marianna was too terrified to speak as Dunsten led her back to her room. Her mind raced. Who was she really in danger from? Dunsten scared her, and she didn't trust him. Still, he hadn't hurt her. And that painting? Maybe Bludington really did meddle with witchcraft.

Marianna's thoughts were cut off by Dunsten's voice. "Here you are Miss Marianna. Remember, it's not safe to wander about at night." He opened her door with a little bow.

"Thank you," she whispered.

He nodded, then turned and left. Marianna scurried into her room and climbed in bed. It was a long time before she fell asleep, and when she finally did, it was restless.

Chapter 35

Light filtered across Marianna's face, waking her. She opened her eyes. Betsy was pulling back the drapes and letting in the sunshine. She squinted at the brightness.

The memories from the previous night came rushing back. She glanced down at her hand. A hardened bit of red candle wax clung to her skin.

She pushed herself to a sitting position. Betsy was already fixing her tea and filling a plate with food from her tray. It was a thoughtful gesture, but at the moment, Marianna was more concerned with getting answers about what was going on here.

"I had a horrible night last night, Betsy. If you know anything about the dangers here, you need to tell me."

Betsy hesitated.

"I know the hallway's real. I found it last night. And don't even tell me it was a dream because I know it wasn't. Tell me everything you know about this place, and tell me the truth."

"Oh, Miss Marianna, I could be in a lot of trouble if I tell you what I know, and it's not much either. I only know what I've been told by others. And if what they say is true, no one really knows the whole story, except for Cook, but no one would ever get it out of her. What I know is the room at the end of that hallway has something to do with Lord Bludington's wives' deaths."

Betsy smoothed out invisible wrinkles in her apron as she continued. "I don't know what exactly. Some say he goes there and tries to bring them back to life. That's why they say he's involved in dark magic. That creepy painting is supposedly a depiction of a dwarf called Bluebeard. He was trying to get all the powers of dark magic for himself by offering sacrifices he killed with his wolf-headed knife. I don't know what it has to do with anything, but Lord Bludington gets mad if anyone talks about that hall."

Betsy gathered the edges of her apron in her hand, clutching it as if it were a lifeline, staring at the floor. "They say he has a lot of servants locked up in an underground prison for talking about it. I believe that because when I'm near his quarters, sometimes I hear screams that sound like they're coming from underneath me."

"But what does all this have to do with me specifically? Why do people keep acting like I'm in danger?" Marianna sat on the sofa.

Betsy's eyes darted about the room as if searching for a way out. Marianna touched her shoulder. "Please tell me."

Betsy sighed. "People say it's bad if his wife tries to talk to him about the room. I don't know why. Please, don't go and ask him. Promise me you won't. I told you I'd try to protect you, and right now this is the only way I know how." She was on the verge of tears as she grabbed Marianna's hand and squeezed it. "You're my friend, the first real one I've ever had, and I don't want anything bad to happen to you."

Marianna pulled Betsy into a hug. "Don't worry, I promise I won't talk to Lord Bludington about it."

Silence fell as Betsy helped Marianna dress. Things seemed to be getting stranger and stranger. Even after the scare last night, Marianna still couldn't shake the feeling that she needed to get into that room. It had to be the key to everything weird happening here, but she couldn't let Betsy know. She was terrified already. Today they would have a relaxing, fun time, and Marianna would worry about things tomorrow.

Marianna cleared her throat and tried to infuse her voice with cheer. "Come on, let's go eat breakfast. We're going to have a wonderful day today. I've decided not to let those horrible stories haunt me. We can go through the gardens and then go riding."

Betsy gave her a wary look.

"Not out to the cliffs this time. I promise we'll go on the normal path. Wherever everyone else rides." Marianna pulled Betsy downstairs, not giving her a chance to protest.

When they reached the dining room doors, Marianna turned to Betsy and said, "Come meet at the dining room as soon as you've finished eating, and we'll go to the stables."

Betsy nodded and then disappeared down the servants' hallway. Marianna smiled to herself, flinging the dining room doors open. She stepped inside and stopped short.

Bludington was rising from his chair.

"Ah, Miss Marianna. I've been waiting for you. Come, sit and eat. You can listen and eat at the same time, right?" Bludington laughed like he had told the funniest joke ever and motioned Marianna forward.

Marianna inched toward her seat. Had he already found out that Betsy had told her about the room? Did he really throw servants in dungeons and beat his wives? Was she next? She swallowed hard as she slid into her chair.

"I must go on a business trip. I'll be gone three or four weeks at least. I wanted to let you know and remind you that this is your home too. If you want to have any guests while I'm gone, feel free to do so, just let Mrs. Strunk know. Also, I wanted to give you this."

Bludington reached down and pulled a key ring from his belt. Twenty or thirty keys of various sizes dangled from the ring. Some were silver and some gold. Bludington reached into the mass of keys and pulled out a tiny golden one.

That was the key to the room! Marianna bit her lip and tried to keep her expression neutral.

"These are the keys to every room in the house. You may use any of the rooms you like, except for the room this key belongs to. Do not open that door." Bludington handed Marianna the key ring.

She lowered her eyes, hoping he couldn't see her relief. She'd thought he was going to say something about her sneaking around last night.

"I hope you enjoy yourself while I'm gone, and don't fret. I won't be gone too long. How are the wedding plans coming along?" A smile covered his face as he said it, and Marianna held back a shiver.

"Umm, fine," Marianna managed to squeak out, schooling her features and hoping he couldn't tell she hadn't done anything related to wedding planning.

He didn't seem to notice or even care about her response as he continued, "Remember, I want you to do whatever will make you comfortable. Anyone you might like to have over, your father or sister or friends, don't hesitate to ask them. I know it's a big place and can get lonely." Bludington smiled again before walking out of the room.

Marianna didn't understand him. She'd hardly seen him since moving here, but he was determined to marry her. Now he was leaving and acting concerned about her well-being.

And why couldn't she go into that room?

Marianna jumped up and went down the hallway, stopping suddenly when she saw Dunsten and Bludington huddled in conversation by the front door. She crept back into the shadows and listened.

"And you sure she's ready?"

"Yes, my lord. I'm positive. She will be exactly as you want her when you return."

"Good, then keep an eye on things, Dunsten."

Dunsten gave a little bow and nodded. Bludington walked out the front door, and Dunsten turned to go down another hallway.

Marianna slumped forward, pressing her palms and forehead against the wall as her pulse raced. What did that mean? Ready for what? Certainly nothing good.

Chapter 36

Marianna hurried down the hallway, away from Dunsten and Bludington. Her heart thundered and her head spun. She knew without a doubt the bad feeling she had all this time was for good reason.

Keys jangled as Marianna lifted the ring and pulled out the tiniest key from their midst to study it. The secret room would tell her what she needed to know. She was sure of it, and now she had access to it.

"Miss Marianna, what is it?" Betsy appeared around the corner. "Is everything okay?"

"Betsy, look what Bludington gave me." She held up the little key, the rest of the keys clanking together as they spun on the ring below.

"He gave you the keys to the manor? Why is that one so small?"

"It's the key to the door in the hallway." Marianna grabbed Betsy's arm and squeezed it.

Betsy's eyes filled with fear, and she took a step back. "No, you can't be thinking of looking in there. It's too dangerous." She wrapped her arms around herself and shivered. "Did Lord Bludington tell you what that key belonged to?"

"No, but it was the only one he told me not to use, and it's the only one small enough to fit in the keyhole of that door."

"If he told you not to use it, then surely you won't use it." Betsy's voice was tinged with desperation.

"Why shouldn't I? I want to know what everyone is trying to keep secret from me. Maybe it will explain why Bludington is so eager to marry me, and yet never comes around."

"Miss, Marianna, you don't understand. There is evil here. All the servants agree. Your life could be at risk if you do this. Why would you put your life at risk for something as silly as satisfying your curiosity?"

"But that's just it. What is this evil? All I've heard is talk, and I haven't seen one shred of actual evidence to support it. How am I supposed to believe all that?" Marianna didn't bother to mention the ominous feeling that never left the pit of her stomach these days, but she was tired of only having a feeling and some servants' warnings. She needed to know what exactly was going on here.

"What about my word, Miss Marianna? I told you I was your friend, and I'll do whatever I need to keep you safe. I wouldn't lie to you."

Marianna sighed. "I believe you're my friend, but you can't even tell me anything more than rumors. You've gotten caught up in the stories the others have told, so much so that you believe them." She walked over to the window seat that looked out on the front drive.

Betsy followed her and laid a hand on Marianna's shoulder. Her grip was firm, and determination glowed in her eyes. "You know there's something to fear here, Miss Marianna. I've seen it in your eyes when you've come back from wandering the halls at night and when you've woken from one of your horrible nightmares. What I can't understand is why you continue to meddle with it. Leave it alone. I beg you, if not for your sake, then for mine."

Marianna knew Betsy was right, but despite knowing she should leave the room alone, something inside her couldn't let it go. It was clear Betsy wouldn't go with her to unlock the room, but she could at least give her peace of mind with a lie. She reached out and squeezed Betsy's hand.

"I guess you're right, Betsy. It's good I have you around to watch out for me. But I can explore any other rooms I want, and since Bludington is gone, come show me around his quarters."

Betsy hesitated a half-second, her eyes still wary, before pulling Marianna into a hug. "Of course, I will take you anywhere you want to go, anywhere but that dreaded hallway."

Betsy pulled away and started toward the door. Marianna fastened the ring of keys to her belt and followed.

They spent the rest of the afternoon exploring Bludington's wing, which consisted of his bedchamber and dressing room, a sitting room, and study. There were also some empty rooms, and some with a few pieces of furniture.

"And this is Bludington's parlor." Betsy led Marianna into the last room.

Dark heavy drapes covered the windows, making it look like nighttime inside. Betsy hurried over to a large side table and lit the chamber lantern. Its pale glow filled the room.

A large chest, the kind you would see on ships, was tucked against one wall, its clasp tightened fast and padlocked. Why did Bludington padlock a chest in his own quarters?

On the far wall hung three portraits. The first one pictured a pale, young woman with bright red hair. The second pictured a girl with mousy brown hair and wide blue eyes. The last pictured a golden-haired girl with sparkling green eyes.

A gasp escaped Marianna. The last girl looked like Annette. How could that be? Why would Bludington have a painting of her sister in his quarters?

"Miss Marianna, what's the matter?" Betsy hurried over to stand next to her. "Oh, these are Bludington's previous wives. Did you know that already?"

Marianna shook her head. Then she noticed the little tag at the bottom of each painting label with the names, Lilianna, Carianna, and Elianna. "Right, of course."

She turned, trying to shake off the unease. It was eerie how much Annette resembled Bludington's third wife, but it had to be a coincidence, right? Especially since Bludington had only seemed interested in pursuing Marianna from the beginning.

She cast a glance around the rest of the room. There wasn't much else in the way of decor. A dark brown loveseat sat in the middle. And over on the far wall was an ajar door. Where did that lead to? Marianna walked to it and peered through the crack.

A long dark hallway ending in a wall with a painting hanging on it. This was it! This was the hallway.

"Here, let's sit a moment." Marianna plopped down onto the loveseat. She rubbed her hand over the smooth silk fabric. It was silk of the highest quality, and hard to come by. They had never had anything this fine in her childhood home.

"How about some tea?" Betsy wiped away invisible dirt from her apron and stayed standing.

"You don't have to go all the way back to the kitchen. I need a little breather and then I'll be ready to go."

"Oh, no. It's not far from here at all. The kitchen, I mean." Betsy hurried over to the corner and grabbed a doorknob. It was so unobtrusive, blending into the wallpaper, Marianna hadn't even noticed it before. Betsy pulled the door open and motioned down the dimly lit hall. "It's down there. I won't be but a minute."

Before Marianna could say anything else, Betsy darted down the hallway and out of sight.

Marianna pulled her journal and pencil from her pocket and scribbled down a map of the passageways. It would be interesting to see where all the servant hallways led. They had their own maze behind the walls of the main house, but there wasn't time for that now. Marianna was sure she could find her way back to the forbidden hallway now.

Betsy popped backed into the room as Marianna was tucking her journal back into her pocket. Betsy set the tray down on the side table and poured out two cups, picking up one and handing it to Marianna.

The sweet scent of lavender mingled with honey rising to greet her in a swirl of steam. Marianna breathed it in. The tension in her neck and back eased and she settled back against the couch. She patted the spot next to her and motioned for Betsy to sit.

Betsy sat down wordlessly. She thumped her right hand against her thigh as she perched on the edge of the seat. The hand that held her teacup shook a little. Was she nervous because she suspected Marianna still planned to open the room?

Marianna cleared her throat. "What are all those empty rooms for?"

"Nothing that I know of. Lord Bludington likes his space, so he had his rooms placed behind several empty ones." Betsy drained her teacup and set it onto the tea tray before clasping her hands together and sitting up straighter.

That was strange. Why would Bludington need that much space to himself in a house this large?

"Hmm," Marianna murmured. She couldn't think of anything else to say, and Betsy jumped up to carry everything back to the kitchen.

Marianna stood up as well. "Here, let me help you."

Betsy shook her head. "Absolutely not! You've met Cook. She'll have a fit if I bring you back to the kitchen." She scooped up the tea service and scurried back down the little hallway.

She returned within minutes. "Didn't you say you wanted to try writing to your family again?"

Betsy scurried over to the door that led back out to the main hallway and pulled it open. "We best be getting back to your rooms so you can do that."

Marianna nodded and followed. She hadn't heard from anyone back home, and she wanted to try writing them all again. Amid her thoughts, Marianna turned to look back the way they had come. Dunsten stood in the shadows, his eyes following every move she and Betsy made.

Had he nothing better to do than spy on her? Marianna turned, running to catch up with Betsy.

Once night fell, Marianna rushed to her room and hastily readied for bed. She was already feigning sleep when Betsy arrived to help her undress.

Betsy walked over to the bed and stopped. Marianna struggled to keep her breath even and deep. Betsy leaned over her and pulled the covers up to her chin.

"Poor girl. This place has been so rough on her nerves. At least she is finally resting properly," Betsy whispered as she blew out the light. Her footsteps shuffled across the floor and after a brief silence, the door latch clicked shut.

Marianna waited in the darkness for a long time, wanting to be sure everyone would be in bed and asleep before she ventured out to the hallway. When she heard the hall clock chime once, she climbed out of bed, only bothering to pull on her robe this time.

She shoved her journal into its large pocket and grabbed a candle and some matches from her drawer. She wanted to be prepared to light her candle again if her flame went out. She unlatched the key ring from the dress she had worn that day and stepped out into the hall. Fastening the key ring to the belt of her robe, she winced at the clatter and paused. The hall was silent, so she lit her candle and consulted her journal once more before making her way through the maze of hallways.

Light footfalls followed behind her. She turned, but no one was there. She started walking again. The footfalls followed her again. She stopped and whirled around. Still, she saw no one behind her. She turned back around slowly, listening carefully. Nothing.

Marianna started walking again, more slowly this time. She strained her ears, and when she heard the footfalls again, she spun around without breaking step. A figure that looked suspiciously like Dunsten disappeared through a door.

He was following her. Her breath caught. He'd tell Bludington, and then who knew what would happen. Would Bludington really beat her? She didn't want to take that chance.

Marianna blew out her candle and tiptoed back down the hall. She was careful to be quiet as she passed the room Dunsten had hid in and didn't relight her candle until she had left Bludington's wing of the house.

Once in her room, Marianna pulled off her robe and flung it onto her bed. She sighed. How was Dunsten always able to follow her?

The next night, Marianna followed the same routine, except when she got to her bedroom door, she peered out into the darkness looking for Dunsten. She didn't see him, so lit her candle and started her journey to the hallway.

When she got close to Bludington's wing, something moved in the darkness ahead of her. Was it Dunsten? She blew out her candle and pushed up against the wall. After her eyes adjusted to the darkness, she was able to make out a figure waiting at the entrance to Bludington's quarters.

So that was where he waited. He must be guarding Bludington's quarters to see if she would try to open the door to the locked room. But why would Bludington have Dunsten do that? It seemed Bludington thought she would try and open the door and wanted to catch her doing so.

Maybe she didn't want to do this after all. It was getting a little too creepy. Marianna leaned against the wall and waited for several minutes. Dunsten was not going anywhere anytime soon, so she turned and went back to her bedroom.

She climbed in bed but could hardly sleep. Her thoughts were a tangle as she tried to sort out what was happening. That locked room had to hold the answers. She had looked at the silver cups, she had gone to the cliffside where Elianna had supposedly killed herself, and she hardly knew more than when she first got here. But Bludington was most certainly hiding something.

The fact that Dunsten was always on guard gave credence to that. Maybe the stories the servants told were true. Maybe it was stupid of her to go searching for answers. Maybe she was putting her life in danger.

She wished she could talk to her father. Or Annette and Susan. She had never gotten around to writing those letters. She should do it now and ask them to come for a visit. Bludington had told her to invite anyone she wanted to Thunderwell.

Inspired by this new idea, Marianna slid out of bed, relit her bedside lantern, and dug out her writing supplies. She wrote to her father, Annette, and Susan, asking them all to come for a visit. As she sealed up the final letter, the heaviness that had settled in the pit of her stomach seemed lighter and when she laid back down, she immediately fell asleep.

Chapter 37

Marianna was grateful when morning came, but even daylight could not calm her thoughts. She was on edge waiting for a reply from her family. The next few days and nights were much the same. During the day, she wandered the castle and gardens, and at night, she tossed and turned, hardly sleeping. All the while, her tumultuous thoughts never stopped.

Every day when the mail arrived, Marianna darted down to check for a reply. But none came. Betsy tried to get Marianna to tell her what was wrong, but Marianna just murmured that she was fine.

One day, while wandering away from the library, Marianna noticed a tiny hallway leading off the one she was in. She had never noticed it before and was sure she had never been down it.

She turned and walked into it, surprised by its narrowness. There did not seem to be enough room for two people to pass each other. The hall was long and twisty, turning this way and that, but finally ended when it met another hallway.

At first, Marianna was not sure where she was. She walked down the new hallway and opened the first door she came to. The room was empty. Not a single piece of furniture—the only décor the heavy black drapes that covered the window.

She was in Bludington's wing. She had to be. His wing was the only place where there were rooms like this. She now had a way to get to the secret room without Dunsten's knowledge. Marianna raced forward looking to see where that hallway might be in relation to this new passageway and soon found it.

Once there, she paused for a moment, pulled out her journal, and scribbled in the new passageways she had found, then hurried to her room to prepare for the trip she was going to make that night.

Rain pattered against the windowpanes as Marianna lay in bed waiting for the right time to get up and find the secret room. She turned onto her side and watched as the torrents streamed down her window. Maybe the noise of the storm would help cover any sound she made. This could be a good thing.

At last, when the large clock chimed three, Marianna climbed out of bed and donned her robe. She gathered her candle, matches, and keys and snuck down to the narrow hallway she had discovered earlier that day.

It seemed longer than it had during the day. Could there be two passages like this in the house? Just when she was sure she had taken the wrong hallway, Marianna came out into Bludington's chambers. It didn't take her long to find the hallway with the painting.

She stopped at the beginning of the hallway, took a deep breath, and nodded. She needed to know what was in that room.

She took another deep breath and crept down the hall. Her candlelight flickered, sending shadows dancing across the wall. Rain beat against the roof. Thunder cracked overhead. The hallway seemed more eerie than it ever had before.

Her heartbeat echoed in her ears so loudly, she was sure the entire house would hear it and find her here. The one place she was not supposed to be. Her palms were slick with sweat.

She swiped her empty hand down her robe and tightened her other hand around the candle base. "Don't drop the candle," she whispered.

The only thing worse than getting caught here would be starting a fire that burned the whole place down.

The ball of nerves in her stomach twisted tighter. She swallowed hard and kept moving forward. Another few steps and she had reached the end of the hallway. She stared at the painting.

Why would someone want a painting of this? It was morbid. What kind of man was Bludington? It seemed he had two sides. The man who catered to her whims and worked hard to impress her family, and the man who enjoyed gruesome things like a room full of taxidermized animals and violent paintings hanging on the wall.

At least she hadn't seen this weird, dark side of him yet. Did she even know him at all?

She shivered as she remembered the way the dwarf had seemed to move and speak the last time she had stared at the painting. To avoid seeing that again, she turned to face the door.

She pulled the ring from her robe, fumbling for the smallest key, but her sweaty palms caused the keys to slip through her fingers and crash to the floor. She jumped at the noise and cast a quick glance behind to be sure Dunsten hadn't somehow heard and come to stop her.

He hadn't. She breathed in deeply and let it out slowly. She could do this. She was going to do this. She needed to do this. She needed to know what was going on here.

Marianna bent down and picked up the keys. She managed to pull out the little one without dropping them again, though her hands shook. She stared at the tiny key before slipping it into the keyhole.

After a moment of resistance, the lock popped, and the door creaked open. A horrible stench came rushing out of the room. She covered her nose with her arm and pushed the door all the way open. The hinges squeaked as if they hadn't been used in ages.

Lightning flashed through the only window in the room, illuminating it clearly. Marianna gasped and stumbled back, grabbing the door frame to keep from falling.

Four skeletons lay across the floor of the room. Blood splattered, ragged dresses still clung to their decimated forms. A small wooden chest sat against the far wall. On the top of it, something shimmered in the candlelight. Marianna took several hesitant steps forward, mesmerized. There were four rings, each with a large purple stone surrounded by smaller diamonds, exactly like the ring Bludington had given her.

In a daze she lifted her hand, just to be sure. There was no doubt. The ring she wore on her finger was a perfect match for the ones on the floor. Bludington didn't just beat his wives, he killed them.

Chapter 38

That thought pounded over and over through Marianna's head as she stood frozen in disbelief. Her breath caught. Her head spun. Bile rose in her throat. Surely she was having another nightmare. But no, the image before her didn't waver. Why were there four? Hadn't there only been three wives before her?

Sense flooded back through her. She had to get out of here before Dunsten came looking for her. She hastily backed out of the room and slammed the door behind her, wishing she could block what lay behind it from her mind.

She thrust the key toward the keyhole, but it caught the doorjamb instead of the lock. Why wouldn't her fingers work right? She tried again but this time the key slid down under the lock screeching against the metal doorplate.

The noise was so loud, she was sure they could hear it in the next wing of the house. She shot a glance over her shoulder, but no one was there. She took a deep breath and pressed her palm against the door, finally managing to insert the key into its tiny lock. She twisted it and sighed with relief when it clicked into place.

She pulled the key out. Something red and sticky covered the end. Was that... blood? How could it have gotten blood on it? She swiped it against her dress, but still the splotch remained. She tried again, rubbing harder. Still there.

She didn't have time to waste standing here. She would have to clean it off in her room. She pulled the offending key from the ring, stashing the rest of them down in her pocket, and clutched the little key in her fist, her nails biting into her palm. On shaky legs, she hurried back toward her room, desperate to wash the red spot away.

Thunder cracked right above the house. Marianna jumped and broke into a run. Her heart raced, and pain pounded her head. She had never been more terrified in her life. Why hadn't she listened to Betsy's warning? What was Bludington planning to do with her? And how exactly had he killed all the other wives? She hadn't married him yet. She could run away.

When she reached her room, she flung her door open and raced inside, slamming it shut behind her. She whirled and pressed her face against the door as if it could erase the image now seared into her brain. The smooth wood was cool, easing the pounding in her head a bit.

A hand grabbed her shoulder. She screamed and jumped.

"Oh, Miss Marianna, sorry. I didn't mean to startle you." Betsy dropped her hand and took a hesitant step back. "What is it? What's happened? You're as pale as a ghost."

Marianna grabbed Betsy and pulled her into a hug. "I'm so glad to see you."

Tears streamed down her cheeks. She pulled back and released Betsy.

"I'm sorry, it's so horrible. I have to leave, but I don't know if I will ever be safe. He'll chase me and hunt me down until I'm like the others, because I know."

"Because you know? What do you know?" Betsy couldn't disguise the fear in her voice.

Marianna hurried over to her wardrobe and pulled out a bag. She grabbed things from hangers and things from drawers without even looking at them, stuffing them inside the bag. Tears flooded her face, and she broke into sobs.

"It's just..." Marianna gasped for the air to finish her sentence. "...he'll kill me," was all she managed to get out.

"Oh, Miss Marianna, I'm sure it can't be as bad as you think." Betsy pulled Marianna away from the bag, motioning to her bed, then went over to the pitcher and poured Marianna a glass of water, and thrust it into her hand. "You need to calm down. Come on, drink up."

Marianna sank onto her bed and accepted the glass with a shaky hand. She reached her other hand up to help support it, dropping the key in the process.

"What's this?" Betsy bent down to pick it up.

"The key to that room."

Her eyes were wide as saucers as she turned to Marianna. "You went into his secret room? What..." Betsy broke off as if afraid to ask the question she clearly wanted to. "That's why you're so upset. Because of what you found... in there."

Betsy slowly sank down onto the bed next to Marianna. She held up the key and examined it. "What is... is this... blood?" She covered her mouth with her hand and thrust the key toward Marianna.

Marianna accepted it. She stared down at it as she spoke. "I'm so sorry I didn't listen to you, Betsy. I should have. You were right. I didn't want to know what was in that room, but now I do, and I need your help. You must help me get this key clean or else Bludington will know I went in there. And if he knows..." She choked on a sob and looked at Betsy pleadingly.

"Of course, Miss Marianna. I would do anything to help you." Betsy nodded her head. "But.." She hesitated, looking at Marianna questioningly, before speaking again. "What was in the room that there is blood on the key?"

"I can't tell you, Betsy. It's too horrible. Please, let's not talk about it. No one can know I went there tonight. Promise me you won't tell anyone, please."

Maybe if Betsy helped her get the spot off, no one would ever know she'd been in the room. There were still some things that didn't make sense. Why were there four skeletons in the room rather than three? Who was the fourth woman? But she didn't have time to think about that now. She cleared those thoughts from her mind to focus on the here and now.

She was counting upon Betsy's loyalty, and while she didn't think Betsy would purposely betray her, she knew how gossip went wild among the servants. The smallest slip could have disastrous results.

"I promise I won't tell anyone, Miss Marianna. I'll go get some of the strong soap Cook uses to clean floors. It can get almost anything up." Betsy fled the room.

Marianna turned to the water pitcher, poured some water in the bowl, and viciously scrubbed the key with a wet rag. The blood still would not come off, so Marianna left it in the bowl to soak.

Betsy entered holding up the jug of soap. "Cook had already mixed some soap flakes in water, so I grabbed it." She smiled.

"That's great, Betsy, thanks. Bring it here." Marianna waved her over. They took turns scrubbing at the blood.

Finally, Betsy held it up triumphantly. "I think I got it all!"

Marianna grabbed the key and examined it. "I think you're right." She set the key on the nightstand and grabbed Betsy in a hug, sighing with relief.

"How.." Betsy gasped as she pulled away, her eyes wide with shock. Marianna turned to follow her gaze to where the key lay. Blood seeped out of the key, as if the key were crying tears of blood."

"How is this even possible?" Marianna sucked in a ragged breath.

"Maybe..." Betsy started then stopped.

"Maybe what?"

"Maybe it's a magic key," Betsy whispered.

Marianna choked on the laugh she forced out. "A magic key? I can't do anything if that's the case. If I can't get this blood off, Bludington will know I went into the room, and he will kill me." She crumpled onto the bed.

"Are you sure he'll kill you?" Betsy said. She picked up the key and resumed scrubbing it.

"Trust me, if you had seen what I saw, you would have no doubt. He'll kill me." Marianna tried to erase the image of the row wedding rings from her mind.

"I know what we can try. Sometimes the maids use this vinegar mixture to clean up stains. I'll go get it." Betsy dropped the key into the washbowl and started for the door.

"Don't let anyone see you," Marianna hissed as Betsy slipped out, bobbing her head in acknowledgement of Marianna's words. Soon Betsy was back with the vinegar solution, and the scrubbing began again.

After working tirelessly for several minutes, Betsy held up the key proudly, her eyes shining. "Look, Miss Marianna, I think it's gone."

Marianna peered at it closely. "You're right. But we better watch a few minutes to make sure it doesn't come back like it did before."

After several minutes when no blood appeared on the key, Marianna took it from Betsy and laid it on her nightstand.

"Thank you so much, Betsy." She threw her arms around the girl, swallowing the lump of emotion that had taken residence there. "What would I do without you?"

A wave of exhaustion flooded over Marianna, and she fought to keep from yawning as she pulled back. "You'd better go back to your room and get some sleep now. Make sure no one sees you."

"I'll be careful, Miss Marianna. I would hate myself if anything bad happened to you because of me. Good night."

Betsy left the room, and Marianna climbed into her bed with a sigh of relief. For the moment she was safe, and tomorrow she could come up with another plan. She laid back against her pillows and soon fell into a deep sleep.

Chapter 39

Marianna woke to sunlight shining across her face. Sitting up, she glanced at the clock. Almost lunchtime. She scrambled out of bed and threw on her clothes.

Why hadn't Betsy come to wake her? This had never happened before. Had Bludington returned during the night? Was he waiting for her?

She opened her door. Distant chatter drifted up the stairs. The usual chatter of the servants tending to their duties. Somewhere far away a door opened and shut. Everything seemed normal.

She darted downstairs and into the dining room. Carrie and Leah were preparing the table for lunch.

"Excuse me, do either of you know where Betsy is?"

Both girls looked up, surprised looks on their faces. They glanced at one another, and Carrie set her tray down, taking a step forward. "She didn't tell you, my lady? She left to tend to a sick relative."

Marianna stared at Carrie. Carrie's gaze didn't waver, but Marianna couldn't shake the unease that started twisting through her stomach. Why didn't she believe Carrie? Why would Carrie lie about something like this?

"Is it her mother?"

Leah pulled out Marianna's chair and motioned for her to sit.

"I don't know, my lady. All I know is that she left to care for a sick relative?" Leah's voice lifted at the end like she wasn't sure she was telling the truth.

Maybe they had been instructed to tell Marianna this. A tight ball of dread settled itself inside the pit of Marianna's stomach. Maybe Dunsten had seen her go into the room last night.

Marianna struggled to keep her face neutral as she sat down and asked, "Who would know more?"

"Maybe, Mrs. Strunk or possibly Dunsten. They're the ones in charge." Carrie placed a plate with a roast chicken sandwich and some strawberries in front of Marianna.

Leah poured her a glass of lemonade, then they picked up their trays and hurried out of the dining room.

Marianna ate quickly before looking for Mrs. Strunk. She found Mrs. Strunk overseeing some maid's chores in one of the sitting rooms. Marianna approached cautiously, remembering that their last meeting hadn't gone so well.

"Mrs. Strunk, I understand that my lady's maid left to tend to an ill relative. Was it her mother?"

Mrs. Strunk stared at Marianna. An unreadable look passed across her face. "I don't know who the relative was, only that it was some distance away, and she expects to be gone for a long while. Should I send for a temporary candidate from the village for you, or perhaps the maids here can take turns assisting you?"

The ball of dread unraveled and twisted through her. She didn't want another maid helping her, not after the way they had acted when she questioned them about the hallway. She didn't trust any of them.

She also didn't want a girl from the village, since she had no clue who those girls would be loyal to. And no one could help her like Betsy did.

Why would Betsy have left without telling her? She couldn't think of any reason she would have done so. Without Betsy, she had no ally in the house.

"No, I won't need anyone to fill in while Betsy is gone. In fact, my sister Annette will be coming to stay. I expect her in three or four days."

Marianna turned, hoping what she said was true, that Annette had already received her letter and was preparing to come visit. But then it might be too dangerous. Maybe she should warn Annette not to come. She hurried to her room to write the letter.

As she bent over her night table to collect her stationary, the tiny key caught her eye. Or rather the large splotch of dried blood that had once again appeared on its surface.

Impossible!

She snatched up the key and carried it to her dresser. Knowing she did not have time to wash it again, she pulled out a handkerchief, wrapped the key up, and stuffed it underneath her clothes at the bottom of her wardrobe.

Then she sat down at the desk to write the letter to her sister.

Dear Annette,

So much has happened here, and I'm afraid. I fear it might not be safe for you to visit. Wait until our brothers return and then send them to check on me. Please don't try to come on your own!

Your loving sister, Marianna

Marianna read the letter, hoping it didn't sound too desperate but was convincing enough to keep Annette from coming. She folded the letter, sealed it in an envelope, grabbed her shawl, and walked downstairs and out the front door.

This time she would take the letter to the post herself. Just to be sure that it went out with the mail. She'd never walked to the village before, but she knew it wasn't far. The only time she had seen it was when Bludington had taken everyone on the outing to the lake. She remembered that it had seemed strangely empty, but surely there was a post there.

After a brief walk, Marianna reached the edge of the village. Several dilapidated shacks lined the edge of it. A hoard of dirty children played in front of them. One boy who looked to be the oldest caught her eye. He wore ragged blue pants and a red vest. A little black cap perched on his head at an angle.

"Um, excuse me, young man," Marianna called out. The boy as well as several other children looked up at her. Wonder covered their faces as they stared at her. Had they never seen a lady before?

"Uh, yes, you, young man, could you assist me?" She motioned at the boy, waving him over.

Without hesitation, he darted over to her and gave a little bow. "My lady, what can I do for you? I never met a real lady afore. Mother always said they was real pretty. You are real pretty too." The boy's eyes shined with excitement.

"And what's your name, sir?"

"Ey, Ben, you 'ear that? The lady called me sir!" the boy yelled to his friends. He turned back to Marianna. "My name's Tom, my lady, but I ain't no sir. My family's real poor."

"Well, Sir Tom, I suppose you can be a sir, if I dub you one, right?"

"I reckon so, my lady. You can do anything you want since you're a lady."

"Well, not quite anything, Sir Tom, but a lot of things." Marianna laughed. She reached down and picked up a long, skinny stick. "Okay, Tom, kneel before me."

Tom scrambled to obey. "I dub thee, Sir Tom, of Thunderwell Manor Village." With the stick, she tapped his right shoulder and then his left. "Rise, Sir Tom of Thunderwell Manor Village."

Tom jumped up and crowed, "I'm a knight. Ben, did you hear that, I'm a knight."

By now all the other children, including Ben were staring at the spectacle before them.

Marianna tapped Tom's shoulder, regaining his attention. "Now, tell me, where is your mother?"

Some of the sparkle left Tom's eyes as he replied. "My mother's dead, my lady. She died of the fever a year ago. It's just me and my brothers 'n sisters."

He pointed to several other children playing in the dirt. "Sally has the baby, Jimmy. Then there's Jon, Peter, and Tessa. Ben's my friend.

"You mean you live all by yourself with your siblings? How old are you?"

"I'm twelve, my lady, but I take good care of my siblings." Tom puffed out his small chest and stood up as tall as he could.

"I can see that you do, Sir Tom, and I have a special job for you today."

Tom's eyes sparkled again as he said, "What's that my lady?"

"I need you to take this letter to the postman for me. Here is your pay for the fine job I know you will do, Sir Tom."

She gave him everything she had with her, which wasn't much, but it would buy some food for the children.

Tom's eyes got as big as coins when he saw the money Marianna handed him. "My lady, I will do the best job ever. Thank you."

He bowed, took Marianna's hand, and kissed it.

"Oh, and Sir Tom, one other thing. Do you know a Betsy Wilem? Or a Wilem family? I think they might live here in the village."

"Uh, I don't recognize that name." Tom glanced questioningly over at Ben. Ben shook his head.

"I'm sorry, my lady, but I don't think they live here. Between Ben and me, we know everybody in the village, and we've never heard of them." Tom shrugged his shoulders.

"It's okay. I'm not sure what village they live in. Thanks for the information and for helping with my letter."

Tom gave her a bright smile before running off to the postman with Marianna's letter. Where had Betsy said her family lived?

As she walked back to the manor, Marianna's thoughts ran wild. Did Bludington know about these parentless children? Wasn't it his job to care for his manor village? It didn't appear that any of the village had been cared for. There were only shacks for housing. The stone path that led into it was cracked and uneven, with rocks jutting out at all sorts of odd angles.

No way anyone could take a carriage down it. Now she understood why they'd only passed the outskirts on the way to the lake. Bludington was probably too embarrassed by the state of his manor village to allow them to see it.

And he should be. How long had it been since the king's inspector had visited here? Marianna thought they were supposed to visit every five years, but the decay she saw had happened over much more time.

How had he managed to hide such negligence? And did no one care? All the servants did what he said with unquestioning loyalty. How could they not know his village was in disarray?

He had a lot of power, so maybe everyone feared him. Maybe that's why no one had done anything. She needed to think about this, wanted to figure out what she could do to fix things.

Marianna turned up the drive to the manor. Something red and white peeked up from the ground, fluttering gently in the breeze. What was it? She walked over and knelt. Her knees sank into the soft ground. Her dress would get muddy, but she didn't care.

She reached out and grabbed the object. It was cotton fabric, and it looked... bloody. It was stuck to the ground somehow. She tugged harder. It still wouldn't come. She crawled closer to the object and examined the ground around it. A large, jagged edge rock was keeping it in place.

She grasped the rock with both hands and pulled. It was so heavy, it knocked her off her knees and onto her backside. The cloth fluttered free and took off on the breeze like it was a kite.

"Oh!" Marianna scrambled to her feet and chased after it. If she believed objects could have personalities, then this piece of cloth certainly did. It taunted her, coming to rest on the ground for a moment, before catching the breeze and floating back up into the air when she got close.

After three unsuccessful attempts, Marianna had enough, and when the cloth next hit the ground, she launched herself onto it, landing on her hands and knees. "Yes," she squealed in delight. The cloth was pinned under her right hand. She sat back and lifted it to examine it.

It was an apron, one like the maids wore at Thunderwell. Droplets of red were splattered across the front. Her eyes followed the droplets down to the little embroidered flower. She fingered the pattern. This was Betsy's apron. But what was it doing out here? And why did it have blood on it?

Her mind whirled and her heart raced as Marianna remembered Betsy telling about her mother sewing the flower onto the apron even though she wasn't well. Marianna's throat tightened. Betsy would never leave this behind. Not of her own free will.

Had something happened to Betsy? If so, it would be all her fault. And she couldn't think of another single reason Betsy's bloodied apron would be left outside like this. Why had it been pinned down? Was someone trying to warn her? Or was it a threat?

Marianna's thoughts were a runaway train she had no way of stopping. Tears flooded her eyes, and a sob escaped her lips. She was so stupid! She had been warned over and over not to mess with the secrets here, and she'd tried to discover what they were at every turn.

There was no hope for her now. She remembered a tale Annette loved to tell about Pandora's Box. Pandora had been warned not to open the box, but instead of listening she opened it and let out all the evil in the world. Marianna had always hated how that tale ended, but now she knew how it felt.

She was Pandora, and she had discovered that evil resided here at Thunderwell.

Chapter 40

Marianna didn't know how long she stayed on the ground crying, but when the sun started to sink below the horizon, she knew she had to get up and go inside.

She picked herself up off the ground, every muscle aching as if she had run for miles. The pounding in her head from last night paled in comparison to how it felt now. And what if her letter to Annette was too late and Annette still came? Or worse yet, Annette didn't listen to her and came anyway? What if something bad happened to Annette?

Her throat closed, and she couldn't breathe. She couldn't let anything happen to Annette. She stumbled toward the house. She had to get some answers. Carrie had been nice that one time, talking with her and answering some questions. Maybe she'd help. Maybe when she realized that this was life or death, she'd help.

Marianna clambered up the steps on the side of the house that led to the kitchen and prayed Cook wouldn't be in there. She sighed when she opened the door and saw only Carrie and two other maids.

She rushed over and grasped Carrie's arm. "Please," she begged. "You have to help me!"

Carrie's eyes widened, and she glanced over at the other two girls. They stood frozen, clearly having no idea what they should do in this situation.

"I need to know if Betsy's okay." Marianna sounded slightly unhinged and probably looked it too, but she was past caring.

"What do you mean? Didn't you see her this morning before she left?"

"No," Marianna nearly yelled. She lifted the bloody apron she was still clutching and thrust it at Carrie. "Look at her apron. It's covered in blood." Her voice squeaked on the last word, and she struggled to hold back tears.

Carrie shooed the other two girls out of the room. "Not a word about this to anyone, do you hear me?" she hissed as they ran out wordlessly, bobbing their heads in agreement.

"Now, Miss Marianna, I don't know what is going on, but you must calm down. If Mrs. Strunk sees you like this, she's liable to cart you off to the insane asylum, and believe me you do not want to go there." She took the apron from Marianna and balled it up, stuffing it down into her own apron pocket. "And you certainly don't want to be flashing this around and making foolish accusations."

Carrie escorted Marianna to a chair and pushed her into it. "Sit and calm down and maybe we can have a reasonable conversation."

"Okay, thank you." Marianna's voice was small. A couple tears escaped, trickling down her cheeks. "Do you know what's in Lord Bludington's secret room?" she whispered.

Carrie took a step back. Fear covered her face, and she shook her head. "Why are you so obsessed with that room? I know everyone here has told you to leave it alone."

Marianna shook her head and didn't reply. Clearly Carrie didn't know what was in the room, only that it was something to be feared. Marianna almost laughed out loud at the irony, but then her reality came crashing back down on her and she felt like sobbing again.

What should she do now? Who *did* know about what was in the room? Probably Dunsten, and there was a good chance Mrs. Strunk knew too. But maybe everyone else was really in the dark as to what was inside. What would Carrie do if she told her? Freak out like she had? Maybe not.

But what kind of position would that put Carrie in? Would she be the next victim because Marianna told her about the secret in the room? She hadn't even told Betsy, and now she was gone. Maybe she shouldn't even be talking to Carrie right now. Maybe a simple conversation with her was enough to endanger someone.

"Here, Miss Marianna, have some chamomile tea. It'll help you calm down. I'll investigate the Betsy situation and see what I can find out. Until then, I can send Leah up to help you if you'd like."

"Thank you for the tea." Marianna picked up the mug and stood. "But I'll be okay. I got overheated, I think." She tried to laugh convincingly. "I don't need Leah to come up. I'll be fine. And don't worry about Betsy either. I just remembered, I did see her before she left, for a quick moment. I was still half asleep. That's why I didn't remember before." Marianna guzzled the last of her tea and set the empty cup onto the table.

"Silly me." Marianna pasted on her biggest smile as she reached her hand out. "Oh, can I have Betsy's apron back, please? She'll be wanting it when she returns. Her mother made it special for her." She hoped it was enough to convince Carrie she was fine so Carrie would return the apron.

Carrie stared at her warily for several seconds. It was clear she hadn't believed a word Marianna had said. Finally, she reached into her pocket and pulled out the balled-up apron. She pressed it into Marianna's hands. "Don't get caught with it," she said as she turned to leave.

At the door, she stopped and turned to face Marianna. "I don't know what all has happened, Miss Marianna, but tread lightly. Don't make any more waves, and you should be fine. That's the one thing they don't like around here—troublemakers."

Marianna had never noticed how bright blue Carrie's eyes were until now, because now they shimmered with tears. Carrie turned and rushed out of the kitchen before Marianna could reply.

Chapter 41

Marianna spent the next few days in an anxious daze. She didn't know when Bludington was going to return, but she was sure Dunsten would tell him she'd been in the room. Only, she hadn't seen Dunsten around. Mrs. Strunk was keeping a close eye on things though, so maybe Dunsten had taken some time off.

She'd had no luck in finding out where Betsy's mother lived. One maid thought she lived in a neighboring manor village but wasn't sure which one. Another thought her mother lived a whole day's journey away either due west or due north, she was uncertain of which. And a third maid had told her Betsy's mother lived in Aberny, a whole other country.

For moment, Marianna considered questioning Mrs. Strunk, but that thought was dashed as soon as she turned the corner. Mrs. Strunk's gaze was icy as she berated a maid.

"There are rules in place here for a reason, Ella!" Her stringent voice made Marianna wince. "Going into rooms you've not been assigned to is cause for termination. You signed a contract when you came on, so I'm sure you are aware of this."

A tiny, blonde maid stood before Mrs. Strunk, shoulders hunched, head bowed, and even from her spot peering around the corner, Marianna could see that she was crying.

"I'm so... so... sorry... Mrs. Strunk," Ella sobbed. Her hands swiped her eyes as if doing so could make the tears disappear. "I... I was... confused. I... th-thought that... was... a room... I w-was responsible for." Ella's shoulders shook as she cried harder. "B-Bridgette... said... it... was..."

"Is Bridgette your boss? No, absolutely not!" She thrust her right hand onto her hip, taking a step closer to the sobbing girl. Lifting her left hand, she shook her index finger at the girl. "This was covered when you were first hired. Don't listen to the other girls' gossip. Your only boss is me, and if you're uncertain about your duties, you're to come straight to me to sort it out."

"Yes... I... understand... now. I-It... won't... happen... again..."

"You're right. It won't happen again because you're fired," Mrs. Strunk snapped.

At that, Ella raised her head, panic in her eyes. Her face was red and puffy from crying. "Oh... p-please, Mrs. Strunk." She clasped her hands together in a pleading gesture. "Please. I... I need this... job. I'm... s-supporting m-y... family. Without th-this job... w-we'll starve!"

"You should've thought of that before you made this choice. Now out!" Mrs. Strunk made a shooing motion and stepped forward. "Out, out!"

Ella stumbled, tears still streaming down her face. Her breaths came out in heaving shudders. She glanced at Mrs. Strunk, but seeming to realize it was hopeless, she walked to the door and pulled it open. She darted through it and disappeared.

"Hmmp!" Mrs. Strunk slammed the door behind her and turned. Marianna sank back against the wall and sucked in her breath, praying Mrs. Strunk would not see her. Mrs. Strunk didn't even glance her way as she stalked into her parlor.

Marianna let out her breath. She was certainly not going to approach Mrs. Strunk now. There might be one other person who'd know where Betsy's mother lived. Jay, the stable hand.

Marianna waited a couple minutes before tiptoeing down the hall to the door and slipping outside. She raced down the path, only slowing when the barn came into view. Caden was carrying a bucket, heading toward the stable doorway.

"Caden." Marianna waved for him to come over.

He put his bucket down and hurried over to her. "Milady, hello." Caden bowed. As he stood, he wrestled with his burlap vest, trying unsuccessfully to smooth out all the wrinkles in it. "We weren't expecting you. Can I saddle your horse for you?"

"Oh, uh no, that won't be necessary. I was looking for Jay, but maybe you can help me."

"It would be my pleasure to help you." Caden smiled and slipped his hands into his pockets.

"I'm trying to find out where Betsy's mother lives. Would you happen to know where that is?"

Caden's face fell. He pulled his hands from his pockets and crossed his arms over his chest. "Oh, I'm so sorry, milady. I haven't been here long. I don't know much about where the others are from." He shook his head.

"Well, perhaps you know where Jay is?"

Caden's face brightened, and he dropped his arms. "Yeah, he's in the barn." He turned and motioned for Marianna to follow him.

Stable hands were bustling around tending to the horses. One horse snorted, while another kicked his stall door impatiently. A couple other horses poked their heads out over their stalls and stared at the newcomers. Horse sweat and a slight odor of manure hung in the air.

She followed Caden as he weaved around the dozen or so stable hands tending to their chores. Near the end of the barn, Jay bent over a shiny, black horse's hoof, cleaning out the dirt and grime lodged there.

As they approached, Jay looked up. "Hello, Miss Marianna."

He gently set the hoof down and gave the horse a pat on the rump. "Good boy, you should feel a lot better now," he murmured before stepping over to Caden and Marianna.

He nodded to the groom who held the horse's lead, and the groom led the horse back the way Caden and Marianna had come.

"Milady, it's nice to see you again. What can I do for you?" He flashed a dazzling smile Marianna was sure brought him more than enough female attention. She smiled back. "No Betsy with you today?"

"Um, no, that's why I am here. Have you seen her lately?" Apparently, Jay wasn't aware of Betsy's trip either.

"No." Jay slowly shook his head, concern covering his face. "Has she not been up at the manor house today?"

"I haven't seen her in several days. They told me that she'd gone to see an ill relative, but she never told me that. It came as a shock, since I find it hard to believe she would leave without telling me. Do you know where her mother lives?"

"Yeah, over in Candera. But she's not come to the stables in over a week. She usually takes the old pony cart to see her mother. I don't know of any other way she could get there. It's a bit too far to walk." Jay rubbed his forehead. "Has something... happened?"

Marianna didn't know what he meant by that question. Was Jay aware of the rumors that circulated at the main house? How much should she tell him? He seemed nice enough, and he was one of Betsy's good friends, but she still wasn't sure she could trust him.

Jay must've seen the hesitation on her face, because he added, "I mean she didn't get in trouble with Mrs. Strunk, did she?"

"Not that I know of," Marianna replied. "But I suppose something could have happened I didn't know about. What happens when the maids get in trouble with Mrs. Strunk?"

She was pretty sure she knew after the scene she'd witnessed, but she was curious what Jay would say.

"Well, they get fired a lot, but there are other rumors..." Jay glanced around. Marianna followed his gaze.

No one was paying them any attention. Jay took a step closer and lowered his voice. "Surely, you've heard the rumors about the dungeon?"

Marianna swallowed hard and nodded. She should have come here in the beginning to garner information about the secrets of Thunderwell. Jay was the first person who seemed to be willing to give them up.

"Well, I'm not sure it's real, but there are more than a few servants who suddenly disappear never to be heard from again, making me wonder if it could be true. The first thing to do would be to verify that there's an entrance somewhere to a lower level in the manor. Have you seen anything like that?"

Marianna thought about the door lodged in the corner of the kitchen. She'd seen it when she'd looked at the silver cups and wondered where it led.

"Possibly," she whispered. "There is one door that's nearly hidden in the kitchen. It could lead below the manor."

"Jay, which horses are supposed to get bathed today?" a young stable boy called as he walked toward them.

Jay held up a hand. "Just a moment, Trent. I'm talking with Lady Marianna. I'll be right over."

Trent nodded and flopped down onto a nearby stool to wait. Jay turned back to Marianna. "We'll have to meet under the cover of darkness. Do you know where the river footbridge is?" he whispered.

Marianna nodded. She'd seen it when she and Betsy had gone riding.

"Meet me there tonight, just after dark. Come here first. I'll have Caden prep your horse. Tell everyone you're going for an evening ride and expect to be back within the hour."

"Okay, but..." Before she could finish speaking, Jay started walking toward Trent. He glanced back at her and mouthed, "Tonight," then turned back to Trent.

Marianna had so many questions. Did she even want to go down this path? Would it help things or make everything more complicated? And how in the world would she get out of the manor after dark without Dunsten or Mrs. Strunk noticing?

Chapter 42

Marianna paced her room, her mind spinning. Should she go meet Jay tonight? Could she trust him? Or should she leave everything alone and hope things wouldn't get any worse?

She knew that wasn't even possible, because as soon as Bludington came back and saw the bloodied key, he would know she had been in that room. That was if he didn't know already.

What if Jay was right? What if there really was a dungeon? Betsy could be locked up in it. But the blood on Betsy's apron seemed to suggest otherwise. Had she been killed?

The air felt thick and heavy. Her heartbeat was so fast, her blood throbbed in her neck and wrists. Sweat beaded her hairline as she struggled to breathe. She had to get out away from the manor even if it was just for a little bit.

Marianna cracked her door and peered out. No one was in the hall. She slipped through and crept over to the door to the servants' passage. She pressed her ear against the door. Nothing. She took a deep breath and pushed into the passage. No one was about.

Well, there really shouldn't be. At this time of day, everyone would have duties to tend to. She hurried through the winding passageways and down the stairs before exiting the manor through the servants' entrance.

The service courtyard was bustling. A group of men unloaded a wagon full of supplies while the cook barked out orders. A few younger maids stood in a huddle giggling and staring at the strongest and most attractive male servants.

"Get back to work! This isn't a social hour," Cook growled.

The maids scattered, some grabbing buckets and mops on their way back into the manor, while others carried laundry baskets out to the drying line. Marianna slipped through the courtyard and out the gate.

She took a deep breath once she'd safely left the manor and broke into a run. Fresh air whipped her hair about, calming her. Even though she was running, it was easier to breathe out here than it had been in the manor. She ran down the path and off into the field beside it. Tall grass nipped at her ankles, but still she kept running.

She didn't stop until she reached the edge of a forest. There was a forest here? She'd never seen it before today. Had she run farther than she thought? She glanced back. She was pretty sure she could find her way back to the manor. And if not, well, perhaps there would be a way to escape her fate within the forest.

Tall pines huddled together, their pointed tops creating an archway over the narrow dirt path that led into the woods. The trees were thick, making it dark and cool. The air was musty and filled with the scent of pine. Tiny bits of sunlight peppered the path intermittently, but other than that, there was no light.

It seemed like another world. Like the forbidden worlds in her fairytale books. Maybe she shouldn't go any farther. She shook her head. She was not ready to go back, and besides it was the middle of the day. What could be lurking in here right now?

She continued, and the forest deepened so that it appeared to be dusk. Sunlight managed to trickle through only a few of the less bushy treetops.

Marianna stopped and sat on an old tree stump to rest. A light breeze rustled through the trees. It sounded like people whispering. Light flickered between the waving leaves creating speckled patterns on the dirt floor, like little fairies dancing about.

A twig snapped behind her. Marianna jumped up and whirled around. A rabbit hopped closer before stopping to nibble on some green grass. Marianna laughed weakly.

"Oh, it's you," she said. "You must think I'm silly jumping around like something is coming for me. But I've seen something horrifying, and I've reason to believe someone might be after me."

She crouched down and crept a little closer to the rabbit. "You're a cute little fella."

The rabbit watched her carefully as he chewed on his grass.

"Things are often not what they seem. Especially in these woods."

Marianna twisted around so fast, she fell onto her backside. An old hag hunched over a crooked wooden cane. Her face was lined with dozens of wrinkles, and grungy gray hair hung over her shoulders. A large wart perched on the end of her nose. Marianna stumbled to her feet and took a step back.

"Who... who are you?" Marianna hated the quiver in her voice. She felt like she was in one of the fairy stories her mother used to tell. Right in the clutches of the evil witch.

"Don't be afraid of me, dear Marianna. There are much worse evils in your luxurious manor."

"Do you..." Her words came out in a rasp. Marianna cleared her throat and tried it again. "Do you know me?"

"I know of you, Dear. You're to be the fourth wife of Lord Bludington, are you not?"

Marianna nodded, still wary. She noticed the old lady hadn't bothered to answer her first question and tell Marianna her name.

"I've been waiting for you," the hag replied.

"Waiting for me?" How could the hag have been waiting for her when Marianna hadn't even known she was coming here herself?

The hag nodded. "I've a message for you. A warning of sorts." The hag's voice was ominous.

"A warning?" Marianna repeated. Why couldn't she think of anything to say? Things had become so fantastical that she was barely managing to process anything anymore.

"Yes," replied the hag. She stood still, staring at Marianna.

"All right," Marianna said. "What is it?"

"Beware the evil blue-headed dwarf with the cairn-headed knife." The hag turned away and plodded off deeper into the woods.

What? What did that mean? Was she talking about the painting? Marianna stood frozen a minute before her curiosity kicked in.

"Wait!" she called, running after the old lady. The hag acted as if she hadn't heard and kept walking, but it only took a second for Marianna to catch her. She laid a gentle hand on the old lady's shoulder. "Please, wait!"

The hag turned, her milky blue eyes settling on Marianna. Marianna fought back a shudder. Could the old woman see?

"Yes?" the hag asked. "Did you need something?"

"Well, it's just..." Marianna sputtered.

"Well? Spit it out girl. I haven't got all day. I've got other ominous messages to deliver."

"Is that all? What does that mean? I don't know any dwarfs." Except the one in the painting. But he wasn't real, was he?

The hag reached out and took one of Marianna's hands into her own rough and wrinkly one.

"You know more than you think you might, girl. You must be brave. You have the courage you need if only you can dig deep enough within yourself to find it." The hag's eyes cleared for a moment, the same tender kindness she heard in the woman's voice glimmered there momentarily.

Then her eyes clouded once more. She dropped Marianna's hand and shuffled away.

"It's only my job to give the messages, not explain them," she called over her shoulder. Her tone was no longer tender but cavalier, and Marianna wondered if she had imagined the clear, kind eyes.

The hag's words stunned her, because they were eerily like some her mother had told Marianna long ago. The memory flooded her mind.

While on her deathbed Marianna's mother had called her into the sickroom. It was unusual because Marianna hadn't been allowed to see her mother during the sickness. But her mother had been adamant that she see her eldest daughter. She had known it would be her last night on earth.

"Marianna, you've had a wonderful life so far, and I hope that will always be the case, but more likely it won't. At some point, everyone faces hardship. When it comes for you, I want you to be ready."

Her mother fell into a coughing fit. A spike of fear shot through Marianna because even as a ten-year-old, she knew her mother was dying.

After helping her mother sip some water, she adjusted the pillows. Her mother scooted up higher and continued speaking. "You have a strength inside of you. I can see it even now. But sometimes it's tricky to reach it so you can use it. I want you to remember your cameo." She lightly touched the cameo where it rested on Marianna's throat.

Marianna hadn't taken it off since her mother had given it to her when she first became ill. Marianna looked down at it, a confused look on her face. "How will this help me, Mama?"

"The cameo is made of a delicate shell, a shell that gets tossed about in the sea. And as if that's not enough, it's harvested, heated, hammered, and shaped to become a beautiful necklace. It has strength despite being delicate. That's what I want you to remember." Her mother reached out and took her hand, squeezing it gently.

"When it seems things can't possibly work out, that's when you will need to reach down deep to find that inner strength. You are stronger than you know, my dear."

That was the same phrase the old hag had used. Chills scampered down Marianna's back, and she hugged her arms to herself. Without thought her hand slipped up to grasp the cameo at her neck.

Marianna decided to take the hag's words as a sign. She would go meet Jay tonight.

Chapter 43

Marianna pulled her horse to a stop before she reached the shadowy figure. The air was humid and warm, and the scent of water lilies and wet dirt lingered. The full moon hung high, casting silvery light across the creek, but it wasn't enough light for her to be sure it was Jay.

What if this was a trap? She had no guarantee that Jay wouldn't turn her over to Dunsten and Bludington. But after waiting several minutes no one else appeared, and the figure moved toward her.

"Lady Marianna is that you?"

Marianna recognized the low rumble. It was Jay. "Yes."

She urged Jupiter forward. Right before the bridge, she stopped and dismounted.

Jay met her as she stepped down. "You weren't followed, were you?"

Marianna shook her head. "I don't think so."

"Okay, great." Jay led her over to the high rail that rose from the footbridge. He pulled out a candle and set it on the rail's ledge, lighting it. He pulled out a wrinkled, folded brown paper, opening it and smoothing it out. Dust flew into the air and a musty odor tickled Marianna's nose.

"I was able to get these from my father's old things. My grandfather was the architect who designed Thunderwell."

"Really? The original blueprints." Marianna was amazed.

"Yeah, they're pretty old, so they might not be completely accurate, but it will give us an idea of where the dungeon could be." Jay ran his hand along the edge of the drawing. It was so old, the ink had faded and in some places was nearly invisible.

"This would be right about where the kitchen is." Jay traced a square near the lower right-hand corner. Jay must have studied it before, because to her the square boxes seemed hardly distinguishable as rooms.

"Right here there is a door that looks like it leads to the basement." The excitement in Jay's voice was contagious.

"So, I was right. That door leads to the dungeons?"

"It looks possible. There's no way to know for sure until we go through it." Jay leaned back and crossed his arms over his chest. "Are you up for a potentially dangerous adventure?" He looked at Marianna, a mischievous smile covering his face.

"You know I'm going to say yes, don't you?"

Jay shrugged his shoulders, dropping his arms as he straightened up and grew serious. "I knew you were committed to this. You met me here, even though you're not sure you can trust me. But it will be dangerous. Even life-threatening. I don't know what will happen if we get caught, but I'm sure it won't be good."

"I know," Marianna replied. "But I haven't got much to lose. I think Lord Bludington plans to kill me, so if I can find a way out, I'll take it."

Surprise covered Jay's face and he swallowed hard before schooling his features. "All right. Anything I can do to help."

They made plans to meet right outside the door the next night at three in the morning since that seemed to be the time when everyone was finally in bed.

"We'll only have a couple hours, because people start getting up around five," Marianna warned.

"Okay, we'll work quick."

Marianna nodded. They said their good nights, and Marianna hurried her horse back to Thunderwell.

The next night, Marianna found Jay already waiting at the little green door. A bag was slung over his shoulders, and he was dressed in all black, from his knitted cap to his work boots.

Marianna felt an urge to laugh. She managed to stuff it down as she softly said, "You look like you're here to rob the place."

"Not quite, but like robbers, I don't want to get caught," he whispered back. "You ready?"

Marianna nodded. "As ready as I'll ever be."

"Let's see how hard it will be to get this door open." Jay tried twisting the knob first, and both he and Marianna took a step back when the door popped open easily.

They stared at one another for several seconds before Jay whispered, "Well, that was unexpected."

Jay pulled a half-melted candle and some matches from his bag. After lighting it, he led the way down the narrow wooden staircase. There was no railing, but the staircase was enclosed on either side by a roughhewn stone wall. The steps creaked and groaned as they descended, and Marianna wondered how old they were. Were they safe?

Marianna reached out, pressing a hand against the cool stone. The air was thicker down here, the scent of something heavy and old filled the air. She kept a hand against the wall, steadying herself as she followed Jay.

"We've reached the bottom," Jay said, his voice echoing even though he spoke barely above a whisper.

Marianna breathed a sigh of relief as she hurried after him, anxious to be off the staircase. There was a loud crack and the ground dropped out from under her.

She smashed into hard packed dirt. Shards of the broken step scraped her back followed by the unmistakable sound of fabric ripping. Cool air caressed her stinging back. How big was the hole? This was embarrassing.

Jay rushed over to her, offering his hand. "Are you okay, milady?"

Marianna nodded, accepting his hand. Once she was standing, Jay shrugged out of his jacket and tossed it over her shoulders.

"Thank you." Marianna gave him a grateful smile. "I hope no one heard that."

Jay nodded, but his expression was doubtful. "Let's keep moving."

The stairs led into a wider tunnel. The same stone walls rose on either side of it. It was cooler now, the air not so thick, though the musty smell still lingered.

Marianna followed Jay through the winding tunnel until they came out into a cave-like room with several more tunnels veering off from it in various directions. The ceiling was higher and seemed vaulted, but it was hard to see any details in the darkness.

Inside the room, Jay paused, casting the light from his candle about the room. There wasn't much. The same stone rocks and hard packed dirt floor. Until his light flashed across something silver. Jay turned his light back. The silver thing moved. It raised a sword.

Marianna gasped. It was one of the old-fashioned suits of armor she had seen in Bludington's wing. Before she could say anything, the suit charged them.

"Run!" Jay yelled. They ran toward the tunnels on the other side of the room. It hadn't seemed so big when they first entered.

Jay pulled her up alongside of him. "We're going to... have to... split up," he huffed as they kept running at full speed.

"Take... that tunnel. I'll lead him away." He pointed to the tunnel on the right, pushing her in front of him. Marianna could hear him behind her as she darted into the tunnel. At the last second, he veered away, running into the tunnel on the left.

Marianna didn't stop though she wanted to. What would she do if the armor followed her? And how was she going to find Jay again? She was out of breath, but she didn't dare stop running, not until she was sure that thing wasn't chasing her anymore.

She ran until her lungs were on fire. Sure they would burst and her legs would collapse under her, she slowed down and listened. Nothing but her gasping breaths. A sudden intense pain seized her side. She stopped and clutched it as she paced back and forth.

After several minutes, she finally felt like she could breathe again, so she slowly started down the tunnel. Now the only way out was to follow this tunnel to its end. At least, she hoped there would be a way out at the end. It could lead deeper into the ground, straight into the dungeon so many claimed Bludington had.

She sighed and pulled Jay's coat tighter around her. She couldn't think like that. Positive thoughts only. She would get out of this. Hopefully, Jay would as well. He seemed strong, like he could hold his own in a fight.

Had there been a person in that armor? It looked strange, moving so slowly and meticulously, and not at all the way a normal person would move. Did Bludington really have access to magic?

First the key that couldn't be washed clean, then the mysterious hag in the woods, and now the suit of armor Marianna had thought was decor. It was too strange and overwhelming to think about. She picked up her pace. Surely this tunnel would end soon.

It seemed like forever before a slight breeze drifted in toward her. The air was lighter, and something pleasant flowed in over the bad smell. Something she couldn't quite place. It was cooler too. She went faster, nearly running as she followed the twists and turns of the tunnel.

There was a distant roar, like running water or something. The new smell was salty sea air. This tunnel was leading her out and away from the manor. Far enough away to be close to the sea. No wonder it seemed she'd been walking forever.

The tunnel widened, and she burst outside. A full moon hung low in the sky casting a silver glow over everything. Waves crashed against the shore, and a couple seagulls called to one another.

Sand rose and fell under her feet, the path leading right to the ocean. She breathed in deeply, the salt air cleansing her senses of the foul smell of the tunnels. The water was dark and murky except for the silver tops of the waves that rolled toward the beach.

Marianna dropped to her knees and laughed with relief. She was okay. She was still alive and now maybe she could get away. She was far from the manor. No one besides Jay knew where she had gone.

She could just leave, follow the shore to the nearest harbor, tell someone about the horrors Bludington was hiding in his manor, and bring in an army to save the people left there. No one would have any idea this was how she got away. They'd think she'd left by the main road, and that's where they would look for her.

She didn't have any supplies, not even any water, so that was a problem. Who knew how far away the nearest town was? She got up and walked along the beach, taking in her surroundings. Another problem. This beach was surrounded by cliffs. Was the only way out by sea or the tunnel?

She spotted a path that led up the cliffside. It was steep and rocky and didn't look easy to climb, but it was at least one way to get off the beach that didn't require a boat or going back to Thunderwell. She didn't dare attempt it at night though. She was at least going to have to spend the night here.

She sank her hands down into Jay's coat, grateful she had it, as it was much colder tonight than it had been during the day. Her hands felt something small and flexible. She pulled it out. Matches! She could start a fire, and even cook some fish if she could catch any.

She'd reassess her situation in the morning, but for tonight she could rest comfortably next to a fire with the sound of the ocean waves lulling her to sleep.

Chapter 44

Marianna opened her eyes. Bright sunlight nearly blinded her as she pushed herself into a sitting position. Sand scraped against her palms and tickled her neck as it fell under her clothes. What was she doing here?

She swiped a hand against her dress, then shaded her eyes as she surveyed her surroundings. Waves rolled in and drifted back, caressing the shoreline. The water sparkled like diamonds.

Right, she'd been in the tunnels trying to escape the living armor and ended up on the beach.

She glanced behind her. The tunnel exit appeared small compared to the rocky cliffs that rose above it. Tan colored stone was broken up by bits of sparse green plant life in a wall that surrounded her. The only way up was a narrow, steep path that didn't look easy or safe to climb.

Her stomach growled as a knot of hunger formed inside it. She sighed and stood up. She couldn't stay here with no supplies or any way to obtain fresh water, so best to start trying to get up that cliffside.

She plodded across the beach and stopped in front of the narrow path. Hard-packed dirt several shades darker than the stone led in a winding path up the cliffside. She could see several places where rocks jutted up out of the path like they were waiting to trip her and send her tumbling back down to the beach.

She sighed again, then started climbing. The first bit wasn't too bad as she was able to walk upright, but the path continued to get steeper and steeper until she was leaning forward and using her hands to grab at any vegetation that looked sturdy enough to hold her weight.

Her skirts bunched up against the cliff, and her foot caught on a rock, sliding out from her, her other foot following. She scrambled to keep from falling, one hand pressing against the rock that barely rose above the dirt, the other grasping for anything to hold her steady.

Her hand caught on something. A skinny tree—barely wider around than a shovel handle—bent under her weight and her feet slipped farther. She drew in a sharp breath then gritted her teeth.

She would not die on this cliff. Not after all she had been through. She dug her toes in, managing to secure herself back on the path. She went slowly, making sure she had a handhold before moving her foot and her feet were solid before moving her hands.

She reached above her head, her hand grasping a cold metal rod. She was so startled she nearly let go. What on this cliff could possibly be made of metal? She pulled herself up. The rod she was clinging to nestled among several others forming a prison window. It was too dark inside to tell what was behind it.

Tentatively, Marianna stretched her other hand through the bars. Warm, musty air rushed up her arm. She pulled herself up farther, pressing her head against the bars, straining to see inside. The same dank stench from the tunnels greeted her, and she wrinkled her nose and tried not to breathe too deeply.

After a moment, her eyes adjusted to the darkness, and she could make out a passageway much like the tunnels she'd come through last night. Was this the prison everyone kept insisting Bludington had in the basement?

Marianna couldn't hear anything but the drip, drip of water falling from the ceiling onto the tunnel floor.

"Hello?" It came out hoarse. How funny a voice could be rusty after only a day of not using it.

Marianna cleared her throat and tried again. "Hello? Anyone in here?" Her voice echoed back to her in a rippling pattern. She hadn't noticed that last night, but then again she'd been running for her life.

She waited another minute, then tried again. "Is there anyone in here? I heard this could be a prison. Do you need help?" Still nothing but an echo.

She waited several minutes, but no reply came. Maybe it wasn't really a dungeon after all.

As she started to climb past the window, a voice called out. "Hello?"

"Yes, I'm still here."

"Marianna, is that you?"

Marianna recognized the voice immediately. "Jay, are you okay?"

"For now." Jay's face appeared. He grabbed hold of two of the bars, his wrists encased in iron shackles. He squinted against the sunlight.

"But that may not last long. There's a lot of people down here. So many friends who disappeared, and Jon, Carrie's fiancé is here. A lot are sick, some injured, and some have been here a very long time." He sighed, lifting a hand and rubbing his forehead. The chains on the shackles jangled.

"Oh, Jay, I'm so sorry I got you tied up in all this. Does everyone have to wear those?"

"Well, all the people who don't have a cell. There's a few of us. We can wander about the tunnels within the dungeon, so it's not so bad." He dropped his hand and gave her a little smile.

"And you didn't get me in this, I volunteered, remember? Betsy's my friend, one of my best friends, and I'd do anything for her."

Hope flickered inside of Marianna, and she leaned closer. "Have you seen her? Betsy? Is she okay?"

Jay shook his head. "I'm afraid not. I haven't made it to every cell, so there's still a possibility she's down here."

Marianna nodded, unwilling to let go of the fragile bit of hope she'd latched onto. "I'm sure she's down there somewhere."

Already plans were forming in her head. Ways to break people out of prison. She would have to go back to Thunderwell now. She had to find Betsy. And even if Betsy wasn't in the dungeon, there was no way she could leave the other people there.

"Who's in charge of the prisoners? Have you seen anyone from Thunderwell down there?"

"I'm afraid not. It's weird, but the only thing I've seen is a couple of those old-fashioned suits of armor. They are in charge down here. I mean, I guess there's people inside of them, but it's hard to tell. They don't walk like normal people, and they never take their headpieces off."

"Do you think they're..." Marianna hesitated, not sure if she wanted to say what she was thinking. But Betsy had believed it was a possibility, so maybe Jay might too. "Magic?"

"I'm ready to believe anything at this point. At least you've escaped. You need to get as far away from here as you can."

Jay could apparently tell what Marianna was thinking by the look on her face. "No milady, don't even think about it. At the very least, you're going to need some help. So you must go back to your family."

"They may already be on their way here. I invited them to come stay." Marianna swallowed hard. "The only thing I can do is go back and see how things stand."

It was her fault everything had started to fall apart. She'd been so insistent about looking in the room despite everyone warning her not to. Would it have mattered? Would she still face the same fate even if she hadn't looked in the room? It certainly seemed so.

"It'll be okay, Jay. I promise, I'm going to find a way to get you out of here and everyone else too. Just because the king bestowed favor on Bludington's family doesn't mean he can use it to mistreat and kill others. I'm…"

"Wait, kill?" Jay interrupted. "Who has he killed?" His eyes were large and worried. "If he's killed someone, you definitely need to leave."

"Oh." Marianna frowned. She hadn't meant to let that information slip. "I mean, I assumed he has," she lied. Badly, apparently, because Jay was shaking his head.

"Milady, I think you need to leave. If you find help, then you could come back and get us."

Marianna didn't answer immediately. If she went for help, that could take days. And who could she trust? It seemed the local authorities hadn't investigated any of the suspicious things surrounding Bludington, including the poor management of the manor village, so maybe they were on his side?

If she went outside of their district, maybe she could find someone who would help, but who knew?

The only thing to do was to go back. She had to assess things. If it was only those armor things moving about, maybe she could slip back into the manor, and no one would be the wiser. No one except Jay and Caden seemed to care that time she and Betsy had been caught in the storm. And Caden, what about him? He could help.

"I'll be careful, Jay. I promise." She reached out and touched his hand. "Everything will be okay."

He shook his head sadly. "I hope so, milady. For your sake and mine."

"Stay strong." Marianna squeezed his hand, then continued ascending the cliffside.

"You too, milady!" Jay called.

"See you soon." She hoisted herself up past the window and out of Jay's sight. She continued climbing in the same careful manner as before.

It seemed to take forever, but Marianna could tell by the sun that only an hour or two had passed. The top of the cliff appeared, amazingly flat compared to the steep, rocky path she had just climbed up. She inhaled deeply, let it out, and pulled herself onto her stomach, rolling away from the edge of the clifftop.

She lay there, catching her breath. She'd done it. She'd made it to the top. Now she had to find some water and food and find her way back to Thunderwell. After several moments, she picked herself up and started walking toward the main road.

Chapter 45

Marianna was nearly to the manor village. Maybe there would be people there who could help her. As she entered, she passed the water fountain. Excited to see fresh water, she darted over to it.

Leaning down she cupped her hands, scooping up water and drinking. It was bitter, with an iron-y, dusty flavor, but it was cool and wet and refreshed her despite its unpleasant taste.

She stood and took in her surroundings. The dull gray rock of the fountain was chipped and worn. A stone woman stood in the center of it, her head had broken off leaving behind an uneven and cracked top.

Had it been like that when she was here days ago? She didn't thought so.

The same group of children from before ran around playing with a worn, dirty ball. Sir Tom was the first to notice her.

"Milady, it's milady," he yelled as he ran over to greet her, the other children not far behind.

"Milady, how are you?" Sir Tom gave a sweeping bow.

"Okay, especially now that I get to see all your lovely faces. How have you been?"

"Good!"

"Great."

"Just fine."

There was a chorus of answers as they all pushed forward, trying to be the closest to her.

"That's good to hear." Marianna sat down on the edge of the fountain and patted the stone next to her. "Come sit."

They moved forward as one unit, squishing in as they clambered onto the ledge.

"Sir Tom, where is the sheriff?"

Tom's face grew serious, and his eyes widened. "The sheriff?"

"Yes, I was thinking he might be able to help with something."

Ben piped up before Tom could say anything else. "Didn't you know, milady? There's no sheriff here."

"Yeah, we haven't had a sheriff here since before I was born," a skinny red-headed boy added.

"Well, who takes care of things around here? Who handles the problems?"

"We all do, milady," Tom replied. "Most of us don't have no parents, and the ones we do have, work all day in milord's mines."

"His mines?" Marianna asked. She hadn't heard anything about this before.

"Yeah, it's half a day's ride there, so our parents stay all week. They come back late on Friday night, are here on Saturday and Sunday, then leave again early Monday morning," the red-headed boy said.

"Ya, we don't really see 'em much at all, 'cept holli-days." This came from a red-headed girl who looked about thirteen or fourteen. She had to be the boy's sister and was the oldest child Marianna had seen.

"I'm in charge of the kids now. Ever since milord declared all the grown people must work his mines. I would 'ave to a gone too, 'cepting they couldn't leave the kids alone that long."

"You mean there are no grown-ups here in town?" Marianna asked incredulously.

How could that be? How had she not known about this? Bludington's evilness was deeper than she thought. How could he leave a bunch of children alone, away from their parents all week, and in the care of a girl barely older than the rest of them?

The girl shook her head seriously. "Just me, milady. I'm real responsible though. No one gets hurt on my watch."

"What kind of mines?" Marianna asked, at a loss for words.

"The luroniam mines," the red-headed boy answered. "They mine the magical blue stone milord needs to keep things running smoothly."

"What?" It came with more disbelief than she had intended, but she couldn't help it. Things kept getting crazier and crazier. She had never heard of either luroniam or a magical blue stone. Not even in any of the fairytales she loved to read.

"Milady, how do you not know the things that happen in your own kingdom?" the red-headed boy asked.

"Jason, no. You can't ask her that. Go tend to your chores." Tom shooed the other boy away.

Jason gave him a dirty look but did as he said.

"The rest of you too. Can't you see milady is tired? Go on, now." Tom motioned them away.

The red-headed girl followed slowly behind them, shooting a wistful glance back at Marianna and Tom.

"Are you all right, milady?" Tom asked. "Is there something I can do to help you?"

Marianna shook her head. "No, I'm afraid the problem is mine. I must figure it out on my own. The only thing..." Marianna hesitated.

"What is it?"

"What do you know about these mines and the magical blue stone your friend was talking about?"

"Oh, that." Tom laughed. "Those are stories. I don't know what's really in the mine. No one will tell me. The grown-ups say that so we won't worry."

Tom's face grew serious. "I don't know what is up in the mines, but I know it's dangerous. That's how my parents were killed - working in the mines."

"I'm so sorry. I didn't know." Marianna laid a gentle hand on Tom's shoulder.

"It's okay. It happened a long time ago." He reached into his bag and pulled out a wedge of yellow cheese and a loaf of sourdough bread. "Here milady, you look hungry. Have a bite."

Marianna wanted to refuse. Who knew if she was taking Tom's lunch or worse yet, his only meal of the day? Her stomach growled loudly, and she knew it'd make Tom feel bad if she didn't accept his offering. And she was starving, having eaten nothing in over twenty-four hours.

The bread was soft and warm, the cheese sharp and full of flavor. It was the most delicious meal she'd ever had, but she supposed that was because she was so hungry.

"Thank-you so much, Sir Tom."

A huge grin covered Tom's face. "You're welcome, milady. I got to go now, but maybe I'll see ya again soon, huh?"

Marianna nodded. "Next time I'm here, I'll look for you."

He darted off down the cobblestone path and disappeared. Marianna sighed. So much for getting help here. It sounded like things were more complicated than she knew. She needed to find a way to help everyone without getting killed.

By the time Marianna reached the manor, the sky was painted with vibrant pinks and oranges. She stopped and stared. As far as she knew, Bludington was still gone. Dunsten hadn't seen her leave. So she could pretend she went for an overnight ride.

She inhaled deeply and let it out, stepping up to the door. As she reached for the knob, it opened. Mrs. Strunk stood in the doorway, an unreadable look on her face.

"Milady, there you are. Out with your horse, I suppose. Well, come on. I haven't got all day, and I need you to approve the dinner menu for when your family comes to visit." Mrs. Strunk motioned her in, seeming not as cross as she usually was.

Marianna followed her, half in a daze. Was Mrs. Strunk being nice to her now? And what did she mean when her family came to visit? Had she received a reply, finally?

"Oh, umm, Mrs. Strunk, did I have any mail today?" Marianna asked.

"No, none at all," Mrs. Strunk replied as she went into her parlor and strode over to her desk. She jerked open the long drawer in the middle and pulled out the house book she was always carrying around. She flipped it open and turned a few pages before coming over to where Marianna stood in the doorway.

"Yes, here it is." She turned the book so Marianna could see.

"Dinner - Roast stew and vegetables with honey rolls and fresh fruit for dessert. Breakfast - Poached eggs and sausage meat pies. Lunch - deli style meat and cheese bar. Tea - lavender honey, orange spice, or black breakfast, variety of tea cookies. Dinner - Full course - cobbler salad, corn chowder soup, filet steak, roasted vegetables, stewed potatoes, strawberry shortcake, and orange sherbet..." Mrs. Strunk continued to rattle off a full four day list of menus, but Marianna couldn't concentrate.

Had she told Mrs. Strunk her family was coming? Why was she suddenly planning meals for them now when Marianna hadn't heard from anyone back home? Did Mrs. Strunk know something she didn't?

"Um, yes, that'll be fine."

"Okay, dear. Thank you. We'll be ready for them whenever they come." Mrs. Strunk nodded, turned without waiting for a reply, and hurried into her parlor, shutting the door behind her.

Marianna stood frozen, staring at the closed door. Had Mrs. Strunk just called her "dear"? She didn't know when her family was coming. She was being proactive as usual, ensuring every avenue had been considered and planned for.

Marianna sighed and shook out her arms. What was the matter with her? She had to get herself together and think clearly. If not, she wouldn't be able to help anyone. She turned and hurried up the stairs to her room.

It was empty without Betsy. Tears pricked her eyes. She swallowed hard. Would she ever see Betsy again? What could she do?

Marianna sniffed and wiped her eyes. She needed a plan. A plan always helped her think more clearly. First, she needed to see how much help she might have here—Caden, possibly Carrie?

She hurried to her nightstand, opening the drawer and pulling out her journal. She carried it to her desk, where she sat and started to plan.

Chapter 46

Marianna stared at the journal page. Despite staying up all night, she only had one feasible idea.

See if Caden or Carrie or any of the servants are willing to help.

Everything else had been scratched out. She tossed the journal onto the bed and sighed. Her eyes were raw and stinging from the lack of sleep, and her head pounded like a foreboding drum signaling death was near. Who knew how much time she had left before Bludington returned and discovered she'd seen the room?

Anxiety swirled up inside her. She jumped up from the bed and began pacing. Her hands formed fists so tight her fingernails dug into her palms. She ignored the pain and pounded her fists against her thighs.

She didn't know who she could trust or how to get to the dungeon where the prisoners were kept. Was that suit of armor still patrolling? How many of those suits came alive? She knew there were at least three located in various parts of the manor, but that was just upstairs. Who knew how many lurked in the dungeon?

Even the servants didn't seem to know what was down there, but they were afraid of it. The idea that any of them would be willing to help her seemed more ludicrous with each passing moment.

She needed some fresh air to clear her head and help her think. She flung open her door and rushed through the hallways and downstairs. At this point, she hardly cared who saw her. She had a feeling nothing would happen, not until Bludington returned.

She stepped into the garden and breathed in deeply. The fresh floral scent calmed her racing heart. She took several deep breaths before walking toward a bench.

It would be okay. She would figure something out. She always figured something out. Like that time when Annette didn't have a dress for her coming out party and no fabric was available because the ports were closed to incoming ships. She'd taken one of their mother's old dresses and remade it into something new. Annette had loved it.

Or that time when a bully had refused to leave Henry alone at school. Marianna suggested Henry show him kindness. She bought some of the boy's favorite candy for Henry to take to him. It'd taken time, but in the end the bully become one of Henry's best friends.

Or when James was failing Grammar Skills. She'd studied with him every night for weeks, making a game of it. He had managed to pull off a passing grade. She'd been so proud of him.

She tried to focus on these things and think positively. But the niggling doubt at the back of her mind reminded her this situation was much worse than any of those. This time she might be in too deep to figure a way out.

The rattle of a carriage interrupted her thoughts and filled her with horror. Had Bludington returned early? She gripped the iron bench, the metal biting into her palms. If he'd returned early, she was out of time.

In a daze, she rose from the bench, plodding toward the front of the house. She barely managed to stop herself from turning the corner where she would be in full view of whoever was coming up the drive.

She pressed against the house. The stone felt cool even through the fabric of her dress. She rested her head against it, allowing the sensation to ease the pain in her head. The clatter of the carriage grew louder. The horses' hooves pounded closer.

"Whoa," the driver yelled.

Everything was silent except for the horses' heavy breathing. Marianna pushed away from the house and peered around the corner.

Wait, was that Wilson climbing down from the carriage? She gasped, covering her mouth as he opened the door and Annette stepped out.

Marianna nearly collapsed in relief. She picked up her skirts and ran.

"Annette, you're here." Her voice broke and tears flooded her eyes, trickling down her cheeks.

Annette turned at the sound of her name. She ran to her sister. They threw their arms around each other and stood that way for several minutes.

Annette finally spoke, her arms still around Marianna. "Why haven't we heard from you until now? I wrote dozens of letters and never received one reply. Then I get this letter about you being frightened, and I was scared witless. I didn't know how I would find you, maybe bound and gagged and locked up in a tiny room. My imagination went crazy. Even Susan said she hadn't heard from you."

Marianna pulled back. "You mean you didn't get any of my letters, except for this last one? Didn't I tell you not to come?"

"Yes, you did write before?" Annette said, ignoring the second question.

"Several other times to you and Papa and Susan." Marianna wanted to scold her sister for coming, especially since she was probably now in danger too. But Marianna felt a little better having her sister by her side.

What had happened to her letters? Had Mrs. Strunk taken them? Destroyed them? She'd acted perfectly fine about her family coming to visit.

"Where is Papa? Did he come? Is he well?" Marianna leaned past Annette, looking at the carriage, but Wilson had already shut the door and was guiding the horses to the stable.

"Papa stayed home. He's doing better. He's still weak, and probably won't ever regain all his strength, but he doesn't cough so much anymore. I didn't tell him what your letter said, because I didn't want to worry him," Annette grasped Marianna's arms.

"But Marianna, no one received any of your other letters." Distress covered her face and tears shimmered in her eyes.

"It must be because I left the letters with Mrs. Strunk. She must not have sent them."

"The housekeeper? Why would she do that?"

Marianna glanced around before dragging Annette back into the gardens.

"What is it? Slow down." Annette stumbled after her, nearly falling, so Marianna slowed her pace but didn't stop until they had reached the end of the gardens farthest from the house. She led Annette over to the bench she had vacated only a few minutes before, and they sat down.

"Something is wrong here, Annette. I found evidence of murders, and if Dunsten and Bludington find out I know, I'm sure they'll kill me. I told you not to come because it's dangerous here."

Annette gasped, clutching Marianna's arm. "Surely, you're mistaken. Your imagination has been working overtime because you've been away from society for so long."

"I saw dead bodies, Annette!" Marianna nearly yelled. She cast a furtive glance around the gardens before sighing and lowering her voice. "I could show them to you, but it was terrifying, and I don't want to ever see that room again. They're..." She didn't know how to explain the horror of that awful room. She stared at Annette, willing her to understand the severity of the situation.

"This is crazy." Annette stared back, her eyes wide, disbelief still hovering in them.

Marianna sighed. How could she explain it all? It was unbelievable. If Annette had been telling her this tale, she wasn't too sure she would've believed it either.

"The bodies were Bludington's wives. They all had the same wedding ring as me. Except there were four of them instead of three, I don't know why. I don't know why Bludington killed them. He's not here right now, so he can't know I went into the room. I think Dunsten is his spy, and he might know, even though I didn't see him watching me that night." She was rambling and this wasn't making sense, but that's how it was in her mind. Nothing was making any sense.

"Bludington gave me a key to the secret room. You remember the room I found during the party Bludington held for us?" She didn't give Annette a chance to answer. She was afraid if she stopped talking, she would break down. "I opened it and found them. The bodies. Then the key was covered in blood I couldn't wash away no matter how hard I tried. And my one friend here, Betsy, is gone now too. Without any explanation, and I found her apron, covered in blood. I think..." Marianna choked up. She swallowed hard and continued.

"I think she's been killed too." Marianna let the words out with a huge breath.

A few tears escaped and trickled down her cheek. "And that's not the worst of it. He has dungeon tunnels underneath the manor filled with prisoners and suits of armor that come alive and chase anyone who goes down there."

"Well, it might be a person inside the armor," she amended.

Annette stared in horror, speechless for several minutes. "That's almost too gruesome to believe, but you're obviously frightened by all this. You haven't gone crazy, have you? What have I done to you?" Annette began crying.

Marianna rolled her eyes, smacking her sister on the shoulder. Leave it to Annette to find an obnoxious way to make her stop crying.

"I haven't gone crazy, and I have proof of this insane story without showing you the room. Stop blaming yourself for my being here. I agreed to come, it was my choice, remember. Now come on." Marianna pulled Annette to her feet, thankful her sister hadn't been the one originally sent into this mess.

"But only after I practically made you agree by saying I would marry Bludington."

"Annette, stop worrying about it. We have more important things to take care of right now."

Laughter drifted from the house interrupting Marianna's thoughts. She and her sister were hidden by the thick foliage of rose bushes, but just because they couldn't be seen didn't mean they couldn't be heard.

She put a hand on Annette's arm and a finger to her mouth. "Shh."

As she rose from the bench, voices carried through the foliage. Voices that were getting closer and closer. Marianna barely managed to stop herself from squeezing Annette's arm painfully. Who was coming down here? Had they heard anything she'd said?

Twigs snapped and fallen leaves crunched. The voices stopped, and Marianna sucked in a breath as two figures stepped around the rose bushes.

Chapter 47

"Miss Marianna, is this your sister?" Carrie called as she and Leah approached.

Marianna nearly collapsed in relief. Still, how had they known she was out here?

Carrie smiled at Annette and dipped into curtsy. "It's a pleasure to meet you, Miss."

"Oh, yes," Leah added, struggling to copy Carrie's perfect curtsy. She wrinkled her nose and gave up, bowing instead.

Carrie smacked her arm. "Stop being ridiculous," she hissed. "All you have to do is smile." She turned back to Annette with a fresh smile on her face. "Ignore her. She's still in training." She cleared her throat and turned to Marianna. "Mrs. Strunk heard the carriage pull up and sent us down here to see who it was and if you needed anything. She's got some soup warming on the stove if your sister is hungry."

"And we can draw a bath for her if she'd like to wash up from her journey here," Leah added, clearly trying to improve upon the first impression she had made.

Annette, ever charming, gave Leah a big smile. "That sounds lovely. Thank you for thinking of me."

Leah returned the smile, clasped her hands together and clapped in excitement.

Annette turned to Carrie. "Hot soup sounds perfect. I'm famished."

Carrie gave her a small smile. "Okay, right this way, Miss." She grabbed Leah's arm, stopping her from gawking, as she pulled her back toward the house.

Marianna put a hand on Annette's arm, holding her back a minute as she whispered, "Don't say anything about what I just told you."

"But they seem so nice."

"Yes, but I don't know who we can trust, so be careful."

"All right," Annette agreed in a miffed tone. "But we don't have to be rude." She pulled away from Marianna's grasp and hurried to catch up with the maids.

As Marianna watched them hurry up the hill, she recalled what Jay had said about seeing Carrie's fiancé in the dungeons. That had to be why Carrie was so emotional when she warned Marianna about the dangers here. But surely if she found out that he was still alive and could be rescued, she would help them.

She had to find the right time to talk to her. A time when no one else was around.

But she could take advantage of this moment to talk to Leah. She hurried up to the girl and tapped her on the shoulder. "Can I speak with you?"

Leah stopped and watched as Carrie and Annette kept moving closer to the house. "Uh, of course, milady."

"This will only take a minute. I wanted to ask that you have the room next to mine cleaned and set up for Annette to stay in."

"Uh..." Shock covered Leah's face, and for once she seemed speechless.

"That's not a problem, is it?" Marianna asked.

"I guess not." Leah lowered her voice and continued. "But are you sure, milady?"

Why wouldn't she be sure? The room had been empty all this time. "Is there something wrong with the room?"

Leah shook her head, glancing back up at Carrie and Annette who were nearly at the manor house. She sighed and turned back to Marianna. "Nothing wrong, exactly. It's just..." She threw another glance toward Carrie.

"Well, it's just what?" Marianna prompted.

"I can't believe no one told you," Leah whispered. She cleared her throat and spoke louder. "That was Lady Elianna's room. It hasn't been used since she... um." Leah paused awkwardly, as if afraid to say the word "died." She took another deep breath. "It hasn't been used since she's been gone."

Since she'd been murdered. Had they seriously put her in the room next to the most recently murdered wife?

Whose idea had that been? Lord Bludington's or the servants? Probably most of the servants didn't know she'd been murdered, but still it was morbid.

"Umm, that's fine." Marianna schooled her features, hoping Leah hadn't been able to tell how shocked she was by this new piece of information. "We'd like to be close together."

"Okay, if you're sure." Leah still looked uncertain.

"Yes, it's perfectly fine." Marianna laid a hand on Leah's shoulder. "I'd greatly appreciate it."

"Sure, I'll get some girls to help me clean it immediately." Leah smiled weakly before hurrying away and up to the manor.

After a quick lunch, the girls retreated to Marianna's room to wait while the servants cleaned the room next door. Marianna locked her door before going to her dresser. She pulled out the linen bundle with the key, unwrapped it, and handed the key to her sister. Annette examined it, dropping it with a little squeal, before snatching it back up and examining it.

"Marianna, there's blood on it," she whispered.

"Yes, and it won't come off. Betsy and I scrubbed and scrubbed, and every time we thought we had it clean, new drops of blood seeped out of the key and settled on its surface."

"That's impossible." Annette's voice was weak. Her eyes begged Marianna to tell her it wasn't true.

"See for yourself. Go try to wash it off."

Annette hesitantly took the key over to the wash bin and began washing it. Soon she was scrubbing furiously, desperate to get the blood off. "It really won't come off. Why won't it come off, Marianna?" Annette's voice was high and strained.

"I don't know. All I can guess it the rumors that Bludington uses dark magic are true, and he's placed a spell on the key. He has a room up in the tower. It's filled with tubes of weirdly colored liquids and things. Maybe he brewed the spell there."

"Seriously?" Annette whispered, her eyes wide as she covered her mouth with her hand.

Marianna nodded and continued. "If someone opens the murder room, the key becomes bloodstained, and nothing anyone does will remove it."

She sighed. "I don't know what to do, Annette. Or if anyone will help. Everyone thinks they're going to be locked up in the dungeon if they betray Bludington and maybe they will be."

She swallowed hard as she remembered seeing Jay's face through the barred window, the shackles clasping his wrists.

"There was one servant, Jay, a stable hand, who was trying to help me. We got chased by that living armor, and he got caught and put in the dungeon. I'd heard strange noises sometimes coming from below us, but I wanted to believe it was my imagination. Clearly, it was not."

"If there's a key like this, I would think all other strange things you think you hear or see would probably be real." Annette wrinkled her nose and dropped the key into the water bowl.

"Why didn't you come home? When you realized things were off here?" She pushed her blonde curls off her shoulder and sank onto Marianna's bed. Marianna shook her head before sitting next to her sister. How could she even explain it?

"Have you heard from our brothers at all?" she asked, changing the subject.

"Yes!" Annette's face brightened. "They're coming home soon. Matthew is coming back with them too. The border skirmish is over, and they're waiting for their orders to return home."

"Annette, that's wonderful. Our brothers are safe, and Matthew too. Maybe now he'll ask you to marry him." Marianna reached over and squeezed her sister's hand.

Annette shook her head. "I can hardly think about that when your life is in danger, Marianna."

"But don't you see, all we need to do is send word to our brothers. They can come and get us. Bludington can't stop them without making a scene, and he wouldn't risk that. He values his status with the king too much. He would have to let me go."

"What about his magic? He could use that to stop them or kill us." Annette's eyes were wide.

"The king will send people to investigate if anything happens to the soldiers, and if Bludington gets caught dabbling with dark magic, he'll go to prison."

Marianna was feeling better than she had in a long time. If her brothers could get here before Bludington, she was sure things would be fine.

"Let's write a letter, and we'll take it to the village to be sure it gets mailed."

Chapter 48

They'd barely finished composing a letter when there was a knock at the door. Annette followed Marianna as she opened it. Dunsten stood there with two burly men.

"Milady." Dunsten gave a little bow. "Your sister, I presume." He motioned to Annette. Marianna nodded. "A pleasure to meet you, miss."

"And you as well, sir." Annette pushed past Marianna to offer her hand. Dunsten took it and lifted it to his lips, not bothering to disguise the smirk there. Marianna glared at Annette, but Annette didn't seem to notice.

Dunsten turned to the men behind him. "This is Rantoo." He motioned to the first man, then the second. "And this is Cardom. We've had some disturbing news. There are thieves about, so they're going to be your bodyguards."

"What?' Marianna gasped. "Aren't we safe inside the manor?"

"Ideally, yes. But to be cautious, I've assigned them to stay with you both for the foreseeable future."

"How kind of you, sir. Thank you for thinking of our safety." Annette smiled.

Marianna stared at her. Had she not heard everything Marianna had told her? Did she not understand the severity of the situation they were in? Dunsten could be in on this whole thing with Bludington.

"If you're ready for dinner, can we escort you down?" Dunsten gave Annette such a charming smile that Marianna nearly laughed. She'd never seen him smile like that.

"Of course, I'm famished! I only had a bit of soup for lunch and no breakfast at all." Annette stepped out into the hall and glanced back at her sister. "Are you coming?"

Marianna nodded mutely, at a loss for words. Dunsten led the way to the dining room, the girls behind him, the bodyguards taking up the rear. Dinner passed in a blur. Annette kept up a lively flow of chatter with Dunsten and the bodyguards as well as with every single servant who entered the dining room. Marianna didn't have the energy to keep up.

If Annette loved this place so much, she should've come here. Everyone here clearly loved her too. She probably never would've entered the forbidden room or found herself in such a horrible predicament.

By the time dinner was over, Marianna was so worked up, she didn't say a word on the way back to her room. She flung her door open, stalked over to her bed, and plunged down on it.

Annette followed, closing the door gently. "What is the matter with you?"

Marianna shrugged her shoulders and didn't reply.

"Seriously, what is the matter? Is there suddenly some new development I don't know about?" Annette put her hands on her hips and stared down at Marianna.

Marianna pushed herself up. "You're not taking this seriously enough. I told you couldn't trust anyone, and you're waltzing about the place like you're best friends with everyone, including Dunsten, who is quite possibly Bludington's henchman."

Annette shrugged her shoulders then crossed her arms over her chest. "It doesn't hurt to be nice to people. If you'd been a little nicer, maybe you would know who you could trust."

Marianna's mouth dropped open. "If I had— I can't believe you! You have no idea what it was like here all by myself. I was nice enough. And I had a friend. I already told you that. Bludington probably murdered her when he found out she was helping me investigate things."

"That's part of the problem too." Annette's voice had taken on a judgmental tone. "Why did you even feel the need to investigate? Why do you always have to snoop in things that aren't your business? And what actual proof do you have that Bludington's wives were murdered? Sure, you say the bodies are in that room, but maybe he's a weirdo who wanted to keep them nearby. Maybe they died from natural causes."

"Ha! Natural causes." Marianna jumped up from the bed and started pacing the floor. "I just... I can't even." She shrugged her shoulders. "You're so judge-y, Annette. I did this for you and father. The least you could do is believe me." Marianna whirled around to face her sister.

"For that matter, why would he give me the key ring and specifically tell me not to go into that room if he didn't have something to hide? Even if he didn't murder them, he certainly isn't innocent. I told everyone from the beginning there was something off about him, but no one wanted to believe it, so I don't know why I suddenly expect you to believe it now."

Annette shook her head. "You always think you know something that everyone else doesn't, Marianna. There's no way to know things before you find evidence of them."

Marianna waved her arm at the dresser where she had hidden the bloodied key. "What about the blood that won't wash off the key? You saw that with your own eyes."

Annette shook her head. "It's still not proof of a murder. And who's to say the blood stain isn't just stubborn and won't wash off." She sighed and walked over to the door.

"I'm tired. It's been a long day. I'm going to bed." She didn't wait for Marianna to reply as she slammed the door shut behind her.

A heavy thump woke Marianna. Everything was dark except for the pale square of moonlight that cast a silvery glow into the center of her floor. What had made that noise? She strained her ears.

Silence.

It'd come from next door. Next door where Annette was sleeping. She threw back the covers and bounded up, fumbling on the nightstand for the matches. Her hand knocked into her single candle sending it tumbling from its holder and onto the floor. She stopped its roll with her foot, bent down, and picked it up, shoving it back inside of the holder.

She slid her hand across the nightstand again, still searching for the matches. An old pencil pricked her palm, giving her a splinter, but no matches. Where could they be? She'd had a whole box sitting there when she went to bed. She pulled her hand back and shook it.

Creak. Creak.

The door must have opened. She looked over at it, her eyes straining in the darkness. Shadows played tricks on her eyes, seeming to grow bigger into something they weren't. Something moved.

"Annette," Marianna hissed. "Annette, is that you?"

Silence greeted her. She thrust her hand back onto the nightstand, ignoring the pain from the splinter. A teacup clanged against its saucer. Her knuckles knocked into the stack of books on the far edge as her fingers grasped the match box. She yanked it open, grabbed a match and struck it against the strike bar. She lit her candle, then blew out the match. Smoke swirled up into her face stinging her eyes and nose and making her cough.

"Are you okay?" A voice startled Marianna.

She barely held onto the candle as she jumped, choking back a scream. Annette stood in the doorway, in her nightgown, her hair a tousled mess, holding her own candlestick.

"Annette, why didn't you answer me earlier? You nearly gave me a heart attack."

Annette rushed into the room, her eyes red and swollen. "I'm so sorry, for everything. Not believing you and saying those things. I just... I..." Tears shimmered in her eyes, as she choked on a sob.

She was clutching some papers. Papers she'd found in the dead wife's room. Something that had caused her to apologize. Dread swirled through Marianna's belly, curling into a tight ball in the pit of her stomach.

"Annette, what is that?" She pointed at the bundle.

Annette shook her head and clutched them to her chest. "They might not be real. You can't freak out."

"Annette, what is it?" Marianna stepped closer to her sister and held out her hand.

"I'm so sorry," was all Annette managed to get out before breaking into sobs. She thrust the papers at Marianna. "They're..." She gasped for air before continuing. "Letters."

Marianna grabbed the papers which were now half crumpled from Annette's fist. She sat her candle down on the nightstand and spread the letters out with her palm. Neat, spidery writing covered the first page along with a date from two years ago.

Dear Elianna,

I'm more scared than ever now. You must come home. Father will forgive you. He has to. He'd much rather have a live daughter than a dead one, I'm sure of that. I'll speak with him, and he'll listen. Please, make immediate plans to come home. It's not safe there. Not with what you have discovered. I'll send Paul to meet you at Tringhill. It won't be a problem at all. Please, please, please, come home!

Always your loving sister,

Lygia

Marianna lifted the page and looked at another letter, dated a few weeks before the previous one.

Dear Elianna,

It sounds a bit terrifying there. Dungeons and stories of ghosts haunting the cliffs. Do you really think it's all true? I'm sorry Father sent you there. He should have been more compassionate and willing to listen to your side of things. You are safe there, though, aren't you? You would tell me if you weren't, right? Do you want me to come and visit? It would be nice to get away from things for awhile. Write soon and let me know!

Love always your sister,

Lygia

Annette thrust some more pages in her face. "More letters?" Marianna looked up hopefully. Annette shook her head, tears still streaming down her face, her breaths coming in ragged gasps.

Marianna took the pages. One side was ragged as if it had been ripped from a book. She quickly put the pages in order, gasping when she came to a full-page illustration—an exact replica of the creepy blue-haired dwarf painting.

This was the key. It had to be. She pulled Annette into a quick hug before motioning for her to sit on the bed.

"It's going to be okay," she murmured. "The answers are here. We have to figure them out." She sat next to Annette and began reading the story.

Chapter 49

The Hag's Tale

There was once an old hag who had plentiful magical talents. People from all over the land would travel to see her. The old hag only had one precious thing, her daughter.

Before she had been a hag, she was a beautiful princess. Princes from every nearby land came to woo her, but only one won her heart. They were married in a lavish ceremony and merriment filled the land. But it didn't last long, for soon a great dark war covered the land and the prince was killed in battle.

The princess's only consolation was the little baby coming. The war raged on, and eventually a beautiful baby girl was born to the princess. The princess knew her baby wouldn't be safe from those who sought the crown, so she took her baby and left the palace in the middle of the night. She ran and ran until she was sure she was far enough away for her baby to be safe.

She found a quaint little village with an inn that needed a housekeeper. The job came with room and board, and so the princess had found a new home for her and her daughter. For many years, the princess lived undiscovered, until one day her daughter fell ill. The princess went to everyone in the village who had any kind of skill as a healer, but none could help her daughter. Just when she was about to lose hope, a wizened old man came to her and asked, "What are you willing to do to save your daughter?"

"Anything!" the princess cried. "Anything, I would give my life for hers. Can you help us?"

"I can," replied the man. "I can give you magic that will save your daughter, but magic always comes with a price."

Without stopping to think, the princess cried, "Yes, yes, give me the magic that will save my daughter!"

"Take hold of my staff, then," said the wizened old man. The princess clutched the staff. A gust of wind blew up around her. It spun around her faster and faster until she could no longer see the old man. A strange calm coursed through the princess's body. She knew this was not normal and she realized she might not live, but she also knew this would help her daughter, and that was all that mattered to her.

As quickly as it had come, the wind disappeared, and the old man handed the princess a worn and tattered book. "Everything you need to save your daughter is in here," he said.

"Where? Where in the book?" The princess flipped through the book desperately. She looked up when the man didn't reply, but he was no longer there.

"What? Where could he have possibly gone?" The princess didn't want to waste time as she feared her daughter's condition was worsening. She ran into the inn and up the stairs to the room where she and her daughter lived. The matron of the inn met her at the door.

"Who are you?" the matron demanded.

"What do you mean?" cried the princess. "I am Brenna's mother."

"Taura?" The matron's eyes widened, and she covered her mouth. "Is that really you?"

"Of course it's me. Why would you even have to ask?"

The matron leaned back into the room and yanked the old, wooden-framed looking glass from the wall and shoved in front of the princess's face.

A hag stared back at the princess. Gray hair as bristly as straw, wrinkled, pock-marked skin, and a long, droopy nose with a wart on it had replaced the princess's youthful beauty. She lifted her hand to the coarse hair then ran her hand over the warty nose as if to convince herself that what she saw in the mirror was real.

"Magic always comes with a price," she whispered to herself. She stared at her reflection, then sighed. "It doesn't matter." She pushed past the matron and rushed over to the bed where Brenna lay. Her eyes were closed, but Taura could still hear her shallow breaths. Taura rested her hand on Brenna's forehead. It was still so hot.

Taura pulled the tattered book up onto the bed and started flipping through the pages: How To Create a Love Potion, Destroying Your Enemies Once and

For All, Speaking to Animals, Creating Everlasting Fire, and finally, *How to Heal the Sick.*

It didn't take Taura long to follow the directions and heal her daughter. A strange energy coursed through her body. Taura felt it when it left her and jumped into her daughter. Only seconds later, Brenna's body temperature had dropped to normal, and her eyelids fluttered open.

"Momma?"

"Yes, I'm here darling." Taura took her daughter's hand and squeezed it.

"You look different, Momma."

"I know, darling. But I'm still the same inside."

"You had to do it to save me." The girl said this matter-of-factly, then sat up and continued before Taura could think of anything to say.

"I'm hungry. What are we having for supper?"

And that was all that was ever said about Taura's change in appearance. It seemed everyone in the village knew she had somehow gained magic, and they brought her all their problems. Some she could help. Others she had to tell that not even magic could help them. She was paid well for her services, and soon she had enough to buy a little cottage for herself and Brenna.

Brenna grew into a beautiful young woman, and she turned the heads of all the boys in the village. Between Brenna's beauty and her mother's magic, it wasn't long before people from other villages began coming to see them. Their fame grew so much that one day a wealthy lord came to see them.

At first, Brenna was excited. "A lord. Just imagine, Momma. A lord coming to see us." Her mother didn't share in her daughter's excitement, and at first Brenna wondered why. Then she met the lord. He was a strange, little man with evil intent, and so Taura refused to help him.

In anger, he stole Brenna away in the night. It was morning before Taura knew she was gone. Taura immediately set out after them, getting directions to where the lord lived from some kind men at the inn.

"But ma'am, you don't want to go there," the first man insisted.

"I must, for he has taken my daughter."

"I don't mean to sound crude, ma'am, but you can count your daughter as gone. If he's taken her, you'll not likely get her back. There's a reason no one ventures out there where he lives. No one lives to come back and tell the tale."

But Taura refused to listen to the man's warning. She gathered some supplies, wrapped her warmest cloak around her shoulders, and set off.

As she had reached the edge of town, one of the gentlemen from the inn came chasing after her. "Ma'am, ma'am, if you insist on going, here please take my horse. You don't stand a chance of getting there in time on foot."

Taura inhaled deeply and rubbed the horse's nose. He was a large, magnificent animal, dappled gray with a snowy white mane and tail. He was clearly worth a fortune in gold.

"But sir, I have no coins to pay you for this fine animal."

The gentleman shook his head. "I don't need any coin. It's my gift to you. And a coward's gift at that. For if I were truly brave, I would go with you. Maybe in my younger days..." His voice was wistful, and a far-off look covered his face. Then it vanished, and he cleared his throat. "Anyway, please take it. I want to do something to help you."

Taura nodded. She had learned not to turn down genuine offers of help. "Then let me give you a little something." She dug through her bag and pulled out a vial of shimmering blue liquid and handed it to the man.

"W-what's this?"

"Something to use in dire circumstances. Next time you find yourself in such straits, this will be whatever you need to get out of them for I have a feeling you might find yourself in such straits in the not-too-distant future."

Confusion spread across the man's face. "I'm done with all of that dangerous stuff. That's why I'm not going with you."

Taura smiled and patted his hand. "But it might not be done with you." Then she grabbed the pommel and lifted herself onto the horse's back. "What's his name?" she asked.

"Aquarius," the man replied. "He loves water."

Taura laughed and kneed Aquarius into action. He sprang forward like a bolt of lightning, and Taura found she had to hold on for dear life.

Aquarius ran like the wind and soon Taura found that they had entered the Old Wood. She pulled back on the reins, slowing Aquarius to a walk. "It's dangerous through here, boy. We must tread carefully."

Aquarius snorted in agreement, his eyes wide, the whites flashing as he danced about.

Despite strange, howling noises and several rustling bushes, they made it through the wood without harm until they came upon a clearing. A large bonfire leapt toward the sky, and before it stood the strange lord. Brenna sat next to him, her hands tied together in front of her body. A blue strip of cloth covered her mouth.

She caught sight of her mother riding up on the grand horse and let out a muffled cry. The lord pulled Brenna to him and placed a dagger against her neck.

"No, wait, please!" Taura jumped from Aquarius's back and ran toward them.

"Back, woman. You're awfully nimble for an old hag. Almost like you weren't an old hag after all. Just made to look like one by magic. I know you have the power to give me what I want. The question is, is it worth your daughter's life to keep it from me?"

"I told you magic is not free. And magic like that comes with a steep price. The price of lives—not only the ones you take to achieve your goal, but also your own. It will ruin you, make no mistake."

"Then that would be my decision, wouldn't it?" He gripped Brenna tighter and pressed the knife harder. A thin trickle of blood dripped down Brenna's neck.

"Okay, okay. I'll do it." Taura sighed heavily and sank to the ground. "It seems the time has come for me to pay my full cost for taking this magic."

"Good." A devilish smile covered the lord's face, and he withdrew the knife. "My boy will be here any minute now, and he will get you the things you require for the spell."

Soon a tall, thin boy with ghostly white skin appeared. He took Taura's list and located every single thing she needed, then disappeared as quickly as he had come. Taura got to work on the spell, anxious to be done with this horrid man. He hovered over her the entire time.

When she had finished, she handed him a vial. "Drink this. It will give you what you want."

Taura looked over to where her daughter had been moments before, but she was no longer there. "Where is Brenna?"

The lord ignored her and tossed back the nasty green liquid the vial contained.

"Where is she, you idiot? You made a promise!"

The lord cackled as his appearance began to change. "You should know better than to trust someone like me. I needed your daughter for the first sacrifice. She is gone already."

Taura fell to her knees. "What? No, it can't be. You promised," she wailed as she watched his transformation continue, but she knew in her heart it was true, for how else had he been able to transform so quickly.

Grief threatened to overwhelm her, but a voice in the back of her head chastised her. "What have I done? How could I have done this? I've unleashed a monster on the world."

She knew there was no way to stop what had already transpired, but there might be a way to stop this evil man in the future. She quickly made some adjustments to her spell and doused the lord with the addendum. He was so ecstatic about his transformation he didn't even notice.

"If only a girl brave enough, true enough, and caring enough would take action, the curse will be lifted, and the lord will return to his natural form." Taura whispered the words into the wind, and she prayed that one day such a girl would exist.

Marianna finished reading the story, her throat tight, tears prickling her eyes. Thoughts raced through her head faster than she could hold onto them. Was this true? It had to be, didn't it? Lord Bludington had kidnapped and killed the old hag's daughter. It had been his first kill. And the hag had to be the same one who had come and warned her in the woods.

But what was Bludington's goal? Whatever it was, he was beyond desperate and even more dangerous than she had imagined. He wanted whatever it was no matter the cost.

He'd already killed four women for it. Five with the hag's daughter.

There was one final page—a letter from Elianna that was longer than the others. Marianna's eyes flew over the page as the knot in her stomach grew into a monster.

My dear Lygia,

I write this from the closet in my room. I haven't got much time. I can only pray this reaches you, if not in time to save me, at least in time to save others. Things are far worse than I realized. Bludington has not only killed his previous two wives, but he also killed his own sister. I'm afraid nothing is off-limits in his quest to obtain the power of the blue Heart Stone. He's sent every grown and half-grown person from the manor village to work in the mine harvesting it. Anyone who has dared defied him has been thrown into the dungeon. Hundreds of servants and townspeople are imprisoned there now even as I write this. But Lygia, this is the most important thing. He must not be allowed to reach the center of the mine where the Heart Stone is embedded. Once he has that, the only other thing he will need is a couple more bodies. If he obtains the Heart Stone, I fear all Anderi will be lost. He must be stopped. Please, whatever you and Father can do to stop him, you must. This is my last request! STOP HIM!

Your loving sister,

Elianna

"The Heart Stone," Marianna whispered. "The people are still working the mines, so he must not have gotten it yet. But what does it do?" She stared at the letter as if it could come alive and answer her.

"Marianna, did you see what it said? We must leave here now. This instant! That crazy man has planned all along to kill you. You must see that."

Marianna ignored her sister, still lost in the whirlwind of thoughts that whipped through her brain. What could she do? She couldn't leave. She knew that much. Jay, Carrie's fiancé, and so many others were still held captive in the dungeon. And Sir Tom and his friends who were left in the manor village to care for themselves.

Annette grabbed her arm and shook her. "Marianna, did you hear me? We must leave now!" Her eyes were wide and still red from her tears, but her sobs had subsided. "What are you doing? Why are you just sitting there?" Her voice grew in intensity and volume, snapping Marianna out of her daze.

"Shh," Marianna hissed. "Those bodyguards out there will hear you, and I'm thinking more and more they aren't actually bodyguards.

Annette gasped. "You're right. How did we not know that before?" Her eyes got bigger and filled with terror. "How are we going to get past them? We're doomed. Lord Bludington's going to..." Her breaths were shallow and ragged. "He's going to... come back... and kill us."

Marianna grasped Annette's shoulder and leaned forward to look into her sister's eyes. "You must calm down. Deep breaths." Marianna demonstrated, breathing with her sister until she had calmed.

"Now, listen, we aren't leaving, but we're not going to get killed either. I have a plan."

Chapter 50

The next day, Marianna led Annette to the library.

"We'll be in here all day reading. I've already alerted the staff and asked them to bring refreshments at the proper time," she informed the guards as she pushed Annette into the room. She followed her sister inside and slammed the door shut behind them.

"That wasn't at all suspicious," Annette hissed at her.

Marianna ignored the comment as she swept her arm out as if presenting the library to a group of onlookers.

Annette gasped, spinning, trying to look at everything all at once. "This is amazing." She ran over to the velvet covered couch, ran her hand along the soft fabric, then twirled around under the large crystal chandelier before dashing over to the sliding ladder. Hopping onto it, Annette laughed as she leaned in, and the ladder rolled along the shelf.

"Why did I never come in here during the party? Now I know why you were always hiding out in here."

Marianna grabbed Annette's arm and pulled her off the ladder. "We don't have time for distractions. Come on." She dragged her sister over to the hidden door and opened it.

Annette gasped. "How did you find this? It's covered in the same wallpaper as the rest of the wall. I would've never noticed it."

Marianna put a finger to her lip. "Shhh, this hallway echoes. We can't risk anyone hearing us."

Annette grew serious, as if suddenly remembering the danger they were in. If their plan didn't work, they wouldn't make it out of this place alive. She swallowed hard and nodded.

Marianna picked up the candlestick from a nearby table and started down the narrow hallway. "Pull the door closed," she whispered.

"All the way? But how will we get back out of this tunnel?"

"Yes, all the way. If the guards happen to come into the room, we can't risk them knowing where we are. We'll be able to get out."

Annette gave her a doubtful look before obeying and shutting the door behind them. The hall went dark, the single flame from the candlestick giving barely enough light to see right in front of them. Marianna paused, allowing her eyes to adjust, then started forward cautiously.

The hall got narrower the farther they went, twisting this way and that. The walls and ceiling were closing in on them. Marianna sucked in a steadying breath. She couldn't freak out now. They had a plan, and she had to see it through.

Annette stayed close on her heels, silent. Marianna glanced back. Her sister looked as serious as she'd ever seen her. At least she'd realized the dire straits they were in. Still, it hurt Marianna's heart to be the cause of Annette's solemn attitude. She trudged forward, hoping this would work and it would all be over soon.

Every so often they passed a little door, an entrance to some other room in the manor. Marianna carefully counted the doors, remembering Carrie had told them to enter the twenty-fourth one. She hadn't been sure Carrie would help them, but she'd taken that gamble and it'd paid off.

Carrie's eyes had shimmered with tears when Marianna told her Jay had found her fiancé in the dungeon. And when she'd proposed her plan, Carrie hadn't even hesitated before agreeing to go along with it. She'd even managed to convince Leah and a couple of other maids to help as well.

Marianna reached the twenty-fourth door, praying she counted right and twisted the knob, pushing into the room. Bright light assaulted her eyes.

"You made it," Carrie's voice reassured her.

Marianna's eyes adjusted, and she sighed in relief. They were in the servants' prep area right off the kitchen. A large window looked out into the servants' courtyard where the chicken coop, goat pen, and cow barn stood. Inside the prep area sat a long skinny table, taking up the length of the back wall. A basket of fresh eggs and a pail of milk sat on top of it. Bits of hay and dirt covered the floor. A rustic, earthy smell filled the little room.

"Are you ready to do this?" Carrie's eyes were bright, her fingers tapping out a nervous beat on the table.

Marianna swallowed hard and nodded, casting a glance back at Annette.

"As ready as we'll ever be." Annette's voice was high and thin, but she had a steely look of determination in her eyes.

Carrie nodded. "Wait here while I check to see there's no one in the kitchen."

Thanks to Carrie's high-ranking position in the servant hierarchy, she'd been able to send all the kitchen maids to tend to other tasks. She'd also volunteered to fill in for Cook, whose daughter recently had a baby Cook hadn't seen. Cook was thrilled and hadn't hesitated to take Carrie up on her offer.

Carrie stepped back into the prep room as Leah charged through the other door.

"He's here!" Leah's face was white, and she was shaking. "L-lord Bludington." She waved her arm toward the manor's entrance. "He came back early. His carriage is coming up the drive now."

Her arm was still waving as she blabbered on. "Our plans are all ruined. He's going to catch us and kill us. I'll never see my family again." She wailed and dropped to her knees, sobbing.

"What?" Marianna whispered.

Annette grabbed her arm, terror in her eyes.

Carrie jumped forward and grabbed Leah's arm, yanking her up off the floor. "Be quiet," she hissed. "We'll get caught with you carrying on like that." She glanced over at Marianna.

"Is anyone in the kitchen?" Marianna asked.

Carrie shook her head.

Fear spiked through Marianna with the force of a lightning bolt. Already things weren't going according to the plan, but maybe she could still salvage it. She took a deep breath, forcing her fear back as she dug into her pockets. She pulled out Bludington's key ring.

It jangled merrily, her hands shaking as she thrust it into her sister's hand. Even the keys were taunting her. But she wasn't going down without a fight.

Annette stared at her, trying to shove the keys back into Marianna's hands. "No," she whispered, a horrified look on her face. "You have to come with us."

"The only way this is going to work is if I go meet Bludington and distract him from finding out what you are doing."

"He'll kill you." Annette's voice cracked on the last word.

"Not if you find everyone first and set them free. Bludington won't stand a chance against all those people." Marianna forced a smile on her face, barely keeping the fear from creeping into her voice.

Annette shook her head vigorously. "No, you can't do this. You must come with us."

"I must do this. It's my responsibility to free those people, and this is the only way."

"But why... why is it..." Annette wrapped her arms around herself and shook her head. "How is it your responsibility?"

"Um, sorry to interrupt, but we don't have much time. If we're going to do this, we have to do it now," Carrie said.

Marianna nodded, pulling Annette into a hug. "It'll be fine, I promise," she whispered into her sister's ear, not sure she it was a promise she could keep.

"What if I never see you again?" Annette whispered back. "I'm so sorry for not believing you and for saying all those things and for forcing you into this horrible mess." She pulled back and looked into Marianna's eyes, tears shimmering in her own.

Marianna nodded, afraid to speak around the knot in her throat. Tears pricked at her eyes, and she knew it'd only take a word or two to release them. She cleared her throat and turned to Carrie who was still holding a distraught Leah.

"You'll be able to handle both of them?" she asked, nodding at her sister.

"Of course, milady. It's been an honor to serve you." To Marianna's shock, she reached out and squeezed Marianna's hand. Marianna had never seen Carrie be affectionate with anyone. "Watch yourself, milady. Use those brains you've been using this whole time, and you may outsmart him." She pulled away, dragging Leah with her, motioning for Annette to follow.

Annette started after Carrie, stopping to squeeze Marianna in a hug one more time. "Be careful. I love you."

"I love you too," Marianna whirled away and rushed out the door before Annette could see the tears that'd escaped.

She drew in a shuddering breath as she hurried to the front parlor. She had to calm herself. It wouldn't do for Bludington to see her upset. He'd suspect she was up to something.

She swallowed hard and took several deep breaths, clearing her thoughts and thinking only of the mission. She pushed open the dining room door and stepped into the hall. She was ready to meet her fate, whatever that might be.

Chapter 51

"I thought you were spending all day in the library." Mrs. Strunk's strident voice startled Marianna, and she took a step back.

"Um, yes, I was going to, but I heard that Lord Bludington had returned." Marianna stumbled over her words, sucking in a gulp of air. She had to calm down or they would know something was going on. "I thought I should greet him since he's been gone for so long."

"Hmm." Mrs. Strunk pursed her lips, staring at Marianna for several beats before nodding approval and turning towards the front door. "That's appropriate. Come with me."

Marianna had to nearly run to keep up with Mrs. Strunk's long, purposeful strides.

"I've already had tea prepared. You may take it with Lord Bludington in the front parlor."

The front parlor? Mrs. Strunk's parlor? She was allowing them to take tea there? She barely allowed the maids in to clean, and she had been quite angry the one time Marianna had approached her there.

Before she could say anything else, they were at the door, and Mrs. Strunk was throwing it open. Bludington stepped from the carriage and hurried up the stairs.

"Mrs. Strunk, how have you been?" He threw an arm around the housekeeper, squeezing her in a hug.

Had he always been so friendly with her? Marianna had never seen such a big grin on Mrs. Strunk's face. He wasn't friendly with many servants, though she thought Dunsten would've been here to welcome Bludington home. Where was Dunsten, anyway? He hadn't been around much lately.

"And Miss Marianna, how lovely to be in your presence again." Bludington turned to her and held out his hand. She accepted it.

He grasped her hand firmly, lifting it and pressing a kiss there. His lips were cold, and a shiver rushed down her spine. She wanted to rip her hand away from the vile man, but she knew that would only endanger her sister and friends and the plan they were attempting to carry out.

She pasted a smile on her face and bobbed into a brisk curtsey. "The same to you, sir."

Bludington's grin widened. "I missed seeing my lovely bride-to-be so much I had to return early." His smile turned into a smirk as he dropped Marianna's hand and turned back to Mrs. Strunk.

Chills spread out from Marianna's spine, engulfing her whole torso. She wasn't sure if she could keep up this pretense.

"Everything is ready?" Bludington whispered as he leaned in towards Mrs. Strunk, shooting an unreadable glance at Marianna.

"Yes, milord, as you requested. And tea is ready for you and the lady."

"Oh, lovely," Bludington cooed.

"Right this way, into the parlor." Mrs. Strunk rushed them into the room, gesturing to the set of straight-backed chairs covered in a pink and white floral silk.

Mrs. Strunk was letting them sit in those chairs? She'd never let anyone sit in them. The maids were always joking about the fact that she had a pair of chairs, but no one to sit with her in them.

Bludington lumbered over and plopped down into the closest one. Marianna swallowed the lump in her throat and followed. Tension crept up from her shoulders and neck and formed a knot in her head. Something seemed off about this whole scenario, but she had no idea why. Maybe Bludington did know she'd already been in the room. And where in the world was Dunsten? She couldn't believe he would miss a chance to gloat.

Mrs. Strunk ushered in a little maid Marianna vaguely recognized. She had mousy brown hair and stood hunched over the tea tray as if afraid her very presence would make someone angry. Her name was Brigid or Brigette, and she spoke with the accent of the Bulgari people. Marianna wondered how she'd managed to find her way here to this creepy place. It was such a long way from her home.

She didn't have to ponder anymore as Mrs. Strunk's irritating voice interrupted her thoughts. "Well, get to serving, girl. You aren't paid to stand around."

The girl ducked her head even lower and hurried over to the tea table which sat between the two chairs. She poured both Marianna and Bludington tea and then timidly asked, "Milk or sugar?"

"Both, thank you." Marianna leaned forward and gave the girl a reassuring smile, but the girl didn't even look at her as she dumped the milk and sugar into her teacup. She started to do the same for Bludington, but he covered his teacup with his beefy hand.

"None for me. You're dismissed." Both the maid and Mrs. Strunk left the room, and Bludington turned to Marianna, a calculating look on his face.

"So, my keys," Bludington murmured, steepling his hands under his chin as he stared at her. His eyes bore through like they could see all the secrets hidden in her mind.

Marianna said nothing and closed her eyes. The tension knot pounded against her forehead, and she couldn't think clearly.

Had Annette and the maids had enough time to find the prisoners in the dungeon? She had no idea. She didn't even know how long it had been since she'd left them in the kitchen. She inhaled deeply, let her breath out slowly, then opened her eyes. Bludington was still staring at her, smirking.

"Are you troubled by something, Marianna?" His voice was mocking, as he blatantly dropped the miss from her name.

"I'm tired, and I have a headache," Marianna snapped, tired of his condescendence. He either knew or he didn't. It was simple as that.

"Oh, pardon me." Bludington's eyebrows rose. He cleared his throat. "It appears the rose has thorns. But anyway, on to the matter of my keys. I believe I left you the caretaker of them, correct?" He stared at Marianna, waiting for an answer.

She didn't know what to say to that, so she nodded.

"Hmm, I thought so." He reached into his pocket. There was a jangle as he pulled out a set of keys. A set that looked exactly like the one Marianna had left with her sister. She choked back a gasp.

But how? How could he have gotten them? Sweat beaded her forehead and her heart kept time with her pounding headache. She'd watched him come in, and he hadn't left her sight since. Maybe it was another set. She was sure she had seen one like it with Dunsten.

Bludington picked up each key and slid it around the ring letting it drop down onto the other side. "Hmm, my quarters, your quarters, the maids' quarters..." he chanted off the location each key unlocked until he reached the end.

The final key clanked against the rest as it fell into place, sending them all swinging back and forth like the pendulum of the grandfather clock in the hall.

"It appears we are missing one." He lifted his eyes and scorched her with them, a fire there she'd never seen before. She swallowed hard, still not saying anything. Pain beat against her head, echoing in her ears.

"The key to the room"—he paused— "the *only* room, I instructed you not to go in. And did you, Marianna, go into that room?"

Bile rose in Marianna's throat. She couldn't speak, so she shook her head. Maybe a lie would buy her some time. She clutched the arms of the silken chair, her nails biting into the delicate fabric. It would surely leave a mark, but at this rate who knew if she would be alive to face Mrs. Strunk's wrath.

"Hmm, well, there's one way to be sure, isn't there, Marianna?" Bludington didn't wait for a reply as he continued, his gaze never wavering. "Where is the key?"

Time stood still as Marianna struggled to command her voice. "Um, I think it's in my room. I must've dropped it or something."

She jumped up from her seat. "I'll get it," she called over her shoulder as she rammed into the door, pushing her way through.

She dashed up the stairs to her room and ran inside, slamming the door shut and locking it. She turned and rested against the wood, then slid down to sit on the floor. She put her head in her hands and massaged her forehead, praying the pain would go away.

She'd had a plan, but now it was ruined by Bludington's early arrival, and she was spinning in the dark, unsure what to do next. But she'd bought a little time. She had these few moments.

Maybe she could find the key and wash it. Maybe it would stay clean long enough to appease Bludington, at least until her sister and the maids could free the prisoners. If that was even still happening. She didn't know if

Bludington had really taken her set of keys. She didn't see how he could've, but she wouldn't have thought he was a serial killer either. She wasn't sure of anything anymore.

Sitting here in fear wasn't going to help. She took a deep breath and then another. The pain in her head eased slightly. She pushed herself off the floor and hurried to her dresser. She rifled through it, not seeing the white handkerchief she'd wrapped the key in.

Where was it? She was sure she'd left it here. She yanked the drawer from the dresser, dumped its contents onto the floor, and pawed through the pile of clothes.

It wasn't there. Not even the white handkerchief she wrapped it in was there. Had she put it somewhere else? She thought back on her movements over the last few days. No, she was sure she'd put it back in this drawer after she'd shown it to Annette. Could Annette have moved it? But why would she have done such a thing?

"Marianna." Bludington's voice floated up the stairs. "If you can't find the key, it's okay, but I do need to speak with you." He sounded giddy and amused, like the wretched Carnevil clown she had seen when she was eight—the one who had given her nightmares for weeks afterward.

Why did he have to speak to her now? The monster of fear inside her rose higher, threatening to melt her into nothing more than a puddle on the floor.

"Marianna," Bludington called again.

He was getting closer. Footsteps thudded against the steps like the tick-tock of a clock.

"Marianna," Bludington called. "Where are you?"

He was outside her bedroom door. She was out of time. She was going to become one of his victims.

Chapter 52

"I'll be there in a minute," Marianna called, her voice strangled. She got up and went over to the mirrored washstand. She splashed water on her face then stared at her reflection. The fear in her eyes mocked her, telling her it was over.

She averted her eyes and took deep breaths, ignoring the fear. She needed her thoughts to be crystal clear, in case she could still find a way out. There had to be something, anything. She wasn't ready to give up. She yanked the towel from its rod and dried her hands before going to the door and flinging it open.

"There you are, Marianna. I thought I'd have to send out a search party. Come, I must speak with you." Bludington's eyes sparkled with feverish glee as he took Marianna's arm. Mrs. Strunk stood half a step behind him, her eyes steely, arms crossed over her chest.

Bludington's grip tightened around Marianna's arm, pinching into her skin as he led her toward his wing of the house. She wanted to yank her arm away but was afraid it would make him mad.

As he trotted faster and faster down the hallways, his coat gaped open. Tucked into his belt was the red-eyed wolf dagger. Marianna could only see the hilt but there was no mistaking the glittering ruby eyes or the snarled teeth that jutted out from the wolf's mouth.

She sucked in a breath, her eyes shooting up to Bludington's face. He didn't even look at her as he chuckled to himself, his eyes filled with half-crazed glee, a lopsided smirk pasted across his face.

"So close," he muttered. So, so, so close."

It was so quiet, Marianna almost thought she'd imagined it. She shot a look at Mrs. Strunk who walked demurely behind them, an unreadable expression on her face.

Once they reached Bludington's wing, he turned into the hall lined with suits of armor. Marianna shrank back, afraid that at any minute they would come alive. Visions of the suit that'd chased her and Jay in the basement filled her mind and her breath quickened.

Had Annette, Carrie, and Leah been able to get past those armored guards? Had they even managed to get to the dungeon? The familiar ball of fear rose inside of her, untangling itself as it reached up through her thundering heart and scraped at her throat. How had she believed they had a chance against Bludington? He had magic at his fingertips and an army of armor.

She coughed, choking on her shallow breaths, unable to get the air she desperately needed into her lungs. Bludington paused, loosening his grip as he stared at her.

"What's the matter with you, girl?" he snarled. "We haven't even gotten to the scary part yet."

Marianna struggled to answer around her coughs. "Water," she managed to sputter.

Bludington nodded to Mrs. Strunk. "Fetch the girl some water. It won't do if she's dead before we're ready."

Displeasure covered Mrs. Strunk's features, but she turned to follow Bludington's directions, and returned quickly with a glass of water.

Marianna gratefully took the glass, taking small sips between breaths, trying to breathe slowly and deeply. She worked to slow her racing thoughts. She couldn't worry about her sister and the others right now.

If they had managed to get to the dungeons, she needed to buy them as much time as possible and the only way to do that was to play along with Bludington and whatever nefarious plan he'd cooked up. She could do this. She would do this.

She cleared her throat as she handed the glass back to Mrs. Strunk. "Thank you, my throat was terribly dry." She rubbed her neck hoping it would help sell the lie.

Mrs. Strunk sneered at her before rushing back the way she had come.

"Better now?" Bludington grunted as he tightened his grip and pulled her forward once more. "Mrs. Strunk can catch up with us."

Why did he need Mrs. Strunk with them? Was she part of this whole scheme too? And where was Dunsten? He had yet to make an appearance.

Bludington yanked a lit candelabra from its stand on the wall and turned the corner into the hallway that led to the forbidden room. His coat flapped open once more, and the candlelight shimmered over the wolf's eyes, making them glow.

He was going to slaughter her in the murder room and leave her there to rot with the others. Marianna cringed at the thought.

Bludington picked up the pace, dragging Marianna along behind him. Had this hallway always been so narrow? The walls looked ready to close in on them. The only light came from the candelabra Bludington held, casting a small circle around them.

As they reached the end of the hallway, there was a loud whoosh. Flames jumped up from two large candles on either side of the painting. The smell of smoke assaulted Marianna's nose, making her eyes water. Firelight flickered over the image of the dwarf threatening the girl. A tear shimmered in the girl's eye before trickling down her cheek.

Marianna couldn't hold back the gasp. Was she seeing things? She glanced up at Bludington, but he didn't react. He was staring at the painting with the same creepy smirk still on his face.

The click clack of heeled shoes came towards them. Mrs. Strunk turned the corner and strode down the hallway carrying her own lighted candelabra. Marianna had never seen this hallway so bright, but it wasn't cheerful. Instead, the light seemed to emphasize the gloom, highlighting the places where the candles burned, casting everything else into shadowed darkness.

Bludington whipped his head around, as if just now realizing Mrs. Strunk was heading their way. "Come along, Mrs. Strunk," he called out in a sing-songy voice, "we haven't got all day."

Mrs. Strunk picked up the pace, the click clack turning to a clickety clack. A grimace covered her face as she replied, "I would've been here the whole time if you hadn't been so busy coddling the girl."

Bludington shook his head, never losing his little smirk. "Now Mrs. Strunk, we may be fearsome, but we don't have to be vicious."

What did that mean? Did Bludington honestly think if he treated Marianna nicely, it wouldn't matter that he was planning to kill her? The man was insane. How had no one realized this?

Bludington dropped her arm and reached into his pocket. He pulled out the tiny, bloodied key and handed it to Mrs. Strunk before grabbing Marianna's arm once more.

Marianna let out a little gasp before she could stop herself.

"Yes, I had it all along." Bludington chuckled as he turned to Mrs. Strunk. "Hurry, what are you waiting for?"

"Why are you doing this?" Marianna blurted out. She couldn't help herself. She wanted to know what he would say when confronted about his behavior, and she needed to waste time. She was afraid once he got her into the room, he wouldn't hesitate to kill her. "Bringing girls here and killing them because they disobey you once?"

"Is that why you think I kill them? Ha, how little you know." Bludington anxiously watched as Mrs. Strunk unlocked the door and pushed it open. Marianna covered her nose as the stench of rust and death swirled out into the hall.

"Then why do you do it?" Marianna asked.

Bludington turned back to her, surprise on his face. "You're the only one to question me about this. All the other girls screamed and pleaded for their life, well, except for the first one, because she didn't know what was going to happen." Bludington laughed.

"Well, since you want to know, I'll tell you. Why not?" Bludington pointed to the dwarf painting.

"See that little man? That used to be me, until I met this hag in the woods who told me she could change me into a real man, not some half, misshapen one. I was tired of being that creature. It was bad enough that strangers and neighbors were cruel to me, but even my own mother and sister were as well." His smirk disappeared as his face twisted in hurt and anger.

"My mother claimed she couldn't love me because I was her illegitimate child—a child who was never supposed to happen. The result of a one-night affair with a dwarf in the mines when my mother was off 'finding herself.'" Bludington spat out the last words, the angry expression turning to disgust.

"Anyway, I did discover one plus side to being half dwarf. I had access to magic, but it wasn't enough. Not to turn me into a full-blooded human, or at least to make me appear that way." He snickered before continuing.

"Then I found the old hag, and she had the answer. But it would have a price. A maiden's blood. So I killed the first girl. She wasn't my wife, just some girl I found in the village—the hag's daughter." He snorted. "People are *so* trusting. It was almost too easy."

"She helped you, so why would you kill her daughter?" Marianna tried to yank her arm away, anger outweighing her fear, but he grasped her arm tighter, his nails biting into her skin.

Marianna pulled harder. "You're hurting me."

"You think that matters to me?" he growled, fury replacing the giddy look in his eyes.

"What are we doing still standing out here?" Mrs. Strunk stepped closer to Lord Bludington and placed a hand on his shoulder. Bludington turned toward her, and some unspoken communication passed between them. He took a deep breath, shook off Mrs. Strunk's hand, and turned towards Marianna.

"Do you want to hear the rest or not?"

Marianna nodded, not knowing what to say. She shot a glance at Mrs. Strunk who had taken a step back. Without sparing a glance for Marianna, she sighed heavily, set her candelabra on the floor, and crossed her arms over her chest. She mumbled something under her breath. Marianna wasn't sure, but it sounded like she'd said, "Guess we'll be here all day."

The smirk was back on Bludington's face as he continued. "So, then I was a man, but that wasn't enough. I needed land and houses. 'Another virgin maiden's blood,' the old hag said. This time I had met a girl I liked, I got her to marry me, then killed her. It was a lot easier to cover up. I told everyone my wife had died of a deadly disease and the body had been burned." He giggled like a little girl who'd just received her first doll.

He was insane, completely crazy. How had he fooled everyone? And it looked like he might get away with it. The fear that'd settled back down into the pit of Marianna's stomach rippled and waved, rising.

She swallowed hard, forcing it down and making herself concentrate on Bludington's story. Maybe he would unwittingly tell her something that could help her get out of this.

"Well, then I decided I wanted the power the hag had to grant wishes. Three virgin maidens' blood was the price this time, oh, and the Blue Heart Stone." Bludington smiled charmingly at Marianna as he continued.

"I bet you didn't know the Heart Stone is the source of all the power for the dwarves. It's ironic, isn't it, that the thing I despise being is actually what's going to give me everything I desire in the end? Any day, my miners will uncover the Stone. I've already gotten the first two maidens. You're the final one. Once you're dead, all the power of the dark arts will be mine."

Her heart raced as the fear bounced around, begging to be let up to overtake her. She inhaled deeply and thought about what he'd told her so far. Now she knew why he wanted the Heart Stone, but she still didn't know what it did. Or if it really existed for that matter. Hadn't it been a myth?

She sucked in a breath then asked, "How do you know it's real? The Heart Stone?"

Bludington snorted again. "Oh, my dear, surely by now you've realized that much more than you ever dreamed of exists."

"I suppose." Marianna shrugged her shoulders, struggling to keep her nerves steady as she continued. "What makes you think the hag was telling the truth? Who is she to grant such a thing?"

Bludington's grip on her arm tightened even more, his nails digging deeper into her skin. Her skin prickled and damp bubbles settled on the surface of her skin. She wanted nothing more than to wrench her arm away and wash off the blood and grime he'd left there.

"And what would you know of such things?" Bludington snapped. "The hag granted everything else, didn't she? Enough talk!"

He pushed her through the open doorway, releasing her once she was inside the room. She wanted to close her eyes so she didn't have to see her fate mocking her, but she needed to see if there was a way out of here. She glanced back at Lord Bludington and Mrs. Strunk.

Mrs. Strunk sighed and grunted. "It's about time we get this moving, but we still don't know where Dunsten is." She looked up and saw Marianna watching them. She lowered her voice and angled her body so Marianna could no longer see her mouth.

"Where did he go?" Bludington whispered.

"Shh," Mrs. Strunk hissed, making her voice even lower as she continued talking.

Marianna scanned the room, careful not to let her gaze rest on the skeletons that lay in a row in the corner. On the far wall, something metal caught her eye.

Was that a doorknob? Yes, it looked like the ones that led to the servants' quarters. Hidden within the wall, surrounded by wallpaper, they were nearly indistinguishable except to the trained eye.

The wallpaper in this room had probably once been beautiful, but the flowers had faded to a dingy gray, and the white background was no longer white, but a dirty cream mottled with a rust color. She didn't want to think about where that rust color came from.

Would that door even open? She couldn't imagine any of the servants had been here lately. Certainly not since the first girl was killed. But maybe it had never been locked. There was only one way to find out.

She glanced back at Bludington and Mrs. Strunk. They were still engrossed in a hushed conversation. She took a step away from them and then another. They didn't even look at her.

She moved away, one step at a time, keeping her eyes trained on them. It seemed like an eternity but had to have been less than a minute for her to reach the door. She shuddered as she reached for the doorknob.

It twisted easily in her hands, and she nearly collapsed in relief. She shot a final glance behind her. Strunk and Bludington were still engrossed in conversation, so she pushed the door open.

Chapter 53

A set of iron stairs greeted Marianna, and she knew at once where they led. The tower room. They twisted upwards and around. Not ideal, but she didn't have much choice. She stepped onto the first step.

"The girl!" Mrs. Strunk screamed.

Marianna glanced behind her. Bludington pushed past Mrs. Strunk brandishing the wolf-head knife. Marianna didn't hesitate. She slammed the door shut and started up the stairs. She grasped the handrail, the iron cool to the touch as she scrambled higher. The staircase rattled and shook, and she prayed it wouldn't collapse.

She'd barely gotten up ten steps when the door thundered open. The staircase swayed as Bludington bounded onto it and charged up after her. His heavy boots pounded against the metal, making the staircase rumble.

Being so much smaller than Bludington, she could take the turns on the stairs much faster. His bulk barely fit in the spiral staircase.

But what was she going to do when she reached the top? She knew there was no escape up there. It was too far to jump, and there was only a single room where Bludington had access to who knew what kind of concoctions.

She risked a glance below. Bludington's face was red, and he wielded the wolf-head knife like a sword. Was he planning to charge and stab her?

"Why are you running?" he yelled up at her. "There's no escaping. Submit to your fate, and things will go easier for you."

She picked up her pace, gripping the handrail for dear life as she sprinted around the twists and turns of the staircase. Bludington's boots rattled with every step, the din causing her head to pound in time with her thundering heart. How much farther was it? She didn't know how much longer she could keep this up.

She shot a glance upward. She still couldn't see the top of the stairs, and her lungs were already burning. She remembered how out of breath she'd been the day she and Betsy had explored up here.

Pain pricked her heart. Had the others found Betsy? Were they okay? Was this all hopeless anyway, and no matter what she did, she was destined to be killed by Bludington?

Her chest heaved as she struggled to breathe through the fear and exertion. Her mother's cameo thumped against her chest. She reached up with her free hand and clasped it.

Unbidden, her mother's words from long ago came back to her. 'When it seems things can't ever possibly work out, that's when you will need to reach down deep to find that inner strength. You are stronger than you know, my dear.'

She clutched the charm tighter as she renewed her efforts, thundering up the stairs, ignoring the rattling and shaking, and focusing only on her goal—to make it to the top. With her other hand she clung to the railing hoping it would keep her from falling.

Her heart felt like it would race out of her chest. Her lungs were on fire, but she could finally see the top of the stairs. She pounded up the final few steps and flew through the wooden door at the top.

She shot a quick glance behind her. Bludington had gained on her and was only a few steps away. She slammed the door shut. It needed a key to lock it. She darted over to the worktable covered in papers and various sizes of beakers filled with red, blue, and green liquids. She shuffled through things, careful not to spill any of the liquid on herself. Who knew what it would do to her skin?

The key. Where could it be? It wasn't on the table. The pounding was getting closer. Bludington had to be nearly to the door. Her eyes shot up as she scanned the room looking for a nail with a key on it.

There on the far wall was a nail with a single key hanging from it. She dashed over and pulled the key from the wall so hard the nail flew out of the wall, yanking the key from her grasp as it sailed across the room before dropping to the floor and skidding into the door.

Marianna followed right behind it, crouching down, she grabbed the key and shoved it into the lock. Before she could turn it, the door slammed into her, knocking her off her feet and onto her backside as Bludington stormed into the room.

He towered over her, clutching the dagger in both hands, he held it above his head. "Are you crazy, woman? You know what's coming, so why fight it? There's no way out of this for you," he growled. He bent forward, the knife coming down.

Marianna scooted back across the floor barely managing to miss the blade as it cut through the air towards her. Bludington couldn't stop the forward momentum of the knife and it crashed into the floor, lodging in the spot Marianna had been sitting moments before, catching the edge of her skirt. She yanked, ripping it away.

Bludington yelled as he pulled on the knife. It took three tries before he got it out of the floor. His face was redder than before, and his eyes looked like they would bulge right out of their sockets. Marianna had never seen him like this, but the state he was in only confirmed that Bludington was indeed crazy.

"I should've known better than to go after you when you were so reluctant to agree. I should've realized then you'd be difficult. Stupid me always having to go after a challenge," he roared as she charged at her again, the knife held aloft, aimed at her heart.

Marianna spun around and rose to her feet, darting behind the table. She searched the room desperately, looking for a weapon or anything that could be used as one. She grabbed one of the beakers of liquid and threw it into Bludington's face.

He howled as the blue liquid hit his skin and eyes. He closed his eyes and dropped the knife, clutching his face with both hands. The liquid sizzled, turning the skin around his eyes flaming red.

Marianna wanted to run for the door, but there was no room to get around Bludington without him feeling her. And even in his impeded state, he'd still be a formidable foe. All he'd have to do is grab her. She was no match for him physically.

Bludington's howling suddenly stopped. He took a deep breath, placing both hands flat against his face covering it entirely. He chanted some strange words. A blue light glowed around his hands for several seconds. The light dimmed, and he dropped his hands from his face. His smirk was back, and the reddened skin now looked normal.

Marianna gasped. Had he healed himself? How did she stand a chance against him if he could heal himself? What else could he do?

Bludington snickered. "You weren't expecting that, were you? I told you it was pointless to fight. You should give up. I promise it will go much easier for you."

"Never," Marianna hissed. "You're a horrible man. Hurting others to get your own way. To get riches and magic, and whatever else. Don't you have any feelings? Do you care about anyone?"

"Well," Bludington chuckled, "I would think you'd know the answer to that by now." He bent down and picked up the dagger. He tapped the blunt side of the blade against his hand and stalked closer to where Marianna still stood behind the table. "Does it seem like I care about anyone else? Do you see anyone else here with me?"

Marianna picked up another liquid beaker and flung it at him. He barely paused as he lifted his palm towards the beaker. Just before it hit him, it stopped and tumbled to the floor, shattering into hundreds of pieces, green liquid rolling across the floor.

He stepped closer as he continued. "I learned early on that the only one who was going to care about me, was, well, me." He snickered again. "So no, to answer your question, I don't care about anyone but myself."

Marianna grabbed another beaker filled with red liquid and hurled it at his head. Again, he stopped it with an upraised palm, the beaker shattering against the floor. Marianna grabbed the rest of the beakers and threw them as fast as she could, hoping one of them would slip through and hit him. But Bludington managed to stop every one before they reached him.

He took another step closer, tapping the knife against his palm. He was two or three steps away from her, and she was all out of beakers. Her eyes darted about the room.

As if he could hear her thoughts, Bludington laughed. "So, what now, Marianna?"

He drew her name out, making it sound like a taunt. His eyes glittered as he stared her down.

"You're out of time." Bludington's voice was sing-song-y as he wagged the dagger at Marianna.

"Is this fun for you? Preying on vulnerable girls. I read about your other wives. They were young, and they trusted you. Elianna was devastated when she found out what you intended to do to her." Marianna scanned the room once more.

A broom sat in the corner next to the balcony window. The window was wide open, a gentle breeze drifted in, belying the circumstances she had found herself in. No weapons anywhere.

Marianna doubted she'd garner sympathy. Bludington was too far gone for that, but talking was the only thing she had at her disposal.

The mad man smirked. "But isn't that how the world works? Men prey on women, particularly the young and vulnerable. And they fall for it." He laughed. "Every single time."

"No. I know men who aren't out to prey on girls, and I've known girls who aren't so easily fooled by men like you."

"And yet, here you are." Bludington shook his head in mock shame. "Preyed upon and vulnerable, and about to face your death."

Marianna darted forward, trying to skirt around Bludington, but he grabbed her arm and pulled her toward him.

"Enough of this fooling around," he growled. "It's time to end this."

He lifted the dagger. Marianna jerked backward out of the knife's path. The blade sliced through her sleeve, nicking her arm. A sticky warmth was followed by a burning sensation, but Bludington's grip had loosened. She yanked away from him, darting to the corner, and grabbing the broom.

He lunged for her again. She held onto the broomstick with both hands, bringing it down as hard as she could, whacking the knife with the flat side of the bristles. It flew out of Bludington's hand and soared across the room straight towards the balcony window.

"No," Bludington screamed as he dove after it. The knife skittered on the edge of the balcony for half a second before dropping over the edge.

Bludington's knees hit the balcony edge at full force. He tilted over it, his arms still outstretched, reaching for the knife as he plummeted through the opening.

Marianna gasped, the broom dropping from her hands. There was no way Bludington could've survived that fall. A fist clenched around her chest, cutting off her breath. She slipped to the floor as she struggled to breathe. She pushed against the wall and sat up straight.

In, out. She fought against the fist, dragging in ragged breaths until she could breathe normally. She didn't want to look over the edge, and yet she did. Was he really gone?

Before she could get up, the door crashed into the wall. Dunsten charged in, holding a sword. Marianna pushed herself up from the floor. Had he come to finish her off?

Chapter 54

"Miss Marianna, are you hurt?" The concern in his voice rendered her speechless. He wasn't going to kill her?

Dunsten scanned the room a final time, dropped the sword and hurried over to her. "Miss Marianna?" He asked as he gently laid a hand on her shoulder. "You're bleeding." He pulled a handkerchief from his pocket and pressed it against her arm.

Marianna nodded. "Bludington." It came out ragged and hoarse. She cleared her throat and tried again. "I don't think Bludington is though..."

She pointed out the window. Dunsten hurried over. A grimace covered his face as he turned away from the window. Marianna walked over to peer down.

Dunsten laid a hand on her arm and shook his head. "You don't want to look, miss." But Marianna couldn't help it. She needed to know if Bludington was dead, so she looked.

His crumpled figure lay on the cobblestone below, a circle of red spreading out around him. She turned her head, satisfied he'd not be coming after her again.

Dunsten awkwardly patted her shoulder. "Come, let's go check on the others."

She started toward the door. A distant clamor sounded. Yelling and... was that cheering? Dunsten's words registered.

"The others?" she asked. "You mean Carrie and Leah, and my sister?"

Dunsten nodded. "Of course, who else?"

Marianna turned and rushed down the stairs.

"Marianna, where are you?" Annette's yells greeted her before she'd reached the bottom.

"Up here. You're all okay?" She scrambled down the stairs and charged through the door, across the murder room, and into the hallway.

Annette met her there, throwing her arms around her sister's neck. "Oh, Marianna, I was sure you were dead." Annette cried against Marianna's shoulder.

"I thought *you* were dead. Bludington had a key ring that looked like mine." Marianna pulled back to look at her sister.

"Those were Dunsten's. He knew Bludington would be looking for the keys in your room, so he hid his set there. He couldn't do anything about the bloodied key, though."

"You're okay?" Marianna's eyes scanned her sister.

Annette nodded.

"And everyone got out okay?"

"I think so. There are still people coming out. Jay and Caden are searching the tunnels. There were hundreds of people down there." Annette's eyes were wide as she lowered her voice. "Where is Bludington?"

"Dead. He fell over the balcony chasing after that creepy wolf-headed knife."

Annette sighed in relief. "I'm sorry, Marianna. But I feel better knowing he's not going to hurt anyone else."

"Miss Marianna, I hate to trouble you, but where is Mrs. Strunk?" Dunsten asked.

Marianna shook her head. "I don't know." She looked back at the murder room door. "She was here before, whispering to Bludington. Talking about you, I think."

"Hmm," was all Dunsten said. "Well, we need to see if everyone has gotten out of the tunnels."

Marianna nodded. "Of course, I'll be right there." Dunsten nodded and started down the hallway.

"What is it?" Annette asked.

"I thought I saw..." Marianna walked back over to the murder room door. There on the floor was something silver. A cup lying on its side. She knelt and picked it up, turning it over. Her name was inscribed on it in an elegant script.

"What's that? Why does it have your name on it?" Annette's voice startled her, and she nearly dropped the cup.

"I'm not sure exactly. I think it might have been to collect my blood. Bludington said something about needing my blood." She shivered, then she tossed the cup into the murder room and slammed the door shut.

She and Annette hurried to the ballroom. People were everywhere. Groups hugging and laughing and crying. More people than Marianna had ever seen at Thunderwell.

"All these people came from the tunnels?"

Annette nodded. "There were still more coming up from there when I left to find you too."

"What are we going to do with all these people?"

Annette shrugged. "I guess that's your problem, milady," she said with a laugh.

"What do you mean?"

"You own Thunderwell now."

"What?" Marianna gasped. "But I didn't marry Bludington."

"Doesn't matter. He'd already signed the papers declaring you the heir. Of course, he thought you weren't going to live, so he had no problem signing the papers early."

"How do you know?"

"Dunsten showed us the signed deed."

"You're friends with Dunsten, now?" Marianna raised her eyebrows.

"Yeah, you were being a bit dramatic about him. He's been on your side the whole time. Bludington had a powerful hold over him." Annette pointed over to the corner.

A little girl squealed as she flung herself into Dunsten's arms. "Daddy, you found us!" She was followed by a slender, strawberry blonde woman who embraced Dunsten and pressed a kiss to his lips.

Marianna's mouth dropped open. She'd had no clue Dunsten had a family.

"Miss Marianna!"

She turned and saw Betsy hurtling across the room. "Betsy, you're okay!" She ran to greet her friend.

"Yes, just got thrown into the dungeon for a bit. But I'm better now."

The next few hours were overwhelming as people were accounted for. Annette helped Marianna set up a system to organize people by family groups and send them to rooms accordingly.

The sheriff from town came to deal with the dead bodies. He had an extensive conversation with Marianna. It was clear there'd been no foul play on her part, and by the time the sheriff left, all criminal proceedings had been resolved.

That night she sat out in the garden, enjoying a cup of tea with Annette, Betsy, Carrie, and Leah.

"Mrs. Strunk was never located?" Leah asked.

"Apparently not," Marianna answered. "Why is everyone looking for her?"

Carrie laughed. "Miss Marianna, she's the one who taught Lord Bludington how to use his magic," Carrie replied. "She'd been with him since he was a boy. Her magic's even stronger than his, and she's most definitely dangerous."

"Why didn't anyone tell the sheriff that?" Marianna asked.

Leah snickered. Carrie glared at her, and Leah straightened up, the smirk disappearing from her face.

"Because the sheriff doesn't believe in magic," Betsy replied. "Most of us barely believe in it."

"So, what does that mean?" Marianna asked. "Is she going to be coming after us?"

"I doubt it," Leah answered. "She's after the Blue Heart Stone. Her focus will be on that now."

"Yeah, what exactly is that?" Annette interjected.

Leah shrugged her shoulders. "I have no idea. Just that it's very powerful. Some think it doesn't exist. Either way, I think you're safe for now, Miss Marianna."

Marianna was quiet, soaking in the gentle night air. The scent of jasmine and roses drifted by, soothing her senses. For the moment, things were good. She was safe. Annette and the others were safe. Her father and brothers were coming to Thunderwell tomorrow to help get things in order.

She lifted her hand to the cameo at her neck. Her mother's spirit lingered with her. She wasn't sure what the future would hold, but after today, she was ready to face anything.

Epilogue

3 months later

Marianna led Jupiter out of the stables. Sir Tom ran past her, laughing with a group of boys as they hurried up towards the manor. She smiled. They were probably late for class.

Over the past few months, she had turned Thunderwell into a boarding school. There were more than enough teachers among the people Bludington had imprisoned in the dungeons, and they were all happy to help, pleased to see a complete reversal of the state of things at Thunderwell.

Carrie made a great headmistress, and Leah was a capable assistant. Dunsten and his family had settled in as well, and his whole demeanor had changed. Who knew the ghostly figure that seemed to haunt her hid a charming and entertaining man.

Marianna climbed up onto Jupiter's saddle and turned him toward the beach. She signaled him into a canter, relishing the feel of the wind in her hair. Bludington had gotten one thing right, finding the perfect horse for her.

Within minutes they had reached the beach. Marianna had asked the groundkeeper's crew to create a riding and walking path that led down to the beach. It was silly to have such a beautiful place on your property and no reasonable way to get there.

She slid off Jupiter's back, dropping her reins to the ground. She would stay within the area, nibbling on the tall sea grass.

Marianna inhaled the refreshing, salty air. Her toes sank into the cool, damp sand. Purple and pink streaked across the sky as the sun peeked over the turquoise water. The roar of the waves soothed away the last of her anxiety.

She couldn't believe this was all hers. A smile crept across her face, and she broke into a run. She loved the rise and fall of the sand under her feet, the roar of the ocean, and the rolling white waves that always seemed to be welcoming her here.

Something glittered in the water, and she skidded to a stop. A glass bottle bobbed along with the tide, getting closer and closer to the shore. Dots of yellow light danced inside the bottle. Marianna stepped into the edge of the water.

The waves rippled over her toes, bringing the bottle within reach. She grabbed it and examined its contents. What kind of light was this? Little bits that could be contained in a bottle?

A browning, crinkled paper was rolled up inside. Marianna popped the cork and tipped the bottle over. The little bits of yellow light faded and turned to yellow dust that sprinkled across her skirt, and the roll of paper landed in her palm.

Carefully, she unrolled the paper and skimmed its contents. The name at the bottom made her eyes fill with tears, and she nearly dropped the letter. Was this for real? She sank to the sand and smoothed the paper out, reading it again.

Dearest Marianna,

I have no idea if this will ever reach you, but I pray it does. Tink, my friend here, has helped me with this and assured me that pixie dust never fails. Yes, pixie dust! I can hardly believe it myself. Tink is a pixie.

I know this sounds crazy, and even if it does reach you, you may assume it's somebody's idea of a bad prank. I assure you it is not. If only I had time to tell you everything, but Tink is here insisting I hurry, or we'll lose our window of time to send this.

So, to get to the point. I'm trapped here in this strange land. Neverland, it's called. I doubt you'll find it on any map. It's somewhere south of Carid. I don't know where exactly, as I was unconscious when I arrived here. And I have no idea if there's any way for someone to get here, but I fear I'll never escape without help.

If you do somehow manage to send someone here, tell them to be wary of everyone, because nothing is like it seems. They can trust no one. I hesitated to even send this. I don't want you to send anyone to a dangerous place to be hurt or worse, but Tink insisted I do something, as now it is no longer only my own life in danger, but everyone else's on this island as well. So, if you do get this, I need help. But no matter what, I'll always love you.

Forever yours,

Will

P.S. The long thin silver thing folds out to a compass. Tink claims it will lead you right to Neverland.

All this time she had been right. He was alive. Will was alive. Marianna laughed out loud. Her mind raced, jumping from one thing to the next. Pixies, and pixie dust? Who would have thought? And that map. She had found the map with *Nerland* on it. That had to be it. It wasn't a hoax at all. Maybe this was why everyone feared the Isle of Carid. And a compass that led there.

She hadn't seen any thin, silver thing inside the bottle, but she picked it up again, examining it. A long, thin silver tube was inside. It took several tries before she was able to remove the tube.

There was a little button on the side. She pushed it, and the tube exploded out into a round disk. On the face of a disk, there was only one letter at the top, a curly N. A red needle danced around it.

Marianna stood up and held the strange compass still. She slowly turned until the red needle bounced over the N. She was facing the ocean, looking in the direction one would take to get to Carid.

Her heart leaped. When it came to Will, she was willing to do anything for him. And she knew she could do this. The compass would show her the way. She had a fleet of ships and more money than she had ever seen before at her disposal. She had navigated a dangerous manor and battled a murderous lord and survived. How much worse could this Neverland place be than what she'd already faced?

Acknowledgements

I'm so excited to see this book reach my readers, and there are so many people I have to thank!

First off, I'm thankful to three college professors, Dr. Miller, Mr. Hain, and Mrs. Beard, who fed my literary hunger and encouraged me to continually develop my skills with the written word.

I want to thank my awesome writing group: Camilla, Jennifer, Natalya, and Sadie. They helped me refine and get this book just right!

Many thanks to my wonderful editor, Natalie Cammaratta. Her eagle eyes caught many things mine had overlooked.

Thanks also to all the early readers on my street team. I appreciate you all!

I want to thank my parents and grandparents for sparking and nurturing my love of reading, which is of course the first step to becoming a writer. I'm especially thankful to my dad for passing on his love of grammar and literary analysis, and to my grandfather for passing on his love of storytelling.

Many thanks to my siblings: Faith, Harold, and Hope. They were my very first readers and are always encouraging and eager to read whatever new piece I foist upon them.

And of course, a very special thanks to my husband, Don, who has always believed in my dreams and inspires me every day to keep chasing after them.

About the Author

Charity loves fairy tales and myths and re-imagining them. When not writing, she takes creative photos, paints, and spends time with family. Charity lives in Maryland with her sassy pomchi and her own charming prince. *The Bloodstained Key* is her first book.

Read more at https://charityrau.wordpress.com/.